# THE
# GOOD
# TRAITOR

# ALSO BY RYAN QUINN

*End of Secrets*
*The Fall*

# THE
# GOOD
# TRAITOR

## RYAN QUINN

**THOMAS & MERCER**

Published by Thomas & Mercer, Seattle
www.apub.com

Amazon, the Amazon logo, and Thomas & Mercer are trademarks of Amazon.com, Inc., or its affiliates.

ISBN-13: 9781503954625
ISBN-10: 1503954625

Cover design by Marc Cohen

Printed in the United States of America

*For the hackers.*
*Be gentle.*

# SHANGHAI

Amid the rigged chess game that shuffled fuselages around the tarmac of Pudong International Airport, a sleek Gulfstream G450 taxied from a private terminal and slipped into position behind a line of wide-body commercial jets. Overhead, the last daylight drained from the waiting sky. Inside the glowing porthole window over the G450's wing sat Greg Rodgers, United States ambassador to China. Graying but still handsome and healthy, Rodgers had eyes that were steady with the patience of a family man, which he was, and lit by the incurable curiosity of an academic, which he'd been before the presidential appointment that had moved him and his wife, Wendy, from New Haven to Beijing. Their two grown sons remained in the States, though they visited often with the diplomat's daughters-in-law and three grandchildren.

During his ambassadorship, now on the eve of its sixth year, travel for Rodgers rarely involved more than a traffic-choked ride in one of the drab diplomatic vehicles that shuttled the ambassador and his security detail around the capital city. But a recent spate of multination trade talks had forced him to the sky, where he'd been wearing out the airways between Beijing, Shanghai, and Hong Kong.

This particular trip was exceptional for its incorporation of the private jet, which belonged to a wealthy Chinese investor named Hu

Lan. Rodgers's first instinct had been to decline Hu's offer to lend him the Gulfstream for the weekend. Posted to a country where hundreds of millions of citizens lived in abject poverty, Rodgers was not the sort of man who felt comfortable indulging in luxury. But Hu was on the list of Chinese politicians and businessmen with whom Rodgers was encouraged to form ties. This was an actual list—classified and delivered to him weekly in encrypted cables from the State Department in DC. Some of the names on this list had obvious diplomatic value; others didn't. Rodgers suspected the latter were placed there by the Central Intelligence Agency. Hu Lan was almost certainly one of the CIA additions.

Aside from reluctantly agreeing to borrow the Chinese businessman's private jet, Rodgers had not given Hu a second thought—until the previous day, when a story had rippled through the international news media that made the trip on Hu's jet more awkward than it had been already. The story originated on the news website Gnos.is and was quickly confirmed by other reputable news organizations. This Gnos.is-led wave of disruptive news stories was starting to feel like the new norm. Gnos.is's reportage was thorough and apolitical, and Rodgers had to admit that on many occasions he'd found the site a valuable resource. But Gnos.is—which, instead of relying on the labor of individual journalists, vacuumed up massive amounts of online data and applied algorithms to sort fact from rumor and even to generate the actual text of articles—had a habit of publishing details that caused headaches for diplomats like Rodgers, whose job relied on state secrets remaining secret. While this particular story didn't cause embarrassment for the US government, it nonetheless promised to complicate Rodgers's life. The Gnos.is scoop was that Hu Lan's majority stake in an American telecom company called InspiraCom had been funded by the Ministry of State Security, China's equivalent to the CIA.

The news story proved Rodgers's instinct right: Hu's hospitality would amount to more trouble than it was worth. But that changed nothing. He confirmed that Hu was still on the State Department/ CIA list, and then he and his staff climbed aboard the plush little jet and pretended to be grateful for the ride, sipping glasses of wine and avoiding discussing anything they wouldn't have said aloud in the presence of a Chinese MSS officer.

Owning a business jet was a hot trend among the Chinese elite, who imported them from the United States and Europe by the hundreds annually. With an operating cost of $10,000 per flight, the small luxury aircraft were by all appearances impractical. But the motives behind keeping up appearances are often exactly that. If Hu Lan wanted to spend $10,000 per flight to whisk Rodgers to Shanghai and back as a symbol of China's ascension in the global economy, who was Rodgers to decline? Diplomacy, he'd discovered, required not only a clear knowledge of one's principles but also a willingness to go along with almost anything that didn't violate them outright. Despite his personal discomfort, he had no political principle against riding in a private jet. At least the G450 was American made.

In the fading daylight, Rodgers watched an Airbus A380, the world's largest passenger jetliner, lumber onto the rubber-scarred runway and rumble to speed before lifting, improbably, into the air. Then a Boeing 777 received the all clear from the tower and roared from land to sky.

Next up was the G450, which looked like landing gear with wings next to these larger craft. The initial thrust pushed Rodgers back in his seat. The jet fought to absorb the contours of the runway as it gathered momentum. And then the ride went suddenly smooth. The Gulfstream climbed steeply into the darkening night, banked away from Earth's most populous country, and darted over the mouth of the Yangtze River before cutting temporarily away from the coast. When it banked back to settle into its flight path over the Yellow Sea, the western horizon tilted into view, glowing in the far distance, enlarging the sky.

Rodgers glanced at his watch. Before boarding he'd called his wife to let her know that the ninety-minute flight to Beijing would get him home closer to bedtime than dinnertime. Rodgers leaned back in his seat, exhaustion weighing on his eyelids. His workday was far from over. Right now it was eight in the morning in Washington, and the deputy secretary of state was expecting a report on the Shanghai meetings. But that was not the sort of cable Rodgers could compose on Hu's plane. He would have to wait until he was inside the secure confines of the American embassy.

The G450 could comfortably accommodate eight passengers in addition to the crew, but on this leg it held only Rodgers, an assistant, and two former Navy SEALs—his protectors, though what they were supposed to protect him from Rodgers did not waste time imagining. His relative solitude was an unexpected pleasure. He almost always traveled with his top aide, Angela Vasser, ever since she'd been sent from DC two years earlier. He enjoyed Angela and had come to rely on her quick, incisive mind. But when they had at the last minute decided she should stay on in Shanghai through the weekend to continue deepening her rapport with her Chinese and African counterparts there, he'd found himself glad at the prospect of some true downtime.

Not that he could allow himself to make use of it. Even as he tried to shut down, Rodgers had begun composing in his mind a cable that outlined the key developments of the negotiations. He was still engrossed in this when, without warning, the plane pitched dramatically upward, hard enough to knock his phone and a small bottle of water from the armrest and send them sliding aft across the cabin floor. In addition to the physical disturbance, he noticed a more subtle change: the hum that had accompanied their forward thrust out of Shanghai had suddenly ceased. This silence, more than the plane's violent bucking, was acutely unnerving, like the sudden absence of a soundtrack in a movie scene. With almost no outward reaction other than a glance at the closed cockpit door, Rodgers calmly acknowledged the wild sinking sensation between his lower stomach and the base of his spine.

"Whoa, there," said one of the security men, playing it cool.

Rodgers imagined that they all must be thinking the same thing: *Turbulence. It's worse in small aircraft, right?* But it wasn't necessary to be a pilot or a meteorologist to understand that this wasn't turbulence.

A second later, there was a noise that was louder than a click but softer than a thud, and the cabin lights went out. Rodgers glanced to the wing but couldn't make out the light that should have been flashing at its tip. The exterior lights had been cut too. Glancing around, he felt both suddenly skilled at diagnosing problems—*Electrical failure! Engine failure!*—and acutely aware that he had no knowledge of how any of these complications might be overcome.

The second security man stood heroically, perhaps because he was trained to do so, and stumbled toward the cockpit, riding the narrow aisle like a bull. By starlight, Rodgers watched him open the door and half expected to see the silhouettes of both pilots slumped over their instruments. He was not prepared for the alternative: that they had full control of their own faculties but somehow none of the plane's. A brief, calm, highly professional conversation between the pilots and bodyguard ensued. It was inaudible to Rodgers except for a curt excerpt from one of the pilots that reached him, and which turned over and over in his mind: "She went into a stall."

Rodgers was afraid to guess where that particular problem fell on the continuum of manageable to catastrophic, but the jet's odd silence was making everything feel inescapably real. He was in the present. This was happening. They were twenty thousand feet above the Yellow Sea, in an aircraft he had not imagined could be so silent as it sailed through the air.

Of the forces imposed upon objects of mass on Earth, gravity is the most predictable. It does not gust or evaporate or ebb or erode. It cannot be harnessed with a windmill or an airfoil or a solar panel. It cannot be voted upon or negotiated or corrupted by money. Struggle against it, and it doesn't surge with vengeance or retreat out of mercy. It merely is. It always is.

For a violent thirty seconds, the fuselage yo-yoed and rattled, an ungraceful dance partner rebelling against the pilots' lead. Soon, the aerodynamic phenomenon of lift was no longer in play and the only relevant force was gravity, which, Rodgers had learned in elementary-school science, accelerates objects in free fall at an exponential rate.

The cabin air grew putrid with vomit. Terror pealed in shouts through the stench. Then gradually the human noises subsided as, one by one, the six souls in their spinning cage in the sky were swallowed mercifully into unconsciousness.

Some seconds later, the ocean's buoyant surface intervened to arrest the plane's free fall and disperse debris across the surface of the water, which was darker than the starlit sky.

# LANGLEY, VIRGINIA

Lionel Bright, director of the Central Intelligence Agency's Office of Collection Strategies and Analysis, paused the video on the operations center's main tactical display and slipped the small remote control into his pocket. "'We grieve with all Americans for the loss of our mutual friend, Mr. Ambassador Greg Rodgers,'" he said, translating aloud the final line from the Chinese president's remarks. This was the fourth time Bright and his team had reviewed film of the press conference since it had been aired three hours earlier by the state-controlled Xinhua News Agency.

He gazed at the dozen men and women around the room through the beat-up glasses that rested on the slope of his angular nose. Bright had begun to notice how common it was these days to be the oldest person in the room. But seniority had plenty of advantages, and few of the side effects bothered him—even his gray-white hair. He had yet to entertain one serious thought about retirement.

In Bright's other hand, he realized, was a coffee mug painted on one side with the phrase "#1 Dad." He was not a father and could not remember filling the mug. He looked down into the tepid liquid before abandoning the mug on the nearest desk, which belonged to one of the East Asia analysts, Wilson Yu. Was it possible Yu was a father? Bright had never spoken to him about anything other than satellite images, transcripts from Central Politburo meetings, and cyberthreats that had been traced back within the borders of the People's Republic. No way Yu had a kid. He was little more than a kid himself, at most two years out of college, and worked sixty-hour weeks.

Bright was in a doubting frame of mind. He was also exhausted. He'd come into work that morning without a care in the world, energized by the improbable success of a second date the night before. After a decade devoid of romance, Bright had found himself on five dates in the past two months. Last night's had been the only repeat customer. He wasn't entirely sure where the impetus to socialize had come from in his advanced middle age, but it was doing him some good. He'd begun to exercise regularly and dropped fifteen pounds. He'd never been overweight, not by American standards anyway, but at an inch shorter than average, fifteen pounds went a long way.

"Look at the panel here," Bright said, nodding at the on-screen image of the members of the Central Politburo's Standing Committee. A flag-draped background blazed red behind the seven men. Everyone in the ops center knew the faces, names, and biographies of even the lowest ranking among them. "See anything out of place?"

It was rare to get a glimpse of the Politburo Standing Committee, which was composed of China's most powerful decision makers. But nothing about the formal, highly staged imagery they were analyzing suggested anything more than the condolences being expressed by the president.

"Let's assume we're not going to get a good look at whatever's left of that plane," Bright said, gazing over the rims of his glasses. He jabbed a finger in the direction of the Chinese politicians on the screen. "And let's assume these guys aren't being straight with us. Can we independently rule out foul play? Do we have satellite pictures yet?" he said, turning to the two imagery analysts working an eight-screen array near the center of the room.

While one of the satellite analysts selected key images and punched them up to the big screen, Bright silently reviewed what they knew. The incident had occurred over Chinese airspace and terminated in Chinese waters. No planes or commercial boats in the vicinity had come forward with witnesses. Chinese military vessels had been the first responders, but they'd reached the scene in the dead of night, and bodies had yet to be recovered. The flight data recorder and cockpit recorder remained lost to the sea. Some of the more buoyant pieces of wreckage had been plucked from the water and would be made available to NTSB investigators, who were en route to Shanghai.

That, at least, was China's version of the story, as relayed through their ambassador in Washington. US agencies working through the night had found only one discrepancy with China's account. The closest American vessel to the wreckage, a *Virginia*-class submarine, the USS *North Dakota*, had directed its sonar toward the crash coordinates as soon as the American embassy in Beijing had alerted Washington of the incident. The *North Dakota*'s sonar picked up something curious: three Chinese military vessels were already circling the coordinates, well before the time Beijing would eventually claim their search-and-rescue boats had arrived on the scene.

"The plane went down just after dusk, so our sats were blind through all the action. At first light the scene looked like this." On the first satellite image, the imagery analyst drew a circle around a cluster of oblong dark spots that stood out against the ocean's deep-green morning hue. "These are the Chinese navy's standard search-and-rescue vessels, the same sort of thing they'd send out for a crippled fishing boat. But the three boats pinged by the *North Dakota* read a lot more like these." A new satellite image filled the screen, this one of Shanghai's bustling port at the mouth of the Yangtze River. The analyst zoomed in on three larger vessels docked along its northern end. "This is daybreak, fifty miles west of the crash site, in a section of the port used by the navy. And here are our three boats. Judging from all this vehicle and personnel traffic around them, it looks like they've returned from working overnight."

Bright looked away from the grainy boats and glanced up at the stringcourse of digital clocks circling the room. It was 0830 hours in Beijing, 2030 hours in Washington. The plane had gone down nearly thirteen hours earlier, and he'd been in the windowless ops center since two hours after that, as soon as the State Department had learned of the ambassador's fate. Eleven straight hours spent among the indicator lights, the glowing maps, the screens and their live feeds. He was not proud of the addictive rush being in this environment provided. Days passed in his sunny office meant that operations were running smoothly and the world was ordered—but those days were often tinged with boredom. What brought him to life were the hours spent in the ops center, which usually meant that a crisis had developed in some critical part of the world. Lives were in jeopardy or had been lost.

Bright shook his head. "So they had boats waiting out there to collect the data recorders. Or they had the plane bugged and were prepared to recover the audio. We'd have done the same thing. Have we confirmed that the plane was owned by Hu?" Bright wanted to bring the conversation back to the Chinese businessman. The crash of Hu Lan's jet was a peculiar development, coming just forty-eight hours after the news story published by Gnos.is had exposed Hu's financial ties with the Ministry of State Security. It was no surprise, of course, that Hu had ties to the MSS. But for China to play in the global economy, it was in their interest to keep secret even the possibility of such ties between the Chinese government and its leading business figures. They might not have any qualms about cheating in the global markets, but they had enough tact to not want to get caught. The news story about Hu was a black eye. America's top diplomat dying in Hu's airplane was another one. Either this was a pile of coincidences, or there had been an uncharacteristic slipup within China's intelligence community.

"Yes, sir, the plane was Hu's. NSA identified the aircraft from activity intercepted from the tower at Pudong. It was a private jet. Tail number registered to Hu's company."

"Do our dips usually fly private?" one of the analysts asked. "Why was Rodgers even on board?"

"Because we asked him to be," Bright said. The room fell into a somber silence. The more he thought about it, the less he liked the timing of all of this—the public revelation of Hu's links to the MSS and then the downed plane—but he couldn't draw a straight line between any of the potential causes and effects. "Any chatter from Hu about the crash?"

"Not yet. We're going back over intercepts from his staff, investment partners, and his wife."

"That news story about Hu came from Gnos.is," Bright said. "How'd Gnos.is get the scoop? A whistle-blower inside Hu's camp?" In addition to generating articles based on facts that emerged from tirelessly mining the Internet, Gnos.is was also a known hub for whistle-blowers and activists who wanted to anonymously submit information that was not already available online. Gnos.is's top-level domain—the ".is"—meant the site was registered in Iceland, where such activity was protected by liberal free speech laws.

"There's no evidence of that yet. But it seems more likely than the alternative—that there's a leak inside the MSS."

Bright feared a more alarming possibility, one that he had so far kept to himself: that the leak of information to Gnos.is had come from one of the men and women within the CIA's China division— possibly someone in this room. Bright and his team had discovered months earlier—well before the Gnos.is story—that Hu Lan had received funds from the Ministry of State Security, funneled to him through the Ministry of Industry and Information Technology. Bright had decided to sit on this bit of intelligence and watch Hu, keeping enough distance to let him attempt to go through with whatever the MSS had in mind for him. But the Gnos.is story had leveled the playing field; Bright's team no longer had the advantage of know-ing more than their rivals thought they knew.

Bright took a call from Charles Kowalsky, the White House chief of staff. The president was preparing a statement, and Kowalsky wanted to know if there were any last-minute updates. Bright assured him there weren't. Kowalsky hesitated before hanging up.

"The president trusts you, Lionel. What's your gut say? Is there any chance that this was an assassination? Any reason why we shouldn't be treating China the same as we were treating them yesterday?"

Bright had entertained and rejected this idea a dozen times since he'd been called into the ops center that morning. "There's no evi-dence to suggest that, Chuck. No logic either." Killing diplomats is not something that governments risk, unless they're trying to escalate a conflict. China wasn't that reckless. Unlike the United States' other tricky adversaries, such as the Russians and Iranians, the Chinese had always demonstrated the discipline to not wade in over their heads. No, Bright couldn't imagine a scenario in which the Chinese government was behind an assassination of Ambassador Rodgers.

"Terrorists?"

"That doesn't add up either. If a terrorist wanted to send a mes-sage to Washington, why make the ambassador's death look like a tragic accident? They'd want to make it a sensation, and they'd be eager to take credit."

Bright told the president's chief of staff that, for the time being, it was best to take the Chinese at their word and try to work back chan-nels to get permission to look harder for those flight data recorders.

# LOWER MANHATTAN

Two banks of elevator doors dominated the lobby of a skyscraper on Pine Street, two blocks from the New York Stock Exchange. As lawyers and investment bankers tapped their ID cards at a row of security turnstiles, computers assigned them to an elevator car, grouping them in a way that minimized the number of stops each car had to make as it whisked the passengers efficiently to offices as high as ninety floors up.

At 9:17 AM a screen instructed fourteen people to crowd onto elevator 2B. The passengers rode in silence, their heads turned down at their smartphones or up at a pair of flat-screens that broadcast CNBC. The car made a stop at the forty-eighth floor, depositing seven people. It stopped again on fifty and a woman disembarked. Four men and two women remained on board as the car decelerated and approached the seventy-second floor. The familiar chime rang and the car stopped, but the doors did not slide open, provoking a moment of weary confusion. This was the final leg of the passengers' morning commute. They'd endured trains and cabs and bagel lines and crowded sidewalks. What else could the city throw at them before nine thirty on a Wednesday morning?

The elevators had been upgraded the previous summer to the automated, hands-free grouping system. This eliminated the need for a panel of buttons inside the elevator, which meant that there was nothing to push in frustration when a door didn't open or close as expected. The only actionable hardware was a call switch below an emergency intercom speaker. The man closest to these flicked the switch. Nothing. Not even a busy tone or an empty crackle. He flipped it up and down a few times in quick succession, but his irritation was met only with indifference. At some point after he gave up and stepped back to let a fellow passenger have a go, but before anyone else could, the elevator car shifted unexpectedly. For a brief moment, innocent confusion reigned. Had any of the six passengers been able to describe it later, they might have mentioned a strange, disorienting sensation in their gut. And then, suddenly, they were weightless. A handbag bounced off the wall and floated slowly toward the ceiling. A man let go of his BlackBerry, and it hung there in front of his face.

These were tricks of perspective.

"Oh my god," groaned the first man to realize. His last word was drowned out by the sudden chaos around him.

The early portion of the descent was surprisingly smooth. The elevators had been well maintained and were designed to slip up and down the ninety-story shaft with a whisper. The passengers, all strangers, screamed together. Around the fortieth floor, the walls began to vibrate from the friction and there was an odor of smoldering metal. The ride was short after that. The elevator car ran out of shaft three stories below the lobby, compacting and fracturing into a shallow crater ripped into the concrete by twisted metal.

# THE VALLEY, RURAL MONTANA

Twenty miles beyond the last gas station, on a plain where gorgeous desolation stretched beyond the horizon in every direction, Charlie Canyon broke off the two-lane highway and pointed the rental car's hood up a narrow gravel road. Soon he passed two small signs nailed to a fence post: PRIVATE PROPERTY and NO TRESPASSING. Then the road began to wind up a wooded ravine, leaving behind the open foothills patrolled by cattle.

This world was a surreal contrast to his life in New York City, which he'd slipped from unnoticed forty-eight hours earlier. The journey had started in his office—a SoHo loft that served as the public-facing headquarters of Gnos.is. After returning from lunch around one, he'd changed into clothes he'd never worn before, including new shoes fresh out of the box, a hat, and noncorrective glasses. He'd packed light—just a backpack with toiletries and two changes of clothes. He did not bring his laptop or tablet; even his phone he left behind on his desk.

He'd slanted the bill of his hat low over his face to shield it from any of the building's surveillance cameras, whose feeds were almost certainly processed by facial-recognition software and available

to several law-enforcement and intelligence agencies. Then he'd
descended to the ground floor via the stairwell and pushed through
a fire exit, where he was immediately swallowed into the heavy sidewalk traffic. He bought a new Metro card—using cash—and took the
6 train up to Grand Central Station, then caught a cab across town
to Madison Square Garden. There, he entered Penn Station and paid
cash for the 3:40 Amtrak train departing for Chicago. The whole
time he remained mindful to keep his face hidden from surveillance
cameras.

The train emerged from beneath the Hudson and accelerated
west. By late evening, when the FBI agents assigned to tail Charlie
Canyon began to wonder why they hadn't spotted him leaving the
office at his usual time, he was two hundred miles away.

The train ride took nineteen hours. In Chicago he rented a car
from a disreputable company that would take his cash. Then he
set out west on the twenty-two-hour drive to Montana, careful to
obscure his face whenever he pulled into a gas station or rolled past
a tollbooth.

And then finally he was here.

When the gravel road crested at a pass, Canyon—thirty, handsome with dark hair and eyebrows and a smattering of chin stubble—
stopped the car in front of a gate. The two earlier signs discouraging
trespassers were reprised here, along with another sign that said BIG
SKY ENERGY. He got out and stood in front of the gate. It didn't look
like much, the gate, but if one thought about it, the thick steel bars
slung across the road were overkill for managing livestock. In a place
where most gates had rusty padlocks, there was instead a sophisti-
cated magnetic latch. There was no call box to announce himself.

Canyon stood for a moment in the dirt, stretching his legs. The
view from the pass was extraordinary. After ten years living in the
city, this scenery was as novel to him as driving a car. The valley
below was walled with ridges slicing into the sky, crescendoing at
three points to form rocky peaks. On the valley's south-facing slopes,

tennis-court-sized solar panels checkered the landscape above the tree line. He spotted a lake on the valley floor. It was the hottest part of the day, and the only thing that distinguished the dogleg body of water from the evergreen woods surrounding it, other than the way it sparkled in the sunlight, was a short dock protruding from the near shore. He noted that none of the recently constructed cabins were visible through the tree cover, though he knew they were down there somewhere. Viewed from above, the valley looked nearly untouched, save for the dock and solar panels.

Just when he started to wonder if he'd forgotten a step in the instructions—instructions that had come in a series of encrypted chat messages, which he'd memorized and wiped from his computer— he heard a metallic clank and the gate yawned open. He got back into the car and eased it forward.

The road plunged below the tree line and then descended toward the lake in wide, gradual switchbacks. It was an old mining road, he'd been told. On the valley floor, the road split in three directions. Sticking to the instructions, he took the one that guided him to a simple, spacious, two-story log house that appeared suddenly from out of the forest. There was no answer when he knocked on the door, but it was unlocked. He called out to announce himself. The house was as silent as the hills. He crossed the room to stand at the large picture windows overlooking the lake. And there he saw it. Far out in the center of the lake, at the tip of a wake's V, a male figure advanced through the water with steady crawl strokes.

Canyon went down to the dock below and joined the man's dog, who was overcome with excitement from tongue to tail for twenty or thirty seconds before sprawling lazily again upon the warm wood. Canyon sat in a chair that had a towel draped over one of the arms and watched the man crawl through the water toward him.

He didn't have to wait long. A minute later, Rafael Bolívar hoisted himself out of the lake. Bolívar wore no swim trunks. Unashamed, he turned around as if to admire the distance he'd come. Canyon watched the water come off his body; pulled from it by gravity, lifted from it by the sun. Canyon enjoyed moments like this, feeling his species' basest yearning. His job was to understand human nature and harness its power on a mass scale. Or, as he liked to tell people with an enigmatic grin, "I work in advertising."

That was true, in a way, though it was only one small piece of the role Canyon played at Gnos.is as the website's only public face— its spokesman and advocate. Gnos.is, in fact, did no conventional advertising or marketing. It didn't need to. The site's performance was enough to capture users' imaginations.

Canyon tossed the towel to Bolívar, who had bent to scratch the dog.

"How was the drive?" Bolívar asked, covering himself and step- ping into sandals.

"Fine, considering you live on the dark side of the moon."

· · · · ·

Canyon was sitting at the dining room table when Bolívar, showered and dressed in khaki shorts and a white T-shirt, joined him. Bolívar was thirty-three, and he'd looked his age in the city, Canyon thought, if not abstractly a little older in his fitted suits and a solemn business stare that guarded not just his thoughts but a headful of proprietary secrets—secrets that, eventually, had driven him to this valley.

Before he'd disappeared from the outside world, Rafael Bolívar had inherited hundreds of millions of dollars from his father, who had founded Venezuela's largest media company. Bolívar had turned those millions into billions by expanding his father's media empire into North America. He had been celebrated in the media industry as a cunning yet principled businessman and in the tabloids as an eligible bachelor. But Bolívar's success in the world of sensational- ized news and reality shows had been a front, a ruthless tactic to raise money on the backs of cultural institutions he saw as depraved.

Secretly, he had been reinvesting that money to fund what he hoped would replace them: Gnos.is.

It had been a little more than two months since Canyon had seen him in person. He thought Bolívar looked much younger out here than he had in the city.

Canyon slid a beige file folder across the table. Bolívar lifted its cover to glance at the first page, then he let it fall closed.

"This is the real reason you're here?"

Canyon nodded.

"What are they?"

"They are the findings of an investigation into Gnos.is by the Senate Select Committee on Intelligence. The committee's chairman, as you know, is Senator Wrightmont of Montana, who would probably not be amused if he knew that you were currently a constituent. I gather they think you're hiding in Iceland." Canyon picked up the file and flipped through it. "The senator has amassed a collection of letters from the attorney general's office along with these invitations from the FBI, CIA, State Department, DHS, and the embassies of most US allies. It's all here."

"Invitations?"

"That's what they're calling them. For now."

"What do they want?"

"They want Gnos.is's sources."

"For which stories?"

Canyon shrugged. "Dozens of them. There's a list of Gnos.is articles that they say exposed classified information." Canyon leaned back, folding his arms over his abdomen. "They did not, however, cite any concrete examples of harm caused by the publication of that information. Most of the stories seem pretty minor to me, just like before. There's one, though, that seems to have especially struck a nerve."

"Which one?"

"It ran last week. That report about the Chinese businessman who invested in an American telecom company with money from China's intelligence agency." Canyon shrugged. "Is that breaking news? I wouldn't have thought so."

Bolívar lifted his eyebrows, but he made no move to review the contents of the file.

"Any warrants or subpoenas?"

Canyon looked hurt. "If a subpoena comes, it won't be served by me."

Bolívar left the file on the table and walked to the window. "They'll come," he said. And then, after a long silence, "Come on, I'll show you the mine."

•  •  •  •  •

Bolívar drove them in a pickup truck. He was silent during the short ride, his arm resting on the edge of the open window, his hair waving in the breeze, his olive skin noticeably darker from a few months in the sun. Canyon looked out at the woods, noting the occasional narrow driveway they came upon and passed. At the end of each drive was a small cabin sheltered among the trees. Bolívar's staff in the valley totaled approximately two dozen men and women who had jumped at the invitation to work for Gnos.is, even though it meant— at least for now—living in hiding and engaging only in activities that didn't risk giving away their location. They lived this way out of necessity, to protect Gnos.is, which, like any good news organization, had enemies who were much more powerful than its friends.

Canyon, in fact, had had to delay this trip to the valley because, as the only person publicly affiliated with Gnos.is, he was under twenty-four-hour surveillance. Government law-enforcement and intelligence agencies watched him, hoping to find a trail that would lead them to Bolívar, and thus to Gnos.is, which the government viewed not as a news organization but as a dangerous leaker of classified secrets. Teams at the FBI and NSA were probably going apeshit right now wondering where Canyon had gone and how he'd slipped their watch. When he returned, Canyon thought, their surveillance would only get tighter, perhaps making it impossible for him to visit again.

When they got around to the far side of the lake, Bolívar steered the truck onto a narrow drive that would have been easy to confuse with any of the other potholed and overgrown paths that sprouted off from the main road. They had to roll up the windows to keep from being slapped by branches. After half a mile, the path opened to a clearing. There was still cover overhead from tall evergreens that let only a few columns of late-afternoon sunlight through their branches. The ground was clear of vegetation but cluttered by small piles of abandoned mining equipment. Moss grew over rusted-out troughs and cables like mold warning of expiration. Bolívar parked next to three other vehicles. Canyon got out of the truck and kicked the dirt and pine needles underfoot, looking up at the trees. He couldn't see the high ridges through the tree cover.

The mining tunnel was on the far side of the clearing. At just the place where the land began to slope up steeply, almost like a cliff, there it was—a rectangular black hole in the earth, framed like a picture with thick posts of wood. The opening was no larger than a one-car garage door.

"It's a little ways in here," Bolívar said, and he disappeared into the base of the mountain.

Canyon caught up with him at a steel door several dozen feet into the tunnel. As he waited for Bolívar to enter a pass code, Canyon glanced back, a little claustrophobically, at the opening they'd come through. It didn't look so far away, but the temperature had dropped quickly with each step. Canyon turned back to the door when Bolívar pulled it open.

They came first to a bright, white-painted chamber. It was small, more like a junction of two short hallways than a room. There was a door on each wall.

"Through there is the lounge and restrooms," Bolívar said, nodding at the door to the left. It was the only door that did not have a keypad lock on it. "This door on the right leads to the Big Sky turbines," he said, referring to the mine's power source, which was made available by Big Sky Energy, an experimental, privately owned company that Bolívar had invested in through a proxy. Big Sky was, in fact, the reason Bolívar had chosen this valley as the spot to anchor Gnos.is. The energy company, whose owner was enthusiastic about Gnos.is's mission, had been seeking a way to test a hybrid of solar, wind, thermodynamic, and other experimental forms of power that, once perfected, would help communities independently source the energy they required. Big Sky needed a guinea pig and Bolívar needed power—a lot of it, and none that came from the main grid. It had not taken long to reach a secret agreement that made Big Sky Energy a cover for the existence of all activity in the valley, providing Bolívar with his power source while maintaining his anonymity.

"Beyond the turbine room is a large hall where we've installed the servers and generators—Gnos.is's brain and beating heart," Bolívar continued. "If necessary, we can keep extending capacity by tunneling deeper into the mountain. But we're going in here," he said, walking to the door directly across from the main entrance. He obliged a waiting keypad and retina scanner and, a moment later, was holding the door open for Canyon.

The chamber inside was surprisingly large. When they entered, a half-dozen men and women looked up from consoles around a long table. The only person Canyon recognized was J. D. Jones, who smiled and came over to greet him. Jones, in his midthirties and presenting a pasty, plain-featured face, had let his hair grow out some, enough that he tucked it behind his ears where the temples of his black-rimmed glasses clung. A veteran of both the NSA and CIA, Jones had been recruited to run Gnos.is's cybersecurity.

Bolívar introduced Canyon to the others in the room. As he did, Canyon realized that he knew everyone by name. Like J. D. Jones, they were all well-known coders, hackers, and cybersecurity experts. It had not been difficult to get any of them to quit whatever corporate or government job they'd been doing and join Gnos.is.

All four walls of the chamber were lined with large flat-screens displaying pages from both branches of the Gnos.is site: gnos.is/fact, the news branch, and gnos.is/truth, a highly curated arts site. Controversy erupted most often from the /fact side, which was dedicated to collecting, verifying, and publishing facts about the world. Where Gnos.is differed from other sources of journalism was in how it carried out this process. Gnos.is worked by filtering as much Internet traffic as it could access through layers of complex algorithms that assigned a truth value to each claim about the world that it scraped from cyberspace. When a truth value became high enough, a claim was ruled a fact and was then incorporated into all relevant articles on the site. In addition to collecting data and evaluating its truth content, Gnos.is's powerful software also absorbed the language patterns it detected across the Internet, a capability that was then reverse engineered to spool out the sentences and paragraphs that formed Gnos.is articles. This meant that human beings were not required to actually write the articles or even the headlines. And it also meant that articles were not static documents. New facts could be introduced into articles as soon as they could be verified, automatically updating the text in real time.

The gnos.is/fact, or news, side of the site was free to users, but only monetarily. Gnos.is did not need money, for it had Bolívar's fortune. Instead, Gnos.is was paid heftily in the currency it most craved: information. And everyone who had ever touched the Internet had paid them in this way, whether they knew it or not.

"So this is where it happens," Canyon said, watching the men and women at work. He thought of the thick file of complaints from the Justice Department. "Do you know how many people would like to get just a few minutes alone in this room with a sledgehammer?"

For a brief moment, Bolívar was unable to suppress a smile.

· · · · ·

After touring the mine, they rode back to Bolívar's log house. It was early dusk, and the only sounds as they drove were the branches slapping against the side of the truck. They sat on the porch as the wide sky changed color. Even framed by the valley walls, the sky seemed a limitless expanse, felt as much as seen.

"Are you coming back?" Canyon asked.

They were drinking beer from bottles. Inside, some of the others were preparing dinner, reading, playing cards.

Canyon's question was followed by such a long silence that he was prepared to just let it go. But then Bolívar answered.

"Not until Gnos.is has proven itself."

"Hasn't it already?"

Bolívar shook his head. "We've proven to ourselves that Gnos.is works. But Gnos.is still scares a lot of people. We need more time." He didn't name the threat contained in the file folder that Canyon had delivered. But that was what he was talking about. The government wanted Gnos.is shut down, and they wanted Bolívar in their custody so they could force him to reveal the website's sources. "As our public face, I need you to remind them that Gnos.is is interested only in facts. We haven't broken any laws, and we don't even know the names of Gnos.is's sources."

Canyon nodded. A little while later, he retrieved his bags from his car and was shown to a guest cabin. The next morning he was gone before sunrise.

# PARIS

The Hotel Victoire on Rue Michel-Ange in the city's La Défense district was a full block of tasteful design and trendy lodging, the sort of place that, in a centuries-old city, had benefited from an architect who knew where to apply restraint even if the developer's budget didn't require it. The interior features were cutting-edge, but practical. Self-tinting windows, environmentally friendly plumbing and lighting, high-speed Internet connectivity—not just for the flat-screens in each room but also for the minibars, closets, air-conditioning, and other utilities. Every variable of the human-designed indoor environment could be digitally adjusted to taste. So what if Victoire had no grand history; it was elegant and expensive. It was the most modern hotel in Paris, and the people who mattered had taken notice.

At a quarter to nine in the evening, a woman left her ninth-floor room after dressing for dinner. In the hallway she pressed the button to call for an elevator and stood back, smoothing her silk skirt, which had been pressed inside her luggage since New York. The woman was on her way to dinner with a man she saw sometimes when she was in town. The thought of him now made it easier to ignore her jet lag, and she chose instead to savor her anticipation.

There was a soft chime and the elevator doors parted. She selected the lobby as her destination and the doors slid shut. She was alone in the car. By the time it started to move, the woman had become distracted with checking the address of the restaurant on her phone. She didn't notice at first that the lift was going up, not down. It wasn't until some twenty seconds later, when she sensed the journey was taking too long, that she looked up.

Floor fourteen was illuminated on the indicator above the door. Then fifteen. She pushed the lobby button again, though it was already illuminated. The car reached seventeen and still it climbed. She jabbed experimentally at a few of the panel's other buttons, but the lift responded to nothing. It wanted only to climb. She stood back, resigned to wait for the car to reach the top before descending to street level.

The elevator finally decelerated and came to rest at the twenty-fourth floor, the top, which hosted the hotel's penthouse suites. Perhaps the elevator gave priority to guests willing to pay 800 euros a night, the woman thought, a little curious to get a glimpse at her wealthy rival for the lift's services. But the doors didn't open. The car hovered silently for a few seconds, and then the woman experienced a very strange sensation. Her stomach turned, and she felt weightless.

# SEATTLE

Kera Mersal sat on a park bench, pretending to read a paperback. Over the rim of the book, and through dark glasses, she eyed a woman she guessed was her own age playing with a toddler near the public sculpture in McGraw Square. Kera had caught herself noticing things like this more often, though she didn't see the point. Her life did not allow for children. It might never. This hadn't given her much pause in her twenties, and now it was too late. Not because of her age—she was only thirty-one—but because of the career path she'd chosen. Under the best circumstances, someone with her résumé would have unique difficulties raising kids. But she'd made choices that put the best circumstances far from reach. Now, seeing the toddler hug his mother's leg, she reminded herself that it was just human nature to want what you can't have.

Kera's real purpose for sitting on this particular park bench presented itself at 6:10 PM. A man came out of the news-and-shine shop across the street and lowered the rolling gate over the shop's entrance. Then he set off in the direction of the light-rail station, just as she knew he would. In twenty years, his routine had not changed. Maybe he'd moved a little faster in a younger body, and of course he'd gone to the bus station before the rail system existed. But this was what he did six days a week. Seeing it again both comforted and saddened her.

When he got on the train at Westlake Station, she boarded the opposite end of the car and watched him from a distance. It was rush hour, but someone had noticed the way he hunched slightly from back pain and had given him a seat. He sat quietly, looking forward.

At the first stop, the seat facing him opened up. Kera took it. She waited until the train was moving again before she removed her sunglasses and forced eye contact with the man. For a beat there was no reaction, just a silent battle: recognition versus disbelief. She remembered now that she'd dyed her hair much lighter than he'd ever seen, but she hadn't done anything else to disguise herself, not today. With widened eyes, he tried to speak.

"Not here," she said softly. "Get off at Pioneer Square and meet me up on the street." He seemed paralyzed. "Will you do that?" Finally he nodded. She held his gaze for a moment to reassure him and was unprepared for what she saw in his eyes: anxiety, fear, confusion. She turned away, then stood and walked to the next car.

She waited for him on the sidewalk in Pioneer Square and then guided him into an alley where a Dumpster hid them from the street. Before saying anything more, she asked to see his cell phone. He produced a flip phone that had to be at least five years old. She removed its battery, ignoring the questions that filled his eyes. Confident that the disabled phone couldn't be accessed by eavesdroppers, she led him back out to the sidewalk. They strolled a few blocks to City Hall Park, where they sat on a bench.

"Are you OK?" he asked her. If she had given him a chance to speak on the train, moments after he'd first seen her, his first words probably would have been different, angrier. But he'd had time to let her presence sink in, and this is what he wanted to know.

"I'm OK." How else could she respond?

"You should have called us. Why didn't you call?"

"I couldn't. I'm sorry."

"You could have, Kera. You could have." He was shaking his head. "We have to call your mother." He looked at the phone and battery in his hands.

"I already spoke to Mom. I just came from the university." Her father's eyes got big. "She's angry," Kera said. Her father nodded. "I understand that. Look, Dad, all of those things they say I've done—" she started, and then stopped herself. She could see doubt in his eyes, sown by all the stories that had been stirred up about her in the media. Her phone records, text messages, e-mails, even her private photos—all of it carefully cherry-picked for release to the media to build the narrative the agency wanted to create. She had no clue how they'd even gotten their hands on most of it. They hadn't done so legally, anyway. But what could she do? Defending herself meant falling into their trap. They were provoking her, trying to draw her out of hiding.

Even if her next words hadn't been stopped by a sudden lump in her throat, she knew there was no way to explain this to her father. "It's not the way they say it is," she whispered finally. "I can't prove that to you now. But I will. Someday this will be over and I'll show you."

Mercifully, the media had been gentle with her parents. Her adoptive parents. The only parents Kera had ever known. Her adoptive mother was a white UW anthropology professor from the Midwest; her adoptive father had run his news-and-shine shop since he immigrated to the US from Egypt when the couple married. Kera herself had been born to a Salvadorian woman; everything about her biological father was unknown. After Kera vanished two months earlier, some professionally distasteful pundits, mostly from conservative radio, had taken the predictable swipes at the mixed-race, Seattle-living, professor-immigrant couple. But for the most part, the media had written her parents out of the drama. Kera was relieved for that, even if she suspected it had to do with the fact that they were not her "real" parents. Could the sins of an adopted Central American child who grows up to be a treasonous spy really be blamed on the loving couple who took her in and gave her a chance at a good life?

Kera had done her best to ignore all of that. What did it matter anyway? The media had been spun and misled so thoroughly that they had no hope of getting the story right. She was just thankful that her parents had been spared the dirty misinformation campaign intended to level suspicion and judgment on her.

She had to look away when she saw the wet shine in his eyes. That's when she knew she had to go. She pulled a folded slip of paper from her pocket. "Here. If you need to reach me, use this e-mail address. But don't use your computer at home. They're watching that."

"Who's watching that?"

"I'm sorry, Dad. Good-bye for now."

"Who's watching us?" he called after her. "Kera, what have you done?"

# LANGLEY

She looked different from her online pictures. Not worse, like the others had; but still, the disconnect had thrown him. Live and in three dimensions, she looked like a distant, older cousin of the woman Bright's imagination had constructed from her dating-profile photos. Now that Bright had spent a few hours in her company, he could see, retroactively, the honest resemblances contained in those photographs. The lines at the corners of her mouth when she smiled. The look in her eyes when she laughed, which was so tied to the sound and movement of her laugh that its identifying contours could not possibly be conveyed in a picture viewed by a stranger.

In the span of their first meal, the dating-profile version of herself had been replaced with the live woman in front of him, and to his surprise, Bright found his curiosity deepening in her presence. She commanded a down-to-earth appeal that he rounded up to beauty. And her eyes cast the hint of a wild drive he couldn't imagine she had a use for in her career as an airline-industry lobbyist. She was the kind of woman Bright could picture equally comfortable watching an opera or drinking pints in a sports bar. On their first date they'd barely glossed over the topic of their jobs. When she asked, he had told her only that he worked at a foreign-policy think tank, his usual cover story.

After he got out of this meeting, Bright decided, he would call her—Audrey—and suggest they have dinner again later in the week.

A mention of the late Ambassador Rodgers by a woman down the conference table nudged Bright back into the present. But the name had only been dropped in the service of making some tangential point, and the woman continued on about chatter the Central America division had intercepted and interpreted as a terror group's ambition to strike the Panama Canal. Bright listened, hoping he wouldn't be called upon to acknowledge that he knew nothing more about the ambassador's death. The meeting he was in was a daily high-level teleconference session between CIA Director Cal Tennison and the director of national intelligence, who delivered the daily security briefing each morning to the president. Bright rarely attended such sessions, but he'd been asked to sit in today in case the DNI brought up the situation in China, which so far he hadn't.

Bright's mind had begun to wander again when the door to the room opened slightly, and his assistant, looking rather sheepish in this company, slipped in.

There was a short list of people for whom Lionel Bright was to be pulled out of any meeting, should they call. James Pollert was not on that list, but that was only because it had never occurred to Bright that the US secretary of state would have any reason to call him. Fortunately, Bright's administrative assistant had taken the liberty of exercising his common sense and, instead of asking the secretary of state if he wanted to leave a message, broke into the DNI briefing to deliver a Post-it tucked inside a file folder.

Bright did a slight double take at the note, then excused himself and retreated to his office. James Pollert and Lionel Bright had been stationed together for nine months in Cairo early in their careers and had grown close. But then Pollert went into politics and made a name for himself, and Bright remained anonymous in the trenches, which was his preference.

Bright hesitated before picking up the phone. Save for comparing notes before congressional briefings on the Hill, it was unusual for their paths to cross on official grounds.

"Jim, I'm sorry about Greg," Bright said into the phone, referring to the deceased ambassador. It was the only reason he could think of why Pollert would be calling. "I know you two were—"

"Have you seen this?" the secretary of state said as soon as he realized Bright was on the line. His tone had more than a little backspin.

"What?"

"Are you near a computer? Look at Gnos.is."

"Gnos.is? Christ, what now?" Bright said. Gnos.is had of course been the cause of several minor headaches for the agency, but his prevailing take was that the website was given more credit than it was due. Sure, occasionally Gnos.is published something that created a stir, but no more often than established news organizations. Bright was not alone in his bafflement about where Gnos.is obtained sources for stories or how it was funded under such secrecy. It was beginner's luck that Gnos.is had managed to stay afloat for as long as it had, Bright mused. He gave it no more than another year or two before it wound up buried in the great start-up graveyard in the cloud.

"It's not just Gnos.is," Pollert said, delivering the name of the site like it was a slur. "The *Post* and *Times* are picking it up too. But Gnos.is broke the story."

Bright was already at his desk. In front of him sat two computers. He reached for the keys of the one designated for unclassified traffic. The other machine beside it was reserved for classified matters, separated from the Internet by an air gap. He opened a browser and selected Gnos.is from the inappropriately named "Favorites" bar.

"OK, what am I looking at?" As soon as he said it, his eyes tripped over the headline.

"US Spy Agencies Target Foreign Journalists," Secretary Pollert said. "We're looking at our worst nightmare."

Bright grazed over the first paragraph. America's spying apparatus was targeting journalists who had access to the inner circles of foreign heads of state, including close allies, the article reported. Undercover CIA operatives stationed at US embassies around the world were aiding the NSA in the program, code named TERMITE. The name had been chosen at random by a computer program, a standard practice that prevented the name itself from revealing even the subject of the operation. As it happened, TERMITE was one of those occasional cases where the name seemed serendipitous.

*Fuck,* Bright thought. Journalists reported constantly on what they thought were classified operations, but rarely with much specificity. Naming TERMITE was a catastrophic level of specificity. And public knowledge of the program was a nightmare because spying on the leaders of countries considered close allies had been banned by President Obama after Edward Snowden's leaks revealed the NSA had been listening in on German chancellor Angela Merkel's phone calls.

"It was my understanding that this would never be a headline," Pollert said.

"Your displeasure is noted."

"*My* displeasure. This office hasn't received this many pissed-off calls from Congress since Benghazi. I didn't call to vent, Lionel. How is it that they're publishing this kind of detail? Why can't we shut them down?"

Bright ignored these questions because his answer for both was *I don't know.* "I wouldn't fault you for venting, Jim. But you called me on a telephone to ask me about classified operations. There's nothing I can say."

"What am I supposed to tell them?"

"Who?"

"Congress. France. Israel. Russia. China. The fucking Vatican."

Bright sighed. "This came from Gnos.is, right? No one reads Gnos.is."

"I can guarantee you that our counterparts in Britain, Israel, Russia, and China are poring over it right now."

"No, I mean that's what you should tell them. 'No one reads Gnos.is.' Tell them that the *Post* and the *Times* should be embarrassed for biting on this story. What is Gnos.is? It's not a legitimate news organization. It doesn't employ real journalists. It's been around for what, a year?"

"That's not the point. There's a fucking leak, Lionel. And having this crap in the news makes my job impossible."

"Well, I have my own job to do. But if I were you, I'd tell my counterparts overseas that the classified operation Gnos.is describes does not exist. If they want a different answer, they can get it from their own fucking spy agencies. End of conversation."

The secretary of state let a beat pass, then he said, "Fuck you, Lionel." That had been the way they spoke to each other those many years ago in Africa. *Good morning, Jimbo. Fuck you, Lionel. Good talk, let's go find some terror-loving terrorists.* In this context, it was an olive branch, a clue to let Bright know that the secretary of state was aware they were all on the same team.

"Look, you've had a hell of a week," Bright said.

When Pollert spoke again, his tone was altogether rehabilitated. "What are you learning about that crash?"

"I'm sure you know more than I do, Mr. Secretary. Last I heard, everyone was waiting to hear all the gory details from the NTSB."

"The NTSB will be lucky if they get the Chinese to give them a tour of Tiananmen Square. Our access to the investigation is a joke. The Chinese had nearly forty-eight hours with that wreckage. If there's anything they don't want us to find, it's gone."

"It'll all come out, Jim. It always does." He'd meant it to signal the end of their conversation, but Pollert wasn't finished.

"Lionel. I'm not saying here that I actually believe foul play was involved—"

"But?"

"This Gnos.is article specifically mentions Beijing as a key target of the TERMITE operation. And last week Gnos.is called out Hu Lan's ties to the MSS. What if the ambassador's plane going down was retaliation?"

*The man needs a vacation,* Bright thought. *A counselor. Something.*

"I don't need to tell you that anything's possible, but assassinating a diplomat hardly serves the interests of the Chinese, and they know it. Let's give it a little time, huh? Planes don't just fall out of the sky. There's a reason it went down, and we'll all learn it sooner or later."

When he hung up, Bright sat alone thinking about what he had to do. There was a leak somewhere—and the exposure of the TERMITE program suggested that it wasn't coming from the Chinese. The leaker had to be someone with knowledge of the program. The good news was that that narrowed down the list significantly. The bad news was that everyone on that list had a TOP SECRET security clearance, or higher, which meant whoever it was had access to a whole lot more than what had so far appeared on Gnos.is. If the goal was to harm the United States by leaking classified documents to the press, he or she might just be getting started.

# THE VALLEY

Rafael Bolívar had never once awoken to an alarm in the months he'd lived in the valley. He was up each morning with the birds and often sat on the dock with coffee until curiosity drove him to his computer to check the overnight developments on Gnos.is. He and his team—"employees" was not a word that did them justice— had relocated to these mountains hastily, and as such Bolívar had underestimated the full range of advantages of the location. He'd been pleasantly surprised to discover that, more than just a private, subpoena-free place, the valley was an ideal setting for thinking deeply and clearly. All the better that this could be done while sitting on a dock thrust out over mirrorlike water at sunrise.

These had been some of Bolívar's most productive months, professionally and intellectually, though they were not without the typical burdens of fugitive life. With the launch of Gnos.is, crimes of corporate fraud and income-tax evasion had been alleged, and then dropped—the former dropped because the media corporation claiming to have been defrauded by Bolívar had gone bankrupt under the expense of defending its own criminal activities, and the latter because Gnos.is earned no income. No, thank you, Gnos.is did not wish to file as a nonprofit, they'd stated in their letter to the bewildered IRS. Perhaps there ought to be another designation: "extra-profit," as in beyond or outside of profit, although that still conceded a position relative to profit, which defeated the purpose. In fact, Gnos.is took no position on profit at all, other than to acknowledge that profit seeking was a uniquely ill-suited mechanism for getting at common truth and personal meaning.

It was not the tarnish of those past criminal charges that kept Bolívar from venturing out of the valley. The concern now, the reality that glared back at him from the lake and the trees and that mountain—underneath which his computers performed some of the most advanced data mining and aggregation in the history of information—was that more allegations and charges would come. Bolívar had become certain of that, even before Charlie Canyon had delivered the government's hyperbolic "invitations" to appear before Congress and in the FBI's interrogation chambers.

On this morning, however, it appeared there would be no such peaceful lakeside contemplation.

Bolívar sat up in bed and waited for the thick fog to lift from his mind. The sound that had disturbed him was a relentless string of crisp beeps, not very loud, but persistent enough to dislodge him from sleep. Facts began to come to him. The tone did not originate from his bedside clock, which told him it was 3:24 AM. Instead, both his phone and his tablet were blinking on the nearby desk in a way he'd seen only once before, when J. D. Jones had demonstrated one of the network's warning systems. But which one? It was certainly not an attempted cyberattack or the detection of a fraudulent source, both of which happened so frequently, and unsuccessfully, that he'd silenced the corresponding alarm tones on his mobile devices. No, this was something else.

Bolívar slid from the sheets and crossed the room to the flashing tablet. A text bar at the center of its screen declared two related alerts: SOURCE COMPROMISED and STORY COMPROMISED. Bolívar studied these for a moment, unable to remember their precise meanings.

Just then his phone rang. It was J. D. Jones.

"This wake you too?" Bolívar asked.

"Yes."

"Any idea what triggered it?"

"No. This one's never gone off. It might just be a bug. I'll go over to the mine and check it out."

"I'll pick you up," Bolívar said. They'd tested the security of the site enough that he knew Jones didn't really think it was just a bug. Besides, now he was up; returning to sleep would be impossible.

· · · · ·

Twenty minutes later they were seated at Jones's console in the chamber buried beneath the mountain. The Gnos.is/fact home page displayed news stories as spheres clumped together in a cloud. High-level algorithms determined the size and placement of each sphere, shifting the spheres' proximity to others in the cluster as the algorithms constantly digested streams of new data scraped and filtered from the world's fiber-optic Internet cables. Stories that impacted the lives of large numbers of people were represented by larger spheres, while less consequential events were contained in proportionately smaller spheres.

The diagnostic warning system pointed them to one of the largest spheres in Gnos.is's global news cloud—a wide-reaching report about corruption by government leaders in China. Bolívar noticed something immediately, even before Jones tapped the sphere and it unfolded to display the story's content in full-screen view.

"This is the same story that reported Hu Lan's ties to the MSS."

"Yes," Jones said, "but the China story is one of our most complex. It's massive. That bit about Hu Lan is basically a sidebar."

"That's not how the attorney general sees it," Bolívar said. He'd eventually flipped through the file Charlie Canyon had delivered.

Jones chuckled. "The attorney general is just doing his job. And we're doing ours."

Bolívar stared at the screen with renewed seriousness. "The story's compromised?"

"According to the alert, yes."

"How?" Tension had crept into Bolívar's tone. He did not need to say aloud that they could not get this wrong. Not a story this big.

"I'm not sure," Jones said, opening the infections log, which recorded every instance of an unauthorized user or virus attempting to penetrate Gnos.is's network. He scanned through the log entries; there were plenty of hits, but none had succeeded. The log revealed nothing out of the ordinary. Jones tapped the screen, returning to the alert. "The system seems to think that a source might have been exposed."

The effectiveness of Gnos.is depended upon the absolute protection of anonymous sources. A government official or low-level employee of a corrupt corporation would be compelled to send Gnos.is information only if his or her anonymity was guaranteed. Building on this principle, Jones had programmed security software to monitor the network for potential breaches to source confidentiality. On a handful of occasions, the computer had flagged a source as compromised, only to rule it out as a false positive a few nanoseconds later. The software protecting both the identity of sources and the integrity of the stories to which they contributed had worked flawlessly from the beginning.

Until now, if this alert was genuine.

"Hold on," Jones said, interpreting the information on his display. "It's not just one source. It looks like three were flagged."

"Three sources?"

"That's strange." Jones had been shuffling quickly through the data, working the touch screen with expert swipes, taps, and pinches of his fingers. Suddenly, he stopped.

"What?" Bolívar followed Jones's eyes to the screen.

"It says they're deceased."

"Since when?"

"All in the past few days. That must be what triggered the alert. I programmed the system to warn us if two or more sources for a story died of unnatural causes within seventy-two hours."

"How'd they die?" Bolívar asked, realizing the answer as soon as the question was out.

Jones shook his head. "Telling us that would compromise their identities."

By design, no one—especially not Bolívar or Jones or anyone who worked for Gnos.is—was permitted to learn the precise source of each piece of information that the Gnos.is computers collected and then used to assemble and prioritize the world's news. This served the central aim of Gnos.is, which was to eliminate human error and bias in reporting.

"Thousands of sources must have contributed to a story like this. Isn't it possible that three of them dying is just a coincidence?"

Jones thought about this. Finally he said, "I could run some statistical models and tell you the probability of that. But that's all it would be, a statistical probability." He glanced up to confirm that Bolívar wasn't interested in abstractions. Then he said what they both were thinking. "We won't know for certain without looking at the actual circumstances."

Bolívar scratched the back of his head, looking up at the story on the big screen for a long moment. Finally he said, "Dammit."

It was technically possible to get the computer to identify the three sources. They'd designed the system, after all. They knew how to get from it what they wanted. But accessing source-specific information was something Bolívar had hoped he'd never have to do. It was a purity that he wanted to maintain. Did he have a choice now? He stared at Jones's screen. *Compromised.* The word seemed a chilly, inadequate label for someone who'd died. If they couldn't figure out what had happened to the sources, they had no way of knowing whether the China story itself was compromised, or whether the damage was contained or had only just begun. Looking into it further suddenly seemed like the lesser of two evils.

Jones must have been playing out this scenario in his head too, because he'd stopped working his screens and was leaning back in his chair. After a few moments, he looked up at Bolívar.

"All right," Bolívar said. "We better have a look."

Bolívar and Jones were the only two people authorized to handle Gnos.is's cybersecurity or integrity issues at this level, and they each had to enter separate security codes to get the system to violate its principle of absolute source anonymity. Discomfort rose in Bolívar as he typed in his twelve digits from memory. He considered it a flaw that the system was so vulnerable to the actions of two people with pass codes, no matter how trusted and well intentioned those people were. If Gnos.is had been designed to eliminate human error and bias when it came to reporting factual information, clearly it was not yet a perfect system.

The pass codes entered, Jones performed the requisite commands. Just like that, the three names appeared, along with links to Gnos.is stories that reported on the circumstances of each of their deaths. Bolívar and Jones leaned toward the screen in unison.

"Oh shit," Jones whispered.

# SEATTLE

Kera had just finished lunch and was walking along Alki Beach when she felt the pocket pulse of an incoming e-mail. At first she assumed it was from her parents, then remembered that the e-mail address she'd given them wasn't linked to the burner phone.

Two days earlier she'd paid cash for three prepaid smart-phones—two for $64.98 each at Walmart, and another for $79.95 at Target—along with three months' worth of prepaid unlimited minutes and data usage. She'd only activated one of the burners, and she intended to use it mostly for mundane convenience: to read the news and listen to podcasts, which she preferred over music. She had not used the phone to make a call or to send a text message or e-mail, and she had given no one the phone's number. As soon as the phone received a call or a text, thereby linking her number to another number, it would be swept into the NSA's intricate contact-tracing soft-ware; she'd have to toss it and activate one of the backup phones.

There was only one Gmail account linked to the phone—an account she'd set up two months earlier on a public library computer in the West Village in Manhattan. Setting up the e-mail account was one of the precautions she'd taken, systematically, as she'd been trained to do, to prepare for going on the run. She'd purchased wigs and colored contacts, withdrawn cash from accounts monitored by the Central Intelligence Agency—her former employer—and spread the money out over several new accounts. She'd established credit lines and created passports and driver's licenses for three aliases, documents she'd stashed in a safety deposit box in a Midtown bank. They'd be there when she needed them.

For now, she was traveling under the name Laura Perez, a fourth identity she'd built up while waiting out the past two months in El Salvador. Admittedly, it was a thin alias—not much more than a passport, a driver's license, and a small wooden cross she wore on a necklace. When quizzed by the customs official at LAX upon her return to the United States, she said that she'd been traveling through Central America as a Catholic missionary and was returning to her diocese to raise more funds for the mission.

Kera studied the e-mail that had just hit the in-box of the previously unused Gmail account she had created for this sole purpose. She stared at the jumble of letters and numbers that made up the sender's e-mail address, which was meaningless to her. There was no subject, and the body of the message was blank.

She hailed a cab and told the driver to take her to the Seattle Public Library. There, she went up to the fifth floor and found an unoccupied public computer. Using a temporary library card she'd acquired under the name Laura Perez, she logged on and clicked away from the library's home page. She wasn't here to check out books.

Working quickly, she established two new e-mail accounts, one with Yahoo, the other Gmail. She named each account by glancing down at the front page of a *Seattle Times* someone had left behind on the desk and selecting the first words her eyes focused on, then tacking on a few numbers to ensure that the e-mail addresses would be unique. She ended up with opposition301@yahoo.com and insists119@gmail.com. For each, she created a different password.

From the "opposition301" account, she composed a new message to the sender of the blank e-mail she'd received. She typed a few lines into the body of her e-mail, pitching a great deal on a safe and effective male-enhancement product. At the bottom of her fake ad, in a tiny font size, she typed the following line, which included the address of the second e-mail account she'd just created:

To unsubscribe from future e-mails please send an e-mail with the word UNSUBSCRIBE in the subject line to INSISTS119@GMAIL.COM.

She hit "Send," then logged off. An elderly woman with a cane and thick glasses took the seat when she got up.

Kera killed twenty minutes reading newspapers off the periodicals shelves before she returned to the computer stations and sat down at a different terminal. She logged into the "insists119" account. There were two messages in the in-box she'd set up not a half hour earlier. She leaned forward. The first was an automated welcome message from Gmail. The second was from another unfamiliar address. It said:

Get your Dodgers tickets. 2 for 1 until Aug 8. Call 866-DODGERS.

This was followed by detailed directions to Dodger Stadium; links to articles about the baseball team's most recent games, trades, and injury reports; and a schedule of the season's remaining home games. Kera ignored all of this, though she was amused by the great lengths the sender had gone through to pad the message with so much extra detail. She focused on two things in the e-mail: the address fields and the first line in the body of the message.

In the "To:" field, three e-mail addresses were listed, including insists119@gmail.com. The other two were made up of random numbers and letters. But the addresses themselves didn't matter; it was the number of addresses that was significant. According to the system they'd agreed to—which was to be used if they needed to contact each other and had not yet established an encrypted OTR

(Off-the-Record) chat protocol—she would use the number three to decode the message. First she wrote down on a piece of scrap paper the third of five gibberish e-mail addresses in the "CC:" field. It was lzrq9g40nv1@gmail.com. Then she combined the third word and third number that appeared in the first line of the e-mail message. This gave her "Dodgers8," which would be the password for the lzrq9g40nv1@gmail.com account.

She logged off. There was no one at the computer to the right of where she was sitting, so she moved over to the open station. On the Gmail home page, she entered the new address in the username bar, taking care to get each of the letters and numbers in the correct order. Then she typed Dodgers8 into the password bar. The combination worked, quickening her pulse.

She clicked into the "Drafts" folder and found his message.

I'VE GOT A PROJECT I'M WORKING ON. WANT TO HELP? CAN YOU MEET ME AT THE SHELL STATION ON HWY 93 JUST NORTH OF MISSOULA, MT? ASAP—YOU NAME THE TIME.

She deleted his draft message and sat staring at the screen. Her training told her that she should stick to her original plan. She'd returned to the States for one reason, and it did not involve a road trip through Montana. Unless, of course . . . *a project I'm working on.* Could that mean what she hoped it meant? There was a good chance they were both after the same thing. If he'd contacted her because he had something that would help clear their names, why make things more difficult for herself by going it alone?

She typed: NOON. TOMORROW.

Instead of sending the message, she hit "Save" to keep it contained within the "Drafts" folder. Then she logged out and returned to browse the periodicals. This time she was too anxious to read anything. She forced herself to flip through a *Vanity Fair* for five minutes before she found a computer she hadn't used yet. She logged back into the coded Gmail account. Per their agreed-upon system, if the message had been received and confirmed, the entire draft would be deleted, erasing all record of it and signaling that the meeting was on.

Kera held her breath. The "Drafts" folder was empty.

She had to get herself to Missoula.

# I-93, Outside Missoula, Montana

It was overcast when the two figures climbed out of their respective vehicles and embraced in the windy parking lot. Had anyone been watching, they might have established that the pair were not relatives. Her skin was too dark, his too pale. But it was clearly a reunion, and the way they clasped each other silently, and for a moment longer than was necessary for a greeting, gave it an air of significance. Maybe they were lovers, or old college friends, or, judging by their plain, dark clothes and sunglasses, perhaps they were gathering for the funeral of a mutual friend.

They were in fact none of these things, but that didn't matter. No one paid them any attention.

"How long will I be staying?" Kera asked, climbing into the pickup J. D. Jones had driven. They'd parked her rental car where it would be inconspicuous overnight.

"That depends."

She took this to mean that he would not be comfortable discussing specifics until they got where they were going.

"You were out of the country?" he said when they were fifteen miles up a two-lane highway.

"Yes. El Salvador." She told him the truth; there was no longer any reason to protect it. She'd returned to the States because she was done running.

He let out a short laugh. "How was that?"

"Boring." With her eyes fixed on the ribbon of blurred pavement that split the wide plains, she experienced the same detached feeling she'd had looking out at the ocean from a balcony for the past two months. There had been only two things to occupy her time in El Salvador: watching the Pacific and culling through news reports in search of a sign that there had been a shift in her case, a softening in the vitriol, a lessening of the use of terms like "treason" and "aiding the enemy."

"No," she said. "It was worse than boring. It was torture."

"Worse than prison?"

"I'm not afraid of prison. And I'm not afraid of the people who want us there." She looked over at him and then nodded at the landscape flying by. "We made it this far, didn't we?"

When he smiled he looked free, she thought. This made her feel optimistic about why he'd summoned her.

For two hours they sat side by side, tracking north across the continent at seventy miles an hour. Out here, Kera thought, space defined everything. Beauty, time, silence. It was all measured by space. The silences in their conversations stretched on for the length of a plain, the width of a mountain range. At one point the sun came out and he rolled down his window. Wind howled through the cabin.

"You look well," she said, just loud enough to be heard. "It's good to see you."

He nodded and smiled, his hair blowing in the wind.

· · · · ·

Jones took Kera directly to the mine. As they descended into the valley, circled a sparkling lake, and parked near a tunnel at the base of a
mountain, Kera made mental notes of all her questions. Everything
made her curious—the conspicuous electronic gate they'd passed
through on their approach, the cabins sheltered among the trees,
the solar panels littering the tundra on the ridges above—but for
now she kept her questions to herself. She trusted Jones; the answers
would come.

It wasn't until they arrived at the heavy security doors inside the
mine that she understood suddenly where they were.

"Is this . . . ," she said.

Jones smiled. "It's not as flashy as our old CIA digs, but it's more
powerful than it looks." Jones typed in a security code and submitted
an unblinking eye for a retina scan. Approved, he pushed open the
steel door.

Had she been given another thirty seconds' warning, her mind
might have better anticipated what lay beyond this threshold.
Instead, she entered the room still thinking about her old job at the
agency, the many task forces she'd been assigned to whose sole purpose was to locate the people and hardware that kept the mysterious
Gnos.is website running—and how all of those task forces had failed.

From these thoughts her mind went suddenly blank. Seated at a
six-screen array at the far end of a long table was Rafael Bolívar. He
glanced up at her entrance, and she saw in his eyes that he had not
been expecting her either.

When time resumed, Kera managed to glance back at Jones, who
was smiling, a little proud of himself for having kept this moment a
surprise.

"Rafa, Kera," he said. "I believe you two have met." There were
a few other people at workstations around the room. All of them
looked up at her entrance, but then went politely back to work.

Bolívar started across the room to embrace her, and for a brief
moment she almost wished he wouldn't. Her mind had worked hard

to put him at a distance; she feared that even a brief moment of physical contact could destroy that. Her body, though, never intended to resist. She felt her arms against his back, her chin pressed to his shoulder, and his precise smell—the one characteristic she'd been unable to re-create clearly in her mind on the occasions she gave in to a wayward thought of him.

"What are you doing here?" Bolívar asked, looking at her with wonderment.

"She's going to help us independently verify the China story," Jones said.

Bolívar turned sharply. "No. No way." He pushed away from Kera to face Jones. The tension was heightened by the sudden lack of activity from the other workers around the room. "How do you imagine that would work? She's about as mobile as you are. Every law-enforcement agent in the country is looking for her."

"Evading detection is among her many areas of expertise. I think her presence here demonstrates that."

"I don't care. Find someone else. Anyone but her."

"Hey, I can hear you, you know," Kera said. "I'm right here. What are you talking about?"

"Three sources who contributed to a story about—"

"Jones," Bolívar said, cutting him off and creating a stalemate.

Kera tossed her jacket over the back of a chair and looked from one man to the other. "You two might have had this conversation before hauling me out to the middle of nowhere. But now I'm here. Please," she said, more to Bolívar. "It's OK. Try me."

With his silence, Bolívar finally conceded. Around the room, the other workers resumed their tasks.

"This story has been building gradually over the past few weeks." Jones nodded at one of the large flat-screens on the wall, where a page from Gnos.is was displayed. Kera read the headline and a few paragraphs. It was all familiar to her; Gnos.is was the first news site she read each morning. The story was about corruption in China's government.

"Not exactly breaking news, is it?"

"Some of it was, apparently. We'll get to that. But generally, no, corruption in China is well documented. The difference is that Gnos.is's account is painstakingly comprehensive—and highly unflattering to a whole bunch of members of the Communist Party." He paused, a small hesitation before getting to the main point. "Two days ago our integrity software detected a problem. Three sources who contributed to this story died of unnatural causes within seventy-two hours of each other."

"Unnatural? That makes it sound like you've ruled out the chance that their deaths were a coincidence."

Jones and Bolívar exchanged a glance.

"What?" Kera said.

"All right, show her," Bolívar said.

Jones went to a console, talking as he tapped out commands on a touch-screen keypad. "We don't like to know the identities of our sources, but given the circumstances, we didn't have a choice. Here they are. Marcus Templeton, a forty-seven-year-old hedge-fund manager. He'd hit a sweet spot recently investing in the telecommunications industry. Net worth cracked a billion last year." Jones tapped his screen, and Templeton's image was replaced with a woman's. "The second is a tech exec, Anne Platt, early forties. She was way up the chain in product development at Apple until she was poached by a private Silicon Valley consulting firm two years ago." Jones looked at Kera. "These two both died in elevator accidents—he in Manhattan, she in Paris."

"Elevator accidents?" Kera said.

"Yeah, if you can imagine that."

"I'd rather not. But I'm starting to see why you don't think the deaths were coincidental. Did the third one get on a bad elevator too?"

Jones hesitated. "The third was Greg Rodgers, our ambassador to China."

Kera's eyes narrowed. "The plane crash."

"Yes."

"That was a hit?"

Jones shrugged. "Unless it was a coincidence."

Kera's mind rapidly shuffled scenarios. "You say he was a source?"

"All three of them were."

"Meaning what? They were all leaking information to Gnos.is?"

"Yes, but not necessarily in the way you mean it."

Kera waited for them to explain.

"There are some people who directly upload information to Gnos.is with the intention that it be used in a story," Jones elaborated. "But they make up only a tiny fraction of the total data that Gnos.is relies upon."

"Right," Kera said. "And the rest comes from . . ." She was generally familiar with how Gnos.is functioned, but did not understand its inner workings the way Bolívar and Jones did.

Jones held out his arms to indicate the atmosphere around them. "The Internet. When we say 'source,' we're including anyone whose everyday digital activity is scraped from the Internet by Gnos.is and used to corroborate background data for a story," Jones said. Kera let him continue. She was listening for a vulnerability in the system. "Most events—from natural disasters to wars to an individual's trip to the grocery store—are digitized in one way or another. And most of that data is linked to the Internet. So, for all intents and purposes, we're all leaking information to Gnos.is, whether we know it or not. Gnos.is analyzes all that information and calculates the probability that each data point is false or factual. Then it discards the false data and describes all the facts in relation to each other."

"If everyone's leaking data online, why were these three killed?" Kera said. "What made them targets?"

"TERMITE," Bolívar said suddenly, participating for the first time. "You've heard about this operation the CIA was running out of our embassies overseas? The one where we're eavesdropping on journalists to spy on foreign leaders."

"Of course. It's been all over the news."

"Well, the highly classified details first appeared in a Gnos.is story."

"*You* published that leak?" Kera said, not hiding her disapproval.

"It turned up in an offshoot of this China corruption story, actually," Bolívar said, nodding at the big screen. "Ambassador Rodgers was one of the few people in a position to know about TERMITE."

"Wait. You think Rodgers gave up TERMITE to Gnos.is?" Kera said. "No way. Rodgers wouldn't do that." Kera had never met Greg Rodgers in person, but as an analyst covering China and Iran, she'd come up in the agency studying Rodgers's interactions with the Chinese during the early years of his ambassadorship. Rodgers blowing open something like TERMITE made no sense. But then again, if Rodgers didn't leak it, someone else at the agency or high up in one of the embassies had, and that reality wasn't any easier to stomach. *People get turned,* Kera thought with a chill. *Professionals. People who are trained in duplicity.*

Jones shook his head, aligning with her skepticism. "I don't know. Even if Rodgers was the leak, then what? Instead of recalling him from Beijing and charging him with violating the espionage statutes, the CIA just shot his plane down?"

"I didn't say that," Bolívar said.

"Didn't you?"

Bolívar let that go. "What about the Chinese? They had a motive. The revelations about Hu Lan were embarrassing for them."

"No," Kera said. "They have too much to lose by starting an overt conflict with the United States. They wouldn't risk assassinating an ambassador."

"Maybe that's why they tried to make it look like an accident."

Kera shook her head. "It's too risky. They're more disciplined than that."

"What about the other two sources?" Jones said. "They couldn't have even been privy to something like TERMITE. Why kill them?"

"That's what I wanted to hire an independent contractor to look into," Bolívar said. He didn't look at Kera.

"Hold on," Kera said. "You're talking as if you don't know what each of these sources contributed to the story. If some of them are leaking data about a trip to the grocery store and others are leaking sensitive classified info, you must know the difference. Who's responsible for what?"

Jones and Bolívar exchanged a glance. "We don't know," Jones said.

"Why not?"

"To protect Gnos.is from human error and bias, we anonymize our sources and what, precisely, they contribute."

"Then how can you verify a story?"

"Gnos.is verifies everything."

"Gnos.is is a computer. How would you even know if it made a mistake?"

Jones shook his head, betraying a little frustration with her. "It can't make a 'mistake.' Unlike a human journalist who is prone to overlook something or forget to ask the right question, Gnos.is literally computes it *all*. Anything it reports as a fact is reported with more certainty than any human journalist ever enjoyed. But we're getting off topic."

"No, we're not. This is relevant. I get that Gnos.is does the legwork, but is there nothing that prevents it from publishing classified information?"

"Gnos.is publishes everything that it can verify as true. It's not an editorial decision. It's either a fact or it's not."

"Bullshit. Don't the motives of people who leak information matter?"

"Not if that information is true. You, of all people, should be sympathetic to that."

Kera was silenced by her own anger. This was the agency's worst nightmare: an anonymous leaker who either didn't know or didn't care that the secrets he or she was leaking could put Americans in the field in danger.

"Look," she said, "I know how it sounds coming from me, but you have to stop this."

"Stop what?"

"Publishing these classified leaks," Kera said.

Bolívar looked at Jones as if to say, *I told you so*. This enraged Kera even more.

"You have three dead people, one of them an American diplomat, and all you care about is preserving some principle of anonymity? It's not even a principle. It's a delusion that some algorithms can make judgment calls better than responsible humans." Neither Bolívar nor Jones said anything. "The information about the classified TERMITE operation and these three murders came to Gnos.is somehow. It's right down the hall sitting in those servers, isn't it? You're just choosing not to look at it."

Bolívar had returned to his workstation and sat down while Kera spoke. Jones averted his eyes.

"Well, *I'll* look at it," Kera offered.

"No way," Bolívar said.

"Don't you see the irony in this? Which principle are you most loyal to: learning the truth, or helping some leaker remain anonymous? It appears you can't have both."

"We have to try" was all Bolívar said. He didn't look up, as if to indicate that the conversation was over.

"I see," Kera said softly. But what she saw, now that her anger had matured past a state that blinded her, was that Jones hadn't brought her here because he had new evidence that could help clear their names. He didn't even seem concerned about that. While she was ready to accept that their own leak of classified files two months earlier, a decision that had ultimately forced them to go on the run, might have been a mistake, his mind had apparently gone the other way. Not only was he unconcerned about their legal status, he was now helping others to commit the same acts. Had he actually made peace with a life in hiding? Or had the reality of that life not sunk in yet?

Either way, that wasn't her; she couldn't do that. And she'd promised herself that of all the people she would no longer betray, she came first on that list.

· · · · ·

"Turn off the lights." Kera had been standing alone at the deck railing when she heard him open the sliding-glass door. It was after dinner and the house was quiet; everyone else had retreated to their cabins, tucked away in the woods that surrounded the lake. The lights went out and she heard him approach in the darkness. Her eyes adjusted quickly under the clear sky. "I've never seen so many stars," she said. "It's beautiful."

Bolívar came up next to her, and for a stretch they stood at the railing looking at the way the stars reflected off the lake. Finally he spoke. "So you're saying no."

Kera nodded. "I can't get involved with this, Rafa."

"You shouldn't, anyway."

"You want to know the most terrifying thing I encountered in my two months in hiding? It's the knowledge that I'm capable of going on like this for the rest of my life. I know how to evade. I know how to survive. But for what? The thing I'm running from is a fraud." She stopped herself to look up at him. "Do you think I'm what they say I am?" she said, immediately regretting it.

"No," he said. "You're guilty of the same thing Gnos.is is: making information public to hold your government accountable. Do you ever read the stories about yourself on Gnos.is?"

Kera didn't answer. She took this as a rhetorical question. Of course she had read all those stories.

"Gnos.is never verified any evidence to support the charges the government leveled against you—except, of course, that you 'mishandled' classified information. Information that I'd say you appropriately handled by making it public. But there was never any evidence of espionage, certainly not the suggestion that you might have been acting on behalf of China."

Kera recoiled at the implication that he was trusting her because his computer told him to.

"That isn't why I know it," he said, resting his hand on her forearm. He left it at that. After several minutes he said, "Your room is comfortable?"

"Yes, thank you." They fell again into silence until Kera couldn't stand it any longer. "Leave me out here alone awhile?"

She held her breath, uncertain how she would react if his face were to move in to meet hers. She'd imagined that happening— maybe a thousand times. But that had always been in the abstract. Confronted with the reality of it now, she knew that kissing him again would be impossible. She wasn't ready. When she closed her eyes now, all she could see was her ex-fiancé, Parker, forever preserved in her mind the way she'd discovered him, lying in the bathtub with a gun resting on his chest. It had only been a few months. She wasn't equipped for peaceful moments under the stars with another man.

She heard the wooden creak of the deck and knew that he was moving for the door.

"Kera," he said from somewhere behind her.

"Hmm." She didn't turn. *He's going to tell me to be careful,* she thought.

"Good luck."

She waited until he slid the glass shut and she was certain she was alone before she exhaled.

# FAIRFAX COUNTY, VIRGINIA

Lionel Bright shuffled down the hall from his kitchen, where he'd just started the coffeepot. The sound of his slippers on the hardwood made him pick up his feet. He wasn't so goddamn old that he shuffled.

Bright opened his front door to a humid morning. It was just after six, still an hour before school buses led the suburban rush-hour parade past his house. For now the neighborhood stirred with joggers and disheveled people walking dogs, plastic baggies at the ready, in the small park across the street.

Wearing only an old Georgetown sweatshirt and the pajama pants he slept in, Bright ventured toward the newspaper at the end of his driveway. As he did, he eyed his neighbors' front yards and drives and failed to spot another paper in any of them. Bright had subscribed to the *Washington Post* for over thirty years. Originally, the subscription had been one of many establishing details in his cover, another physical thing bearing the name and address he presented to the world. The subscription was paid for with a credit card associated with the Spurkland Institute, a foreign-policy think tank the agency had long maintained as one of its proprietaries. But Bright, who now consumed all other text on his tablet, had cemented a habit of browsing the broadsheet with his morning coffee. Though he knew better, the newspaper made the world seem so orderly and comprehensible, laid out like that in neat columns that could be rolled up in a rubber band and tossed onto his driveway. With the rise of the Internet, he'd assumed that he was doing the *Post* a favor by renewing his subscription annually. Now, gazing at his neighbors' empty driveways, he wondered if maybe he was actually a burden on the newspaper, which had to send a delivery van out to his neighborhood just for him, just so that he could maintain the simple pleasures of a morning stroll to the end of his driveway and back and a few minutes with his coffee and the previous day's news.

He was bent over with an outstretched arm when he saw the front page and felt his breath catch in his throat.

He picked up the paper and looked around, aware now that he was being watched. For a few moments he stood there in his slippers, looking anew at his surroundings. He saw her, finally, sitting on a bench in the park. She wore sunglasses, and her hair was different— light, almost blond.

He crossed the street to her.

"Your paper," she said, handing over that morning's actual *Post*. She nodded at the *Post* in his hand, which was dated two months earlier. She knew him well enough to know that he'd once used his newspaper to signal meets and drops, though it had been a while since he'd done that. He preferred not to bring others in his line of work that close to his doorstep. "I know it's a risk for you to talk to me," she said. "Nod right now and I'll walk away and you'll never see me again."

He kept his head still.

"They made you help them write it, didn't they?" she said, removing the sunglasses.

Her amber eyes looked darker, Bright thought, but the rest of her face projected the youth and beauty he remembered. Bright looked down at the outdated paper in his hand. Seeing the headline now felt just as unreal to him as it had two months earlier. EVIDENCE LINKS MISSING AMERICAN CYBERSPIES TO CHINA.

"Kera—"

"It's OK," she said. "You didn't have a choice."

*We always have a choice,* he thought. Like right now. He shouldn't be talking to her unless he planned to bring her in—and it was too early to say what he would do about that. She'd been smart to catch him like this, phoneless, practically in his underwear.

"For what it's worth, I never thought you'd turned," he said, sitting down next to her on the bench. "If you'd wanted to betray your country, you wouldn't have transferred to HAWK in the first place. You would have stayed inside the agency where you might have done more damage."

"Thanks for that vote of confidence."

"This isn't about confidence, Kera."

When she looked at him now, her eyes were pleading. "What did the agency's investigation really determine?"

"That you and J. D. Jones leaked the HAWK files."

"Of course we did. That isn't the part that needed investigating."

Bright paused. And then he told her the truth. "There wasn't an investigation. There wasn't time."

"No?" she scoffed. "But apparently there was time for a disgusting smear campaign."

"The mess you left us with had to be cleaned up. That was the direction they took. I didn't endorse it."

"Oh, how courageous of you. This was their idea of cleaning up a mess? Throwing two of your best under the bus and managing to escalate tensions with China in the process?" She nodded at the headline on the old paper. The treason accusations were the most serious, legally, but far from the most salacious. Private details had been released, selectively, to suggest a narrative that starred Kera and Jones as duplicitous philanderers and mentally unstable outcasts.

Rather than confront its own domestic-surveillance scandal, the agency had manufactured a new scandal that they thought would play better in the media. They'd been right.

"Like you said, Kera, I didn't have a choice. The HAWK operation was classified. You didn't have the authority to make public what you witnessed there."

"The authority? None of us had the authority for the kind of surveillance HAWK was doing. Not on American soil, Lionel. Don't talk to me about who's got authority." Kera paused as a spandex-clad woman clutching a yoga mat walked by. "I warned you personally about what was happening within HAWK, Lionel. When nothing was done about it, Jones and I had to act."

Bright remembered well the last encounter he'd had with Kera. Sitting in a back booth at a Manhattan diner, she'd outlined the disaster unfolding within the classified black op known as HAWK. The problem, from the CIA's standpoint, was that in order to evade congressional oversight, the HAWK operation had been moved off the agency's books. Officially, it didn't exist. To admit that the operation had gone rogue was to admit that it had existed in the first place, which the agency refused to do—and which Kera and Jones had decided to do on their own, by releasing evidence to the press in the form of classified files.

"You should have come to us with all the HAWK files first," Lionel said. "Let us vet them."

Kera almost laughed. "We were spying on Americans, Lionel. Do you understand? We broke laws. You, me—all of us. And the agency got burned—HAWK played us all, and it was too late to pull them back. What do you imagine the agency was going to do with evidence of that? Release it? They're at least smart enough not to fess up to their own incompetence."

"Something might have been worked out."

"I hope so." She looked at him. "That's why I'm here."

At first he didn't understand. And then he did and looked pained. "Kera." He had to be honest. "That's impossible. They think you're a traitor."

Two more women cruised by in shorts and tank tops, talking loudly.

"You're in a position to convince them I'm not," Kera said when the women had passed.

*She can't be serious,* Bright thought. "The director—hell, even the president—is intent on making an example out of you. This administration has already prosecuted more leakers than any before it." He shook his head. "The best thing you can do, Kera, is turn yourself in. The government wants a headline, but they don't want a trial, not one where they'd have to make public a bunch of classified documents in order to make their case against you. You can graymail them into a generous plea deal." Graymail was a strategy defense attorneys used to secure lesser charges for their clients by threatening to expose classified material at trial. What Bright meant was that the more serious charges against Kera—conspiring with China, for example—would be difficult to prove anyway, and they'd be impossible to prove without the government acknowledging the depths of the intelligence community's corruption and negligence in the HAWK case. She'd probably face something more benign, like "mishandling classified information."

"Forget it. If I come forward, it will be so that I can have the opportunity to serve my country again. Not," she said, patting the two-month-old *Post*, "to refute some story the agency cooked up about me working for China. I need some assurance that I have a future."

"I can tell you right now you don't have a future at Langley. Look at this." He held up the old newspaper so that she could see her picture on the front page. "It doesn't matter how this happened or whose fault it was. This is out there now. You've been compromised. I'm sorry, Kera."

A man walking a boxer came within earshot and they fell silent again. The man lingered, bending to collect his dog's waste. Bright recognized the man. He lived half a block down from him. If the man registered anything untoward about Bright sitting in the park in his PJs, talking to a woman half his age, he didn't express it. They exchanged good-mornings as the man passed, and then Bright and Kera were alone again.

"Please think about it, Lionel. That's all I'm asking. You trained me to focus on the mission, to always remember that it's our job to protect—"

"My job, Kera. Not yours anymore."

"Exactly, because while real cyberterrorists in China, Iran, Russia, and elsewhere are planning attacks against the United States, the CIA is wasting its time trying to cover up every ugly truth that might embarrass them." With that, she stood and covered her eyes again with the sunglasses.

As unprepared as he'd been to see her, he was now equally unprepared to see her leave. In a softer tone, he took one last shot at appealing to her reason, what might be left of it after the disorienting hell she'd been through. "Kera, stop running. What good is it doing?"

"It's keeping me alive and out of prison, for one," she said, walking away. But then she turned suddenly and retraced her steps. "One other thing. About Ambassador Rodgers. Do you know anything about that plane crash that hasn't been released to the public?"

"Like what?"

"Like why it went down."

Lionel stared back at her. "You know I can't talk about that. What are you dancing around?"

Kera shrugged. "Forget it. I'm sure you have as many people working on that as you do trying to find me. One only hopes they're better at their jobs."

This time she committed to her retreat and set off across the park. He considered his options—either following her in his pajamas or doing nothing—and, as she vanished down a path, he decided that it was best to go on with his day as if their conversation had never happened.

# MANHATTAN

The official headquarters of Gnos.is—in fact, the only listed address affiliated with the site—was a loft in the SoHo neighborhood of Manhattan. The work space was only one room, but it was vast. Oversize flat-screen monitors filled the walls between broad windows that offered views of the narrow streets and tightly clustered buildings outside. The grand width of the loft was marked at one end by the entrance; at the other end an assortment of seating faced a large desk.

It was at this desk that Charlie Canyon sat, reviewing figures that illustrated the growth of traffic to Gnos.is's site, when a tone sounded on the wall intercom, indicating a call from the doorman. He tapped a button on a touch screen to open the line.

"You expecting any visitors, Mr. Canyon?"

"No, Khaled." There were no meetings on his schedule.

"I figured as much. These guys don't look like they had an appointment. They're asking about Mr. Bolívar."

"Who are they?"

"The man says he's the assistant attorney general."

"Of New York?"

There was a muffled exchange before the doorman came back on the line.

"Of the United States of America. He has three federal marshals with him. I checked their badges. Shall I suggest to them that this is a bad time?"

"No, it's all right, Khaled," Canyon said, wondering again how much Bolívar paid for the loft space. The building's staff members were a class act. "I'm sure they just want to chat. Send them up."

*Here we go,* Canyon thought. He darkened the windows, which had a tinting mechanism built into the glass. Then he tuned all the flat-screens in the room to Gnos.is/fact, the news side of the site, and adjusted them to display an assortment of stories he judged to be most objectionable to representatives from the Department of Justice. The last thing he did was glance at the computer network's intrusion log, which J. D. Jones had designed to record and categorize malicious breach attempts. It was no secret that Gnos.is was a target for cyberattacks, and the US government was high on the list of motivated adversaries with the potential capability to crack Jones's security wall. To counter this worst-case scenario, Jones had nested a suicide pill within the system. If the Feds raided the loft or got a hacker inside the network, Canyon could, from his desktop computer, quickly strike a command that would encrypt the entire local network in a manner that couldn't be undone. The data would be gone forever, but at least it couldn't be seized.

Looking at the intrusion log, Canyon didn't expect it to come to that. Certainly not today. The log was reporting no hostile activity—at least none outside of the common denial-of-service attacks that Jones's cybersecurity system easily beat back. If the US government ever launched a strike at Gnos.is, it wouldn't be with anything as rudimentary as that. Canyon logged off the computer and was reclined in his chair with his feet on the desk when he heard the bell and buzzed the men in.

"Charlie Canyon?" the first man to enter called out. There was half a basketball court's length of concrete floor between the men and Canyon's desk.

"That's me."

The men, four in total, marched toward him with heads swiveling at their surroundings. They stopped a dozen feet before Canyon, where four chairs were arranged around a coffee table. Canyon did not invite them to sit down.

"I'm Lance Bitman, assistant attorney—"

"Assistant attorney general," Canyon said, waving away the man's badge. "I heard. Can I get you anything? Coffee? A drink? A copy of the First Amendment?"

The man smiled combatively. "No, thank you. I don't drink coffee or booze." He took several seconds to gaze around at the headlines glowing down at them from the screens. "I'll be direct. We need to speak with Rafael Bolívar."

Canyon shrugged. "He isn't here. Would you like to leave word or come back later?"

"Cut the bullshit, Charlie. We both know Bolívar isn't going to be here if we come back later. Where is he?"

"If I knew, I wouldn't tell you." This was at best a half lie, and Canyon preferred avoiding those when dealing with people who doled out felony charges for a living. "Is there something I can help you gentlemen with?"

Bitman exhaled, regaining his professional composure. "We're looking at a gravely serious national security breach. We believe a person with access to highly classified files is using news organizations like Gnos.is to disseminate state secrets. It is crucial to identify the leaker before more harm is done. We're looking for Gnos.is's cooperation."

Canyon nodded at the thick manila envelope the AAG was clutching at his side. "I hope what you've brought there are specific examples of the harm that's been done to national security."

Bitman narrowed his eyes. "Think about this very carefully, Mr. Canyon. Do you want to live the rest of your life knowing that you endangered Americans—even when you had the opportunity to help them?"

"Which Americans have I endangered? Can you name any of them?"

"I would think that from your own perspective, handling the PR angle for Gnos.is, you would want to avoid the fallout of Mr. Bolívar and Gnos.is appearing un-American in the eyes of the public. I realize you are new to the news game. There is no shame in cooperating with the government in scenarios like this. The *New York Times* is cooperating, as are other news organizations."

"Gnos.is is not like other news organizations."

"You're right." The AAG stepped forward and slid the thick envelope across the desk toward Canyon. "You'll want to read that carefully and comply with each court order within twenty-four hours. That includes the subpoena for Bolívar, who is now required to return from Iceland"—the AAG paused briefly to read Canyon's reaction to this, but Canyon's smirk was indecipherable, so he kept going—"or wherever he is hiding. We will have him extradited, if necessary."

Canyon opened the envelope but was in no hurry to absorb its contents.

"We are prepared to argue as high up as the Supreme Court," Bitman continued, "that Gnos.is is in fact not engaged in the practice of journalism and therefore does not have the protections afforded to journalists by the First Amendment."

With tedious indifference, Canyon unpacked the envelope, laying out the separate documents across his desk as the men watched. When he'd finished, he made a little show of reclining in the chair. He put his hands behind his head.

"Then we'll wait twenty-four hours," Canyon said, "and see what happens."

"I'm sorry?"

"You are giving Gnos.is twenty-four hours to censor itself voluntarily, and I'm telling you that won't happen. We're not taking down any stories. And even if we knew the names of our sources, which we go to great lengths *not* to know, we wouldn't reveal them to you. If you have evidence against people who have illegally disclosed classified information, indict them, not us." Canyon leaned forward and pushed one of the documents back toward the AAG. "As for that subpoena, you'll have to deliver it to Bolívar yourself. I won't play middleman."

The AAG and his marshals had not even made their way past the lobby doorman before Canyon began scanning the documents and uploading them to Gnos.is for publication. And because he never missed an opportunity for free publicity, he also attached PDFs of the documents to e-mails, which he fired off to the *New York Times*, the *Washington Post*, the *Wall Street Journal*, and a dozen online news sites.

# I-70 WEST

It was Lionel who had taught her how to run. Over two decades in the field, he'd accumulated a cache of knowledge that he'd ingrained into her. Where to purchase untraceable passports and driver's licenses. In what sort of banks to stash money and documents and how to access them. How to avoid surveillance cameras, and when you can't, how to tilt your head at just the right angle to foil facial-recognition software. When to sleep and when to move. When to act in the way your pursuers expect you to, and when to do the opposite.

Kera didn't know what to make of the fact that law enforcement had not descended on Lionel's quiet neighborhood in the minutes after she'd left him in the park. Apparently, he hadn't hurried inside to phone in the traitor sighting. But had he called at all? Had he ordered them to pursue her quietly? Or did he just let it go, believing she would not be found until she was ready?

Training had taught her how to prioritize the retreat points from the park and slip away. But she had not worked out any concrete details beyond that. She'd vanished into the cover of the Beltway's teeming suburbs only to face a new and unfamiliar threat: What to do next? This lack of foresight was more than carelessness; it was an indictment of her state of mind. She had wanted to find Lionel receptive and forgiving. She had wanted it so desperately that she hadn't seriously considered any alternative.

*You have no future at Langley.*

Kera needed to drive. It went against her training to move without a destination or a safe path to get there, but she couldn't summon the discipline to override her instinct to get on the road.

For twelve hours she drove, stopping only for gas. When finally she stretched out on a scratchy comforter at a highway motel and turned on the television, her mind was foggy from a day worrying over the what ifs and now whats. At some point she thought she heard Rafael Bolívar's name and was certain she'd lost touch with her faculties. Lionel had taught her ways to test her mental state, and wearily she began to cycle through them. Did she know her precise location? Did she clearly remember her mission? How long before she was expected to check in with her superiors? Could she monitor her heart rate for a full minute without touching a hand to her throat or chest?

She could not.

But then the television newscaster repeated the name, and Kera sat up. She wasn't imagining it. Bolívar's face was on the screen. She forgot all about Lionel's insanity tests.

She activated one of her two remaining prepaid phones—she'd discarded the first before leaving Seattle—so that she could read online the details of the indictments against Bolívar and Gnos.is that had been handed down by the Department of Justice. She read through the night, and with each hour that passed she began to feel more herself again, more confident of what she had to do next.

# LANGLEY

Lionel Bright's encrypted satellite phone rang, mercifully, fifteen minutes into a briefing with the agency's public relations director. Given that Bright's job was not supposed to involve any relations with the public, these meetings were, under normal circumstances, notorious for their bureaucratic bullshit. But like a weatherman in a hurricane, the PR department was basking in the shitstorm created by the TERMITE scandal. And, of course, they were under the impression that crafting a statement for the press could somehow make it better. The PR director and her staff had come armed with several drafts, all of which were shot down by the spies. At the moment Bright's phone vibrated in his pocket, one of his colleagues was reminding the PR flacks of the only phrase they needed to know to do their jobs: "The CIA does not comment on clandestine operations."

Bright glanced at his phone's illuminated screen. The number itself was unfamiliar—it was associated with a single-use SIM card—but the display indicated that the call was coming through a secure satellite link originating in Beijing. The only people who had the number for this encrypted sat phone were Bright's men and women in the field.

Bright excused himself, drawing envious glares from his colleagues, and swiped the phone's screen to engage the call before it rang out. "Hold on," he said. He walked down a long hallway and through an exit that took him to the cafeteria kitchen's loading dock. When he was confident he was alone, he said, "OK, I'm here."

"This is BLACKFISH." The voice from seven thousand miles away was cool and accentless.

"Authenticate BLACKFISH."

"Two roads diverged in a yellow wood."

"What color is the sky today?"

"Red. Bright fucking red."

It was BLACKFISH, all right, Bright thought. He hadn't seen the man in over a year, but his mind produced a vivid memory of broad shoulders, a flat nose, and ginger goatee. "Go ahead."

"What the fuck, Lionel?" BLACKFISH hissed.

"You've been reading the papers?"

"These stories blew us wide open. My team is gone. Do you hear me, Lionel? They're gone. Missing. This is not a country where you want to go missing."

Lionel shut his eyes. *ZEUS and HORNET.* The other members of his covert Beijing team. The three of them had been instrumental in establishing the TERMITE program in China, where it had been extremely effective. "Can you get to the embassy?"

"I'd rather not, thanks. It hasn't been a great week for people coming and going from that compound. How did this happen?"

Bright sighed. "There was an online news story. It mentioned details of the TERMITE program. Then other news sites confirmed—"

"I read the goddamn Gnos.is story. And all the rest. But where did it *come* from? Because if this is another civil liberties coward trying to play hero, now they have to answer for two Americans who are being tortured in a Chinese prison."

Bright permitted this venting session, even though they both knew that no one would be called upon to answer for ZEUS and HORNET, who didn't exist, not officially. This was the fucked-up thing about leakers: they presumed they were doing good only because they weren't deep enough in it to even imagine the bad.

"We don't know where the TERMITE leak came from. We're working on that."

"And ZEUS and HORNET?"

"We're working on that too."

"Christ, Lionel. Working on it?"

"It's China. We can't just fly a Predator drone over the Great Wall. It's delicate, all right? In the meantime, you're our key man there. I'm depending on you. ZEUS and HORNET are depending on you. You know more about the situation than anyone."

"The situation is that we got fucked by our own goddamn media."

BLACKFISH was isolated, pissed off, and likely sleep deprived. But in the agent's spirited complaints, Bright was relieved to hear a man who had his wits about him.

"You're in a safe place?" Bright asked.

"Safer than others here, I'd say."

"Thanks for checking in." Bright started toward the door that would take him inside.

"Wait. I didn't call just to bitch and moan," BLACKFISH said. He paused. "I've got something burning a hole in my pocket."

Bright stopped at the door, then wandered back out across the loading dock. There was no one around. "Go ahead."

"Before that Gnos.is story broke, I picked up a drop from a contact. It contained a communication from Uncle Orwell that references the ambassador's plane crash." Uncle Orwell was the name they had given to Feng Xuri, the minister of state security, China's equivalent to the American CIA director. "Are you there?" BLACKFISH said.

"Yeah, I heard you. So what? Everyone in Beijing and Washington is talking about that plane crash."

"They are now, sure. But this communication took place three days before the plane went down."

Lionel squinted. He was silent for a dozen seconds. "That's true? You're sure of that?"

"Yes. It's a text exchange between Uncle Orwell and a man he calls Peng. I have the screen grabs right here."

"Screen grabs?"

"My asset took pictures of Uncle Orwell's phone screen when he went to take a piss."

"Your asset. This is the hooker?" Bright had been briefed before on a young woman BLACKFISH had recruited who was said to be in the employ of several Communist Party leaders.

"She's an escort, Lionel. A professional. And incidentally, she was one of our best assets. I don't think we'll hear from her again, though. Not after that fucking story."

Bright cursed to himself. "Just read me the exchange. Is it long?"

"No, a few lines. Hold on. Here it is." BLACKFISH read aloud the texts that he would later forward to Langley.

AND THE AMERICAN FROM THE EMBASSY?
[PENG]

IT IS SET. SHE IS GOING TO SHANGHAI
ON THUR. OUR MAN WILL GET IN THE
PLANE WHILE IT IS GROUNDED THERE.
[UNCLE ORWELL]

AND HE IS CONFIDENT ABOUT THIS?
[PENG]

YES HE IS SKILLED. HE SAYS THE PLANE'S
SYSTEM IS NOT COMPLEX. IT IS SET.
[UNCLE ORWELL]

"Is that your translation from the Mandarin?" Bright asked.

"Yes."

"Did you say, 'She is going to Shanghai.' Not 'he'?"

"That's what it says. But you know . . . text messages, autocorrect. The punctuation in these things is a mess. The guy's got an escort in the room. Maybe he was distracted and typing fast. The point is, they're discussing tampering with the ambassador's plane a few days before it crashed."

"Who is Peng?"

"Don't know. I'll send you the screen shots when I can get proper encryption."

Bright thanked BLACKFISH and hung up, making a mental note to check with the NSA to see what they could do to identify "Peng." For a few moments, he stood on the loading dock, thinking. Then he returned reluctantly to the PR meeting and sat thinking some more while the flacks rambled on about strategies for winning back the news cycle.

Bright was pulled from his thoughts when several smartphones rattled and chirped suddenly in quick succession, beckoning the attention of their owners.

"What the hell is that?" the head PR spokeswoman said, losing the room to their phones. Bright felt his own phone twitch inside his pocket.

"FBI Director Ellis is starting a news conference," someone said, summarizing the alert he was reading as the PR spokeswoman switched the screen on the wall behind her over to the news conference. "DOJ's twenty-four-hour deadline for Gnos.is has passed. The classified content is still live. The Feds are going after Rafael Bolívar."

"Good luck finding him," someone else muttered.

Bright was a patriot from head to heart. A prerequisite of that, he believed, was a firm belief in the First Amendment—a belief he couldn't ever remember questioning before. But then again, he'd never worked so close to such a serious leak of classified files.

"Eventually we find everyone," he whispered, gazing up at Bolívar's picture on the news broadcast.

# THE VALLEY

What kept Bolívar awake through the night, first restless in bed and then under a heavy jacket in a chair on the dock, was not any three-letter agency headquartered in Washington. He'd expected the subpoenas and indictments—expected them sooner than they'd come, even. The real wedge in his mind was something that Kera had said, days earlier, when she'd appeared in the valley for a few surreal hours and then retreated back into oblivion.

*Which principle are you most loyal to: learning the truth, or help-ing some leaker remain anonymous? It appears you can't have both.*

*You can't have both.* The words beat like a mantra through his head, hour after hour, until he could no longer picture her face with-out hearing them. At some point, as he and the dock and the earth beneath the lake all rotated under the stars, Bolívar realized that Kera was right: he had to choose between the truth or the leaker's ano-nymity; he couldn't have both, and it was too dangerous for Gnos.is to have neither. By dawn it was obvious what he would have to do.

In the prelight he left the dock and drove his truck to the mine. Jones was already there, had perhaps been there all night, and he looked up when Bolívar entered.

"You too?" Jones said. Bolívar couldn't be certain if Jones meant he was restless because of the subpoenas or the deceased sources or just because of Kera. Maybe it was everything.

Bolívar crossed to his workstation on the far side of the room. Without speaking or sitting, he logged in and pulled up the China story and the profiles of each of the three deceased sources. For Jones's benefit, he displayed them all on the wall screens. Then he stood with his eyes shifting in a calculated way from one screen to the next.

"Suppose our biggest problem is not that one of these three sources provided Gnos.is with classified information, and that they did so with the expectation that their anonymity was guaranteed."

"OK." Jones recognized the loaded tenor in Bolívar's voice and knew it meant he was circling an idea. He waited for Bolívar to come around to it.

"What if there's something even bigger going on?" Bolívar turned from the screens to face Jones. "You would know if our network had been hacked, right?"

"Sure. The system would have warned us of that."

"Well, what if it *has* warned us?"

Jones's eyebrows drew together in confusion.

"Those alerts about the three sources," Bolívar continued. "What if that's the only way the system has to communicate the sort of breach that's taken place?"

"I'm not following."

"Your network security is too good to permit a conventional malware attack or some other remote intrusion. But couldn't a similar effect be achieved by manipulating sources?"

"Manipulating sources? You mean killing them."

"Yes, in this case. Say you wanted to stop Gnos.is from publishing a potentially damaging story, and you're unable to do so by hacking the site. The only option left might be cutting off the critical sources of the information before it can even be fed to Gnos.is."

Jones shook his head. "Three dead people is some pretty high-value collateral damage."

"Is it? It might sound that way to us. But we don't yet know who stands to lose and gain from the TERMITE story. What we do know is that Gnos.is has upset people who clearly have a lot at stake—enough that they resorted to killing our sources. We can't just let that continue. If we're truly going to protect our sources, I think we have to go inside Gnos.is and see how this China story came together."

"You want to identify which one of the deceased sources is the leaker?"

Bolívar hesitated, even though he'd spent enough of the night certain of his decision. "I don't think we have a choice. The actual leaker is only one part of it. If someone is willing to kill to distort a Gnos.is story, I can't imagine they intend to stop there. They're not finished yet. Whether we like it or not, we're playing an intermediary role in these deaths. I think, in this very narrow case, our duty to uncover the truth outweighs any expectation an individual has for anonymity."

Jones made a few more attempts at playing devil's advocate, stressing that they were talking about crossing a point of no return. But he eventually had to admit that the only alternative to what Bolívar was suggesting was to just sit back and wait to see what happened. And that, they were in agreement, was not an option.

Finally Jones shrugged. "All right, then. Let's have a peek under the hood."

While Jones turned to his screens, Bolívar used his phone to send out a message to everyone scheduled to arrive for work in the mine that day. His message instructed them to stay home. He wanted to minimize the number of people exposed to the information they were about to examine. With that done, he sat down in a chair next to Jones. In the bluish LED glow, they entered the necessary pass codes to access data that, though it sat in servers behind locked doors just down the hall, they had never intended to view.

Before they could begin to orient themselves to the breadth of the task in front of them, they were startled by an electronic warning tone. Out of instinct they both looked up at the small ceiling speakers, from which the tone pulsed with urgency. A few seconds later Bolívar felt his phone vibrate in his pocket and he reached for it. Jones swiveled to an adjacent screen to call up the valley's security interface.

Bolívar felt a sinking stillness in his chest. "It's a perimeter breach," he said, reading the alert from his phone, which did not provide any more detail than that.

"I've got it here. It's a vehicle."

"On the road to the pass?"

"Yes." Jones looked up at Bolívar, and he could see that they were both thinking the same thing: *This is it. It's all over.*

An unofficial agreement had arisen between them to not discuss the government's charges against Gnos.is. Separately they had each read the indictments and subpoenas, which had been published on Gnos.is and elsewhere: Bolívar had been ordered to appear before the US District Court in Manhattan, and Gnos.is was ordered to remove all stories that contained "dangerous" classified information as well as to reveal to the attorney general and the FBI the names of the leakers who had provided them with that information.

Bolívar and Jones had not needed to discuss whether they would comply with any of those demands. They both knew they would not. And now, in this moment, Bolívar was relieved to discover that he did not regret that decision, even as the consequences were closing in around them.

"Have they reached the first camera yet?" he asked Jones.

"No."

"Put it up on the big screen."

A few seconds later, an image of the tranquil country road flickered onto the main screen. It looked almost like a photograph except for the leaves that could be seen swaying gently in the breeze. The two stared at the screen in silence.

Finally, it appeared. A gray sedan charged into the picture ahead of a billowing tail of dust.

"Jesus. They're coming in fast," Bolívar said.

"The plates aren't in our system." An edge of panic had crept into Jones's voice. "Should we evacuate and lock up?"

Bolívar made a face, part anger, part anguished defeat. For a moment, they both thought he was going to say yes. "Have any other perimeter sensors been tripped?"

Jones checked his screens, swiping through a series of surveillance images and motion-sensor readings. He shook his head. "Nothing." He flipped the image on the big screen over to a new feed. This one provided a view of the gate where the road crested the pass. It was the only other camera they had out on the road.

The men waited again in silence until the gray car sped into view. They leaned forward as the vehicle slowed and then stopped for the gate.

For a few seconds, nothing happened. Then the driver's door swung open and a figure stepped out.

•　•　•　•　•

Bolívar opened the gate remotely and was waiting outside the tunnel to the mine when the car swept into the clearing. He watched her get out and walk toward him on a narrow path worn through the moss.

"I changed my mind. I want in," Kera said, answering the question written all over his face. "The ambassador, and your other sources. Let's find out what happened to them."

"Kera. Please, don't do this."

"I've made up my mind."

"It's too dangerous."

"That's irrelevant," she said, and walked by him into the tunnel.

. . . . .

"Go through it again," Bolívar said. "We missed something."

Jones and Kera exchanged a weary glance. Five hours before, the three of them had sat down at separate screens to review every bit of data that had come to Gnos.is from each of the deceased sources. That had taken only minutes. Marcus Templeton, the hedge-fund manager killed in the Lower Manhattan elevator fail, had guarded his private and business lives closely, permitting only a digital trickle to escape. From him, Gnos.is had referenced a series of investments Templeton made in publicly traded companies, trades that Gnos.is had used, alongside similar orders from thousands of other investors in the public record, to confirm an increasing bullishness toward the telecommunications industry. China was a major global player in telecom, which is how Templeton's investments had been relevant, albeit tangentially, to the China story. Nothing about Templeton's trades or how they became available to Gnos.is suggested that he'd ever had access to any classified information about TERMITE or anything else. He wasn't the leaker.

Anne Platt, the technology consultant who had been the sole victim in the Paris elevator, had been only slightly more prolific as a source. Gnos.is's mining of her digitized activity had yielded dated quotations from interviews she'd given to tech-industry publications. Her name also turned up on the programs of a few international conferences, in Dubai, in Shanghai, in Paris. Like Templeton, Platt had volunteered nothing to Gnos.is's servers directly. She wasn't the leaker either.

Ambassador Rodgers, predictably, had the biggest digital footprint of the three. Official itineraries, quotes excerpted from speeches, press releases, and the like represented dozens of points where the ambassador's diplomatic activity had corroborated foundational facts within the China story. But it was immediately notable that he too had never directly submitted any information to Gnos.is—let alone classified secrets. All of his contributions to the China story had been delivered via passive digital donations, seemingly innocuous facts vacuumed up by Gnos.is from the public record.

"So the leaker wasn't one of these three at all?" Kera said, looking from Bolívar to Jones to make sure her imperfect understanding of how Gnos.is worked had not led her to the wrong conclusion. It hadn't.

"Apparently," Jones said.

"Well, someone had to have leaked the classified information about TERMITE, right? Isn't there a record of everything that's uploaded to Gnos.is directly?"

Jones shook his head. "Not a reader-friendly one, no. Remember, identifying individual sources is something we go out of our way to avoid." He paused and seemed to be considering something. "But the data exists, which means it can be searched. Hold on." He swiped a new screen to life.

Bolívar and Kera sat back, waiting. Seconds accumulated into minutes. Then suddenly Bolívar stood up.

"What?" Kera said.

Bolívar fidgeted over Jones's shoulder. "How much longer?"

"A minute, maybe two. I need to make sure the search is narrow enough to be useful, but wide enough to catch what we're looking for. It's a large story; the source material comes from millions of data points."

Bolívar nodded and walked away looking restless. Kera, who had been watching Jones's monitors intently, now watched Bolívar pace along the row of large screens on the main wall, taken aback by the whir of activity behind his eyes.

"All right, here we go," Jones said, drawing her attention back.

"What are we looking at?" she asked. The screen filled with a large three-dimensional network of points connected by lines.

"This is the full piece on Chinese corruption, fragmented so that claims made in the story can be traced back to their source material."

"There are so many."

Jones clicked on a few points that represented intersections within the network. "This stuff's all benign," he said, scrolling through a few of the documents: official minutes from government meetings, court transcripts, itineraries. Nothing classified. "Let me try isolating just the paragraphs of the story that first mentioned the classified surveillance program."

It took Jones a quick series of swipes and taps to execute the new query.

"Huh," he said, squinting at the error message flashing on-screen. Kera glared at it in confusion too. Bolívar wasn't looking at the screen. He was still pacing.

"What does that mean?" Kera asked.

"No matches."

Bolívar stopped pacing.

Jones checked his work and retried the query. When the computer gave him the same result, he leaned back in his seat, defeated. "This system wasn't designed for queries like this. I must have introduced a glitch when I tried to rig the search function."

"There's no glitch," Bolívar said. He was standing halfway across the room, backlit by a large screen. "And there's no leaker. There never was one."

Kera and Jones looked at him, not following.

"Think about it. The CIA drew up this TERMITE operation, named it, planned it, and classified it as TOP SECRET—all activities that took place offline behind closed doors. But as soon as they began rolling out the operation in the real world, it started to leave traces of itself. How could it not? Hundreds of real people were acting and reacting; information was being exchanged. Just because Langley insists the operation is classified doesn't make traces of the operation invisible. Now, maybe no human being is in a position to notice those traces and piece them all together. But Gnos.is is."

A comprehending grin crept onto Jones's face. "And what Gnos.is put together was evidence that the CIA and NSA were spying on foreign journalists who had access to key politicians. In other words, Gnos.is noticed TERMITE's shadow."

Kera shook her head. "But details about TERMITE were published that could only have come from inside Langley. Like the name of the operation itself."

"That's true now. But remember, the original Gnos.is story didn't have any of those details. All it had was a broad outline of the operation, which it mentioned in an obscure paragraph within the larger piece. The name 'TERMITE' only surfaced after the *Washington Post*, following up on the Gnos.is story, got a source on deep background to confirm the program. But the *Post* never would have even asked the right questions if Gnos.is hadn't spotted patterns that hinted at the existence of the program in the first place."

"So you're saying no one at all came forward to tip off Gnos.is about the TERMITE program? It just figured it out on its own?"

"That's right," Jones said with uncharacteristic excitement. "There was never a leaker on the TERMITE story, and it didn't take a leaker to connect the dots between Hu Lan and the MSS either. Gnos.is put it all together, just like it does with any other part of any story. In this case it just happened to come up with a pretty good scoop."

Kera wasn't sure whether she found the implications of that alarming or fascinating. But there was a problem with what Bolívar and Jones were saying. "Hold on. If Ambassador Rodgers, Marcus Templeton, and Anne Platt never uploaded secret files, what made them a threat to whoever killed them?"

"I don't know," Bolívar admitted, looking up at the China story displayed on the main screen. "On that, Gnos.is has been silent so far."

# LANGLEY

Lionel Bright looked up from the transcript he'd been handed after reading only a few lines.

"Who is Angela Vasser?" he asked, turning to Henry Liu, the lead analyst assigned to the investigation into Ambassador Rodgers's death.

"The luckiest American diplomat in China. She wasn't on the ambassador's plane. Decided to stay in Shanghai through the weekend, apparently at the last minute."

"She was supposed to be traveling with Rodgers?"

"Yes," Liu confirmed. "She was the ambassador's top aide."

Bright considered this. "And they were in Shanghai for what, precisely?"

"Trade talks about development in Africa."

"Why didn't she get on that plane with the rest of the embassy staff?"

Liu flicked his eyes involuntarily at the pages in Bright's hand, which contained the answers to all of these questions, but then went ahead and summarized what he knew anyway. It seemed prudent not to test Bright's patience. "The Kenyan and Chinese delegations were staying over for a few extra days, so while Ambassador Rodgers had to return to Beijing, Ms. Vasser stayed back to give us a presence at any informal talks that might have continued through the weekend."

"And this is the first we're hearing about her?" Bright looked in disbelief at the faces of the people he'd summoned to his office. They were his three best analysts: Liu; Rob Anderson, a senior analyst who specialized in China's military strategy; and Judy Huang, a Chinese American woman who was the agency's top expert on China's foreign policy. "This Vasser woman had been in high-level meetings with the ambassador throughout his final day alive? She was possibly the last person to talk to him—and we didn't know her name until *today*?"

"We asked DOS about that, sir," Huang said before Liu could attempt an explanation. Liu shifted uncomfortably at the mention of the State Department. "They were less than—well, they indicated that updating us on every detail of the Rodgers tragedy wasn't very high on their list of priorities. They seem to be upset about the recent headlines describing secret CIA and NSA programs in countries with whom they're—"

"I know what they're upset about, and it's goddamn childish. We're an intelligence agency. We spy. And our allies know better than to expect a free pass. Find me one country with a GDP bigger than North Dakota's who isn't spying on *us*?" Unburdened of that frustration, Bright looked down at the tablet Liu had handed him along with the transcript of the FBI's interview with Vasser, which had taken place two days earlier in Beijing. On the tablet's screen were a headshot and several candids of a young African American woman. Her round, curious eyes stood out against the angular features of her face. "Is this her?"

"Yes, sir," Liu said, eager to be back in less contentious territory. "We managed to obtain her full file—in spite of our peers at State."

"Where is she now?"

"Beijing," Liu said. "She cut short the weekend in Shanghai, obviously, to be with her colleagues and the ambassador's family, though

I gather she wasn't recalled only for moral support. She apparently has made herself essential to our diplomatic mission in China. In the void left by the ambassador's death, she's keeping a lot of heads straight over there."

Bright tossed the unread transcript onto his desk as if to signal a transition in the conversation. He leaned forward to address the three analysts.

"I called you three here for a reason. I'm assigning you to a new case. It's classified, code named MIRAGE. For now, I'm keeping the BIGOT list very small," Bright said, referring to the strictly enforced list of people who would be cleared to know about the operation. Though the term "BIGOT" had British origins dating back to World War II—it was said to have been a secret mission code word derived from "British Invasion of German Occupied Territory"—American intelligence officials had adopted the term and commonly used it when designating a select group of "need-to-know" people for a particularly sensitive operation. "MIRAGE will involve only the people in this room, plus BLACKFISH, who is operational inside the PRC. Our task is to determine as quickly as possible exactly how and why Hu Lan's plane went down while our ambassador was on board."

Liu and Anderson looked confused. While they hesitated, trying to read Bright's mind, Huang voiced the question they all had in mind. "What makes this different from the investigation we're already advising on for DOS?"

"The difference is that we're going to assume, until we have solid proof otherwise, that Ambassador Rodgers's death was not an accident." Bright logged in to his computer and swiveled the monitor around for the three analysts to see. "These are screen grabs from Feng Xuri's phone, three days before the ambassador's death." He gave them a few moments to read the exchange. "If Beijing had a hand in crashing that plane, as these texts suggest, it will permanently change the United States' relationship with China. It's our job to know that before anyone else. Understood?"

The three members of the new MIRAGE team nodded in unison.

"Let's get started. Henry, see if we can set up a call with Angela Vasser without causing a meltdown at the State Department. I know the FBI questioned her, but we know things they don't. She might be the only one still alive who was in a position to recognize that something was amiss before that flight."

"Yes, sir."

Bright studied the photographs of the texts that BLACKFISH had received from Feng Xuri's escort. *The plane's system is not complex.* Did that mean what he thought it did?

After the analysts filed out of his room, he took the elevator to the subterranean floor where the ops center was located. Once he'd keyed in his pass code, he went directly to Jason Hernandez, his top cyber guy, whose workstation was in the near corner.

"Hernandez, if you had access, could you get into a Gulfstream's computer and write a bug that would—"

"There you are."

Bright stopped short at the sound of his boss's voice. He hadn't noticed CIA Director Cal Tennison standing in a group at the front of the room. Now he saw also that the large screens on the wall were tuned to the major news networks.

"What's all this?" Bright said.

"We found our leaker."

# THE VALLEY

"Who's reporting this?" Bolívar said. He stood behind Jones in the control room buried in the mountain, watching the bank of monitors. Kera was seated at a workstation across the room.

"The AP was up with it first. But now it's the top story everywhere."

Jones put a few of the cable news networks up on the wall screens. Photos of a young African American woman were cut into montages of network anchors reporting vague details alongside hastily summoned experts who'd been cut loose to speculate on those details. Both the anchors and their telegenic guests wore earpieces and wide-eyed stares that occasionally lost focus as they were updated by the producers in their ears.

"Who is she?" Kera asked, breaking the televisions' spell. Kera had been at the console they'd set up for her, studying police and fire department reports from the two elevator tragedies, but now she was alongside Bolívar.

"Angela Vasser. A special assistant to the ambassador. She was supposed to be on that doomed flight, apparently. Undergrad at Georgetown, PhD from Berkeley. Her dissertation was on China's influence over developing economies in Africa. She's—" Jones paused. "She's only thirty-six. That's quite a career for someone her age."

"Any of this on Gnos.is yet?" Bolívar asked.

"No." Jones shook his head. "Gnos.is isn't reporting any of it. The woman's name comes up a few times in reference to other stories about our diplomatic mission in China, but nothing that points to her leaking details of the TERMITE surveillance program."

"So either the press throughout the entire free world is getting it wrong, or Gnos.is is," Kera said, with more of an edge than she'd intended. This earned her a pained look from Bolívar. And then he broke eye contact and returned to his workstation.

Kera studied the images of Vasser that the media had raked up out of the past—State Department personnel photos, a driver's license, a passport. In most of them, Vasser posed with an obedient, stilted smile. There was one candid, though, that drew Kera's attention. It had been taken at a panel discussion at her alma mater convened to debate some subtlety of globalization. The photo was a reaction shot, Vasser slightly off to the right of the picture, looking at the speaker, who was in profile. Vasser's eyes looked impatient and adversarial, Kera thought, like she was three steps ahead, just waiting to mount a takedown of the speaker.

"They're accusing her of what, exactly?"

"She sent e-mails to a non-US citizen that clearly mention the classified TERMITE program—e-mails that every news organization but Gnos.is seems to have received," Bolívar said from his workstation.

"What do the e-mails say?" Kera looked to the broadcasts on the wall screens, but found only talking heads. E-mails didn't make for good television, apparently, even if they were precisely the issue at hand. Bolívar opened a link on the AP's site and put the e-mails on the large center screen. There were a total of five short messages, all part of the same back-and-forth exchange between Angela Vasser and someone named Conrad Smith. She read them in chronological order.

"Who's Conrad Smith?" she asked when she'd finished.

"He's a South African contractor, an economic consultant who has done projects for a handful of governments—including ours. And China's."

Kera read the e-mail chain again. The tone in the exchange was bare, free of the false pleasantries customarily present in cooperative, professional e-mails. References to the classified surveillance program were poorly veiled for someone who ought to have known the consequences of what she was doing. It made the back and forth seem almost transparently conspiratorial, like bad dialogue in a daytime soap.

"How does the AP say they got these?"

"An anonymous source. I'm guessing that's why Gnos.is isn't biting. If Gnos.is can't independently confirm or corroborate the claims made in the e-mails, it won't publish."

That restraint, at least, was refreshing, Kera thought, looking away from the e-mails. She stood in silence for a long moment, biting her lip and thinking. Then suddenly, she spoke up. "So this woman, Vasser, works in the American embassy in Beijing, where she somehow acquired knowledge of the CIA's TERMITE surveillance operation. And then she decided to share this classified intelligence with a foreign contractor. In an e-mail." She paused before shaking her head. "No fucking way. I think it's the other way around. There's a witch-hunt on for a leaker already, and then these e-mails turn up, and now you have pundits on TV absolutely giddy over how suspicious she looks. Hell, the fact that she's *alive* is suspicious. After all, she knew just when not to board the ambassador's plane, right?"

"The media's only accused her of putting classified information in an e-mail," Bolívar said, cutting short Kera's sarcasm-laced summary of the events. "What are you suggesting?"

"Oh, I think the media is accusing her of much more than that. And they seem perfectly gleeful about it. What's *she* saying about all this?" Kera wondered aloud. She only needed to glance up at the cable news broadcasts to get her answer. "None of this coverage is even attempting to share her side of the story." And then suddenly she realized something. "Oh shit."

"What?" Jones asked.

"Didn't you say she was mentioned in the China story?"

"Vasser? Yeah, she comes up here and there. But nothing related to the surveillance program. She didn't leak that."

"No one did," Bolívar reminded them. "Gnos.is pieced it together on its own."

"Right, but she *has* been a source for Gnos.is stories, right?"

Bolívar shrugged. "I'm sure she is, in the same way anyone in her position would be."

"In the same way the ambassador was?"

Bolívar and Jones exchanged a glance. "She *was* supposed to be on that plane," Bolívar said. He reached for the nearest computer. "Where is Vasser now?"

They split up, searching Gnos.is, the AP, the *Guardian*, the *Post*, the *Times*—anyone who was doing real reporting on Angela Vasser—but came up empty-handed.

"Got her," Jones said a few minutes later. "She's on a commercial flight out of Beijing. It took off two hours ago."

"Where's it going?"

"SFO. Her itinerary continues on to DC."

"She's coming home, then," Bolívar said, surprised.

"How do you know she's on that flight?" Kera asked.

"I plead the fifth on my methodology, but the felony-free version is that airlines and transportation security organizations keep databases of flight manifests."

"And you can access them?"

"The fifth," Jones repeated, pursing his lips.

Remembering now what it was like working with Jones, Kera held up a hand as if to say she didn't want to know any more than that. "That means we're too late."

"For what?"

"To warn her. She'll be detained at customs in San Francisco."

"You want to warn her that being accused of mishandling classified information could get her detained at a US airport?"

"No. I want to warn her not to get on any elevators."

# FBI Interview Transcript (Excerpt)

DETAINEE: ANGELA VASSER
AGENTS PRESENT: BENTON, CHU, WILLIAMSON, LEE, TOMS
START TIME: 1148 HRS PST
END TIME: 1730 HRS PST
LOCATION: SAN FRANCISCO INTERNATIONAL AIRPORT

ANGELA VASSER: Is Ben OK? Does he know I'm here?

AGENT BENTON: Ben is . . . ?

VASSER: My partner?

BENTON: Partner?

VASSER: Yeah.

BENTON: I see. I'm sure he's fine. We can have someone contact him if you like.

VASSER: I want to talk to him.

BENTON: Later.

VASSER: Am I being charged with a crime?

BENTON: It looks that way, yeah. This is serious. These e-mails—here, I'll ask you to look at them again—in these e-mails you discuss highly classified information—

VASSER: Which I was never privy to. I couldn't possibly have authored these e-mails. I wasn't even aware they existed until you put me in this room.

BENTON: So you deny writing them?

VASSER: Yes. If there's a way to make that clearer to you, I can't conceive of it now.

BENTON: But you don't deny that they were written in your name and were sent from your e-mail address?

VASSER: I'll have to take an agnostic position on that. The documents you've shown me appear to support your theory, but I didn't write them and I can only speculate about who did.

BENTON: Go ahead, then.

VASSER: I'm sorry?

BENTON: Speculate.

VASSER: You're serious. OK. I'd start questioning people who had the appropriate security clearance. Which I did not.

AGENT CHU: I think what Agent Benton is asking is whether there is anyone who would have had both the motive and technological prowess to do what you're suggesting.

Vasser: What *I'm* suggesting?

BENTON: Well, if you deny sending them yourself, how else do you explain them being sent?

VASSER: I can't explain it sitting in this room. I just stepped off a fourteen-hour flight to discover that I was the last person on earth to know about these e-mails. And now you've confiscated my computer and phone. I take that to mean you're accepting the burden of explaining it.

CHU: So you can't think of anyone, then?

VASSER: When I do, I'm sure I'll let you know.

BENTON: Who is Conrad Smith?

VASSER: He's a contractor. A consultant. Based out of Cape Town.

BENTON: So you do know him?

VASSER: Yes, I haven't denied that, have I?

BENTON: And he works for the Chinese government?

VASSER: He works for the Chinese government, and for the governments of Kenya and South Africa, and a number of private foundations. Some of them are American, I might add, since you seem to be suggesting some conspiracy along nationalistic lines. Conrad is an economist and telecom consultant, not a political operative.

BENTON: It sounds like you're defending him.

VASSER: I'm correcting your misunderstandings. They are rather numerous.

CHU: Why weren't you on the plane?

VASSER: I'm sorry?

CHU: With the ambassador.

VASSER: Oh. What does that have to do with this?

BENTON: We're just doing our jobs, Mrs. Vasser.

VASSER: Miss.

BENTON: Ah, yes, we'll get to that in a minute. You flew to Shanghai with Ambassador Rodgers, but you weren't on the return flight, which went down in the Yellow Sea.

VASSER: Look, I went over all of this with your colleagues in Beijing a few days ago.

BENTON: The context has changed since then. We want to clear up a few things. This is one of them. How come you weren't on that flight?

VASSER: My Chinese and Kenyan counterparts remained in Shanghai over the weekend. I didn't want to lose any of the progress we'd made. So Greg—Ambassador Rodgers—and I agreed that I should stay and continue to build relationships.

CHU: You told the agents who spoke with you at the embassy this week that you were at the Park Hyatt when you learned that the ambassador's plane was missing.

VASSER: That's right. I got a call from the embassy's chief of security. I remember clearly looking at the clock. It was 11:25 in the evening.

BENTON: Is that the hotel you'd stayed at the previous evening?

VASSER: No.

Benton: I see. As you can imagine, Mrs.—*Ms.*—Vasser, we've had some agents speak with Conrad Smith since these e-mails between you two surfaced. Conrad Smith is in Hong Kong now, but he mentioned that he was in Shanghai last week. It seems he had a room at the Park Hyatt on the night of the ambassador's plane tragedy. Is that a coincidence?

VASSER: Which part?

CHU: Were you with Mr. Smith that night?

VASSER: Yes, I was. He happened to be in town on business. Coincidentally.

BENTON: And was it a coincidence that you stayed in his hotel room?

VASSER: No. That part was not a coincidence.

BENTON: You're unmarried?

VASSER: Yes. Is that a crime too?

CHU: You admit to being with Mr. Smith at the Park Hyatt as the flight you were initially scheduled to be on crashed into the ocean.

VASSER: You have a way of making facts sound like accusations.

BENTON: We just want to get everything straight. You're saying that not only were you sleeping with someone other than your partner—that's the word you used for, uh, Ben, isn't it?—but that this was the man to whom you then disclosed highly classified information.

VASSER: I was sleeping with someone other than you, which makes that none of your business. I've been as clear as I can be about the classified information. I didn't write those e-mails. I couldn't have.

BENTON: Yet here they are.

Versions of this conversation repeated itself for over five hours. Vasser was then charged with mishandling classified information and flown to a federal prison in Fort Meade, Maryland. The full transcript was published on Gnos.is.

# GEORGETOWN

Lionel Bright waited anxiously, ensconced in the private booth he'd wrested from the tight control of the maître d'. He'd invested an unusual amount of care in planning a successful evening, enough that rearranging his day to guarantee he'd be on time—something he rarely did for social commitments—had delivered him twenty minutes early. The final thing to do now was to make it look like no planning at all had gone into the date, which his early arrival clearly contradicted. To avoid mulling over his expectations for the evening, he ordered a whiskey. The concentration required to pace his sips over twenty minutes provided the needed distraction from his anxiety.

She appeared on time and he rose to greet her. Audrey. She was a touch underdressed, but he suspected there was less to read into that than there might have been with other women. He didn't know her to play games, at least not the subtle sort. Besides, if she turned any heads, it was because of her simple, uncultivated beauty, not for the offense of some common pantsuit that didn't quite live up to the candlelight and thick tablecloths. She initiated a hug before he could. And then he gestured formally, lamely, toward her side of the booth, feeling awkward without the physical prop of a chair to pull out for her.

They sat for a minute beneath the dim, low-hanging light fixture as Audrey spread her hands on the plush tablecloth and glanced
around the opulent dining room, then down at the neat rows of cur-
sive printed on the menu. She looked up at him with a wry little
smile.

"Christ, Lionel. You're laying it on pretty thick. Do I come off as
someone who's difficult to impress?"

"I—" He hesitated. And then, as he'd done several times in her
company—and in no one else's—he said exactly what he was thinking without any premeditation for what might happen next. "I'm terrible at this. This is my first third date."

She cocked her head. "Your first third . . . ?" That smile again.
"That's weirdly endearing."

"Would you like to go somewhere else?"

"No. Now I've got my eye on the surf and turf." Her face soft-
ened. "You're doing great."

The rest of the meal went splendidly, enough so that he never
thought of time passing or even much about the food, which came
in three exquisite courses. He never even thought about work, except
for once, when his smartphone trembled in his pants pocket. While
the waitstaff cleared their picked-over entrées, he stole a discreet
glance at the phone. It was a notification of a text message from
Henry Liu, his top China analyst. It was not unheard of for Liu to
text him after hours. What was unheard of was for Bright to have
the attention of an interesting and beautiful woman. He didn't have
time to open and read Liu's message before the waitstaff retreated
and Bright was again alone with Audrey, who he suspected would
not hold back her disapproval if she caught him reading texts on his
phone during dinner.

Perhaps another half hour passed before they'd finished coffee
and trading bites of a raspberry tart, and Bright excused himself to
use the restroom. Would it be too forward, he wondered, to suggest

that he could drive them both to his house and then back again in the morning to retrieve her car before work? She—

He'd not noticed the figure enter the men's room ten steps ahead of him until Bright himself entered, his fingers already tugging at his zipper. The physical reaction came first: a rising, inflating sensation in his chest that he would not have categorized as healthy. But then his mind caught up and his calm was restored.

"Henry. Jesus, you scared the hell out of me."

"Sorry. I would have just approached the table, but I didn't recognize the woman. I didn't mean to interrupt."

Bright looked around. "Clearly you did."

"You got my message?"

The text. Bright remembered now. He hadn't read it. And now suddenly, with Liu in front of him in a men's room, he understood how out of character he'd begun to act in Audrey's presence. Who was he, ignoring work messages for more than an hour? Bright extracted his phone, activated it with a thumbprint, and opened his messages. Liu's text had contained a single word—"Potomac"—which was their code word to arrange a secure call urgently.

"Well, now you've got me," Bright said, beginning to understand that this run-in wasn't going to be as simple as a few words exchanged in front of a bank of urinals.

"It's MIRAGE, sir. I think you'll want to come back to the office."

Had it been anyone other than Liu, Bright would have dressed him down for sabotaging the evening. But he could see in Liu's eyes that this was different.

*Fuck,* Bright thought, uncharacteristically frustrated with the work intrusion. Why couldn't they live in a world where planes sometimes just fell out of the sky?

"I have to take a leak," he said finally.

"I'll pull the car around."

• • • • •

"Something's come up." Bright stood over the booth, unable to bring himself to sit and look Audrey in the eye.

"Now?"

This one syllable, delivered in this way by a woman, stirred up thirty years of solid rationale against dating. Relationships for someone in his line of work were inhumane, if not impossible.

"I'm afraid so. I don't know what to say. I'm sorry."

"You're not a senior fellow at the Spurkland Institute, are you?" she said.

He'd expected her to try to read something else into his abrupt departure, that she'd think he was changing his mind about their prospects for the evening and beyond and was choosing a cowardly excuse to bow out. He was caught off guard by her striking much closer to the truth.

"I don't know what you mean," he said. They both knew he sounded ridiculous.

"Yes, you do. Go ahead. Go on," she said, catching him glancing at the door.

He'd been in this situation before with women, and on all previous occasions he'd walked out without thinking twice.

"You're right," he said, surprising them both. "I'm not a senior fellow at the Spurkland Institute. I can't get into that now, though. I really do have to go—"

"I'm not a lobbyist."

"What?" he said.

"It's only fair for me to tell you now, since we're clearing the air. I'm not a lobbyist for the airline industry."

"Who do you work for?"

"I don't suppose you're going to tell me what you do?"

"I—I can't. Honestly. I know that sounds ridiculous."

"Which part is ridiculous—that you can't tell me, or that you want me to believe that you're being honest now when you weren't before?"

"Either. Both." The phone vibrated against his thigh with its special insistence. What was it about the design of this inanimate object that pulled people from significant face-to-face interactions with one twitch? "I'm sorry, Audrey. I have to go."

"It's Karen, actually."

"Oh." So he wasn't the only one with a hidden life. He suddenly had questions he wanted to ask. But there wasn't time now. Instead, he smiled, hoping he didn't look as flummoxed as he felt. "OK. Karen, then. I was having a good time."

A transition had come across Audrey's—Karen's—face so that when she shrugged, Lionel could see she'd already retreated into herself, into the way she would be a minute from now when he was no longer there to impress her or lie to her. She looked disappointed, not in him, but in herself, and the shrug seemed to be her way of telling herself to buck up. What had she expected? This wasn't just dating in a city steeped with power and politics; this wasn't just online dating, or dating in middle age. This was all of the above. The power of those cupid algorithms wasn't in the algorithm at all; it was in the capacity of humans to delude themselves.

"I was having a good time too," she said, to herself or to him, and he turned toward the heavy doors at the front of the restaurant. It wasn't until the car was on the George Washington Memorial Parkway heading to Langley that Bright realized he hadn't paid the check.

# LANGLEY

From what Liu had explained in the car, Bright expected to walk into an assemblage of the appropriate people from the China division, who were indeed present in surprising numbers given the hour. But the three figures Bright had not anticipated—though of course he should have; their kind seemed drawn into everything lately—were the pale cyberspecialists sitting along a bank of consoles near the front of the ops center. Just five years earlier, these men had been indistinguishable to Bright, with their matching shiny, indoor complexions and incidental-seeming bodies, soft for their age around the torsos. But as he'd come to depend on them, they'd become easier to identify.

The cyber men worked unfazed through Bright's entrance. They sat hunched over keypads beneath six-screen arrays, so detached from the hubbub around them that Bright wondered if they were actually working as furiously as they seemed to be, or if they simply lacked the social acumen to engage the other human beings in the room. Bright had long marveled at how, even in the highest-level meetings, the cyber guys never seemed to be able to share in a productive interaction with their colleagues without a few gigaflops of computing power as a go-between.

This combination of disciplines—China and cyberespionage—rendered the presence of the youthful brunette planted at the center of the room inevitable. With her thick-rimmed glasses and one wavy, almond-colored lock descending along a delicate cheekbone, Amy Bristol stood over the main terminal, coaching a technician on what to display on the big screens at the front of the room. She looked up when Bright entered and, straightening slightly, nodded hello, which Bright acknowledged with a moment's eye contact but did not reciprocate. Bristol had come to the agency as a young doctoral candidate brushing up a thesis on Chinese foreign policy, and in two years she'd leapfrogged into a senior analyst position by virtue of her superior comprehension of computer networks. In Bright's time coming up through the agency, you had to luck into some life-threatening fieldwork to get promotions that swift. Now you just had to know how the Internet worked, which everyone under thirty-five seemed to.

A quorum attained, the room settled and Henry Liu signaled for Bristol to begin.

At the click of a small handheld remote, the wall screen filled with the now-familiar text exchange that BLACKFISH had acquired from the smartphone of China's minister of state security. "The man on the other side of this intercept, called Peng here by the state security minister, is in fact Zhau Linpeng, a high-ranking officer in BYZANTINE CANDOR," Bristol said. BYZANTINE CANDOR was the name US intelligence agencies had given to Unit 61398 of the People's Liberation Army, a secret bureau of China's top cyber-warriors, also known as Advanced Persistent Threat 1. Bright had first incorporated into his job description the tracking of advanced persistent threats, or APTs—highly capable groups intent on targeting sensitive intelligence via cyberespionage—when BYZANTINE CANDOR was discovered back in 2002. Since then, he'd worked with the NSA and private security contractors to uncover a handful of attacks that had targeted the networks of US businesses, media organizations, and the military. Nearly all of those attacks had been designed and executed by Unit 61398 from their headquarters in an unassuming twelve-story building on Shanghai's outskirts.

A click of Bristol's remote brought Zhau Linpeng's photograph onto an adjacent screen. "Zhau's been having off-campus communications with a Russian national named Anton Kozlov, who goes by Allegro." Another photograph appeared, this one of a slim, blond-haired young man with sickly white skin. The image was accompanied by a profile that, though incomplete, provided Kozlov's birth date, which was half a decade earlier than Bright would have guessed from looking at him.

"What did you say he goes by?" Bright asked. He started spelling out the alias printed alongside the photo. "A—one—one—E—"

"A11Egr0," she said, again pronouncing the word as *Allegro*. "It's leet, an alternative alphabet that substitutes numbers and other symbols for letters. It's a hacker thing, one of the ways they set themselves apart." *Set themselves apart from clueless people like you,* her tone seemed to suggest. "The spelling of a11Egr0 has many variations, but this is the one Kozlov is best known by."

"I see. Go on."

"Kozlov studied programming at MIT for three years, but he was expelled for using school computers to hack corporate targets. As you can imagine, that made him virtually unemployable—at least by noncriminal entities—and he was eventually deported after his student visa expired. We think that's when he became a11Egr0. It's certainly when he started getting popular in the international hacker community. This business with Zhau is the first time a11Egr0 popped up on our radar, but apparently NSA has been tracking him for years."

"For years?" Bright said, digesting the data on the big screen. "He's twenty-five."

"These hackers are like gymnasts, they peak young. And, as with gymnasts, both Russia and China mine their populations systematically for elite talent."

"Whereas the US apparently deports them," Bright noted before moving on. "So what's a11Egr0 doing in China?"

"We think he was granted asylum there two years ago. At least one of our sources in Moscow says a11Egr0 made enemies with the SVR"—the Russian intelligence agency that replaced the KGB—"after he penetrated some of their most sensitive computer networks. When he fled, he didn't even try to come back to the States. China took him in. And now—well, this text exchange is interesting. It clearly suggests that the Chinese planned to have someone access Ambassador Rodgers's plane in Shanghai. And Zhau's communications with a11Egr0 suggest that a11Egr0 himself was the person they had in mind for that. The thing is, I don't know if I fully buy a11Egr0 working directly for the Chinese, despite his contact with them. It goes against everything we know about hackers like him—"

"Hold it. I warned you," Liu said, cutting off Bristol. He turned to the room. "I warned you all. Each of you is here for a very specific reason, and that is to share with us your particular expertise. You are not to speculate on the wider nature of this case. This is a briefing, not a brainstorm."

"I agree," Bright said. He and Liu were the only people in the room on the BIGOT list for MIRAGE—that is, they were the only ones cleared to even know about the secret investigation into China's involvement in the ambassador's death. To keep their inquiry from becoming widely known, a meeting like this was necessary—a way to siphon, in essence, the knowledge of analysts and other experts without reading them into the case. "But I do have a question about what Ms. Bristol just said." He turned to her. "If a11Egr0 did in fact have contact with Unit 61398, is there any reason to believe he *isn't* working for the Chinese?"

"Sure. That's where this gets interesting," Bristol said. She gestured at the young man's picture on the screen. "Hackers generally see it as their duty to keep the Internet free from the control of governments and corporations, and a11Egr0 has always projected himself as the gold standard of those principles. He's built his reputation on it. We know he's hacked targets in the US and Russia, and the NSA says they discovered his shadow on a handful of cybercrimes in Europe and Asia—DDoS attacks, corporate espionage, identity theft, that sort of thing. His trademark seems to be zero-day attacks that—"

"Hold on. Zero-day?" It was a term Bright had heard thrown around, and he was annoyed with himself now for not knowing precisely what it referred to.

Aggravatingly, Bristol seemed to enjoy the opportunity to conduct another tutorial. "He chooses targets that have never been hit before and designs viruses and worms that are novel and thus undetectable until after the fact, usually when it's too late."

Bright could feel the discourse sinking into a technovacuum. He wanted to make sense of this on the macro level first. "So a11Egr0 gets in over his head playing pranks on the SVR and, with his life in danger, finds a sudden friend in China. Which is problematic, at least for his hacker reputation. But he's not too idealistic to recognize that turning a few tricks for China is better than the gulag. Is that the theory?" Bright looked around the room. Most of the heads were nodding in agreement.

"That explains a11Egr0's motivation," Bristol said. "But not the Chinese's unusual behavior. A guy like Zhau Linpeng doesn't usually turn up chattering away about business via text."

"Zhau is who again?" Bright asked.

"Zhau is 'Peng' on those text messages. He's high up the chain at Unit 61398."

"Right," Bright said, remembering. "And the NSA had him making contact with a11Egr0."

"No, actually," Bristol said. "The NSA didn't intercept the intelligence about the meeting between a11Egr0 and Zhau. That particular intel was the agency's own handiwork. It apparently came from one of your men in the field."

*BLACKFISH?* Bright thought. He glanced up at the string of digital clocks on the wall. It was just after 10:00 AM in Beijing.

"I need to clear the room. Hank, you can stay."

Resentment flickered in Bristol's eyes, but Bright had long since overcome his vulnerability to that. She knew the drill as well as anyone else in the room. Most of everyone's daily movements throughout the Langley campus, into and out of certain meetings at certain times, were dictated by three words: "Need to know."

"See if we can get BLACKFISH on the line," Bright said when the others were gone. He went back to reading the intel the analysts had surfaced on Zhau Linpeng and Anton Kozlov, the Russian hacker known as a11Egr0. US intelligence agencies had unraveled relatively little about BYZANTINE CANDOR, and Bright was far from the foremost expert on the secret PLA unit. But were the Chinese getting sloppy? If so, why? He'd never heard of the Chinese importing Russian espionage talent—they had plenty of their own homegrown stars and were too disciplined to trust foreign nationals, especially those who had worked in intelligence. He'd also never seen people like Zhau Linpeng and Feng Xuri be so careless with their use of texting, even when they believed the content of their messages was safely encrypted. On the other hand, Bright reckoned, there was no encryption that protected what a hooker saw if you left your phone out when you went to take a leak.

In the background he could hear Liu on the phone, running through authentication phrases. A few moments later, BLACKFISH was swearing over the speaker.

"I thought you'd never call. This is some shit, Lionel."

"You're on speaker with me and Hank Liu."

"Is that name supposed to mean something to me?"

"No. He's been read into MIRAGE but not half the other shit you're hip deep in over there. So watch your mouth."

"Ignorance is bliss, Hank, whoever the hell you are," BLACKFISH said. "Sweet, forgotten bliss. Get yourself transferred to a station somewhere exotic where nothing happens and no one tells you anything."

Henry Liu, who had never worked in the field, said nothing. He looked to Bright for some sort of a cue, but Bright was already launching into the purpose of the call.

"We're connecting some of the dots you've given us," Bright said, both hands planted on the desk so he could lean over the speaker-phone. "But I'm not sure I believe the story line that's emerging. That young Russian you connected to BYZANTINE CANDOR, Kozlov, he apparently has a reputation with computers. He goes by the name a11Egr0 in those circles." He provided the childish spelling of the hacker's alias. "But it's a little out of character for him to make friends with regimes like China's that censor the Internet. So we're a little confused about what he's doing there. We need you to find out if the Chinese were able to turn him. And if so, what do they have him doing?"

"A11Egr0?"

"That's the name he uses, yes."

"And how the fuck does he spell it?"

Lionel again spelled out the numbers and letters.

"Christ, Lionel. I know that cyber is supposed to be the sexy new thing right now, but tell me you see the irony in the fact that these geeks are the world's largest collection of self-made virgins. No offense, Hank. You're not in cyber, are you?"

"Sorry, sir, that's classifi—"

"It's a joke," Bright said. "Forget it."

"You think this Russian kid's in Shanghai?" BLACKFISH asked.

"We don't know that. But we think he was in Shanghai the day the ambassador's plane flew out of there. We think a11Egr0 is the guy Uncle Orwell and Peng mentioned in that text exchange."

From the silence that followed, Bright knew he'd gotten BLACKFISH's attention. This wasn't another monotonous fringe op where the goal was to chat up the escort who occasionally slept with a corrupt commie who might eventually end up in the same room with the Chinese president—just so you could report to some analyst in Langley how everyone took their tea. No, this was for real. If BLACKFISH understood correctly, Bright was asking him to track the suspected assassin of an American diplomat. It was the sort of mission men like BLACKFISH had joined the service for.

"I'll start in Shanghai," BLACKFISH said. "There must be airport surveillance footage. Your theory is that a11Egr0 planted a bomb on the ambassador's plane while it was on the ground?"

"Not exactly. Do you know anything about computer viruses?"

"I know a lot about free Internet porn. I don't use computers for much else. They're not safe."

"You're right about that. I doubt a11Egr0 put explosives on that plane, if he in fact had anything to do with it at all," Bright said, vocalizing for the first time the theory he'd been developing in his head. "But I think he may have planted a software virus. The guys here call it a logic bomb. Or a zero-day exploit. Or both. I can't keep all that straight. Whatever it is, it programmed the plane's computers to bring the thing down."

Another silence on BLACKFISH's end. Then only, "I see."

Bright told him everything Amy Bristol had come up with about a11Egr0's relationship with China, which wasn't much, and promised they'd send him more when they could. It was nearing midnight when he started to end the call.

"Hold on, Lionel," BLACKFISH said. "I almost forgot. That woman from the embassy here—Vasser. What's happening with that?"

"I gather they're putting together a case," Bright said. He had to tread carefully on this turf.

"There's something a little strange about it, don't you think?"

"I haven't really had time to think about it," he lied.

"There were only five people at the embassy over here who knew about TERMITE, and she wasn't one of them."

So Bright wasn't the only one whose bullshit detector had been set off by those stilted e-mails purportedly exchanged between Angela Vasser and Conrad Smith. As eager as Bright had been to nail down the source of a potential intelligence leak, the e-mails bearing Angela Vasser's name had not been written in the tone of an accomplished diplomat—even one depraved enough to betray her country. Bright would have picked up the receiver at this point, had there been one attached to the conference-call device, or he would have at least muted BLACKFISH if he knew how the futuristic-looking speaker unit worked. Instead, he looked down at the poorly labeled buttons and winced.

"All I'm saying is, it doesn't make sense," BLACKFISH continued. "She couldn't have been the leak."

"Stick to your beat," Bright snapped and then wrapped up the call. After they'd hung up, he turned to Liu. "You didn't hear that last part."

"Hear what, sir?" Liu responded predictably.

Though Liu's play-it-by-the-book style was valued in most situations, Bright suddenly found himself longing for a deputy who wasn't too cautious to go out on a limb when something felt off. But maybe he was just being a sentimental old man, he thought, silently cursing himself. It wasn't fair to Liu to compare him to the previous operative who'd worked under Bright on China and cyber. She would have had as many questions for BLACKFISH as Bright had come up with, maybe more. And he would have trusted her to ask them. He had to admit that he missed her. For a moment he wondered where she was.

But then he stopped himself. There was a team working on that; if there was any update, he'd be the first to know.

# THE VALLEY

Bolívar came to Kera's cabin on her fifth night in the valley.

"How are you?" he asked when she opened the door. Her chest tightened at the sight of him in jeans and a white T-shirt.

"I'm great. The place is perfect. I have everything I need."

"No. How are you?" he said more softly, lingering on the final word.

"I—" She couldn't think of a word to say.

"Can I . . . ?" He gestured inside. She stepped back to let him in. "I brought you a phone," he said, pulling it from his pocket. "Jones finished installing the encryption program this afternoon."

The device looked just like the satellite phones she'd seen Bolívar, Jones, and everyone else in the valley use to communicate with each other. Though the phone was roughly the size of any modern smartphone, Jones had explained to her that it avoided eavesdropping-friendly cell towers by routing communications through secure satellites. The satellites also allowed for reception in remote areas, like the valley.

Kera turned the phone over in her hand. "Does this allow you to track my location?" she said, meaning it as a joke even though she failed to scrub the edge from her voice.

"You don't have to use it if you don't want to. But unless we're in the same room together, it's the only safe way to communicate."

She slipped the phone into her pocket. When she looked up, his eyes were on hers, a shade more intensely than they'd been a few moments earlier.

"Do you remember the last time we spoke? At my place in New York?"

She nodded and whispered, "Of course."

"I told you then that I hoped someday we would meet again when the circumstances were different."

She nodded again.

"You've been through a lot, Kera. And right in the middle of it, I just disappeared. I'm sorry."

"You had no obligation to me."

"I know. But the whole time, I wished there was something I could have done. I thought about you. The least I can do is let you know that."

She bit her lip. He was right; that was the least he could do. But he could not possibly have imagined how much it meant to her to hear him say that. They were still standing near the cabin's entryway when she asked him on an impulse how long he planned to remain in the valley. He shrugged, but she caught the sly smile at the edges of his mouth.

"As long as it takes."

"As long as what takes?"

"Gnos.is will never be a source of perfect information. There will always be facts that exist that cannot be recorded digitally—that is, they cannot be expressed in a way that Gnos.is can process them. And at every moment in time, an entire universe full of new, recordable events takes place. We're maybe five years away from having the computer power that can even attempt to compile all of that in real time. But we can get pretty close. We will reach a point where, for all intents and purposes, Gnos.is will be able to articulate to us nearly every demonstrable fact that is knowable about our universe."

"And then what?" she asked.

"Then there will no longer be winners and losers in the information game. Everyone will have free access to the same accurate information. When I am confident that Gnos.is is not in danger of being seized by a government or a corporation that would use it as a tool of power, it will be safe for me to leave this valley."

Kera studied him while he spoke. His passion made him look to her like a man ten years younger. She wondered which of them was more naïve—he for believing in what he was saying, or her for doubting him.

"Do you think that's really everything—harnessing the universe's facts?" she asked him. "So what? Will Gnos.is be able to articulate the point of it all? Will it tell us what, if anything, is meaningful?"

"No," he said quickly, as though he'd already thought plenty about this. "Would you even want it to?" He paralyzed her with a look. His eyes were vulnerable and questioning, as if looking wasn't enough and he was seeking permission for more.

"I'm not sure what I want anymore," she said.

And then suddenly they were both aware that they'd been stalling and now they'd come upon the moment to say good night. They shifted awkwardly; the recently assembled lumber squeaked underfoot. Finally, Bolívar excused himself.

Closing the door behind him, Kera stood with her hand on the knob listening to his footsteps. She heard them pad against the wooden porch steps and then crunch onto the gravel drive. They crunched once, twice, and then a third time. But the fourth step did not come.

She'd been holding her breath. She realized suddenly what was about to happen.

She had the door open before he'd returned to the welcome mat. She let him kiss her as he backed her up against the kitchen counter.

She pushed back, and then she began removing his clothes, hastily, the way she had the first time, back in New York, before everything else in her life had come apart.

·  ·  ·  ·  ·

She had difficulty sleeping, but that wasn't anything new. She lay awake most of the night, her thoughts paced by the sound of his steady breaths beside her. On several occasions she came within a moment of slipping out of bed, but she feared waking him and having to explain what she intended to do next. Finally, though, she succumbed to sleep, and when she woke it was he who had gone.

It was still before dawn. She showered and packed quietly, though the nearest cabin was a hundred yards away. Then she put her bags in the car and drove without the headlights on until she reached the base of Bolívar's driveway. She left the car idling there and got out.

His house was quiet and she assumed he must have already gone to the mine. But then, as she was leaving the note she'd prepared for him on his kitchen table, she looked out at the lake and caught a glimpse of a figure sitting in a chair alone at the end of the dock.

# MANHATTAN

Her instinct to leave the valley had come suddenly—and it wasn't only because of the guilt that accompanied her desire for Bolívar's touch, when only months had passed since the man she'd once been engaged to was murdered. Staring at screens in a windowless room buried under a mountain was not an efficient way to investigate assassinations that had taken place on three separate continents. And then there was the nagging echo of Lionel's words—*There is no future for you at Langley*—which she knew had been spoken with a finality that she'd not yet accepted. Whatever the cause, the aimlessness she'd been sentenced to over the last few months was suddenly intolerable. She had to act.

If Bolívar and Jones had a surveillance system that alerted them to her departure, they had not tried to stop her; neither had contacted her to try to get her to change her mind. They knew better than to tell her how to do the work they'd hired her to do. They trusted her capabilities. Each, though, did send her an encrypted OTR message asking her to be careful. She acknowledged their messages with a short response that assured them she'd be in touch soon.

Kera sat on the bed in her Midtown hotel room with CNN droning on at low volume from the television. Her attention was devoted to her laptop, on which she composed a report to Bolívar and Jones that described what she'd learned about the catastrophic Lower Manhattan elevator accident that had killed Marcus Templeton, the second of their deceased sources. The short version of her report was that it had been no accident at all, which of course had been her expectation. What she'd really come here to find was evidence of the how and why—and she'd found it, at least the former. She laid out those details in an orderly report, which she still needed to finish and send via OTR chat. It was 10:40 AM; she had to be checked out of the room in twenty minutes.

On the two-and-a-half-day drive from Montana, she'd stopped twice at trucker motels where she'd fallen asleep memorizing the key facts of the Pine Street elevator incident, most of which came from NYPD and FDNY reports, as well as news articles: Fourteen people had boarded the elevator in the lobby. Eight souls had disembarked on various floors during the ascent. Marcus Templeton had been among the six remaining commuters in the car when it came to rest on the seventy-second floor a few moments before it plummeted. Since there had been no evidence of a mechanical failure, the police had concluded that a freak software glitch was responsible. WhisperLift, the designers of the cutting-edge elevator system, were being sued by the victims' families.

After arriving in the city, Kera had gone down to Pine Street in Lower Manhattan. She stood gazing up at the ninety-story building where, two weeks earlier, Templeton had perished. She wore her hair forward in a tight frame around her face, with a hat and large sunglasses that further manipulated her silhouette and obscured her face. She knew all too much about the facial-recognition software that processed hours of footage every second from the city's thousands of surveillance cameras.

Posing as a bike courier, she had tried and failed to gain access to the building's operations department—the windowless, subterranean cluster of rooms adjacent to the mail room. Operations was responsible for regulating the building's heating and cooling systems, power, and other utilities, operating the servers that stored data from the security cameras, and running the software that controlled the cars that lifted tenants up and down the skyscraper's ten elevator shafts with computerized efficiency. Before the incident, the operations center had no doubt been an overlooked and relatively unsecure facility. Kera now found it to be closely guarded and inaccessible to uncredentialed personnel. The failed elevator remained out of service, she discovered on a swing through the lobby, though the rest of the building appeared to hum along apace, as New Yorkers were accustomed to doing in the wake of freak commuting tragedies.

Unable to access the computers that housed the building's elevator software in person, Kera knew there was nothing more to learn from the site. Had evidence of foul play been discovered in the crater caused by the impact of the stricken elevator car, it would have by now been made public. She knew the evidence she was looking for would be elsewhere.

She went back to her hotel room, and using the most basic spear-phishing ploy in a hacker's arsenal, she e-mailed three lower-level employees at WhisperLift, disguising the e-mails as messages from the employees' bosses. Each e-mail contained text obliging the employee to click on a link that opened a Dilbert cartoon about quirky human behavior on elevators; Kera had found the cartoon using a simple Google Image search. Clicking the link also installed on each employee's computer a small, invisible program that gave Kera remote access to their machines. The first employee clicked on the link three minutes after the e-mail was sent, immediately opening communication between the company's computer and Kera's. The two other employees opened the message and clicked on the link later that afternoon. By four o'clock she owned all three computers. Now she just had to wait.

She went down to the West Village and sat alone in her favorite Italian restaurant. It was one she'd patronized almost weekly when she lived in the city. She always ordered the pepperoni pizza.

It tasted as exquisite as she'd remembered, but inevitably the taste of the food, along with just being back in the neighborhood, triggered darker memories. For months, she'd attempted to suppress these, but this time she let them consume her. Maybe this had been the main reason she'd wanted out of the valley. She sensed it was time to make peace with the parts of her past that were good but were now gone forever, and to confront the parts that might always haunt her. That would be the only way to reclaim her life.

Kera returned to her hotel room at six to find that all three of the WhisperLift employees she'd targeted had logged out of their computers and left the office for the evening. With a few keystrokes, she woke up their machines and began to explore. She was able to access the company's main network and all the files related to the contract with the skyscraper on Pine Street. There were also records of the ensuing lawsuit, plus data for the company's entire range of elevator software technologies and services.

In a chain of e-mails between WhisperLift's CEO, general counsel, and other executives, Kera learned that the company intended to offer a settlement to the families as soon as possible. Remarkably, the one thing that could limit their liability for the alleged software glitch had apparently not even occurred to them: that an outside party had breached their boilerplate security firewalls, disabled the elevator's backup safety systems, and ordered the car to plunge seventy-two stories. It was both a failure of imagination and over-confidence in their software's security. And it was about to cost them tens of millions of dollars.

That was not Kera's problem. She took the appropriate notes, then covered her tracks and exited the network. She was hardly any closer to a hypothesis about who might have been behind the elevator hack, but now at least she had confirmation that the WhisperLift software was indeed vulnerable to such an attack.

Her computer was in the final stages of encrypting the e-mail report to Bolívar and Jones when the narration from the CNN broadcast captured her attention. She squinted at the headline beneath the newscaster and reached for the remote to turn up the volume:

NEW LEAK HAS INTELLIGENCE COMMUNITY ON EDGE

# CAPITOL HILL

One by one, twenty men and four women checked their smart-phones at a bank teller–like window outside of Hart Senate Office Building 219. They proceeded through soundproofed double doors that led to a bland room, which had been swept twenty minutes earlier for eavesdropping devices. Behind the beige walls, steel casing prevented electromagnetic transmissions from escaping, and special panels absorbed and retained sound vibrations generated within the chamber. These walls could not talk.

Hart 219 was a Sensitive Compartmented Information Facility—a SCIF—and it was the primary venue for closed hearings of the Senate Select Committee on Intelligence. Like most SCIFs, Hart 219 displayed no architectural flourishes, nothing to detract from the room's main purpose: to keep secrets.

This was the third time in a week that the members of the Senate Select Committee on Intelligence had assembled for an emergency hearing with an all-too-familiar purpose: to evaluate the damage caused by a new intelligence leak. Overnight, Gnos.is had published a CIA report that cataloged, in devastating detail, the projected cyberespionage and cybersecurity capabilities of US intelligence agencies over the next five years.

The committee members, led by Chairman Larry Wrightmont, the senior Republican from Montana, sat in a horseshoe formation on a platform overlooking a witness table. Today's witnesses included CIA Director Tennison, bitter over another of his agency's classified initiatives coming to light before it could yield any measure of success; the NSA director, furious that the new leak might leave key infrastructure and other targets more vulnerable to a major cyberattack; the deputy secretary of state, confused and defensive, if less brazen ever since Angela Vasser—one of their own—had been charged with espionage; and FBI Director Ellis, caught off guard by the occurrence of a new leak while their lead suspect for the first was in custody.

"You're claiming, Director Ellis, that this woman, Angela Vasser, may also be responsible for this new leak?" Wrightmont asked, addressing the FBI man. "That she's, what, sending classified reports telepathically to journalists from her prison cell?" Closed hearings were often less scripted and more frank than the grandstanding on display at televised public hearings.

"She could have had the foresight to put the new report in a time-release file. Or she might have given a journalist the password to access it. She also might have a confederate."

"In which case there could be still more leaks to come?"

"That is our concern, Chairman."

"This woman was not cleared to Top Secret/SCI," Wrightmont pressed. "She's been on the ground in Beijing for two years. How did she get her hands on this intelligence she's alleged to have leaked?"

"Actually, today's leak may have provided a clue about that," Ellis said. "The main focus of the story published today by Gnos.is is the very sensitive IKE program, which you are all familiar with." IKE was a massive classified program, headed by the Department of Homeland Security, which had been charged with modernizing the nation's cyberinfrastructure, from water and power grids to fiber-optic Internet cables. IKE was still in its infancy—studies were being done, models were being tested on computers, bids from tele-com and software companies were being evaluated. "The report that Gnos.is published includes the names of several private contractors hired to consult on IKE. One of them is Conrad Smith."

"This is the man Vasser was having an affair with?" Wrightmont asked. He'd grazed the Gnos.is story but hadn't had time to digest the full leaked report.

"Correct."

"But hold on. The e-mail exchange between Vasser and Smith dis-cussed TERMITE, not IKE. How did they get access to TERMITE?"

"We're working on that," Ellis said.

Chairman Wrightmont shook his head. "What has she said about this?"

"Vasser? She denies it, of course. But the evidence suggests oth-erwise," Ellis said.

"The evidence being the e-mails published last week?"

"Yes, those. And now the affair has new significance. You've seen the transcripts. Our agents spent hours and hours questioning this woman. She's hiding something. I'm confident the case we build against her will be quite devastating."

"OK, OK," Wrightmont said. He sounded skeptical but wanted to get on with his day. "Before we excuse you, can you make a pre-diction about the ultimate scope of this intelligence breach? Have we seen the worst of these leaks, or is this only the beginning?" The senator had put this same question to each of the hearing's witnesses, and, like the others, FBI Director Ellis confessed that he simply didn't know. Wrightmont was one of the few people in the world who knew the combined budget of the US intelligence community, which was a figure that could only be discussed inside a SCIF like Hart 219. More mind-boggling than that multibillion-dollar figure was that none of these so-called intelligence agencies could provide even an educated guess about the extent of a leak supposedly caused by a junior diplomat.

At the hearing's conclusion, the senators collected their smartphones and returned to the outside world to find their secretaries' phone lines jammed with calls from angry constituents—a harsh reminder that the world had carried on without them for the last few hours. Another, particularly stinging reminder of that was the breaking news that Senator Wrightmont discovered when he was reunited with his phone. A judge had ruled that, given the new leak, the evidence in support of detaining Angela Vasser was now insufficient. She would be released, though not permitted to leave the District of Columbia, pending the outcome of the FBI's investigation.

"Should I cancel your lunch?" Senator Wrightmont's secretary asked.

Wrightmont's first instinct was to say yes; the hearing had already busted the day's schedule. Lately, every trip he made into that vacuum chamber left him less certain that what the intelligence boys were telling him made sense. At the beginning of the week, he'd been assured that the first leak, while irritating, had been contained with the arrest of Angela Vasser. But now he got the sense that this scandal was far from over. It would be wise to play the long game.

"No. Let's not overreact. We'll carry on as usual."

* * * * *

Senator Larry Wrightmont browsed no fewer than five of the major news sites daily, though he never admitted this to anyone. Outwardly he carried himself as though he was above the horse race, impervious to the Beltway's chattering class, which manufactured, reported on, and talked about "news" in a wonderfully amusing—and profitable—closed system. For three terms the senator's above-the-fray act had worked. As a reward, he was the horse his constituents bet on, and the Beltway press corps seemed an agreeable coconspirator, rarely calling to attention the fact that in a race of ruthless horses, the indifferent one never wins—certainly not three times in a row.

This careful image crafting was an example of one of Washington's open secrets, and trafficking in such secrets was a skill at which the senator excelled. In his freshman years in the Senate, his abilities on this front had blossomed in ways that surprised even him. Now, like any instinct, it was difficult for him not to take his political talents for granted. Washington was a game; secrets were the play money. Each secret gained or lost value like a stock depending on its moment-to-moment relevance. If one hoped to succeed at this game, reading the news was necessary due diligence.

Wrightmont's habit was to read on his tablet, which he scrolled through constantly in the car. It had been years since he'd actually sat idle and watched the capital's streets roll by. This afternoon—it was just past noon—he told his driver the name of a familiar restaurant and began to read as the car picked its way up Massachusetts Avenue. The *Post*, the *Times*, the *Journal*, *Politico*—they all reported essentially what he'd spent all morning being told by the intelligence directors: that an anonymous leaker, leaving no clue as to his or her rank, location, or motive, had acquired and released in full a collection of detailed briefs about cyberespionage and cybersecurity programs in both operational and planning stages. The competing page-one story in all cases announced the abrupt release of Angela Vasser, who had as of yet made no statement to the press, a fact that only encouraged pundits to debate the plausibility of her innocence.

The car was stopped at a light when a sudden, sharp rapping on Wrightmont's window brought his head up with a snap. Before he could register the source of the sound, he confronted something even more alarming—a black handgun within the car, at eye level, a foot from his face. It took him a moment to comprehend that the hand gripping the gun belonged to his driver and that the weapon was pointed at a figure standing in the street outside his window. Wrightmont had known, intellectually, that his driver carried a firearm, but seeing it for the first time shook him more than he'd have anticipated it might. Keeping his eyes on the weapon, he managed a dismissive gesture at the beggar, forgetting that the window was heavily tinted. The figure did not move. Finally, Wrightmont got a real look at the man and saw what the driver had seen all along—that this was no beggar. The man was in his late fifties, five years younger than Wrightmont, but tours of duty in his youth had long ago collected debts beneath his eyes, around the corners of his mouth, and in rings on his thick neck. He wore a long jacket over a sharp suit.

"It's OK, Jordan," the senator said to the driver. The gun finally vanished. Wrightmont rolled down his window. "Hi, Rick." He tried to remember the last time he'd seen Rick Altman. There had been a black-tie event six months earlier, at which they'd spoken briefly. He couldn't remember about what. They'd shared a couple of lunches over the past few years, and the senator had let Altman express his opinions on one bill or another. Altman was in defense, the private sector. The profit sector.

"Mind if I get in?" Altman said.

Wrightmont felt his driver tense again. The light changed and the car behind them honked. The driver was responsible for the senator's physical safety. But what about his political well-being? Within a fraction of a second, the instinct that gave function to Wrightmont's political organs weighed the risk of being caught with a defense contractor in an illicit conversation against the potential to gain an information advantage over his political adversaries. Calmly, he asked the driver to unlock the doors as he slid over to make room for Altman.

"What's this about?" Wrightmont asked when Altman had settled in beside him and shut the door.

"Her," said Altman. He thrust one thick finger at the tablet, which Wrightmont had forgotten since the firearm had made its appearance. The tablet was still illuminated, resting on the senator's lap. The photo on the screen was of Angela Vasser.

# WASHINGTON, DC

Using cash provided to her by Bolívar for expenses, Kera bought an Acela ticket from Penn Station to DC.

She had intended for New York to be a forty-eight-hour working layover on her way to Paris, where she planned to examine the elevator software of that city's most modern hotel. She hadn't made plans beyond that. Perhaps a trip to South Africa would be advantageous if Conrad Smith, the contractor whose name had turned up in the FBI transcripts as well as in the latest leak of classified files, began to figure into her investigation.

The trip to Washington had been an urgent, last-minute addition to her itinerary. Before leaving New York, she'd gone to the Midtown bank where, months earlier, she'd rented a safety deposit box. From the box, she retrieved documents that supported two of the three aliases Kera had established after it became clear that HAWK was going to implode and she better prepare for the worst. She chose the first alias, Nina Salazar, figuring that she'd need a valid credit card while in DC. She retrieved the driver's license, passport, and credit card of the second alias, Abigail Dalton, as a safety net in case something went wrong. The documents for the third alias remained locked in the bank; she would need them when she was ready for international travel.

Kera had deliberated with herself whether dipping into the aliases was a good idea. Her resources were finite. But once the opportunity presented itself and lodged in her head, she knew she had to give it a try.

At first she did not tell Bolívar or Jones that her plans had changed. She didn't need their input and didn't want them to worry. But while reading Gnos.is on the train, she stumbled upon a new story related to Angela Vasser's arrest and release. At first it appeared to be only a tangential thread. But then she read more, and before long it consumed her.

By the time the train glided to rest at Union Station, she had messaged Jones with a request. It took him twenty minutes—the time it took her to check into a hotel—to pack a zip drive full of background material on Vasser's partner Ben Welk and her apparent lover Conrad Smith and encrypt it in a message back to her. If Jones was curious about her motive for the request, he didn't say so, and she didn't ask him how he'd acquired all the files. It was almost like old times, Kera thought, remembering the months they'd shared working together on HAWK.

Seated at the small hotel-room table in the Adams-Morgan neighborhood where she'd lived when she worked at Langley, she plowed through the files from Jones. After three hours of searching, she identified her opening.

· · · · ·

At dusk two evenings later, a car driven by Ben Welk came out of the subterranean parking garage of a residential building near the Georgetown University Medical Center. Angela Vasser was in the passenger seat. Though Kera had had no one to wager against, she would have bet that Vasser would be with Welk tonight. She'd prepared for either eventuality—that Vasser would accompany her partner to the keynote gala of a conference on neurology and ethics, at which Welk was being honored for research he'd recently published, or that Vasser would stay home and continue to avoid the media and other inquisitors. The latter option presented a more difficult approach for Kera; surely the agency and the bureau had redundant teams watching the condo, which would make knocking on the embattled diplomat's door risky. But after reading the transcripts from Vasser's FBI interrogation at SFO, Kera was beginning to understand that Angela Vasser was not the kind of woman who liked to be confined to house arrest, not by members of the press or the Justice Department or anyone else.

In anticipation, Kera had used the Nina Salazar credit card to purchase tickets to the gala—two, as Salazar would need a husband for the evening, at least on paper—an outfit for the black-tie affair, and a hotel room just one floor above the relevant ballroom. A good cover wasn't cheap. At $1,000 a plate, this one was getting absurd. As a result, a disconcerting feeling had begun to taint all of her preparations: doubt. Was this diversion a mistake? The decision to come to DC seemed more and more like one she would have vetoed had she thought it through more carefully. But now she was here. The money was spent. The Nina Salazar alias was activated. Walking away would only guarantee that all of it had been a waste.

She entered the hotel a few minutes before the Welk-Vasser couple, dressed in an elegant but conservative navy-blue dress that she'd chosen because it was plain and would not stand out. Kera pulled up short at the sign in the lobby directing gala attendees to a ninth-floor ballroom. A few smartly dressed couples had gathered at a bank of elevator doors, waiting. She looked back. Still no sign of Vasser or Welk. When Kera had entered the lobby, the couple's car had been fifth in line for the hotel's valet. Kera had beaten the crowd by leaving her rental car with the valet at an Italian restaurant across the street.

A chime drifted across the lobby. Kera turned back to see the couples shuffle through the elevator's sliding doors. "Hold, please," she heard herself say, doubling her steps to catch them. One of the men noticed her and held the door ajar with his forearm. With only a slight hesitation that none of the other passengers noticed, Kera willed herself into the car. Even though Washington's zoning laws did not permit skyscrapers, the terror of falling even a handful of stories in a metal box came sharply into focus. The doors slid together with a whisper behind her. Kera eyed the panel of buttons. The number 9 was already illuminated. She noted that the hotel had fourteen floors. Her center lurched as they were lifted skyward.

When the chime came again, the doors parted to a spacious lobby filled with black suits and colorful dresses cascading from bare shoulders. Kera planted her pumps, one after the other, on the firm tile floor and stepped forward to a podium where a young woman with a headset matched the name Kera provided with one on the guest list. Kera told the woman that her husband would be coming late. Then she slipped into the near fringes of the crowd where she could keep an eye on new arrivals.

Several minutes passed and she began to worry that she might run out of plausible ways to look occupied standing alone. She took a short loop through the crowd, eyeing the elevators from a distance and growing more anxious each time a pair of doors parted and the handsome neurologist and tall, striking black woman did not emerge.

And then finally they did.

Kera folded herself into the crowd, ordered a club soda and lime from the bar, and stayed out of sight for the remainder of the cocktail hour. When the announcement for dinner came, she had planted herself across the room from Vasser, whose posture beside Welk was as elegant as her silk red dress. The event came off as preposterous to an outsider like Kera, with its hordes of scientists, disproportionately male—and none of them much to look at. Ben Welk, with his dark hair and earnest eyes, was a startling exception to this—even more so in person than in the dozens of photos she'd studied. And Vasser, against all odds, seemed to be enjoying herself. She must have been aware of how everyone in the room eyed her, either with suspicion or simply as amusing ballast to the tedious business of academic research. And yet she carried herself with a warm composure, revealing her bone-white smile in strategic bursts, like muzzle flashes that might cut down her critics. Kera couldn't help but feel a growing respect, even fondness, for her.

The first opportunity for an approach came at the en masse transition to the ballroom for dinner. Kera had predicted that this would be a logical time for Vasser to use the restroom, given that she'd be occupied in Welk's spotlight for the remainder of the evening. Kera's heart quickened in anticipation. But then she saw Vasser eye the sudden line at the ladies' room and decide to wait. There was a brief moment when Welk and Vasser were separated—enough of an opening that Kera might have pulled Vasser aside before she could enter the ballroom. But she was acutely aware that the moment of making contact was the point of no return. As the moment presented itself, her confidence, as if on a roller coaster, plummeted into a valley, leaving her stomach in the lurch. She watched Vasser work her way into the ballroom and toward her seat near the front. Kera exhaled and then began the project of talking her courage back up. It was better to wait anyway, she told herself. This would go much more smoothly if she could get the diplomat alone.

Kera found her place at the table she'd been assigned to in a far corner of the chandeliered room. There was a salad course, during which Kera was forced into small talk with her tablemates. She made apologies for her tardy husband, who she said was on the editorial board of *Nature* magazine and had been waiting for the right time to run a feature on what neuroscience might contribute to our understanding of ethics. This explanation had its desired effect; the scientists around her were more comfortable discussing their own work with each other and, beyond a dull instinct for common courtesy, had no use for the spouse of an absent editor who worked for a non-academic journal. They left her alone.

The windup to the keynote began with a series of remarks made by distinguished researchers and fund-raisers in the field. The moment Kera was waiting for came after the conclusion of a garrulous welcome speech made by a chair of some committee, his cheeks rosy from the cocktail hour. Vasser stood and made her way from the honorees' table to the back of the room. After a few moments, Kera excused herself and followed her toward the lobby restroom.

This time her confidence did not waiver. Delaying her entrance until she heard a flush and the closing of a stall door, Kera stepped through a short corridor that opened to a long, eight-stall affair with generous lighting and baskets of cloth towels. Vasser was leaning over a distant sink, looking directly at herself in the mirror as she rinsed her hands. They were alone. Kera wasn't going to get a better shot than this.

Removing her wig as she walked, Kera moved toward Vasser, shaking out her hair. She stopped a few paces from the diplomat, making herself obvious but leaving an unthreatening gap between them. Vasser looked at her in the mirror, making eye contact, and then tried to look away, as if to telegraph that she wasn't interested in a conversation. But then her eyes flicked back with a glimmer.

"Do you know who I am?" Kera said. Vasser would have been overseas during Kera's and Jones's first few weeks as fugitives—traitors—when images of them had permeated the airways and the front pages of newspapers worldwide. The story had amused Beijing; state-run news outlets had devoted hundreds of hours and column inches to portraying the missing Americans as defectors with anticapitalist motives. Vasser surely would have remembered the coverage.

"What do you want?" Vasser said.

"I rented a room one floor up. Can you get away to talk with me in private?"

"Certainly not." She reached for a towel and worked it quickly over her hands. "Excuse me."

Kera had rehearsed contingencies in the event that Vasser would decline her invitation. She appreciated in full now what had come through in the FBI transcripts as a feature of Vasser's personality: decisive and direct, no bullshit. Vasser wasn't bluffing; she was about to walk out. Just like that, Kera was forced to deploy her contingency of last resort. "The plane crash was a hit."

Vasser stopped at the exit and turned. "A hit?"

"An assassination. And I think you—"

"I've been accused of a lot of unflattering things," Vasser interrupted. She looked Kera up and down with new disgust. "But that's a new one. And from you, of all people—"

"No, you misunderstand me. I think you might have been the target."

Vasser hesitated, her eyes locked on Kera's, examining them closely for the first time.

"Both of you. You and the ambassador," Kera said.

Now only genuine confusion. "Why?"

"Was there anything unusual about your trip to Shanghai?"

"Nothing as unusual as what's happening right now," Vasser said, remembering herself.

"If there was a better way to approach you, I would have tried it. Give me twenty minutes. Please."

"That's impossible. What do you want?"

"I want to find out who murdered the ambassador—and who intended to murder you too."

"This is crazy. You know I can't talk to you."

"I don't think you leaked those files. Even if you had access to TERMITE, why expose yourself by mentioning it in an e-mail sent to a man you would see face-to-face a few days later? It doesn't make sense." Vasser didn't respond, but Kera could tell that this had won her some extra time. "You saw Conrad Smith while you were in Shanghai. In the FBI interrogation you were never asked whether you knew why he was in town. Do you?"

"He has nothing to do with this."

"I'm just asking. The way it looks right now, you were blowing apart a top-secret CIA op around the same time you conveniently missed the flight that killed the ambassador. I kind of like your whole tough-girl act, but it's missing a few simple answers about how all this might have happened."

Vasser's eyes narrowed. "I hope the investigation answers your questions. I can't."

"The investigation? That's what you're waiting for?"

"I have to trust that the justice system will sort it out."

Kera shook her head. "I thought the same thing, and look where it's gotten me. This goes way beyond the justice system."

"I'm here, aren't I? I'm no longer in a cell."

"That's true, but you might have been safer on the inside."

"I need to get back. I think I've indulged your intrusion into my evening for long enough."

"Wait." Kera held out a slip of paper. "If you change your mind, that's how you can reach me." Vasser eyed the note suspiciously, and then, to Kera's surprise, she took it. "Be careful."

"'Be careful'? Are you threatening me? What is that supposed to mean?"

"Stay out of airplanes and elevators." Now it was Kera who walked away, arranging the wig hastily over her real hair.

"Elevators?"

"My note, Ms. Vasser," she said, nodding back at the slip of paper. "Read it." From the restroom she walked directly to the stairwell and descended the nine floors on foot.

Outside, she did not cross to the valet where she'd left her car. Instead, she walked three blocks to a garage where she'd parked a different car that she'd rented under a different name. She was outside of the District before the keynote, "The Moral Brain and the Illusion of Free Will," concluded to lengthy applause.

# LANGLEY

Bright ran her phone number. He had told himself that he wasn't going to do that. Not until things between him and Karen—whom he'd only known as Audrey—got serious. *If* they got serious. He didn't know yet what he wanted, but he knew better than to sabotage his relationship with this woman before he gave it a real chance. The problem was that ever since the unexpected parting conversation he'd shared with Karen/Audrey at the restaurant, his curiosity had been driving him mad.

Running her cell phone number through the system only confused him further. The number was a match to an Audrey Potter of Arlington, Virginia. In the career field, the system noted that she was a registered lobbyist.

Then what had been the point in telling him her name was Karen and that she wasn't a lobbyist?

Bright could think of one more resource at his disposal—and it too was one that the average person didn't have in his arsenal of online-stalking tools. Overriding his guilt, he scrolled through her dating-site profile, singling out clear photos of her face. He selected three and downloaded them onto a flash drive, which he took downstairs with him to the ops center.

"You got a second?" Bright asked one of the familiar technicians. Because so many of the agency's surveillance targets had multiple identities, they had developed a database—or, more accurately, a network of databases—designed to sort out these webs of aliases and true identities.

"Got anything more than this?" the tech asked after he'd opened the flash drive and found that it contained only three JPEG files.

"No, just the photos."

The tech shrugged. "Well, that'll keep it pretty straightforward." What he meant was that he had only one option: facial-recognition analysis.

The facial-recog search was complete in a matter of seconds. Unsurprisingly, there was a positive match for Audrey Potter. The familiar phone number, address, Social Security number, and career information came up. But there was also a second hit: Karen Lessing. Bright stared at the screen. It was her. Karen Lessing was her name. Her real name. But the database wasn't much help beyond that. The most recent updated field noted Karen Lessing's graduation from a UCLA doctoral program in neuroscience—three decades earlier. There was no employer after that, no current address, nothing else.

Bright interpreted this to mean that Karen Lessing had assumed the Audrey Potter cover identity and maintained it for thirty years. That was long enough that the details of her cover had practically eclipsed all record of her real identity.

"Want to save a copy of these?" the tech asked him.

Bright almost said yes. There was a Social Security number attached to the real Karen Lessing. And with that he could have run background checks, credit reports, call logs, etc., even though none of the data would be current. Instead he said, "No, that's all right. Thank you."

He didn't want her old metadata or shopping habits, he realized. But then what *did* he want? This longing, this feeling of helplessness, was unfamiliar to him. There had been hundreds of people he wanted desperately to know more about. But never like this; never someone who was not the target of an intelligence case. He'd wasted an hour prying into the details of her two lives before he realized the proper way to get what he truly wanted was to see her again, to spend time with her, as soon as possible. He reached for his phone.

Voice mail. The outgoing message, he noted now for the first time, was a standard automated one. It was not recorded in her voice and did not give her name. After the beep he apologized again for having to abandon their last evening together so abruptly. If she'd forgive him, he wondered whether she would let him cook her dinner the night after next.

The phone rang so suddenly after he disconnected the call that he assumed it was her. The caller ID display brought him reeling back into his workday. It was a secure call coming from the office of the director of the FBI.

"Can you hold, please, for the director?" a male voice said when Bright answered and identified himself.

"Lionel." The director's voice came over the line a minute later. "I thought you'd want to know. I've just spoken with Angela Vasser."

Bright leaned forward, fighting distraction. His mind raced. When you got a call from another agency, most especially from its director, there was always more going on than it seemed. Ever since Angela Vasser's release—even before her release—Bright had been trying to get a meeting with the diplomat. Vasser had been the last person to talk to the ambassador before he got on that buggy plane. She had to know something useful about what had happened. He wasn't sure what he expected her to remember that she hadn't already told the FBI, but maybe she'd see it differently if she knew they were eyeing the case as an assassination rather than an accident. The trouble was, the BIGOT list for MIRAGE was so pared down that arranging a meet with Vasser required a cover story, and so far every time they'd presented a watered-down story to the bureau, they were told to wait in line. The FBI wasn't letting anyone piss on their territory in the middle of a very public investigation. Vasser herself wasn't encouraging visitors, and she rarely left her condo. Hell, Vasser herself wasn't even a BIGOT—meaning she wasn't permitted to be read into the case. Bright still hadn't figured out how he was going to get around that when he did meet her face-to-face.

"Kind of you to think of me, Director, but we've been following INR's lead on all that," Bright said, referring to the State Department's Bureau of Intelligence and Research, their in-house liaison with the intelligence community.

"I know. This is something else," Director Ellis said. "Vasser had contact last night with Kera Mersal."

The name came in from such a distant context in Bright's mind that at first he didn't register the significance of what the director was saying.

"Vasser told you this? That she spoke with Kera?"

"Apparently. Vasser—who hasn't been very forthcoming about anything, mind you—just turned up at my office without an appointment to tell me that Kera Mersal approached her in a hotel ladies' room last night."

"They met *in person*? She's sure it was Kera?" Bright could picture Kera sitting on the park bench across the street from his house, holding his newspaper. For an instant Bright wondered whether this call from the FBI director might be a trap. Did they know Kera had approached him too?

"That's what she said."

"Can I have a word with Vasser? Don't let her leave."

"Too late, she left fifteen minutes ago."

"Dammit. What about Kera?"

"We've got teams at the hotel, airport, and train stations. But she's got a fifteen-hour head start. I don't need to tell you that she can disappear in a fraction of that time."

"What did they speak about?"

"Vasser says that Mersal wanted to know more about what happened in Shanghai. She tried to bait Vasser by claiming the ambassador's plane crash was a hit. Can you believe that?"

"Jesus Christ."

Bright thanked the director for letting him know, and the director said he'd send over the hotel's surveillance tapes, from which they hoped to confirm Kera Mersal's presence. Bright hung up already convinced that it was her. But what on earth was she up to?

# WASHINGTON, DC

Angela Vasser stepped from the sidewalk onto the escalator and let it carry her down into the Archives Metro station. She had expected to feel better than she did right now. She'd expected to feel the way you were supposed to feel after doing the right thing. Ben had convinced her, finally, after a blur of sleepless hours, that she must go to the FBI and tell them about Kera Mersal. Maybe she shouldn't have told Ben that the fugitive intelligence operative had approached her. She could have kept it to herself for a little while, waited to see how things played out.

But no, that wouldn't have been right. She never kept anything from Ben; this seemed a silly thing to withhold. She'd done the right thing. And Ben had been right to persuade her to go to the Feds. Not doing so was equivalent to aiding a fugitive—a traitor—wasn't it? And beyond that, what better way was there for Vasser to show that she was being cooperative and patriotic? Certainly her lawyers would have given her the same advice Ben had.

Vasser felt a bitter sting. It stung to discover how easily one's patriotism could be put up for debate—not just a debate, but a sham trial where the evidence, one's entire career in the diplomatic service, was negated by howling Beltway lifers who all shared a brain and who seemed to demand that the burden was on her to prove her innocence while simultaneously hinting that no proof could change their opinions.

Through a tunnel, down another escalator, onto the crowded platform. Vasser was wearing dark glasses and kept her head down. She wandered to a spot that was less crowded and looked down at the tracks. If she'd done the right thing, why did she feel this nagging sensation to the contrary? Something about Kera Mersal unsettled Vasser. Something about the way Mersal had approached, about the confidence in her gaze. Vasser didn't have intimate knowledge of the HAWK case that had ensnared Mersal in her current legal trouble. She'd read about it in the news like everyone else. And, like everyone else, she'd accepted the narrative that had emerged—that Mersal and a colleague named J. D. Jones had betrayed their oath to their country by exposing classified information, and that they were perhaps in the pocket of the People's Republic of China.

Maybe it was because Vasser now had more sympathy for just how unfair the tide of press coverage could be, but she couldn't shake an intuition that the woman she'd spoken to the evening before did not fit the mold of a traitor. Why had Mersal risked coming to DC for a few fleeting moments of conversation with Vasser? Just to suggest that Greg's plane going down had not been an accident? To warn Vasser that her life was in danger? To give her a piece of paper with the names of two other people who had recently died?

Vasser had not told Director Ellis about the note with the names on it and the detailed instructions for making contact with Mersal, should she want to do that. At one point the director asked her whether Mersal had indicated any way she might be contacted. Vasser had said no. Lying had felt wrong in the moment, but now it was the only thing that felt right. She slipped her fingers into her pants pocket and felt relief at the touch of the folded slip of paper. She had not told Ben about the note either. Why that, of all things? Right and wrong felt upside down.

Wind moved through the cavernous Metro tunnel, rustling her hair. Shivering, she stepped back from the edge of the platform. Anonymous commuters swarmed around her, angling for a seat on the train.

She disembarked at Foggy Bottom and took more escalators to the street. From there it would be a hike back into Georgetown, but she was in no rush to return home. No matter where she was, she was a prisoner in waiting—waiting for the investigation to clear her name. Walking the streets at least kept her restlessness at bay.

As she turned up Wisconsin Avenue, her mind was back in Shanghai, searching for an overlooked detail that might provide some clue as to how this baffling chain of events had been set in motion. The Shanghai meetings had been only two weeks before, though it seemed like years. They'd flown down from Beijing on the private jet, which, Vasser remembered vividly, was an accommodation that had made Greg uncomfortable. But Greg had insisted on keeping their travel plans, and Vasser, suspecting this was because he'd been given orders from above, did not belabor her objections. Debating their transportation to Shanghai was not something either of them considered worth their time. In any case, the Hu Lan controversy seemed to be a red herring, even in retrospect. She remembered the fleeting, shameful thrill of the plane's trivial luxuries—glassware, swivel armchairs, imbedded television screens. But while flying private was atypical, nothing struck her then or now as suspicious.

On arrival they'd gone to the hotel and met immediately with the Kenyan and Chinese delegations. She had made presentations, forged connections with her counterparts. She tried to pace her memory, to scrutinize everything that had happened right up until her parting words with Greg as he and the others left for the airport. She'd checked her phone then, just after Greg had left, and had seen the message from Conrad. He was in Shanghai and had heard that she was too.

Had anything been out of the ordinary?

She'd run through this exercise a dozen times already, of course, both with the FBI and alone in that cell before her release. But everything looked different now. Different ever since Kera Mersal had walked up to her and spoken those words.

Prompted by the traffic signal, Vasser stepped off the curb and into a crosswalk. Her peripheral vision detected fast-approaching harm, confirmed by a quick glance left. Her body took over from there. The car braked and swerved dramatically, nosing itself violently into a van in the adjacent lane. With a pitiful whimper, Vasser threw herself backward, landing in a sprawl on the relative safety of the sidewalk. From that perspective, she began to assess the situation. First herself—no apparent injury there—then her surroundings. Her eyes swung to the far traffic signal. She would have bet her life—in fact, she had—that the light had been red, indicting the reckless driver. But it was green. Had she been so lost in thought that she'd misread the pedestrian signal?

Finally, time began to move forward again. Not more than an instant had elapsed. A surge of vehicles rolled into the intersection suddenly, with engines accelerating from all directions. Then, just as abruptly, the air pealed with the high-pitched cries of pavement stripping rubber from tires. A half-dozen metallic thwacks brought the unluckiest of the vehicles to rest. Horns vented confusion.

Vasser sat up. Her eyes darted. The walk signal was illuminated. So too was the trio of green lights directing cross traffic. The lights perpendicular to them? All green too. Every traffic light around the intersection signaled green, beckoning vehicles toward disaster. Without realizing why, Vasser thought suddenly of the elevators. That morning, after Ben had left for work, she'd Googled the two names on the slip of paper Kera Mersal had given to her. They meant nothing to her. They were both American; the man ran a hedge fund, the woman had been an executive at a technology company. Vasser saw nothing remarkable about them, except for the grim fact that within forty-eight hours they had both perished in freak elevator failures on opposite sides of the planet.

Movement approached in a blur from her left. A motorcycle. In conspicuous contrast to the paralyzed traffic in and around the crippled intersection, the bike sprang forward, roaring through an aisle between cars. Vasser caught sight of the driver, covered from helmet to boot in thick black combat gear and wearing what looked like a computer bag slung across his body. He leaned hard into a sharp turn to cut through the line of cars and hop the bike onto the sidewalk not a dozen feet from her. At first she thought, *Police!* because the bike had wide carbonate saddle boxes and a thick antenna extending skyward behind the driver. But there were no official markings, no lights or sirens.

A scream from a nearby pedestrian was the only thing that let her believe that what her eyes saw next was a true representation of reality. The man on the bike removed one hand from the handlebars; a moment later it reappeared clutching a handgun. What saved her was an instinct to dive forward, rolling into the street and the narrow space between two idle vehicles, rather than reeling backward defensively on the open sidewalk. The unanticipated motion forced the shooter to redirect both the bike and his aim. She heard the weapon report twice—two pops, implausible to her even as she was rolling away from them. She assumed neither hit its target, though she didn't completely trust her senses. Her brain was not interested in sensations; it hungered only for as much adrenaline as it could coax from the relevant glands.

Over the screams of bystanders, she heard a loud thud punctuated with a metallic tear and then tinkling glass. The shooter, she realized, must have lost control of his bike while readjusting his aim at her. She could no longer hear the bike's motor. Resisting an urge to stand up and run, Vasser rolled from the protection of one vehicle's undercarriage to the next. Was the shooter now on foot? Was he injured? She thought she heard a motor struggling to start. It was difficult to be certain with all the ambient shouting. And then—

Sirens. For the first time since seeing the gun, she believed the odds of surviving the next few moments might swing in her favor. She wriggled left and right, checking her ground-level sight lines. The shooter, stuck with a stalled getaway bike, must have taken off on foot rather than risk capture while trying to finish the job.

Vasser closed her eyes, breathed deeply, and then opened them. She was beneath a taxicab, the grime and rust of its underbelly an inch from her face. She waited, listening to the sirens grow louder, trying to remember an identifying characteristic that could help the police nail this bastard.

Then she remembered the note in her pocket and she got another idea.

# LANGLEY

"That's her?" Bright asked. He'd expected a disguise, of course, but this was impressive. He wasn't confident he'd have registered the woman on-screen as Kera if he'd passed her on the street.

"Yes, sir," the young analyst said, tempering his excitement as he cued up a chain of clips on adjacent screens. After Kera Mersal and J. D. Jones had first gone missing, a team had been assembled for the sole purpose of tracking them down. Embarrassingly, aside from the morning Kera had approached Bright outside his house, an incident he'd kept to himself, the call this morning from the FBI director about the Vasser-Mersal rendezvous had been their only concrete lead. "She enters the hotel lobby at 1813 hours. Here she is five minutes later up on the ninth floor. She hangs out in view of the elevators there until Vasser and her boyfriend arrive. Then she just sort of wanders for a bit."

"Tell me you can see them make contact."

"Not exactly. But it's close enough. Here. At 1920 hours Vasser gets up to use the ladies. And . . . here. See, Mersal follows her."

Bright watched the screens, squinting at the female figure striding into the ladies' room. It was her, all right. He recognized her not so much from her face, which was obscured and heavily made up, but from her tradecraft. Her positions in the room, the way she stood at ninety-degree angles from the surveillance cameras, her detached expression that hid her watchful eyes.

"And then, six minutes later, Mersal emerges and goes straight for the stairwell. This is our last look at her." The grainy perimeter camera had captured a female figure exiting the stairwell door onto the sidewalk and then walking calmly out of frame.

"What have we got on the alias?"

"Nina Salazar. A credit card in that name paid for the gala tickets, a hotel room, and a rental car, which was abandoned at the valet stand across the street. Beyond those transactions, 'Nina Salazar' exists only on paper."

Bright couldn't suppress a thin smile. Kera knew exactly the methods they would use to look for her, and she knew exactly how to thwart them. Of course she did—that's what they'd trained her to do.

Bright returned to his office only to have his assistant confirm that none of the afternoon's back-to-back meetings had been canceled. He trudged off to the first one, which was interrupted ten minutes later by one of the junior case agents who worked under Henry Liu. The young man was breathless from the dash up the stairs from the ops center.

"Sorry, sir," he told Bright in the hallway. "You said you wanted to know right away if we picked up anything unusual with Angela Vasser."

What Bright had actually said was that he wanted Vasser tailed until they'd figured out a way to get a face-to-face meeting with her. Vasser was not only the last person to talk to Ambassador Rodgers but also now the last person they knew of who had spoken to Kera Mersal. Bright had to get to her, even if it meant surprising her in a ladies' room himself.

He entered the ops center hopeful that he was about to hear one of two things—a viable plan for approaching Vasser, or another sighting of Kera. He realized quickly that neither was likely.

"Lionel, there you are," Liu said. "I'm not sure what to make of this."

"What happened?" Bright felt his stomach clench in anticipation of bad news.

"Well, we're not sure, actually. Look at this." More surveillance footage. The feed came from a Department of Transportation traffic cam mounted over a busy Georgetown intersection. "OK, so this is Vasser over here," Liu said, pointing to a tall black woman waiting at the crosswalk. The angle wasn't great because the camera was aimed at the vehicle traffic, but near the edge of the picture Bright could clearly see Vasser, head down, waiting for the walk signal. "Now, just watch what happens."

Bright watched with his arms folded over his stomach. He jerked upright in surprise when Vasser stepped off the curb and was nearly clipped by an SUV that had sped into the frame from off camera. He raised his eyebrows at Liu, who nodded for him to keep watching. Vasser, apparently unharmed, was in a reclined position on the sidewalk, resting on her elbows. Bright was distracted just then by a surge of action elsewhere on-screen. Vehicles converged on the intersection all at once; several of them collided. Bright leaned toward the screen, trying to make sense of it. Movement from Vasser's quadrant returned his attention there, just in time to see her dive forward into the street. A motorcycle entered the picture just as suddenly, and— was that what he thought it was? Two flashes from the weapon, and then the bike swerved but couldn't avoid making contact—hard— with a parked car.

"Was she hit?"

"We don't think so. No hospitals are treating gunshot wounds."

"When did this happen?"

"About forty-five minutes ago."

"Where is she now?"

Liu shook his head. "The team covering her condo is trying to figure that out. District Police and the FBI are on it too."

"She left the scene?" Bright looked back to the spot on the screen where Vasser had disappeared underneath a vehicle. Between that spot and the edge of the frame were two disorganized rows of cars. Had she crawled out of sight and then fled? "She didn't go home?"

"Apparently not, sir."

"Back it up. I want to watch it again." The analyst working the touch-screen keypad obliged and Bright studied the scene, this time anticipating the motorcycle. He watched Vasser dive out of sight just before the bike slammed into the stopped vehicle. "Hold on. What's he doing right there? The shooter?"

"Trashing his equipment, apparently, before he takes off on foot."

"What equipment?"

"It might be too early to say, but the Feds called in a cyber team. They won't know more until they get the bike into the lab, but the agent I talked to said the thing was rigged like a cell tower on two wheels."

Bright went still inside and out. He was staring at the frozen image of the perpetrator, who was bringing the butt of his handgun down hard against the contents of the open saddle box. Bright noted the large antenna mounted behind the bike's seat and the computer bag slung across the perp's chest.

"The traffic signals," Bright whispered. He hadn't noticed the first time around because he'd been distracted by the shooting—and also because the surveillance video was in black and white. But even without color it was clear that the bottom light on each of the signals was illuminated.

"That's right," Liu said. "They all turned green right before Vasser was attacked. We're already in contact with DOT. Their grid was hacked."

# CAPITOL HILL

Mid-adagio movement of Haydn's Concerto no. 2 in D Major, op. 101, Senator Larry Wrightmont received a text message. He checked it discreetly.

MEET ME ON THE ROOF.

At intermission, the senator excused himself from his wife and the couple they had come with and, grumbling, made his way to the Kennedy Center's roof terrace. Rick Altman was leaning on the railing, gazing out at the dark Potomac.

"This sneaking up on me has to stop," Wrightmont said to the defense contractor.

"Would you rather we discuss it on the phone? Or maybe I could just swing by your office or house?" When the senator didn't reply, Altman dropped the sarcasm. "What are you hearing?"

"You know damn well I can't talk about what I'm hearing."

The truth was that what he was hearing was insane. The FBI had prepared a classified report for the members of the Select Committee on Intelligence that contained exactly everything that was being reported on CNN. It characterized the Georgetown incident involving Angela Vasser as chaotic and troublesome. The shooter's identity and motive were both unknown. The FBI's cyberlab confirmed that servers at the Department of Transportation had been accessed by an outside party, who had orchestrated the traffic-signal chaos that preceded the shooting. The FBI had not, however, been able to recover any identifying data from the shooter's damaged and abandoned equipment. If the shooter was foreign, he'd disguised it well. He was clearly a professional. But what sort? That question had sparked a hot debate. Most agents working the case believed that the DOT hack pointed to the work of a professional cyberterrorist and not, as other agents argued, a professional hit man, given the two errant close-range shots.

The classified report prepared for Senator Wrightmont's committee claimed that Angela Vasser had survived the attack, though she had apparently vanished. The NSA had used GPS tracking on her phone to guide the FBI to a Georgetown street corner, where they dug the abandoned device out of a trash can. This fact had inspired a mountain of loose speculation from investigators who, under pressure to provide answers to people like Senator Wrightmont, began to shovel paranoid bullshit into the void created by the lack of an intelligible narrative built on real evidence.

"You know what I think?" Altman said, challenging the senator with unblinking eyes. "I think the only thing you know that the rest of us don't is just how far the FBI is from having a clue about what's going on. This case is pandemonium. It's fraught with incompetence. And"—he paused to let the senator hang on his words—"it's overdue for some leadership. Are we on the same page, Senator?"

Wrightmont shook his head. He didn't like Altman's attitude. "I was clear about my reservations. I won't risk getting on the wrong side of this."

"The wrong side of this? Jesus, Larry, she's on the run. What else do you need? Either you take ahold of this thing, or you're just another asshole bitching about what a shitshow it all is. I need to know now that we're on the same page. Senator?"

A commercial jet banked through the airspace above the winding Potomac and then swung toward Reagan National. "Yes," Wrightmont said finally. "All right."

"Then we'll go ahead, as discussed. Is that your recommendation?"

"It's your goddamn plan, Rick. I told you, no matter what, I'm not getting my hands dirty."

"I understand, Senator. But your nomination to head the NSA moves to the front of the line if we get out in front of this. If we don't, you face a reelection campaign. You're looking at losing a primary to someone who thinks his great-grandparents had pet dinosaurs. Are you willing to leave your career in the hands of the good primary voters of Montana? All I need is assurance from you that you'll take leadership on the Hill to get our surveillance bill passed." The vote on the surveillance bill—which, if it passed, would free up hundreds of millions of dollars to be spent on private defense contractors like Altman's company—would be brought to the Senate floor within weeks. "Once you've moved into Fort Meade, we can talk more about our ongoing business together." Another pause. "Shall we move forward, then?"

This was repulsive, Wrightmont thought. On the other hand, though, he had encountered few decisions in life that were so crystal clear in their distribution of costs and benefits.

"Your guy at NSA has access to her files?"

"He does, and he's already made me a copy of them. Took him a couple of minutes out of his day. And Larry, wait till you see this shit. This woman—"

"No, don't tell me. The less I know, the better. You have a journalist willing to cover it?"

"Willing? This story's huge. It will launch his career."

Wrightmont turned from the view. Intermission was over; he had to get back to the chamber music. "All right, nail her. I'll take care of the surveillance bill. And Rick? Don't fuck this up."

# NORTHERN VIRGINIA

A cab from the city rounded the corner, cautious, as if intimidated by the idyllic suburban streets, and then turned into the parking lot of a ten-field recreational soccer and baseball complex. The tall black woman paid in cash, just as she'd promised the driver she would. He'd been more than a little reluctant to take her twenty-five miles out of the city, but she'd shown him the bills and he'd shrugged and programmed the GPS.

The cab sped away and the woman looked around, orienting herself. The parking lot was only half-full. Behind her, from the direction she'd come, was a quiet residential neighborhood. Leafy green woods surrounded the sports complex in every other direction. Through the trees on one side, she caught glimpses of cyclists and joggers on a path.

She was relieved to see right away how clear the instructions had been. She began walking, past the baseball fields and out to the farthest soccer field, where a children's game was in progress. Bursts of affirmation rose in shouts from the sidelines. She stood on the outer edge of the field, a ways off from the nearest cluster of parents, and waited.

· · · · ·

Kera Mersal watched from the protection of the woods more than a hundred meters away. She'd spent several days casing the complex, learning the patterns of the players, parents, referees, and grounds workers who came and went from the fields. And now, ever since she'd received the call from Angela Vasser on a new burner phone she'd purchased and activated for this sole purpose, she'd been circling the wooded perimeter of the complex, searching for any changes in those patterns. She detected none. No strange vans or SUVs with tinted windows. No fluctuation in the pedestrian traffic on the adjacent bike path. No loiterers or bird-watchers or generic maintenance crews.

She watched Vasser for twenty minutes and carefully reviewed in her mind everything the woman had told her.

The burner had rung the afternoon following her approach in the hotel ladies' room—much sooner than Kera had expected. When she answered, Vasser said, "I've done a terrible thing," by which she meant that she'd gone to the FBI and discussed the conversation she'd had with Kera. She was blunt about what she'd told them— that Kera had approached her, claiming the ambassador's death had been a hit and that Vasser might also be in danger. Vasser apologized to Kera for going to the Feds; the night before it had seemed like the appropriate thing to do.

But now the situation had changed. Someone had tried to kill her. And Kera was the only one who had warned her about that.

"How did you know I was in danger?" Vasser had asked after she summarized her conversation with the FBI director. It sounded like an accusation.

"Listen to me. This is very important. Did you tell them how to contact me?"

"The note you gave me? No. I didn't tell anyone about that, not even Ben. It hasn't left my possession."

Kera had to make a decision: to believe Vasser, or to walk away and not risk drawing half of the intelligence community onto her trail. Talking about it over the phone wasn't helping.

"Where are you now?" she'd asked. "No, wait, don't tell me. Are you safe? Are you alone?"

Vasser indicated that she was.

"And no one knows you're calling me from that phone? There are no cameras around you?"

"No. I got away after the shooting. There's no one here. No cameras."

"What about your own phone?"

"I threw it away, like you said."

"Where?"

"A block or so from the shooting. I followed all of your directions."

"Good." Kera gave her the address and instructions for what to do when she arrived at the sports complex. She detected reluctance in the silence that came over the line.

"How did you know about the gunman?" Vasser demanded. "Who was he?"

"I don't know who he was or who sent him," Kera said.

"Then how did you know I was a target?"

"I can't explain that over the phone. There isn't time."

"Then I won't meet you," Vasser said. It sounded as though she meant it. Kera leapt at the opportunity to test her.

"Very well," Kera said. Almost immediately, she regretted it. After all this trouble, she'd practically opened the door for Vasser to simply walk away—with no plan to reestablish contact. She shut her eyes, listening for the line to be disconnected. But after a pause, Vasser reversed herself and said she was getting in a cab.

Though better than the alternative, that outcome came with its own set of red flags. Vasser's willingness to meet her left open the possibility that the Feds had enlisted Vasser to lead them to Kera. Could they have put a plan like that together in less than an afternoon—including the bizarre hit man on the motorcycle? Kera doubted it, but it was still a possibility. She would have felt safer had Vasser seemed genuinely tempted to back out of the meeting.

• • • • •

Each side scored a goal, and Vasser applauded the kids on both occasions. But Kera knew the diplomat wasn't really watching the game. Her eyes shifted constantly; she fidgeted with her arms. Kera eventually became confident that an immediate ambush was not in the works, and retracing her steps to the bike path, she circled around to a point where she could come up behind Vasser from the woods.

Vasser heard her approach and turned, wild-eyed, her nerves still on edge after being shot at. Fear melted to relief when she recognized Kera. They stood side by side for a moment, two alleged traitors watching kids chase after a soccer ball.

"Were you followed?" Kera asked.

"No."

Kera believed her. Ducking surveillance was a habit picked up by anyone who worked in an overseas embassy. But believing Vasser and trusting her were two different things.

Kera pulled out a radio frequency signal detector she'd purchased for $300 cash at a Best Buy in Reston near Dulles. The handheld sweep unit was about the size of an iPhone with a short, walkie-talkie-like antenna. Vasser eyed it with a mix of fear and suspicion.

"Look at me," Kera said. "Like we're just chatting." She aligned herself so that Vasser's body shielded Kera's hands from any of the soccer fans who might have glanced at them across the field. Then she turned the dial on the device and let it fall at Vasser's feet, as if by accident. She bent over and, working slowly up the diplomat's legs and then torso, watched the device. The bars on the frequency display did not fluctuate. She put the device away, satisfied that Vasser had nothing on her person that could transmit RF signals.

"What happened in Georgetown?" Kera asked. She'd read about the incident online, but the details were vague and didn't add up to a narrative that satisfied her common sense.

"The lights all turned green."

"I know that. Tell me about the shooter."

"When the traffic jammed, a man appeared on the motorcycle. He came straight for me." Her fear consolidated this time into suspicion and she glared at Kera. "You knew it would happen."

Kera shook her head. "I didn't. I told you what I knew—that the ambassador's plane going down was no accident, and that whoever brought down the plane expected you to be on board." What she didn't spell out for Vasser was the pattern that had emerged: a plane, elevators, and now traffic lights.

"What do you want with me?" Vasser asked.

The final whistle had been blown on the field and young soccer players were starting to be led by their parents back to the parking lot.

"Let's go somewhere more private. I have a safe place where we can talk."

• • • • •

Between the sports complex and the sweeping Potomac, which marked the state line between Virginia and Maryland, Algonkian Regional Park—on the Virginia side—provided dozens of acres of woods, a golf course, a picnic pavilion, and a low-grade water park. The road into the park ended at a string of cottages tucked into the woods along the riverbank. Kera had rented one of these for the week under the name Laura Perez, the skeleton identity she'd created to get back into the States. She'd paid in cash after explaining to the reservations employee that spotty travel in Central America, on account of missionary work, had resulted in the temporary suspension of her credit cards.

Vasser sat down on the couch at Kera's invitation. Large picture windows dominated the living room, overlooking the Potomac as it rolled by, slow and brown. Kera took the easy chair, which, when she faced Vasser and glanced out the window behind her across the room, provided a view of the narrow road that led to the cabin. The road was still.

Vasser noticed the small television and asked if they could turn it on. Without her phone, she'd lost all connection to the world. She wanted to know if any new footage had emerged that showed her leaving the scene in Georgetown, or if there was any word on the identity of her attacker. Kera tuned the flat-screen to CNN and sat back for a few minutes to let Vasser watch. She was impatient to question the diplomat, but she could tell Vasser would be distracted until she knew something more about what was going on. After several minutes spent churning through the day's other news stories and a commercial break, Vasser got what she was waiting for: the network replayed the only images it had of the incident—the DOT surveillance footage—while an anchor explained that the shooter had escaped on foot and had yet to be identified. Kera watched Vasser squint at the corner of the screen. The commotion with the motorcycle was visible, but the vantage wasn't good enough to provide any useful detail. At a commercial break, Vasser looked away, shaking her head. Kera muted the television.

"You're not going to find what you're looking for on that surveillance clip," Kera said, nodding at the screen but watching Vasser. "The answer is back in China."

"You would know, I suppose," Vasser said, her gaze suddenly piercing and accusatory.

Kera shook her head. "You and I are in the same boat—"

"Bullshit. You exposed classified files and fled. I don't have any idea how I got here. Don't try to tell me our situations are the same."

Kera clenched her jaw until the pain became a distraction. Clearly, appealing to Vasser's reason by offering help wasn't going to work. She had to take a harder line. "How we got here doesn't really matter. The fact is, our government considers both of us traitors. So does the press. If you're in denial, you can hold out for the official charges to be filed, but it's obvious they're eager to try you for treason, aiding the enemy, mishandling classified documents—should I go on?"

"There isn't proof of any of that. I'll be cleared."

"There are e-mails. There are missed flights. There are affairs with private contractors who have worked for China." Vasser tried to jump in with a protest, but Kera held up a hand to cut her off. "I'm just telling you what they'll say. I know you didn't write those e-mails. And I know that if you didn't have your country's best interests in mind, you wouldn't have gone straight to the Feds after hearing from me."

Vasser considered this in silence.

"So don't turn on me," Kera said. "I want to help you."

"How do I even begin to trust your motives?"

"Start with the fact that I'm here. If I were working for China, I would be there, where it would be safe for someone who—" Kera stopped herself. Something occurred to her that made her forget for a moment what she'd been saying to Vasser. It wasn't until Vasser spoke again that Kera emerged from the distraction.

"Why are you here, really?" Vasser said.

Kera spotted a familiar mix of fear and aggression in Vasser's eyes. But she also saw an opening.

"It's important to me to clear my name," Kera said. "They've left me with no choice but to prove to them on my own that I'm a patriot."

"And you plan to do that how?"

"By figuring out who killed Ambassador Rodgers and why. I don't need to tell you that the whole framework of our relationship with China is at stake."

"What do you want with me?"

"You worked closely with the ambassador. You were the last person to talk to him. I know you already went over all of this with the FBI, but that was when they were accusing you of leaking state secrets. Will you go over it again with me—not as a defendant in an interrogation but as a witness to the final hours before the assassination of a US ambassador?"

Vasser's eyes drifted to the TV and then to the window and the river beyond. "Where do you want me to start?"

"Unless there's someplace more obvious, start with Shanghai. Think back, look for details that may not have seemed significant before."

Vasser went through the trip, from the routine preparations to the meetings to the hotel accommodations. Kera stopped her when she mentioned that she'd stayed the night with Conrad Smith.

"Look, I don't mean to pry."

Vasser nearly laughed. "You're the only one, then." She shook her head. "Conrad and I are lovers. That's all there is to that."

Kera waited for more, but further details weren't offered. "And your partner? Is that what you call him?"

"Ben. Yes. Ben is completely aware of it, of course. He has his own lovers; I have mine."

"So it's . . . an arrangement?"

"It's honesty and communication. We like each other and we like our relationship. But I travel a lot. It's our way of getting what we want without putting our relationship on the line."

Kera nodded. "You explained this to the Feds?"

"I tried. But of course they just obsessed over the sex. They assumed that if they treated it as a dirty secret, it could be used as leverage against me. Well, that's their baggage, not mine. It's unhealthy, and it's bad detective work. They'd be better off focusing their investigation into the TERMITE leak on more relevant leads."

"Like?"

Vasser shrugged. "There must be a list of everyone who knew about the program. They might have started with those people."

Kera nodded. "You wouldn't have been on that list."

"Exactly."

"Then why do you think the Feds came after you to begin with?"

"The e-mails, apparently."

"Which you didn't write."

"That's right."

"Did the Chinese know you weren't on the ambassador's plane when it left Shanghai?"

"What do you mean?"

"Your hosts at these meetings. The Chinese delegation. And the Kenyans. Did they know you'd skipped out on the flight?"

"Yes, I had dinner with them right after Greg left."

"But it was last-minute, your decision to stay an extra night?"

"Yes." She looked down at her hands in her lap. "You mentioned the other night that you thought I might have been the target of that plane crash. Do you really think that? I thought you were crazy then. But now I've been shot at. I just can't figure out *why*."

"The most obvious reason is TERMITE."

"I've told you, I wasn't responsible for that leak. I couldn't have accessed—"

"I know that. And not just because I'm taking your word. I happen to know that the first public descriptions of TERMITE, which appeared in a news story on Gnos.is, did not come from any one human source. They were pieced together by a computer—a lot of computers, actually." Vasser's expression went blank with confusion. "That's how Gnos.is works. But that doesn't matter. What matters is that the sensitive nature of the information in that story created the appearance of a leaker, which is why everyone is looking for one."

"And someone wants to make it look like it was me?"

"Yes. That would explain the e-mails manufactured in your name." Kera encouraged the silence that followed. It meant Vasser was thinking.

"Those two names you wrote on that piece of paper you gave me. Where did you get them?"

"Marcus Templeton and Anne Platt. They were killed within a day or two of the ambassador. Did their names mean anything to you?"

"Not until I looked them up. The woman, Anne Platt, had spent her career developing phones and other devices that laid the foundation of the modern telecom industry. And the man, Marcus Templeton, made billions investing in telecom."

"How about the ambassador? Did he have any stake in telecom?"

"Sure." Vasser shrugged. "No financial stake, of course. That would have been a conflict of interest. But telecom was a big part of our development initiatives with Africa and China. It's in America's own interest to have a global cyberinfrastructure that's compatible, efficient, and that can drive commerce back to the States. That's what Conrad had been hired—"

"Conrad Smith?"

Vasser nodded. "You saw the latest story in Gnos.is? It mentioned that Conrad was working as a consultant on a classified government program called IKE."

Kera nodded. "Did he ever discuss that with you?"

"No. It was classified. It didn't occur to me that he would even know about IKE."

"Wait. So *you* knew about IKE before the story broke?"

"Only the broad outlines. It informed our long-term policy positions with China and Africa."

"What are the broad outlines?"

Vasser hesitated.

"The program is public now. Can't you discuss it?"

Another pause for internal deliberation. Perhaps Vasser was rehearsing which parts of the program were classified and which were not. Or perhaps she was weighing whether Kera's question was actually a trap to test how easily Vasser would give up classified details. Candidness won out.

"More and more devices," Vasser began, "well, practically everything we come into contact with each day—from our televisions to our cars to our refrigerators and bedroom thermostats—are becoming linked via the Internet. This is great news for the future of the telecom industry. Investments and profits have already started to explode. But connectivity is expanding much faster than security. Basically, when it comes to online security—both individually and at the level of the Internet's infrastructure—we've maintained a pre-9/11 mentality. Instead of building security software that becomes outdated in the time it takes to install it, we need to engineer all of our new devices and vehicles and appliances with fundamental security built in."

"This is what Conrad Smith is advising the US government on for IKE?" Kera asked. She had been plenty aware on her own of America's dire cybersecurity position, but she had not heard of the IKE program until the CIA documents were leaked.

"I imagine so. I didn't know he was involved with IKE until I read his name in Gnos.is. We never speak about work, not in that way. We can't. Both of us are too involved with sensitive stuff."

"Did Conrad say why he was in Shanghai on the night you were there?"

"Work." Vasser shrugged awkwardly, sensing that her answer seemed flimsy. "He was there for some meetings. Like I said, we didn't press each other on details. Why?"

Kera leaned forward. "By my count, there are only five people who know you're innocent. You're one of them. I'm one of them. Two others work with me." She watched Vasser do the math.

"And Conrad."

Kera nodded.

"I need to talk to him," Vasser said suddenly.

"Have you spoken to him since your release?"

"No. My calls, my e-mails, they're all being monitored. I have to assume everyone I contact right now is subject to invasive scrutiny. I wanted to spare Conrad that, though I imagine they're already all over him. But this is different. I need to warn him."

"That's impossible. You don't know his role in this."

"What do you mean?" Vasser's eyes narrowed. "What are you suggesting, that he's in on it?"

"I'm suggesting that contacting him is not a risk we can take."

"We?" Vasser said. "I just met you. I *know* Conrad. Don't you have anyone you trust? Do you have any relationships built on that?"

Kera smiled bitterly and stood. "I'm going to get some rest. Your room is at the end of the hall. I got groceries yesterday; help yourself if you're hungry. Don't go out."

·  ·  ·  ·  ·

Left alone, Angela Vasser's eyes drifted back to the television. Every fifteen minutes or so, the familiar banner popped up on the lower third of the screen—BREAKING NEWS: VASSER AND SHOOTING SUSPECT BOTH MISSING AFTER ASSASSINATION ATTEMPT—though there were no new "breaking" developments being reported. With the TV on mute, she occasionally heard a creak or rustle from the upstairs master bedroom where Kera Mersal had gone. Vasser got up and switched off the TV.

The exhaustion hit her then. In the last twenty-four hours, she had confronted the most primal challenge of any species: survival. Now lesser needs presented themselves. A shower. Sleep. Her body suddenly ached for these things. She had no personal belongings with her, and she was wearing the outfit she'd put on the previous morning. In the bathroom, she removed her clothes and washed them in the shower, a chore she lingered over, savoring the warmth and the isolation of the cascading stream. She imagined this would be the appropriate time to break down, to unleash a good sob in the relative safety and privacy of the bathroom. But tears would not come. Her body knew it wasn't time to let go; this wasn't over yet.

Wrapped in a towel, she padded down the hallway to the guest room, pulled toward the queen bed by the promise of imminent sleep. That's when she saw the cottage's landline phone under the lamp on the nightstand.

# SAN FRANCISCO

The flight from Chicago felt short, and not just because Conrad Smith was accustomed to transoceanic travel. What Smith most wanted right now was to be invisible, anonymous, indefinitely thirty thousand feet above it all. Unless you lived in the African bush or the Amazonian rain forest, a plane was about the only place you could credibly claim anymore to be unreachable by phone or e-mail.

And even that would change soon—thanks in part, ironically, to the formerly secret project on which Smith had been advising the US government. Though travelers would welcome the ability to surf the Internet and send text messages in-flight, Smith suspected that the change in regulations was hardly being made on their behalf. From what he'd witnessed in his work on the IKE project, the catalyst driving the policy shift was the fact that the NSA went into withdrawal every time a passenger got on a plane and was forced to stop using his or her phone. The new in-flight electronic free-for-all would provide the agency with the desired uninterrupted stream of data from citizens—some of whom might be terrorists, the agency and its defenders were always quick to point out.

Conrad Smith sat in first class, but only because it had become nearly impossible for him to book a ticket in coach with as many miles and rewards points as he'd accumulated. In fact, he'd thought he'd succeeded this time in doing just that, but at the gate the air-line had given him an automatic courtesy upgrade. He switched off his phone well before the flight attendant's announcement to do so and leaned back in his seat, avoiding eye contact with any of his fellow travelers shuffling down the aisle toward their coach seats. The day before, a classified report mentioning his name in connection with the IKE project had been published on Gnos.is. Ever since, he'd fielded panicked calls from the Department of Homeland Security, which was trying to manage the intelligence leak, as well as inquiries from his overseas clients. And of course, there was a new wave of messages from the FBI agents who had been interrogating him for more than a week about the fake e-mails between him and Angela Vasser. When those e-mails had first surfaced, he'd been immediately suspended from work on the IKE contract. Luckily, he'd been in South Africa at the time, or else he would have been detained the way Vasser had been. But Vasser was finally released and the credibility of the e-mails was challenged.

Just a few weeks earlier, his consulting business had been booming. And then it had all come apart. His involvement with IKE was over. His name was forever linked to news stories of illegal leaks and extramarital affairs. Now, with this trip to San Francisco, he was being forced to plead with his remaining clients not to drop him.

For a few blissful hours, Smith read a book, occasionally glancing out the window where the American plains gave way to mountains and desert and then, finally, the fog-shrouded, verdant coast. Walking from gate to curb, he resuscitated his phone. It twitched frantically. There were a dozen texts and two voice-mail messages. The texts were mostly from harmless friends who'd read his name in the news again and were calling more or less to marvel at this fact. He looked at the voice-mail display. One message was from his former client at DHS, no doubt with instructions for how to handle news of the leak in that afternoon's meeting. The other voice mail was from a Virginia number; probably a journalist or, worse, another FBI agent with follow-up questions posed in the form of accusations.

Smith located his waiting driver and parlayed a greeting into small talk, relieved for another excuse to delay the requisite electronic correspondence. He could return the phone calls when he got to his hotel room.

# LANGLEY

"What's he doing?" Bright asked.

The analyst shrugged. "Nothing. Same thing he's been doing all day." The analyst's screens showed video feeds from inside the home of Ben Welk and Angela Vasser. Welk was seated at the kitchen table with a mug of coffee, staring out the bay windows. Since Vasser had gone missing, he hadn't left the house.

"Put yourself in his shoes. What would you be doing?" Bright said.

"Same thing, I guess. Waiting by the phone. Checking my e-mail, Facebook."

Bright studied the screen. The man's phone and laptop were within arm's reach on the kitchen table. "Why isn't she contacting him?" he wondered aloud.

Bright and the analysts who worked in the ops center were desensitized to the shame that any decent civilized person would experience while witnessing another's private life. Bright had long ago lost the urge to look away out of decency. Ninety-nine percent of the time, it was boredom that turned him away; the vast majority of people's outward lives were that mundane. After a few minutes of watching Ben Welk stare out his dining room window, Bright got restless.

"Where are we with the other likely points of contact?" he said, addressing the analysts he'd assigned to each target. The responses came in quick succession.

"No one at the embassy in Beijing has heard from Vasser since she got on the plane home last week."

"Her parents say they last heard from her two days ago—before the Georgetown attack. Their phone and e-mail logs confirm that."

Ever since the gunman's attempt on Vasser's life—and her subsequent disappearance—Bright had ordered round-the-clock monitoring of anyone whom Vasser might conceivably reach out to.

"And Conrad Smith?"

"He just landed in San Francisco."

Bright suspected that Conrad Smith was as likely as Welk to be contacted. "Do we have phone and e-mail coverage on him?"

"Yes, sir. He's a foreign national contracting on IKE; we own his devices."

Bright knew that the analyst was using the hacker's definition of the word "own," meaning that they had installed malware in Conrad Smith's phone and computer that allowed them to access it whenever they wished.

"In addition, the team you requested will be on him within the hour."

"Anything in the metadata?" Bright said.

"This is what I've flagged so far. There's a call from earlier today that I don't know what to make of," the analyst said.

Bright leaned over his shoulder to get a look. Among calls from clients and the FBI was an incoming call that had originated from an entity listed as "Northern Virginia Regional Park Authority." The duration of the call was sixty-four seconds.

"That's too long to be a wrong number. Do we know what they talked about?"

The analyst shook his head and pointed at the call's time stamp. "I don't think they talked. The call came in after he'd powered down his phone for the flight to San Fran."

"A voice mail, then?"

"That'd be my guess."

"Can we access it?"

"Should be able to, yeah." He paused. "Would you like me to try?" Accessing the actual content of electronic communications on American soil was a step deeper into controversial territory than simply analyzing its metadata. Since the public outcry over domestic surveillance brought on by Edward Snowden, this had become a sensitive enough topic that analysts knew to ask their superiors for permission before proceeding.

"Will he be able to tell if we access it?" Bright asked.

"No. Our malware prevents his phone from ever shutting down fully, even when he powers it off. No matter what he's doing with it now, we can still connect to the baseboard chip without tipping him off."

"All right. Go ahead." Snowden or not, they still had the Patriot Act, which allowed foreign nationals under investigation, like Conrad Smith, to be monitored if someone like Bright thought they should be.

"Yes, sir." The analyst clamped large headphones onto his head. "This might take a few minutes."

Bright wandered across the room, eyeing his own phone with suspicion as he turned it over in his hand. This was the world they were operating in. An agency cybersecurity tech had once walked him through the inescapable vulnerabilities and the procedures for how to counter them. The malware they were currently using to monitor Conrad Smith's smartphone, for example, and which any foreign agency would love to get into a phone like Bright's, could be overridden by plugging in the phone and holding down the power and home buttons in a particular sequence—a sequence that Bright could no longer precisely recall. That was supposed to render the device benign, incapable of transmitting data to an eavesdropper. But there were a dozen other procedures for a dozen other vulnerabilities introduced by the mere possession of these phones, none of which were intuitive to Bright. So he kept things simple. When he needed to ensure he wasn't being tracked, he left the phone at home; when he wanted a conversation kept private, he made sure the phone was in a place where the conversation couldn't reach it.

While the tech worked on pulling data from Conrad Smith's phone, Bright found Henry Liu at the workstation he'd commandeered for MIRAGE. Liu had an update from the NTSB team in Shanghai. "They just wrapped their guided tour of the projected crash site."

"And?"

"They saw a lot of water. No physical evidence."

"What about the submersible?"

"It's standing by, but still hasn't been cleared to get in there. Beijing is stalling. Should we put more pressure on State?"

Bright had stopped listening. "Where's this?" he said suddenly, walking toward the front of the room. Three screens on the big wall were tuned to live feeds from the major cable news networks. All three were showing the same thing: a swarm of emergency vehicles, lights ablaze, in front of a building on a busy city street. The answer to Bright's question was soon revealed in the headline running across the bottom of one network's coverage: SAN FRANCISCO ELEVATOR TRAGEDY IS THIRD THIS MONTH; FOUL PLAY SUSPECTED.

Bright swung around. "Where did you say Conrad Smith is right now?" he called up to the analyst who was monitoring the surveillance on Angela Vasser's contacts.

The analyst was already standing. He ignored Bright's question and instead held out an outstretched arm, offering up his headphones. "I found the voice mail. I think you'll want to listen to this."

# ALGONKIAN REGIONAL PARK

Kera came out of a spoiled dream, groaning at the cheap digital watch on the nightstand. It was beeping again. Had it already been an hour? Outside it was still daylight. Running a hand through her hair, she swung her legs over the side of the bed and sat for a few seconds, listening, scanning the view from the bedroom window. The house was silent; the surrounding woods were still but for the slow roll of the muddy Potomac, visible through the woods where the tree cover thinned.

She performed a similar scan from the window in the master bathroom, which looked out at the opposite side of the cottage. Then she went downstairs and repeated the sweep, moving systematically from one window to the next. Nothing amiss. She hesitated at the closed door of the guest bedroom. The silence suggested Vasser was asleep. Kera weighed the risk of diverting from her own routine against allowing Vasser another hour of sleep. She thought she heard a rustle from Vasser's room as she retreated down the hallway, but Kera had made up her mind to let her rest—only this once. Vasser wasn't trained to handle sleep deprivation the way Kera had been.

The last stop on Kera's hourly rotation was the television, which was her only safe source of information about the outside world. Phones and computers would have been more efficient, no doubt, but they were a two-way link to the world—a path that could lead anyone who knew what to look for right to the cottage's doorstep.

The news from the TV was not good: there had been another elevator failure.

Kera rushed to turn up the volume on the muted TV, desperate for details that she knew would not yet be available. What was known was that a hotel elevator in San Francisco had plummeted two dozen stories. It was thought that as many as three people were in the car; rescue crews were still trying to unpack the wreckage.

Kera heard a gasp behind her and turned to find Angela Vasser wrapped in a towel. One hand covered her mouth; her eyes filled quickly with a fear that put Kera on edge.

"Conrad," Vasser managed to whisper. And then a sob, choked back too late, dislodged from her throat, surprising them both. Her breath looked caught in her chest. "I—I tried to warn him."

Kera forgot about the TV and the elevator. She crossed to Vasser, gripped the diplomat's shoulders, and looked her in the eye.

"Warn him how?" Kera said coolly. "What did you do? Did you call him?" Even as she said it, she felt that she was overreacting, that it was impossible that this woman who had worked in the American embassy in Beijing would consider using any sort of communications device, not in the situation she was in.

But Vasser nodded. Another choked sob escaped from her hand covering her mouth.

"You called his cell phone? From where? What phone did you use?" Besides the cottage's in-room landline phones, Kera had two phones—the satellite phone from Bolívar and her last prepaid, unused burner smartphone, both of which she'd stashed in the freezer after adjusting the thermostat to a safe temperature. If Vasser had used either, she'd have to throw it away.

Using a hand wet with tears, Vasser indicated in the direction of her room down the hall. "I'm sorry. I was trying to help. You don't think my call—oh God, what have I done?"

"Go put your clothes on. Now," Kera said in a chilly, calm voice that was much more effective than a panicked shout. She could tell that Vasser was still worried about Conrad Smith. But they had other problems now. "We have to go."

# LEESBURG PIKE

On the ride out from Langley, colored lights flashing from the windows of a black SUV with government plates, Bright sat in the passenger seat with his smartphone pressed to an ear. The FBI's special agent in charge on the Vasser case had given him listen-only access, via an encrypted satellite link, to the communications between the tactical team on-site and the FBI's command and control center. It was difficult to hear the proceedings over the highway noise. The voices he struggled to make out were calm and measured. Like the armed commandos who stormed unfamiliar buildings for a living, the men and women supporting the raid on the back end were trained to release ice into their veins when the pressure started to build.

Bright gathered from their exchange that an eighteen-man SWAT team had arrived at the address and circled the building with no resistance. As the black SUV sped onto a dirt road leading toward a row of secluded cottages, Bright heard the command given to enter. He strained to hear what followed. There was no loud banging, no gunfire; just a lot of boots clobbering against wood and then the shouts of "Clear!"

Bright hopped out of the SUV as it rolled to a stop at the perimeter of the scene. He flashed his agency ID and caught up with the SAIC on the porch steps. "Rooms are clear."

"I heard."

"The phone you traced that call to is in the guest bedroom. This way."

Bright followed the SAIC inside. The cottage was still crowded with bulky SWAT guys clutching their H&K MP5 submachine guns and looking disappointed that there hadn't been anyone around to apprehend. The cottage had simple furniture and a dated television. It felt closer to something you might find in the rural wilderness than in a DC suburb. Bright was shown down a short hallway and into a small room with a queen bed, desk, chair, and nightstand, on which sat the phone—a cheap receiver and cradle set connected to the landline. Two technicians with FBI windbreakers were scrutinizing the receiver for fingerprints. Their initial examination came up empty.

After the phone's existence confirmed that they were in the right place, the phone became the least interesting thing in sight. Bright noted the comforter and sheets pulled back. There was a towel thrown over the back of the chair. From the way it was hanging—he knew better than to touch anything—it looked a little heavy: still damp. To corroborate this, he backtracked to the bathroom and found that the shower floor was wet. In the kitchen he used the unbuttoned cuff of his shirt to open the refrigerator door. Milk, bread, cheese, deli meat—all neatly shelved. The trash can had a single gum wrapper in it.

Everything was a little too neat, Bright thought. The phone wiped of fingerprints, the empty trash can. Nothing he'd seen actually identified Angela Vasser. He wasn't betting that the forensics team would succeed on that front either.

Had he underestimated Vasser?

Finally, he went upstairs and peeked into the master bedroom. The sheets hadn't been pulled down, but the surface of the comforter was wrinkled in a way that suggested someone had slept there. Standing over the upstairs bathroom sink, which also was wet, he looked out the window, thinking. So Vasser wasn't alone; she was getting help. Bright had a good guess from whom, but all the other questions that surfaced in his mind just collected there, unanswered.

# I-81, Central Pennsylvania

"Where are we going?"

"Why? Is there someone else you'd like to call and give a heads-up to?" Kera said, regretting her tone as soon as the words came out. Rebuked, Vasser fell silent.

They were in a Honda Civic Kera had rented for the week and parked on a residential street a half mile from the cottage. The parking location had been ideal because none of the park's three roads fed into the residential neighborhood. Anyone traveling by road from inside the park would have to backtrack out through the park's main entrance and then skirt a wide arch of suburban obstacles—strip malls, retirement homes, schools, churches, dog parks—to reach the street where Kera had stashed the vehicle. There was, however, a short wooded running trail that cut almost directly from the cottage to the car. Kera had discovered it on one of her jogs to scout the area for choke points and escape paths.

They had left the cottage in a dead sprint. Breaking out of the woods, feet from the car, they had heard the approach of a small fleet of vehicles tearing up the park's gravel roads. Vasser glanced back after she'd climbed into the passenger seat.

"Don't look," Kera warned her calmly and put the car in drive. Vasser obeyed. "If we hit a checkpoint, we belong in this neighborhood. Just heading out for some Starbucks," Kera said. "Got it?"

But the Feds had not had time to expand their perimeter to include the neighborhoods adjacent to the park before Kera and Vasser slipped away, moving a few miles per hour under the speed limit.

"Did my call make Conrad a target?" Vasser asked when they'd driven a half hour. She seemed more stoic now, as if she was looking to take responsibility.

"We don't even know if he was on that elevator."

"He was. I know it," Vasser said softly.

"Your call didn't make him a target. Whoever is doing this is plenty capable of killing Conrad without your help. Your call made *us* a target."

Kera drove north, keeping to minor highways and two-lane country routes, avoiding toll roads and rest stops, which were well covered by surveillance cameras. When she stopped for gas along a busy stretch of strip malls in a Maryland town, she retrieved a blond wig, sunglasses, and baseball cap from her duffel bag and eyed her reflection in the car window to adjust the disguise. She filled the tank and then used a pay phone to make a reservation at a safe place where they would stay that evening. A block up the road from the gas station, she pulled into a narrow lot and parked in front of a small electronics store sandwiched in between a barbershop and Dunkin' Donuts. Without explanation, she left Vasser in the car. She came out three minutes later with a cheap, prepaid flip phone and a prepaid card with sixty minutes of calling time on it.

Kera was about to climb back into the car when she noticed something. Across the street was the town's humble public library.

"Wait here. I'll be back in five minutes."

In the library, Kera found the public-access computer—there was only one—near a bulletin board advertising private guitar lessons, a local theater production, and a community arts festival that had already happened. She directed the Internet browser to Gnos.is and clicked to Gnos.is/fact, the news side of the side. It took no digging to find what she was looking for. The news of Conrad Smith's death was a bigger story than she'd expected. She only had to read the first paragraph to understand why. Unlike the previous two elevator failures, the fatal incident in San Francisco was being reported as a murder, not an accident. And for the first time, Gnos.is had confirmed what other news organizations had begun to speculate about: the three elevator catastrophes were related.

To print the article, Kera had to give fifty cents to the librarian, who collected the pages for her off the printer.

"I'm sorry," Kera said, handing the article to Vasser as she slid back into the driver's seat. She guided the car out of the parking lot.

When Vasser saw his name, she made a muffled sound, part pain and part anger. Kera kept her eyes on the road. A few minutes later, Vasser wiped moisture from her eyes.

"I can't do this," she said suddenly. "Take me to the police station."

"No," Kera said.

"I won't involve you. But I have to turn myself in. If I don't, who else will they kill? Ben? The next person whose name is published by Gnos.is?"

"Turn yourself in for what? Leaving the District while you're under investigation? That's the only thing you've done wrong— except associating with me, and that might be the only thing keeping you alive. Turning yourself in won't protect you or anyone else from whoever's trying to kill you. To stop them, we have to figure out who they are and why they're doing this."

Vasser fell into a troubling silence, but at least she wasn't begging to be in police custody anymore.

"I didn't have time to read the article," Kera said. "What else does it say?"

"It says the link between the victims is InspiraCom," Vasser replied without consulting the pages in her lap. She was looking out the window.

"InspiraCom? How?" Kera looked over when Vasser didn't answer. The look on the diplomat's face had changed. She was no longer fighting tears. Her eyes were narrowed in concentration.

"It might be possible," she said finally, more to herself.

"What? Tell me."

Vasser scanned through the Gnos.is story again, summarizing it for Kera. A year earlier, the booming American telecom company InspiraCom had purchased a Silicon Valley smartphone and tablet manufacturer whose president of development was Anne Platt, the woman killed in the Paris elevator. Platt became involved in InspiraCom's efforts to get a smartphone to market, although she clashed frequently with her new bosses over the phone's security standards. Platt wanted to prioritize security while InspiraCom's management was more focused on growing the company's market share. Meanwhile, Marcus Templeton, the hedge-fund manager who perished in the Wall Street elevator, had become bullish about InspiraCom and was thought to have been angling for a majority stake. He was never able to achieve that, though. The man who beat him to it was Hu Lan, whose private jet had been loaned to Ambassador Rodgers and was never returned.

Kera felt like she was seeing through a window that had just been wiped clean of fog. What if Hu's investment in InspiraCom was more than just a wealthy businessman's bid to expand his holdings? What if it was an early stroke in an orchestrated plan by the MSS to gain control of a vulnerable segment of America's infrastructure—its telecom network? "What about Conrad? What's his role?"

"IKE. Just like that leaked CIA document said, Conrad was advising the US government on its major cyberinfrastructure modernization project. InspiraCom was bidding for the job, and Conrad had apparently voiced opposition to their bid. He thought InspiraCom was rushing their designs to market too quickly, and he didn't think security was at the center of their design philosophy. They relied too much on security software to fix flaws after the fact. That's too late when you're up against hackers capable of zero-day attacks." Vasser stopped. She looked at Kera. "So that's it? InspiraCom is just eliminating its critics to win a telecom bidding war?"

There was a lot of evidence to support that theory, Kera thought. Except for one thing. "No, it can't be that simple. Why kill the ambassador, then? Why try to kill you?"

Vasser shrugged. "Because of my ties to Conrad?"

"But you didn't have any professional ties to Conrad or his work, right?"

"Right, but those e-mails that were planted in the press—those made it look like I did."

"But that doesn't explain why the ambassador would be a target."

Kera spotted the police cruiser coming from the opposite direction too late to tell Vasser to duck and hide herself. If the cops were on the alert for a white woman and a black woman traveling together, it would look less suspicious if they were casually chatting in a car, not ducking at the sight of cops.

"Don't look at them," Kera said. She checked her speed: fifty-one in a fifty-five zone. "Forget InspiraCom for a minute. Start over for me. What was your role in our diplomatic mission in China?"

"What?" Vasser asked, distracted as the police car flew by.

Kera checked the rearview. No brake lights.

"Why were you in China to begin with? Your parents, Ben— your life was in Washington. Surely you could have landed a job doing research or teaching in DC."

"I hate academia."

Kera nearly laughed. "For a woman who hates academia, you sure submitted yourself to a lot of it."

"I had to. It helped that my parents had connections through the World Bank. But I'm still black and I'm still a woman. I needed more degrees than the other candidates. I played their game because it was preferable to sitting on the sidelines. But I don't like all the rules."

"So why China? What were you doing in the ambassador's office?"

"Economic development in China, Africa, and India will have tremendous consequences for the United States. Our way of life is linked inextricably to our economy. And our economy is linked to the rest of the world's. So to say that our future way of life depends on the prosperity, equity, and accessibility of the global economy is an understatement. My academic focus was China and, to a lesser extent, Africa. But actually facilitating an emerging economy is not about imposing academic theories. It's about solving problems. And not by paying people off. Corruption is one of the biggest problems plaguing emerging economies. To deal with this, American foreign policy generally assumes two approaches: military dominance and bribery. These might be effective and acceptable strategies in certain circumstances, like in a short-term humanitarian crisis, but not in fostering new, stable economies. The few examples where we've been most successful—politically and economically—we've exported innovations that cheaply improve the quality of life for local people in a fair way. Put another way: if we're not improving the lives of cit-izens in countries we engage with on a scale that is proportional to what we're getting out of it, it doesn't work."

"Was this the topic of your conference in Shanghai?"

"Yes, more or less."

"Did it go well, or were there problems?"

"There are always problems. China and Africa are steeped in corruption. Hu Lan's use of Chinese government money—or, more accurately, the Chinese government's use of Hu Lan as a cover—to gain a controlling stake in an American corporation is an example of that. But American-style capitalism isn't innocent. Corporations see foreign investment as a zero-sum game—and Washington is run by corporations. Every contract a US corporation wins in Africa is one that China didn't win. And vice versa. And since that's the only way we care to measure success, we have everyone bribing and killing and spying their way into markets that need whole armies of security contractors and surveillance experts and cyberspies to prop them up. Meanwhile, the people of China and Africa are forgotten. You can call me a China sympathizer, but anyone who thinks the global economy can work without them succeeding is naïve. We don't just need their oil or cheap labor or loans, we need their people to have economic stability and dignity. Not because we're charitable, but because it's in our best interests. And anyway, no offense, but you can learn a lot more about an ally or an adversary by working on the ground to build economies with their people than you can by tapping the phones of a whole continent."

"Have you ever thought of running for office?" Kera said.

"You're joking, right?" Vasser laughed. "A godless and childless black woman in an open relationship with a white man. I'm completely unelectable. And that was before I was accused of treason."

Kera smiled. "That'd make for a hell of a campaign slogan. But at least it's honest, which is more than any actual politician can claim."

"Can I ask you something?" Vasser said.

"Try me."

"What really happened with HAWK?"

"Oh . . . that." Kera realized that she'd not had the opportunity to give her side of the story to anyone but Lionel—and he hadn't exactly solicited it from her with empathetic intentions. Jones and Bolívar knew the truth, but that was only because they'd been a part of it. And like Kera, that was why they remained in hiding.

Kera gave Vasser a summary, beginning with her recruitment to HAWK, the cyberespionage black op where she'd met J. D. Jones. After Kera and Jones were nearly killed for what they came to learn about HAWK's illegal domestic surveillance practices, they'd opted to expose HAWK rather than turn over the evidence to the CIA, where they feared it would be obfuscated.

"So you did take the classified files from HAWK. And you passed them on to Gnos.is."

"We did, yes. We did it not only because HAWK was targeting and spying on American citizens, but because they'd partnered with a corporation that was selling American citizens' private data to anyone willing to buy it—including foreign intelligence agencies."

"What about your ties to China?" Vasser said.

Kera looked over at her. "What did you hear about that?"

"I was in Beijing at the time. Chinese state media celebrated the scandal. Most people in our embassy assumed that you and Jones had, at the very least, fled to China and sought defection. The CIA's Beijing station chief had instructed everyone working at the embassy to alert him immediately if any of us were contacted by you."

Kera bit her lip. It was one thing to have the media ranting and raving about treason based on a false narrative peddled by the CIA, who were desperate to cover their own asses. But it was something else to hear that a knowledgeable, respectable diplomat from one of America's most important embassies had bought this story line.

"I see. So you thought I was a traitor?"

"I didn't pay close enough attention to form any strong opinions on the evidence. But honestly, I was dubious of that part of the story. The MSS doesn't take volunteers from foreign spy agencies. They're not like Russia and the US. Your Beijing station chief liked to tell a story about a thousand grains of sand. Have you heard it?" Vasser looked over at Kera. "Kera?"

"Yes, of course," Kera said. She remembered a day, very early in her training at Langley, when Lionel Bright had first explained to her the thousand-grains-of-sand concept, which illustrated the differences in the espionage strategies of the world's superpowers. Imagine, Bright had said, that a certain beach had become an intelligence target seen as highly valuable to the US, Russia, and China. How would each nation approach the mission? The US, he said, would fly drones and satellites overhead and use electronic surveillance to collect a server-farm's worth of data, costing taxpayers billions of dollars. Russia would offer money to one of the American intelligence analysts or blackmail him with prostitutes. Meanwhile, China would quietly send a thousand tourists to the beach and, afterward, ask them to shake out their beach towels.

# MANHATTAN

"For the United States to be competitive," Charlie Canyon's guest was explaining, "we cannot have a Congress that strangles innovation with excessive regulations. The makers of old technologies have too much control on Capitol Hill. Disruptive new technologies need a voice too."

Canyon's guest was Bill Orson, a fit-looking Asian American around forty who was the founder of a tech start-up that developed software that—well, Canyon wasn't entirely sure what Orson's company did. The man had called two weeks prior, requesting a meeting with Rafael Bolívar to discuss some kind of coalition. Canyon had been surprised to find that Orson would settle for a meeting with him instead, if that's what he could get. Orson insisted that he preferred in-person meetings and that making the trip from Silicon Valley was no trouble for him. So here they were.

"You're proposing a lobbying effort," Canyon said.

"Of sorts, I suppose. Is it such a bad word?"

"It is. But I can get over that. The more relevant concern is whether a news organization like Gnos.is ought to be lobbying a political body it covers. It reeks of conflict of interest. We have the First Amendment; we don't need lobbyists."

"And yet Gnos.is is unable to practice its innovative form of journalism in the open. Mr. Bolívar and his staff are in hiding, are they not?"

"That's true," Canyon conceded. "But not because they've done anything illegal. Gnos.is has found very effective ways to hold powerful people, governments, and corporations accountable. That makes them unpopular. So be it."

"Face it, Mr. Canyon. When the government has subpoenaed half of your staff and has declared openly that you should be shut down, it is not just your popularity that has been injured. Your credibility is also at stake."

"I don't see how pandering to Capitol Hill would strengthen Gnos.is's credibility."

Mr. Orson leaned back in his chair with a sportsmanlike smile. "I admire your principled stance. But I hope you'll think about it. Take it to Mr. Bolívar."

"I will, of course. Can I ask what entities make up your coalition? I didn't see that listed on your website." In fact, the website Orson had directed him to during their initial phone call provided very little information at all beyond skeletal biographies of Orson and links to a few other secretive start-ups, all of which had websites that provided vague mission statements laden with lofty predictions of technology's potential. True, Gnos.is might have once been described in just that way, but at least now it was a household name. Not that that had earned them much sway in Washington. Canyon hadn't spent more than a few minutes browsing Orson's website before, bored, he abandoned it and decided he could wait until their meeting to learn the important details of what the man was proposing.

"It's very early stages, you see, but I've had similar meetings with other tech companies," Orson explained. "There's a growing list of retailers who are eager to operate drones, automobile companies are on the verge of introducing autonomous vehicles, computer companies have already invested billions in artificial intelligence."

A burst of pulses from Canyon's smartphone, which was lying on the desk in front of him, divided his attention. He glanced down at it. The screen displayed a cybersecurity notification. *What now?* The security system, custom-built by J. D. Jones, was notoriously burdened. Gnos.is's network faced cyberthreats almost constantly, usually in the form of commonplace denial-of-service attacks. Jones's security system discharged these threats so routinely that, to Canyon, the steady flow of reports that popped up on the network's intrusion log had become little-noticed background noise.

What was this, then? A denial-of-service attack was no cause for an alert to be pushed to his phone. The notification said only that the attack had been flagged as "novel," meaning its origins and intentions were unfamiliar to the security software.

"Excuse me for one moment," Canyon told Orson, who had paused midsentence at the distraction.

"Of course."

Canyon swiveled to his keyboard and brought the screen to life. As usual, he was prompted immediately to enter his username and password. He did this with the ease of second nature. Then he clicked on the icon that opened the intrusion log. Lines of data appeared. The entries were listed in chronological order, beginning at the top with the most recent. *That's strange,* he thought. The log reported nothing unusual. No novel intrusion attempts were listed among the common malware and DoS attacks. If the notification sent to his phone had not come from the intrusion log, where had it originated? He clicked on the system's activity monitor to see if it contained any clues. Maybe the issue was local and didn't affect Gnos.is's wider network. Maybe it had been a false alarm altogether.

His machine's activity monitor was teeming. That was unusual. He wasn't aware of any programs that would have been running while the computer was in sleep mode during his meeting with Orson. He scanned through the most recent entries, at first still searching for anything related to the phone alert. Nothing. Then he slowed down and began reading for other details.

"Oh shit," he whispered. The computer was in the process of uploading files. But how? To whom? The most recent entry in the log said that "C. Canyon" was sending a zip drive full of files to a remote user named "a11Egr0."

When Bill Orson rose from his chair on the other side of the desk, the movement caused Canyon to glance up. That's when he saw the handgun. It was in Orson's right hand, pointed directly at Canyon's chest.

"You don't need to do anything," Orson said. He looked as calm as he'd been when they were discussing Congress. "Just move away from the computer."

In the span of a few seconds, the situation shifted in Canyon's mind from impossible to hard reality. This evolution brought with it understanding. His phone, he realized, must have been hacked. The notification that interrupted his meeting with Orson hadn't been a warning of an ongoing attack, it had been a ploy to entice him to log in to his computer. Then a hacker working remotely had begun accessing files. But it had happened so fast. How? He thought of the website Orson had directed him to. He'd used this very computer to visit the site two weeks ago. When he did, malware must have uploaded itself to his computer and lain dormant, waiting to communicate with the remote hacker who could piggyback onto Canyon's session as soon as he logged on, tricking the system into believing that Canyon himself was responsible for all the commands. It was a bold way around Jones's security system. To pull it off, the hacker needed only two things: The first, getting Canyon to log into his computer, was easy; he did that all the time. But the hacker also needed time to let the attack run its course. The risk was too great that Canyon would notice something amiss right away and shut the whole thing down. Orson—or whatever his real name was—and his gun were here to prevent that.

Given the government's interest in Gnos.is, Bolívar and Jones had warned Canyon that they should expect very capable cyber-attacks, if not court-ordered seizures, from the FBI, NSA, or other agencies. Such attacks would have to target Canyon's office in New York because the loft there was the only physical presence Gnos.is was known to maintain. Because of this, Jones had created a last-resort solution in the event of a raid or some other sudden threat: an instantaneous way for Canyon to permanently encrypt everything on the computers in his New York office. The encryption lock, if executed, would essentially destroy all of the locally stored data and cut off Canyon's office from the wider Gnos.is network.

Orson wasn't giving Canyon the vibe of someone affiliated with the FBI or NSA, but he didn't see how that mattered just now.

Canyon's hand shot to the mouse next to the keyboard. In two clicks he launched Jones's system-wide encryption program. A window opened: "Are you sure you wish to continue? This command cannot be undone."

The first spit of lead from the weapon surprised them both—Orson, because he'd assumed Canyon would back away at the sight of the gun and had fired instinctively when Canyon did the opposite; and Canyon, because his choice and its consequences all happened too fast to seem real. His left arm sagged. A searing, tingling sensation not unlike a hard strike to the funny bone engulfed his left shoulder. But the fingers on his right hand had found the "Enter" key. Fighting his body's impulse to react to the pain, he glanced at the screen. It had gone black but for a simple message bar at the center, which announced that the encryption process had begun.

Canyon's lingering interest in the screen, despite his shoulder wound, must have made obvious his intention to spoil the attack, because Orson squeezed off a second round and followed it up by coming around the desk to kick Canyon's chair backward, away from the keyboard. The force of this strike dislodged Canyon, who found he no longer had control of his posture, and sent him sprawling to the floor. An instant earlier, he'd been certain that the second shot had hit him too. He'd felt the air go out of his lungs. There had been an abrupt pain, sharp as a blade, tearing up the area around his collarbone. But now the pain had dulled. He couldn't be sure where he was wounded. The last thing he was aware of, lying on his back, were the ceiling lights, three of them in a row between two steel beams. They swayed, then they grew fuzzy as they dimmed, shrinking to tiny white points.

# CATSKILL MOUNTAINS

They rode mostly in silence. Every ten or fifteen minutes, Kera would think of another question about Vasser's post in Beijing and they'd talk until the hum of the road lulled them back into an introspective trance. Finally, Kera decelerated to match the speed limit of the small town they were entering. They weren't far from their destination.

It was late afternoon when they turned off the state highway onto a landscaped drive that wound discreetly into the woods. An understated sign tucked away in a flower bed said SUNDOWN SANCTUARY. When they were out of sight of the highway, Kera pulled the car over and got out. She glanced around to make sure they were alone. In each direction, the shaded drive was quiet. Opening the trunk, where she'd tossed her duffle when they fled, she replaced her blond wig with a brunette one and slipped a green contact into each eye, blinking away a well of tears. Finally, she grabbed the unused prepaid smartphone. Then she got back behind the wheel and followed signs to guest registration, where she parked in front of a small vine-covered building. She told Vasser to wait in the car.

Inside, she gave the conservatively dressed receptionist the driver's license that identified her as Abigail Dalton of New York City.

She'd established this identity specifically to open a fake corporate expense account that she could link to the Sundown Sanctuary. After a great deal of research, she'd identified Sundown as an ideal place to retreat to and maintain a low profile.

The Abigail Dalton alias was tailored to fit Sundown's target demographic: overworked and overpaid Manhattanites who needed to drop off the grid once or twice a year to prevent or nurse a nervous breakdown. Signage in the lobby tastefully compelled guests to forfeit their smartphones, tablets, and laptops for secure storage in an assigned safe. The safe could be accessed upon request, and electronic devices could be used in a small study off the lobby, but the devices were not permitted anywhere else on the premises. Exhaling as if with relief, Kera handed over the phone she'd brought with her. "Can I pay an extra fee and just have you destroy this?" she said.

The woman smiled politely, as if either she had no sense of humor or because she'd heard the joke a thousand times. "How many keys will you need?"

Kera thought she saw the woman glance outside in the direction of her parked car.

"Two, please. I have a guest staying with me." Kera declined help getting their luggage to the cabin she'd rented for the week. Then the woman gave Kera the key cards and, on a map of the resort, drew a line to the guest parking lot and, deeper into the property, their cabin.

Kera parked the car in its designated spot and sat for a moment, surveying the route from the car to the cabin. Vasser sat quietly, waiting for instruction. Kera observed the resort staff and security personnel who whisked themselves around on silent electric golf carts. The staff seemed to outnumber the guests. She spotted two middle-aged women walking together, tennis racquets in hand; an Asian man in flip-flops and a still-dripping bathing suit; and a thirtysomething man with a paperback novel sitting on a bar's patio.

Getting out of the car, Kera gave Vasser a baseball cap and sunglasses from her duffle.

Included in the resort's nightly rate was the use of a golf cart to get around the expansive property. As the woman at registration had instructed, Kera located her assigned cart among the neatly parked fleet. The vehicles were all identical but for a unique number printed on the back bumper. She stared at the cart, which she saw could be operated by tapping the key card to a magnetized strip on the electric cart's dash.

"Let's just walk," she said, leading Vasser down paths, past pools and cafés, over a creek, and a down a quiet, narrow drive. Their dwelling was a New England country-style cottage with a large deck and brick chimney. White clapboard was trimmed with forest green accents to match the hedges that lined the drive.

"What is this place?" Vasser asked inside, looking out a window that provided a view across one of the thirty-six fairways that littered the property.

"It's the safest place for you to be right now. No phones, no computers, no NSA. Everyone here is completely disconnected. Oh, and"—she paused in the midst of unpacking her duffle to look at Vasser—"no elevators."

Vasser peeked into each of the two bedrooms and then returned, pacing nervously. "There's not even a television?"

"That's a feature, not a bug. We're surrounded by people who haven't been watching the news."

In her duffle, Kera found the satellite phone Bolívar had given her in the valley. A few days earlier, after she'd updated Bolívar and Jones about WhisperLift's elevator vulnerabilities and given them a vague outline of her itinerary—an itinerary she hadn't followed for even a day—she'd promised them that she would turn on the phone three times a day in case they needed to get her a message. Over the past few days, they'd left several text messages asking whether she was OK. She had ignored them all. When she powered up the phone this time, it spasmed to life with yet another notification. CALL ME. URGENT, Bolívar's text said.

Kera felt a familiar clash of emotions. On the one hand, the guilt she felt for not checking in with Bolívar and Jones grew daily. She knew they were genuinely worried for her safety, and her silence was causing them undue stress. But on the other hand, Conrad Smith's death pointed to a troubling pattern: all of the murders had been preceded by the publication of classified information by Gnos.is. If Gnos.is had refrained from publishing certain things, would these people still be alive? Maybe the answer to that question was complicated, but in any case it had left Kera uncertain of how to address the matter with Bolívar.

She powered down the satellite phone and then put it and the cheap flip phone in the refrigerator.

"Phones are high-level contraband around here. I feel like I'm squirreling away booze at a twelve-step recovery retreat." She could feel Vasser watching her. "They should be clean, anyway, but there's no reason not to be extra safe."

After she took a shower, Kera found Vasser on the couch studying the printout of the Gnos.is article about Conrad Smith's death. Vasser looked up when Kera entered and sat in the chair across from her.

"There may be something here," Vasser said.

"Oh?"

"The first two elevator attacks and the ambassador's plane crash. They all happened within a day or two of each other. They were spaced out geographically across the world, leaving no obvious link between them. They were smart hits, meticulously planned out and so highly technical that no one would suspect foul play, right?"

Kera nodded.

"But killing Conrad in exactly the same way a week later exposed them all. It totally undid everything that was so brilliant about the first round of hits. Why go through so much trouble to disguise the first attacks if you're just going to tip your hand a week later?"

"Maybe something changed."

"Like what?"

"Like Conrad Smith's name turning up in a classified document published on Gnos.is," Kera said. "For whatever reason, that made him a new target."

"Sure, but if they had just wanted to kill him, why not hire a shooter like they sent after me? Or why not make it look like a suicide or a car accident? Hacking an elevator is too unique. It's too deliberate. It's like leaving a signature or something, as if they're trying to send a message."

Kera shrugged. "Maybe you're giving them too much credit. The elevator hit on Conrad could have been a desperate blunder. Or just an act of ego. It's possible that after the first attacks went off so well, the attacker started craving attention, wanting credit that would never come so long as he or she was anonymous."

"Maybe," Vasser said. "But wouldn't that suggest this was just the work of some cyberpunks showing off their nerd skills? I think that's too simple an explanation. These targets weren't random. Their connections to InspiraCom suggest that."

Kera found herself eyeing the fridge while Vasser talked. She couldn't get Bolívar's latest text message out of her mind.

"Give me a few minutes," Kera said, retrieving the satellite phone and powering it back up. She stepped out the side door and went around the back of the cottage, which faced the woods, so she wouldn't be seen using the banned device in view of any of the resort's other guests or security guards. Bolívar answered on the second ring.

"Kera. You're OK."

"Yeah. Won't your all-knowing computers alert you when I'm not?" she said, immediately regretting the bite in her tone.

"We have a problem," he said, brushing aside her cool greeting. "Charlie locked all the Gnos.is data stored at headquarters three hours ago. He hasn't checked in since."

"Locked the data?" Kera was aware that Charlie Canyon remained Gnos.is's only public figure, working out of an office in Manhattan, but it was not totally clear to her what he did there. She also had not forgotten her first interactions with Canyon, which had ended with him disappearing for months as part of a PR stunt to gain attention for Gnos.is. What was he up to now?

"The computers in Charlie's office receive hostile intrusion attempts almost constantly. Because of that, Jones created a last-resort command that Charlie could use in a crisis—say, a raid or some other security breach. If executed, this command essentially encrypts everything on those machines, permanently—and then destroys the key. It's catastrophic for the data, Kera. More permanent than burning the place to the ground. Something's wrong."

*What's wrong*, Kera thought, *is that Gnos.is keeps publishing things that turn people into targets.* But she refrained from throwing that in Bolívar's face right now.

"I'll check it out," she said.

"Kera—"

"No. Don't tell me to be careful."

"You're angry," he said.

She nearly hung up on him, but stopped herself. As infrequent as their direct communication was, she knew that cutting out on a bad note would only create a source of regret that would torment her until she could speak to him again. She realized after a few seconds that he'd fallen into an odd silence. A muted ruckus could be heard in the background.

"Rafa?"

"Turn on the news," he said. His voice was low, the confrontational tone of their previous conversation completely gone.

"What? I can't. There isn't any news here. What's wrong?"

"Charlie's—" he started. "They're saying Charlie's dead."

Kera's throat constricted. She covered her mouth with a hand. In a span of several seconds, she experienced a surreal shock that morphed into a very real anger. After determining that Bolívar didn't have any more information, she got off the phone and went back inside.

"Change of plans. I have to go to New York," she told Vasser in a voice she hoped masked her shock.

"What about me?"

"You're staying here."

"No way. You said we're in the same boat. We're doing this together."

"Together? I have established aliases. I have cash I've stashed away, bank accounts I can access, places to hide that only I know about if something goes wrong. I'm assuming you haven't made sim-ilar preparations?" Kera's loss of temper drove Vasser into silence. "You're a liability. You can stay here, where you're as safe as I can help you be. If you don't like that, you can turn yourself in and try your luck with the FBI. But I wouldn't count on them being very sympathetic."

If Vasser had been about to protest, she changed her mind as she watched Kera repack her duffle bag with urgent purpose. Kera retrieved the cheap burner flip phone from the fridge and entered its number into her satellite phone's contacts. She put the burner back into the fridge before issuing her instructions to Vasser.

"Take that phone out of the fridge every hour on the hour for three minutes. I'll call you in that window if I need to. At all other times, the phone stays in the fridge. Leave the cabin only if you must, and only in disguise. If you need food, try to order in and charge it to the room. Our reservation is under Abigail Dalton. If anyone asks, that's me. You can say I went on a drive in the mountains. There's a small grocery store on the property somewhere," she said, tapping the resort map. "You can get toiletries or whatever else there. Just try to avoid interacting with the staff. I doubt they're on the same sabbatical from the Internet and cable news as the guests are."

"I need clothes."

"I was getting to that. There's a gift shop. Charge whatever you need to the room."

Vasser rolled her eyes.

"I'm dead serious. If you leave this resort, you are more likely to run into someone who has seen your face in the news." Kera put a short stack of bills into an envelope. "If there's an emergency, here's two grand in cash."

"When will you be back?"

"Don't know. I'll call you."

# MANHATTAN

Kera reached the city at dusk. After abandoning the Civic in a church parking lot in Spring Valley, New York, she'd taken Metro-North into Manhattan, where she transferred to a downtown subway. After days in seclusion, the stimulation of the train—its sweaty crush of passengers, its mind-splitting metal clacking in the tunnels, its cameras in every corner—felt claustrophobic and overwhelming. At the same time, she craved information. Her eyes were pulled in the direction of any screen that might provide her with more news.

Surfacing at Houston and Lafayette, Kera faced a deluge of memories. This had been her neighborhood during her two years in New York City, after being transferred from Langley to work on HAWK. This was where she had shared an apartment with her then fiancé, Parker. Where she had discovered him in the bathtub, his head savaged by a bullet. Under normal circumstances, it would have been difficult to prevent those horrible images from resurfacing. But now—given the news of Charlie Canyon's murder—it was impossible to suppress them.

She turned downtown into the heart of SoHo, hugging herself against a chill that could not have come from the still-humid fall air. She stopped behind a police line at Spring Street and peered down a block lit up by emergency vehicles. Above them, on the north side of the street, she could see the windows of the loft that Charlie Canyon had maintained as Gnos.is's small public headquarters.

The coroner's van, apparently not yet burdened with its fare, was parked cockeyed in the street. A handful of men and women, cops mostly, stood around chatting in the glow of swirling red and blue. Every few minutes, someone decked out in the FBI's navy-blue jackets with yellow lettering emerged from the building carrying computer equipment—hard drives, monitors, routers, CPUs—all tagged and bagged inside translucent pink antistatic pouches. They'd find fingerprints, Kera thought, but not much else. What they were really after was no longer accessible. Based on what Bolívar had described, Canyon had—in his final moments alive—managed to activate the cryptographer's version of a suicide bomb within those machines, wrapping every bit of sensitive information in an encryption capsule for which there was no key. Like Canyon himself, the data was now irrevocably gone, no longer reachable by any means known to this world.

Kera watched the scene for longer than she needed to, indulging her anger, permitting it to steer her thoughts. What had she expected to achieve by coming here? Proof that it was real, maybe? She would have to wait, like everyone else, for any useful information about what had happened. Thus far, the police had no leads as to the identity or motive of the suspect.

Her anger showed no signs of subsiding on its own, but eventually she put it at arm's length in order to focus on something more productive. When she began to think clearly, her first thought was that neither the Feds nor the NSA would have acted in a way that might have caused Canyon to lock that data. Surely the FBI and NSA had been trying mightily for some time to infiltrate the Gnos.is computers in Canyon's loft—remotely and anonymously—but she didn't think they were stupid enough to attempt a physical strike against Canyon. The risk was too high that Canyon could destroy what they were looking for—which is exactly what he'd ended up doing.

No, the mortal threat that had forced Canyon to lock all the data must have come from someone else. Who had so much to gain from these murders?

Motivated by a renewed burst of anger, Kera reached for the satellite phone, stepping back from the crowd of people gathered along the police line so her end of the conversation wouldn't be overheard.

"How high does the body count need to get before you stop publishing?" she said when Bolívar answered.

"Kera. Where are you?"

"Where am I? I'm looking at the fucking van that's going to haul Charlie's body to the morgue. That's where I am. Where are you? Hiding away in a cave? It's a little hypocritical, don't you think, for someone who fancies himself a champion of transparency?"

Bolívar had no response.

"Who's next?" Kera said. He had no right to be silent.

"You can't possibly think Gnos.is is responsible for these—"

"I thought the common denominator was InspiraCom. But not anymore. Charlie had nothing to do with InspiraCom. Now the only thing all the victims have in common is Gnos.is. You used them as sources, Rafa, and it got them killed. Take down the China story, please, at least until we figure out who's doing this."

Because he paused, she thought that maybe he was considering doing just that. But then he said, "Everything in the China story is accurate. It's verified. If we take it down, how do we answer to that precedent?"

"You answer to it by saying that it will save lives."

"Will it? And won't others be lost?"

"Don't patronize me. This isn't a philosophical thought experiment."

"I didn't commit these murders, Kera, and I didn't create the world they were committed in. None of us did."

"You'd feel different about that if it were your own life at stake."

"Don't kid yourself. All of our lives are at stake. Yours, mine, Jones's." He didn't say Canyon's name, but it hung there, implied, in the beat of silence that followed.

"I can take care of myself," Kera said. "But these other people— the ambassador, Conrad Smith, Vasser—they didn't choose to risk their lives for your principles."

"What happened to Vasser?"

"She's alive, for now. Look, I'm getting off the phone."

"Kera, wait. Drop this case. Please. We'll still pay you. Just come back here, or walk away, if you'd rather, but get out now."

"I can't do that, Rafa. You're not the only one with principles."

When she hung up, she braced for tears. A few months earlier, turning away from him like this would have been more than she could bear. But things had changed.

·  ·  ·  ·  ·

Kera made it to the bank just before it closed. Access to safety deposit boxes had already ended for the night, but she persuaded a teller that she knew exactly what she wanted. She wouldn't need more than a minute alone with her box.

Once he left her in the small privacy room, she removed the remaining items from the box: a passport, driver's license, and credit card under the name Sabina Francis, along with a dozen business cards identifying Sabina Francis as a travel writer. She locked the empty box and thanked the teller again as she left.

In the taxi, Kera watched the clock. A few minutes before nine, she pulled up the number in her contacts, but she didn't push the "Call" button right away. A minute passed, then another. The taxi was on the freeway, Manhattan behind them. At 9:01 she placed the call. It rang only once before Vasser answered.

"Kera—"

"No names," Kera said. She knew her satellite phone calls were heavily encrypted when communicating with the other sat phones that Jones had rigged for them. But the burner she'd left for Vasser wasn't capable of encryption. If Vasser were to call someone she knew from that phone, the burner's number would turn up in the NSA's servers. Once they knew your number, they knew where you were. But the last person Vasser had tried to call—Conrad—wound up dead, and Kera didn't think Vasser would make that mistake again. Kera had to assume the burner was still clean and that the risk of their conversation being overheard was acceptably small.

"What's happening?" Vasser asked.

*The isolation is getting to her,* Kera thought. She could hear it in Vasser's voice. "There's another victim. A Gnos.is spokesman."

Vasser hesitated, absorbing this, then abruptly she said, "I need to speak with Ben."

"No. You can't do that."

"They'll go after him too."

"I don't think so," Kera said, and wasn't lying. "Ben is fine. The FBI is watching him around the clock." She lowered her voice to make it unintelligible to the cabdriver. "Listen, do you have any contacts within Chinese intelligence?"

"What? No. I—I wasn't a spy."

"I know. But as a diplomat you were certainly an intel target. You must have known that many of the Chinese people you routinely interacted with—politicians, businessmen, and others—were reporting back to the MSS."

Vasser did not deny this.

"I need a name," Kera said. "The highest-ranking person in Hong Kong you can think of. Preferably someone you were friendly with. And if you don't know anyone based in Hong Kong, I'll make do—"

"No, I do."

Kera waited. The taxi split off the freeway at the exit for JFK.

"Ren Hanchao," Vasser said.

The name rang familiar to Kera, an echo of a memory from her casework at the agency three years earlier. It was difficult to confirm these things, but they had suspected that Ren Hanchao was a senior intelligence officer in the Ministry of State Security's Third Bureau, which covered operations in Hong Kong, Macau, and Taiwan. "Ren. Yes, that just might work."

"What might work?"

Kera ignored the question. She was thinking it was possible that if Ren had performed well as an MSS officer a few years ago, he might now be in a position that reported directly to Feng Xuri, China's minister of state security.

"Kera, what will happen to him?"

The cab pulled up to the international terminal at JFK, and Kera paid the driver in cash, collecting her duffle from the seat next to her. "You were friendly with Ren?"

"At most, friendly acquaintances. He turned up often, friendly but uninvited, when the ambassador traveled. Will he be harmed?"

Kera took it as a good sign that Vasser was worried about the man's safety. It meant that Vasser liked him and had perhaps even let him hang around. This was a reflection that Ren had been good at his job. He would be valued within the Ministry of State Security. "Not by me. I'm going to get him a promotion."

"Is that a PA announcement? Are you at the airport?"

"Listen to me. It's important now that you don't know where I am or what I'm going to do. I will check in with you as often as I can. When I do, never say my name and never ask about my location."

"What am I supposed to do?"

"Exactly what you're doing. Stay out of sight."

# LANGLEY

When news of Charlie Canyon's murder arrived in the ops center, Bright leaned forward and squinted at the big screen. To those who looked to him for orders, he appeared concentrated, perhaps a shade bewildered. Inside, though, he felt an unsettling stillness. Diversion after diversion, from Angela Vasser to Kera Mersal, to Vasser *and* Mersal, had siphoned their resources away from the real issue—which was whether the Chinese had assassinated Ambassador Rodgers and, if so, why.

And now there was another body. Another likely diversion.

The details from the scene of Canyon's death, when they finally came from the FBI, served to further justify Bright's fear that the situation was worse than any of them had imagined. The building's doorman said an "Asian-looking" man had arrived for a meeting with Canyon. An hour later, the doorman said, he'd watched on his surveillance monitors as the visitor left hastily through a fire exit. After three failed attempts to reach Canyon by phone, the doorman had gone up to the loft to investigate. He'd found the door unlocked and Canyon's body on the floor behind his desk. He'd been shot twice; apparently there was a lot of blood.

Bright whispered to Henry Liu to assemble the MIRAGE team immediately. When they were all together in a windowless, soundproof conference room, he pulled up the text messages between Feng Xuri and Zhau Linpeng on the conference room's monitor. Alongside that, he displayed the Gnos.is article linking Hu Lan's business investments to the Ministry of State Security. "Whatever other leads you're pursuing, drop them. From now on, we are looking for more evidence of this: that members of China's intelligence and business communities are behind these murders, beginning with the ambassador's and stopping, one hopes, with Charlie Canyon's."

"With respect, sir, in the absence of clear evidence of that, I don't buy it," Judy Huang said. She was Bright's top expert on Chinese politics and foreign policy. "Beijing has too much to lose by assassinating anyone, especially Americans of this stature. They simply wouldn't do it."

Bright couldn't blame her for this analysis—he'd thought the same thing all along. But they couldn't afford to get this wrong any longer. "Maybe. Or maybe that thinking is exactly what's stalled our investigation. We have a growing body count, almost all of whom are American citizens. I don't want to hear any more about why the Chinese *wouldn't* do this; it's time to start considering why they *would.*"

# WASHINGTON, DC

Reese Frampton pulled an exhilarating all-nighter. At 7:00 AM he was at the small dining table in his one-bedroom apartment hunched over his laptop. Balding at forty-three, he wore glasses, a white undershirt, and charcoal slacks he'd put on twenty-four hours earlier. The table was buried under documents. He'd spent the night reading them furiously, one by one as the predawn hours ticked toward the deadline he'd agreed to. He had two hours left.

Another surge of adrenaline. Another pot of coffee.

This was without a doubt a once-in-a-lifetime break, and he was trying not to think about the fact that it had simply fallen into his lap, more or less out of the blue. No matter—he'd had his share of bad luck. What was wrong with seizing the opportunity when his luck took a turn for the better? The story had come to him from a source who needed to remain anonymous because he was a senior NSA contractor at a private defense firm. Frampton had crossed paths with the man at a handful of industry conventions and knew only enough about him to know that he had tremendous access within Fort Meade. In the past, though, all of Frampton's attempts to court the man as a source had yielded nothing. Each time he'd been blown off.

And then this, out of nowhere. The source had called him around seven the previous evening and, as instructed, Frampton had gone immediately to retrieve a package from the concierge at the Grand Hyatt near Capitol Hill. Then he hurried home and began reading its contents.

That's when he realized the true scope of what he had on his hands. He thought about how his former colleagues at the *Washington Times* would react, the ones who had offered nothing more than sympathetic pats on the back when he'd been sacked in the annual downsizing season that seemed to coincide with every release of the paper's earnings reports. Some of them would see it as ironic that he, now a self-employed blogger, would scoop the Washington journalism establishment. But that's not how Reese Frampton saw it. To him, this was a sign of the changing times. He'd landed on the right side of history.

After indulging in them briefly, Frampton set aside these thoughts of his former employer. There was no need to be bitter. He had his scoop now, a story that mattered. It would play nationally for weeks, maybe longer.

Fact-checking the thing overnight had been a heroic ordeal. Three times—at midnight, 1:30 AM, and 4:45 AM—he had called a second source, a man he knew and trusted at the NSA. When the man didn't answer, Frampton had to get creative with his attempts to independently verify the story told by the documents in front of him. For example, he pored through the private phone records and e-mails to pinpoint nearly a dozen key meetings between the Vasser woman and Conrad Smith, the now-deceased South African contractor. Then he cross-checked those dates with her credit card records and, sure enough, found charges at hotels in Hong Kong, Shanghai, and outside Beijing where the two had spent time together. In addition to Conrad Smith, Frampton used the provided text messages— many of which included unpublishable photographs—to identify the numbers of two additional men whom, it seemed rather obvious,

Vasser had met under intimate circumstances. And then of course there were the e-mails between Vasser and Smith that the world had already seen, in which Vasser discussed the classified TERMITE files. The story line practically wrote itself: this woman had taken a real spin on the dip circuit, fucking her way from one Far East city to the next.

At 7:15 AM, the NSA source awoke to Frampton's voice-mail messages and called him back, a mixture of concern and annoyance in his voice. "I need a favor," Frampton said. "No, not a favor. I just need a yes or no." He had been typing and reading for nine hours straight. Switching suddenly to conversation with another human being strained his ability to be coherent. "I have some documents. I can't tell you how I got them, but I need to know if they're authentic."

"What are you talking about?"

Frampton had had all night to winnow down what he needed the NSA man to confirm. From the documents approved for publication—many had been marked for use only as background— he'd set aside three that, viewed on their own, wouldn't hint at the full scope of his story. He'd taken pictures of them with his cell phone, careful to show details like the classification codes and serial numbers at the top of each page. "I'm texting you some images. I want to know if these files look legit."

Frampton heard the man juggle his phone, then several long moments of silence while he viewed the images on his phone. When his voice returned, he said, "You shouldn't be texting these. It isn't secure."

"I intend to publish them this morning. It hardly matters if they're in a text."

"Well, I don't want them connected to me," the man shot back. Then, more calmly, "Can we be off the record?"

Frampton shut his eyes. To independently verify the story, he really ought to have a second source on the record. But maybe that wasn't necessary. Perhaps it was enough, for his own peace of mind, just to get this guy's off-the-record affirmation. After all, the deal he'd agreed to had been clear: he wasn't supposed to talk to anyone about this until the story was published. "Sure," he heard himself say.

"Where did you get these?"

"I can't reveal that."

"Are you willing to go to jail over these? Because publishing them could earn you a subpoena."

*Jail?* What was he talking about? His original source had given him thorough instructions, but he'd said nothing about subpoenas. "I just need to know. Are they for real or not?"

"They're for real, all right. And whoever gave them to you broke some choice laws. This is very targeted, private data on a US citizen. NSA isn't supposed to be storing stuff like that, let alone—"

"And yet they do. Look, I got a deadline. I appreciate you calling me back."

"Wait. I'm going to hang up in a second because I don't want anything to do with this. But my advice to you: I think you should think real hard about this before publishing. This is going to do more harm than good."

"You're in the business of protecting secrets, and I'm in the business of uncovering the truth. I don't expect us to see eye to eye on this."

"Very well. We never spoke, OK?"

"Huh? Oh, right. I got it. Have a nice day."

An hour later the article was finished. Frampton read it from beginning to end, then reread it, tinkering each time with the occasional typo or improving a turn of phrase. Satisfied, he copied the full text and pasted it into his blog's template. He tapped out the title that his source had insisted upon: DOCUMENTS REVEAL DEVIOUS LIFE OF CLASSIFIED LEAKER. He leaned back and stared at the "Publish" button. It was not a moment of plumbing the depths of his conscience; it was a moment to savor the anticipation.

Then it was done. He tweeted the link and e-mailed it to his subscribers. He wasn't sure what to do next. He poured a cup of coffee. But he'd been drinking coffee for twelve hours, one cup after another. It didn't seem up to the occasion. He found a bottle of twenty-year-old scotch that someone had gifted him, still in its fancy box. He poured two fingers over an ice cube in a tumbler and stood at the window, wondering what would happen next.

The phone rang for the first time seven minutes after the article went live. It was a rival reporter at the *Post* who'd been assigned the task of confirming the story. Before that call ended, inquiries began to bombard his in-box and Twitter account. It had begun.

# CATSKILL
# MOUNTAINS

The clothing options could have been worse. From the resort's pro shop, Vasser selected a fleece pullover with the Sundown Sanctuary emblem, a tank top, and ladies' golf shorts. Next door, the decidedly high-end convenience store sold yoga apparel. She put a pair of stretch pants in her basket, along with some cheese, a baguette, orange juice, and bananas.

The clerk at the checkout register, a middle-aged Filipina woman sporting the resort's conservative uniform, watched her approach. Turning her eyes down, as if trying to hide them with the bill of Kera's hat, Vasser slid her basket onto the counter. The woman began to ring up the items, but when Vasser looked up a few seconds later, the clerk was still watching her. Vasser looked down, her heart thudding. Hadn't Kera said they'd be safe here? That no one would recognize them?

The woman bagged Vasser's supplies slowly, securing each item with gentle precision into its place in the brown paper bag. When she finished, they both stood there for a moment, neither of them moving or speaking.

In a voice as calm as she could summon, Vasser gave the woman her cabin number and the name under which Kera had registered. She signed the bill with an illegible scribble. To mask her anxiety, she offered a smile that she knew too late must have appeared forced.

The air and sunlight outside helped to steady her pulse. She reasoned now that there were dozens of reasons the cashier might have been staring at her—and it seemed equally likely that Vasser's own imagination had exaggerated the entire encounter. Still, she took a route through a small garden, avoiding the paths with high foot traffic. Looking back once, while crossing the small footbridge over the creek, she saw one of the resort's security guards about fifty yards back. He was not rushing toward her in pursuit, but he definitely had been looking in her direction. Her mind reverted quickly to worst-case scenarios. Had something terrible happened to Kera that put their story front and center in the news cycle? If something *had* happened, she'd be the last to know. She walked faster and didn't look back again until she was on the porch of the cabin. The security guard was still in sight, though he'd fallen back farther to allow distance to open between them.

She pulled the blinds over the windows and peered out from between the slats. The guard had vanished. But Vasser could no longer talk herself out of the anxiety she felt. She was trapped, claustrophobic. Her fellow resortgoers may have sworn off news from the outside world during their time here, but surely the resort's staff came and went from the premises daily. This felt suddenly like a dangerous disadvantage. For twenty minutes, she went from window to window, alternating glances between the cabin's quiet surroundings and the clock on the stove.

At one minute to four, she removed the little flip phone from the refrigerator. She turned it on and set it on the counter. She watched the device, willing it to vibrate with a call from Kera.

But the minutes passed and no call came.

# HONG KONG INTERNATIONAL AIRPORT

Kera awoke at thirty-five thousand feet from the best sleep she'd had in weeks. She should fly more often, she thought, checking the alignment of her wig in the dark window's reflection. Airports were risky, but once you were within the contained environment of an airplane, your fate was sealed for at least the duration of the flight. Might as well get some rest.

The route map on the seat-back screen told her that they were still three hours from Hong Kong. That meant she had slept nearly twelve of the scheduled sixteen hours. Cathay Pacific's JFK-to-HKG haul was one of the world's longest nonstop flights. She felt a growl of hunger and wondered whether her body thought it was time for breakfast, lunch, or dinner. Tapping the screen's navigation menu, she replaced the map with the satellite television feed. It was already tuned to CNN, the channel she'd watched briefly on the ascent out of New York, before the call of sleep promised higher returns than the repetitive non-news being trumpeted with exaggerated headlines and recycled footage.

She sat through a report on receding polar ice caps and then an interview with a congresswoman who had just announced her retirement. At a commercial break, she got up to stretch her legs and use the restroom. Back in her seat, she had to wait until just after the top of the hour before the news cycle spun around to her story. When it did, Kera could tell quickly from the rotating headlines on the bottom of the screen that there had been a development. An anchor was replaying an interview with a man named Reese Frampton. They were talking about Angela Vasser. Kera was reaching for her headphones when, without warning, the network cut away from the image of the puffy, balding Frampton in a DC studio to display a series of photographs taken by a smartphone. In each of the photos, Angela Vasser was unclothed before a hotel mirror. CNN had blurred the predictable areas, probably out of deference to the FCC, Kera guessed, since the decision to show the photos at all exempted the network from accusations that they'd handled the story with any decency. The Internet would be far less discerning. Kera shuddered to think of how the uncensored photos could have already spread.

Instinctively, she reached for her pocket before remembering that she'd thrown away the satellite phone at JFK, along with everything else that she didn't want the TSA to get too curious about: an extra wig, her colored contacts, driver's licenses for both Laura Perez and Abigail Dalton. The only thing she had on her now was the duffle filled with clothes and toiletries and the passport and other documents that identified her as Sabina Francis.

Kera shut her eyes and felt sick at the thought of Vasser holed up at that resort, possibly one of the last people on the Internet-connected planet to learn that her private photos had been stolen and released.

It wasn't just photos, as it turned out. This Frampton character was apparently the journalist who broke the story—if he could be called a journalist and if this could be called a news story. He was explaining to the anchor how he'd acquired access to a trove of

Vasser's personal files from a source whose identity he would not reveal, and he seemed to have no reservations in defending his decision to publish most of the material on his blog. Kera's hand went to her mouth. The files this man had made public included photographs and videos Vasser had exchanged with Ben Welk and several other men; text messages; credit card transactions that revealed her travel habits; e-mails in which she said undiplomatic things about friends and colleagues; lists of Google searches she'd run, including a query for the name of a common STD; and even a selective history of contraceptives and other medications she'd been prescribed. It was all newsworthy, Frampton argued, because Vasser had made herself a public figure by leaking national security secrets.

"No citizen who makes public classified information should have a reasonable expectation of privacy," Frampton was saying in a way that sounded rote, as though he'd uttered the same clunky phrase to a dozen other media outlets in the last few hours. "These records, this evidence of Ms. Vasser's reckless associations, paint a pretty disturbing picture of a woman we trusted to represent the United States to the world. Look, there's an inevitable tension between privacy and national security. I get that. But that's not the real issue here anymore. This evidence came to light; we can't reverse that. The only thing we can do—we must do—is take all of this information into account when we assess Ms. Vasser's guilt or innocence on these very serious charges."

Kera felt her anger come back into focus, this time backed up by a passion fueled by twelve hours of restful sleep. This was not news. It was a meticulously designed smear campaign, assembled illegally and handed off to a self-proclaimed journalist Kera had never heard of. The government's message was clear: Go ahead and hide. We don't even need to prosecute you to ruin your life.

But where had this come from? Not the CIA; they preferred to keep things quiet. Securing approval for a tactic this depraved seemed like a long shot at the FBI, where too many risk-averse bureaucrats would have had to sign off. There was only one entity on earth that could acquire this amount of this type of information on a target. But what did the NSA have against Vasser? It didn't add up. The smear felt like a new, and much more political, dimension to the case. *Fucking Washington,* Kera thought. No doubt pressure was building for someone to stop both the classified leaks and the rising body count. And since no one was succeeding there, they were all desperate to keep shifting the focus, redirecting the blame.

The Boeing 777-300ER touched down on Chinese soil at dawn. When she disembarked, it was 5:57 AM, local time, which was thirteen hours ahead of Eastern Standard Time. Kera pictured Angela Vasser removing the phone from the refrigerator, eager for news. Kera could purchase a calling card and call her from a pay phone. But what would she say to her? What good would it do?

Kera walked right past the pay phones and proceeded to customs.

# CATSKILL MOUNTAINS

Sundown brought with it a decision. Staying in place was no longer tolerable. Vasser felt more and more certain she'd been recognized and followed by the resort's staff. She had no contact with the outside world. And Kera hadn't called in over twenty-four hours. What if Kera had been followed too? Or arrested? Or worse? Vasser would have no way of knowing. It was time to move. She would leave as soon as darkness set in.

A few minutes after the top of the hour, Vasser set the phone back in the fridge and packed her old clothes, which she'd changed out of after purchasing the resort wear. She checked that the doors were locked and turned out all the lights except for one in the living room. Then she reset the timer on the stove for fifty-five minutes, giving Kera one last chance to call, and she lay on the couch to rest. The sun was already down, but daylight would wane gradually to dusk for another hour or so.

· · · · ·

Despite the adrenaline cycling through her, she must have dozed off while working out in her head where she would go once she left the resort on foot. The next sound she heard was a heart-stopping crash that jolted her from sleep. The front and back doors to the cottage were breached simultaneously, their locks ripped from splintering frames. In the time it took her to sit upright, eight men dressed in black tactical gear with automatic weapons drawn entered the room and circled the couch. It was over before Vasser could even scream.

"FBI! FBI!" the intruders were shouting. "Put your hands behind your head."

Vasser obeyed, and through her exhaustion the only feeling she could summon was relief.

# HONG KONG
# INTERNATIONAL
# AIRPORT

Signs in Chinese and English directed all international travelers through baggage claim and into the expansive, high-ceilinged atrium that housed the airport's busy immigration and customs checkpoint. Passengers burdened with luggage flowed around Kera, who had almost none and who had slowed to study each of the eight customs officials ensconced in their glass boxes, working passport stamps with grave, unchanging expressions.

Instead of falling into one of the lines, Kera stepped aside and entered the ladies' restroom. She found an empty stall and removed the Sabina Francis passport. She pried at the top of the toilet paper dispenser until the thin metal bent up, exposing a sharp corner. Scraping gently against the surface of the passport's main page, Kera removed the control digit for the date of birth within the passport's Machine Readable Zone, or MRZ, the two rows of information along the bottom. Satisfied with the obscured digit, she slipped the book back into her pocket. From her wallet she removed Sabina Francis's driver's license, credit card, and business cards. She considered trying

to flush them down the toilet but then thought better of it; there
was probably a reason signs in public restrooms pleaded with people
not to flush trash. She didn't want to risk a scenario that ended with
her rolling up a sleeve. Instead, she bent the license and credit card
until they were severely damaged and marked with hard, permanent
creases. Then she wrapped each of them in a paper towel and buried
them deep in the trash can by the sinks.

*That was expensive,* she thought, exiting the restroom.

She walked directly to lane 6. It was slightly longer than the
others because, as Kera had observed earlier, the buzz-cut officer in
booth 6 took his job very seriously, scrutinizing not just the passports but also the faces of each traveler, as if he actually suspected
every man, woman, and child might be an imminent threat to the
security of the People's Republic.

The line inched forward. Kera had easily picked out all of the
surveillance cameras, and, forcing herself to buck habit, she refrained
from tilting her head or turning away her face. Instead, she kept her
eyes up, looking forward.

Several people abandoned the line ahead of her in search of
swifter passage elsewhere, leaving her waiting on deck. An elderly
couple was now before the officer. Kera watched the interaction,
rehearsing in her head the answers to the questions they were asked.

"Hi," she said when they'd shuffled off, passports stamped, and
she found herself face-to-face with the customs official. She slid her
passport across the counter.

"Where are you traveling from?"

"New York."

"Where is your final destination?"

"Kuala Lumpur."

"So you will not be staying over in China?"

"No."

"What is the purpose of your travel?"

"Business, mostly. I'm a travel writer."

During this exchange, Kera had been aware that the officer had attempted to scan her passport twice. Though his expression had not changed, he eventually paused his questioning to give the passport page a cursory once-over. Observing nothing wrong at first glance, he tried the scan again. Again it failed to read. This time he examined the page more closely, paying special attention to the MRZ lines. Kera performed an exaggerated yawn. She watched him out of the corner of her eye so that she saw the exact moment he did a subtle double take and then ran his thumb slowly over the scarred digit. When he looked up at her, she averted her eyes and scratched her head nervously, tilting her wig ever so slightly.

"Is there a problem?" she said.

The man picked up his phone and said something into it that she could not hear. When he looked back at her, all he said was, "One minute, ma'am."

It took much less than a minute for the officer's supervisor to arrive. He inspected the document, squinting at the unreadable digit and then looking up at Kera. His tone was friendlier than his colleague's.

"Did you alter this on purpose?"

"I'm sorry? I don't understand."

"See this scratch? It looks very deliberate."

"No, I didn't do that," she said, looking at the passport page as if she'd never even noticed the digits before.

"The scanner cannot authenticate the passport without that number. Has this been in your possession throughout your flight?"

"Yes, of course."

"Do you have another form of identification?"

"Other than my passport? No. What more could you need?"

"Not a driver's license? Nothing?"

"I'm afraid not."

"I see." The two men exchanged a few words in Cantonese. And then, "You'll come with me."

"Oh. Will this take long? My connecting flight leaves in less than an hour."

But the man did not answer her. He didn't give the passport back either.

*Here we go,* she thought.

# FORT MEADE, MARYLAND

"Ben!" She ran to embrace him. "I'm sorry. I'm sorry." She said it over and over, her head buried in his shoulder.

The reunion occurred in a small, windowless room at a federal detention center in Fort Meade where she was being held for violating the terms of her previous release, which had stipulated that she not leave Washington, DC. Now that she had proved to be a flight risk, she would be held at least until the government either dropped its espionage charges or lost their case against her in court. She had not seriously contemplated the prospect of a conviction.

"It's OK," Ben said. "You're safe now."

She wasn't convinced of that, but her main concern now was Ben. She pulled away from him, just for a moment, to look him in the eyes. Throughout the ordeal, she'd been plenty aware of what he must have been going through. But seeing it now on his face was heartbreaking.

"I didn't have a choice," she said. "I wanted to call, but I was afraid they'd come after you too."

"Who?" he said.

She wiped tears from her cheeks. "I don't know. They killed Greg, Ben. I don't know how, but that plane crash wasn't an accident. And Conrad. I'm sure of it. Has there—" She stopped herself. There was a guard in the room, but the lawyers had left them alone. No one had told her whether she was being recorded. She leaned in and whispered in his ear. "Has there been anything in the news about Kera Mersal? Her whereabouts?"

Cupping her shoulders in his hands, Welk held her at arm's length with an expression that was unrecognizable—part confusion, part concern. She realized that he was looking at her as if she were mad.

"What is it? Did they get to her too?"

"No," he said. "No—or, I don't know. I don't think that's been reported. But . . . when was the last time you saw the news?"

"Two days ago. Briefly, after I was attacked. What is it?" She noticed the guard look down at his shoes. "You're not telling me something."

"Your phone was—well, it's more than just your phone. There was a leak of private records. *Your* private records."

"What are you talking about? Jesus, stop beating around the bush. Just tell me."

Welk turned to the guard. "Can we get a TV in here?"

It took a few minutes for someone to rule that the detainee was permitted to see the latest news about herself on TV. Rather than set up a television in the interrogation room, they simply escorted Vasser down the hall to the visitors' waiting room, which they'd cleared to give her privacy. She was about to discover the irony in that.

Vasser watched the coverage in clench-jawed silence for fifteen minutes, until her lawyer rejoined them. When he entered and saw Vasser and Welk, and the TV tuned to CNN, he froze, looking for a moment like an innocent passerby who'd stumbled into a domestic dispute. He tried to back out of the room, but Welk waved him in.

"Sorry to interrupt," the lawyer said. "We'll get to the bottom of this thing with Reese Frampton—"

"This has nothing to do with Reese Frampton, whoever the fuck he is," Vasser said. "We all know that a washed-up blogger doesn't have access to my phone, my medical records—" Her voice broke.

The lawyer appeared flustered, no doubt hung up on what everyone else seemed to be hung up on—the photos and hotel rooms that Vasser had shared with men who were not Ben Welk—which was not remotely the most objectionable issue.

Recovering, the lawyer said, "This will strengthen our case in the end. If the government had evidence of you doing anything illegal, they'd release *that*, not . . . this."

"He's right, babe," Welk said, embracing her. "This might play in the media for a day or two, but legally it's practically an admission that they've got nothing. It's all over now."

"They've offered a plea deal," the lawyer announced self-consciously, as if he was trying to justify his presence. "It's very generous. But"—there was the slightest pause—"it involves giving up Kera Mersal."

Vasser stiffened in Welk's arms. Over his shoulder she could see a photo of herself, blurred in places, being broadcast on live cable news. "No," she said then, and the tone of her voice startled both Welk and the lawyer. "They've taken any hope of a plea off the table." And then, in a whisper to Welk, "I'm sorry, babe, it's not over."

# Hong Kong
# International
# Airport

*This is the most dangerous part,* Kera thought.

She was in a spotless, white-walled room in a sector of the airport most travelers never see. The tile floor was shiny and smelled of bleach. There was a camera in the corner opposite the door, which she'd turned and gazed into for a few seconds after she was left alone.

When the customs supervisor returned, he sat down across the table from Kera in the center of the room. Two guards hovered placidly by the door. The supervisor had in front of him the passport, as well as a printout he'd acquired in the ten minutes he'd been gone. Eyeing the page from where she sat, Kera saw Sabina Francis's name typed into a field near the top, but her passable proficiency in Cantonese did not allow her to quickly read the full document upside down. She guessed it was some sort of background check.

When the supervisor finished scanning the information, he looked up at her and smiled. "I hope I'm not being indelicate if I say that I noticed you're wearing a wig. Why are you traveling under disguise?"

Kera looked him in the eye. "I don't see how it's any of your business."

"With all due respect, ma'am, you are no longer in New York City. You have a faulty passport, and I'm told you have a plane to catch. You will please be cooperative and remove the wig. Routine procedure, I assure you."

"Look, I'm tired. I've had a long flight," she said, which did not inspire any sympathy. Finally, she sighed and peeled the wig from her head. After wearing it for twenty hours, the cool air up top felt good. She undid the tight bun and shook out her wavy Earl Grey hair. For a moment, the man's face expressed generic satisfaction—here was another American, a woman, obeying his orders—but that was followed quickly by an involuntary slackness that resolved itself into recognition. He straightened, barked something to the guards, and then left the room in a hurry.

Kera glanced again at the surveillance camera in the corner.

• • • • •

She was made to wait in the room with the guards for another ninety minutes. They escorted her to the bathroom twice when she asked, but they were unmoved by her concern for the connecting flight that boarded and left without her. Then, without warning, the door to the interrogation room opened and a slender Chinese man in a gray suit entered. He appraised her tentatively from just inside the doorway as if perhaps he'd half expected to have been on the bad side of a prank. But then he approached and sat down across from her at the table.

"Hello," he said. "Kera Mersal." He pronounced each syllable slowly.

"Who are you?"

"I am Gao Dalei. It is a pleasure to make your acquaintance. May I ask, what brings you to China?"

"I'm only passing through. I had a connection to Malaysia."

"It is an interesting choice, though, to connect through Hong Kong. Perhaps you intended to meet with someone here? Surely you've read in the press about what your own government thinks you are up to."

They were both dancing around the issue. Kera smiled. "Mr. Gao, we both know I'm not a spy for China, as some news organizations have been encouraged to suggest. I'm not working for you, nor am I running from you. It is true, I am wanted by the US government. That is the purpose of my travel. I just want to survive and live freely." She yawned again. The scarred passport—now confiscated—the disheveled wig, the lack of backup cover identification—she hoped all of this appeared to be the careless mistakes of an exhausted and desperate fugitive.

"I see. And where were you planning to go . . . to live freely?"

"My flight is to Kuala Lumpur. You understand it is not safe for someone like me to divulge anything more specific than that."

"Yes, of course," he said. He excused himself then, without explanation. She was left to wait for another hour.

When he returned, he assumed his place across from her at the table, as if he'd never left.

"Ms. Mersal, we can help you live freely. If you are interested."

She studied his eyes, saw in them discipline and patience—but also a shade of anticipation that he could not mask. Softly, she said, "How would I know I have friends in China?"

"It is our custom to be friendly to those who are friendly to us."

"I would like to speak with Ren Hanchao," she said suddenly.

The man swiveled to exchange a glance with the supervisor who had first interviewed her. Neither of them were disciplined enough to contain their surprise at this request.

"Do you know Mr. Ren?"

"No. Please tell him that we have a mutual friend: Angela Vasser."

Gao's eyes expanded and then he smiled. He slapped the table with a hand as if this was just the damnedest thing. And then he left the room for a period that was shorter than the other stretches, but long enough that by the time he returned, she'd leaned back, slumping in her chair.

This time Gao did not sit down.

"We will take you to Mr. Ren."

# HONG KONG

A young man appeared. He was around Kera's age, handsome with short, neat hair and earnest eyes. He might have been her onetime counterpart in the Ministry of State Security, she thought, before her career track at the CIA was shattered. He instructed her to put her wig back on and contributed sunglasses and a hat stitched with the airport's logo to strengthen her disguise. Then he led her down a series of hallways and through a door that opened to a busy baggage claim area. On the curb out front they got into a waiting town car. The driver did not ask their destination. Without a word he pulled away from the curb and into a river of red cabs flowing toward the city.

"First time in Hong Kong?" Kera's escort asked. His gaze was polite and not intrusive.

Kera shook her head. She'd been to the city on two occasions while employed by the CIA. He either knew that already or he didn't. It mattered little either way.

"Did you grow up in Hong Kong?" she asked, retaliating with a question of her own.

"Shenzhen," he said.

"How long have you been in the MSS?"

"Perhaps you misunderstand," he said, though they both knew she hadn't. After that, he stopped asking questions.

They rode in silence, edging into the heart of the city and then finally sweeping up beneath the entrance of the Island Shangri-La Hotel. In the two-story marble lobby, her escort approached the registration desk and returned with a small envelope containing her room's key card. He suggested that she could make herself comfortable while she waited for Gao Dalei, the MSS officer who'd last questioned her at the airport, and Ren Hanchao, the senior officer whose name Angela Vasser had given her. The room number was written on the outside of the envelope: 3915. Kera took a few steps in the direction of the elevator bank before she stopped. She could see from the indicator panel over the elevator doors that there were fifty-six floors.

"Everything OK, ma'am?" her escort said. He'd hovered back, watching her. Was he waiting because he'd been given orders to see her safely to her room? Or was he waiting to send word to someone sitting at a computer with access to the elevator's software?

"Yes, I'm fine. When should I expect Mr. Ren?"

"Twenty, maybe thirty minutes."

"Thank you. I slept through the last meal on my flight and I'm hungry. I think I'll sit in the lobby café and have lunch."

This appeared to cause the young man some stress. But she was not a prisoner. What could he say?

"As you wish. I will stay out of your way. Don't hesitate to let me know if there's anything you need." He followed her into the café and chose a seat several tables away.

Kera sat with her back to the wall so that she had a full view of the lobby, including the hotel's main entrance. She ordered a coffee and a sandwich—she was, in fact, hungry—and charged it to the room. She hadn't finished eating when she spotted Gao Dalei enter the hotel with another gray-suited man whom Kera took to be Ren Hanchao. Tailing them were four men wearing sunglasses and radio earpieces. Kera's escort glanced up at her from the nearby table, but when he saw that she still had food in front of her, he followed her lead and stayed put.

She waited for Gao and Ren and their bodyguards to cross the lobby to the elevator bank. Just as Gao reached out and pushed the call button, Kera rose suddenly and hurried toward them.

"Mr. Gao!" she called. All six men spun around. One of the guards took a step toward her, putting himself in front of the two spies. "I was just heading up to the room myself. I'll ride with you." She smiled pleasantly.

The escort caught up to them then, red in the face from embarrassment and apologizing to his superiors.

"It's OK," Gao said in Cantonese, indicating to the guards that he didn't consider her a threat. He flashed Kera a wry, sporting smile that made her wonder if he was conceding that she'd played this well.

The elevator chimed, and a few seconds later the doors parted. Gao took a half step in and held the door with his arm.

"Please," he said in English, beckoning them aboard. "We're all going to the same place."

In the elevator, Kera caught Ren studying her. He was middle-aged with serious black eyes and thinning black hair. She took the fact that he'd actually shown in person as a promising sign that they hadn't planned to kill her. When they reached the room, Kera swiped her key card and invited everyone in. On Gao's orders the guards and the escort were made to wait outside in the hall. That left Kera alone with the two men inside the room, which turned out to be a spacious luxury suite. Gao extended the proper introductions. Ren was still eyeing Kera strangely. Then she remembered her wig. Removing it, she shook out her darker natural hair and sat on the couch.

The suite was easily a thousand square feet, with full-length windows and a hand-painted mural in the master bedroom. The living area where they sat provided dramatic views of Victoria Peak soaring over the city's narrow band of skyscrapers.

"You are a difficult woman to pin down, Ms. Mersal," Ren said, leading the conversation. "An international enigma." He spoke easily in English, using a soft, even voice and a showy vocabulary. "We're honored to have you pay us a visit."

"I did not intend to visit Hong Kong. I was detained at customs."

"No one has been detained." He opened the file on his lap and read the name on the top page. "Sabina Francis was *questioned* at customs. Because she was suspected of not actually existing. A small technicality."

"What do you want?"

"What do *we* want? Didn't you ask to meet with me?" He leaned forward, smiling at her warmly. "I saw the security tapes from the airport, Ms. Mersal. Your performance was masterful. And it's gotten you what you wanted, hasn't it?"

Kera knew Ren was not naïve and that he would not have interpreted her customs foibles as mere coincidence, but they were playing a game. She did not break character. "I was interrogated for hours. When I realized I'd missed my flight and that my delay was going to drag on, I remembered that Angela Vasser had spoken kindly of you. No offense to Mr. Gao here, but I thought it might be in my interests to make contact with a friend of a friend."

"I'm glad that Ms. Vasser considers me a friend." Ren smiled briefly, but an unhappy expression followed. "You are aware that Ms. Vasser has been detained by your government?"

In her shock, Kera allowed a telling beat to pass.

"I see. Then you didn't know," Ren said. "She was detained on charges not dissimilar to those you have endured, if I remember."

Kera shook her head. "How typical of the American government. They have grown too fearful. Their solution to every threat is to lock someone up, to erode more freedoms and privacy. I'm sure you are aware that the charges against Vasser are false, as are the charges against me—though for now she is safer in custody. Her life is in danger."

"You don't have a similar fear for your own life? Or are you just braver?"

"Neither fear nor bravery has anything to do with me being here. I've already told you, I didn't plan to stay in China. I'm not here on a professional basis."

"Where were you headed?"

"You know the destination of my next flight. I'm not going to tell you any more than that. I would not be alive if I was in the habit of keeping intelligence agencies apprised of my location."

Ren chuckled at this. He seemed to appreciate her sparring attitude. "You've survived this long. You must be doing something right. Have you considered the possibility of remaining in China? Perhaps it would be safer than wherever you were headed?"

Kera stared at him, signaling that she knew what he was getting at. "The United States mishandled my case, and that has left me disillusioned. But if I'd wanted to betray my country for the benefit of yours, you and I would have spoken much sooner and under much different circumstances."

"What do you want?" he asked her directly.

"I've been traveling for almost twenty-four hours, and now you've made me miss my flight. I want to get a good night's sleep."

"Very well," Ren said, rising. Gao looked up in protest, but Ren beckoned him to stand as well. "We'll go." He took a few steps toward the door and then turned back to face her. "If you'd like, we can talk again in the morning. Sleep on it. Is that the expression?"

Kera studied him. "And if I decide tomorrow to continue on to Malaysia?"

Ren shrugged. "Then we'll give you a ride to the airport."

*He's bluffing,* she thought. *He's testing me.* Would they really let an American intelligence agent just walk? Not a chance. They knew what kind of opportunity they had on their hands. And she'd just bought them another twelve hours to figure out how to take advantage of it.

When they'd left her, she looked around the luxury suite, wondering whether the Ministry of State Security made use of this room regularly, or if they'd managed—in the time it had taken to get her here from the airport—to install hidden cameras and mics in the walls, lamps, and furniture. If it was the latter, they were good. They'd left no trace.

To keep the pressure on them, she picked up the desk phone, which was almost certainly bugged, and called the airline. She apologized for missing her flight on account of a customs mix-up and asked them to rebook her to Kuala Lumpur the following day.

# MINISTRY OF STATE SECURITY COMMAND CENTER, HONG KONG

Ren Hanchao returned to his office in a tower in the Wan Chai District. He sent word of his meeting with the fugitive American spy to Beijing and then sat waiting for his orders.

Ren was fifty-three and had been stationed in Hong Kong for five restless years. There had been flourishes of promise, signals from Beijing that his service was highly regarded. But the lack of anything concrete had begun to agitate his feelings of restlessness. Ultimately, he'd been disappointed with the posting to the Third Bureau in Hong Kong. The Third Bureau spent a lot of time spying on domestic political dissenters in Hong Kong, Macau, and Taiwan, intercepting and blocking their communications to make it more difficult to organize protests. Ren would have preferred an assignment with the First Bureau, based out of headquarters in Beijing, where he might be noticed more quickly and promoted into Feng's inner circle; or a posting to New York or Washington with the Second Bureau, which handled foreign intelligence and might have given him an opportunity to prove himself in the field.

When he'd received the call that Kera Mersal, the notorious ex-CIA operative, was being held at the airport and had asked for him by name, he immediately hoped it might provide more than just a welcome change from days spent monitoring the social media networks of college students with strong opinions about Taiwan and democracy and Beijing's political influence over Hong Kong. After speaking with Mersal himself, he began to hope that she might be a legitimate walk-in. If he handled this right, it might even earn him a transfer of his choosing. He grew anxious waiting for a reply from Beijing. He was eager for things to proceed quickly.

An hour after he'd cabled Beijing, he got what he wanted—and more.

A secure teleconference link was established so that Ren could brief a dozen senior officers and analysts at headquarters. The first thing he noticed on the conference room's large screen was that Feng Xuri himself, the head of the Ministry of State Security, was seated at the head of the table. Ren's chest swelled and his thoughts swirled. This was significant. The MSS was a government bureaucracy; things typically moved much more slowly than this.

Ren spent fifteen minutes summarizing the circumstances under which Kera Mersal had appeared to them as well as the conversation he'd had with her. He could tell from their questions that consensus in Beijing was split. Did they treat this like a walk-in, a foreign agent who was eager to offer intelligence on her home country? Or was there a risk that she was being dangled by the CIA as a double agent? Or perhaps they could take her at her word that she was neither and had just been passing through?

When the debate subsided, Feng asked Ren to stay on after the others cleared the room.

"What does your gut say?" Minister Feng asked.

The video and audio connections were good. Feng's voice was clear, and Ren could see the minister scrutinizing him on the HD picture. Ren had reported directly to Feng Xuri on several past occasions, which put him in elite company. His relationship with the minister, though, was still formal. Several key operations—operations that Ren could only imagine were some of the MSS's most sensitive—required a competent point person in Hong Kong, and Ren had been called upon to carry out those duties.

"She is tired," Ren said. "She knows she can't run forever. She harbors bitterness for the way the Americans have treated her. Do I think she came here seeking to harm the United States? Not exactly. But perhaps we have planted in her mind a glimpse of a life that is safer and more stable. She might see that it's worth it to cooperate with us."

"If she cooperates, how could we possibly trust her information?"

"It's true that it would be unwise to trust her at face value. But she is still valuable to us." Ren hesitated. He was on the verge of broaching a topic that had not come up in the larger meeting, mostly because he didn't know who was cleared to discuss it. It concerned a secret operation—one that he knew Beijing was handling very delicately. He'd at first been grateful to be given a role in the operation; he felt his contributions were important and he knew they were being watched closely by Beijing. And then recently, very suddenly, things had gone sideways. "I think she might be able to help us with our other problem."

Feng was silent for a long moment, thinking. Ren could tell that his idea had not completely surprised the minister. Finally, Feng responded. "I am beginning to think we would be better to simply get rid of the other problem."

Ren nodded. "With respect, sir, it is my understanding that we need him. For technical assistance. Just for a little while longer. He is crucial to the final phase."

Feng shook his head. "The young Russian knows too much. I was assured that wouldn't happen."

Ren had no idea who had given the minister that assurance, but he was glad it wasn't him. "I don't think anyone could have foreseen the complications that developed. But that is the reality we face. If I may, sir, I might have an idea to fix it."

"An idea?"

"A test. For both the American and the Russian. Remember, each of their lives is in our hands. That makes them very motivated to please us."

"What sort of test?"

"We want to know if the Russian went out on his own and initiated that most recent attack. The elevator in San Francisco. And, separately, we want to know if Kera Mersal will be valuable to us. I propose a meeting between them, arranged so that they might reveal each other's loyalties. Under our close supervision, of course."

Feng did not think about this for very long. Perhaps he'd conceived of something similar on his own ahead of time, or maybe it was immediately clear to him that of all their troubling options, this one had the greatest potential for an upside. "Go ahead. But if it goes bad, the Russian is done. We'll find a way to finish the operation without him."

# FORT MEADE

"I want to ask you a few questions about Kera Mersal."

"Who are you?"

"My name is Lionel Bright. I was Kera's mentor while she was with the CIA. Do you know where she is?"

"No. I already told them that."

"I understand. I apologize for any redundancy. We're all trying to be thorough here. We don't want to miss anything."

"Near as I can tell, you're missing just about everything."

Bright's eyes narrowed. So this was the trademark defiance that he'd heard about from everyone who'd interviewed Angela Vasser. "Then perhaps you can help us find our way. You met with Kera last week in a hotel restroom in DC."

"She approached me. It was not a meeting."

"Did you see her again after that?"

"No."

"I see." Bright glanced down at the file he'd received from FBI Director Ellis. "I understand you were detained last night in a cabin reserved under the name Abigail Dalton." Bright held up the Xerox copy of Abigail Dalton's driver's license, which Sundown Sanctuary had turned over to the FBI. "This is a picture of Kera Mersal." He turned the page so he could look at the photo. He smiled at it, a little proudly. "Not a bad disguise. But I can tell it's Kera. There's no doubt." He paused to give Vasser a chance to respond, but she just stared at him, expressionless. "The Feds found something else interesting in the cabin. In the refrigerator, I'm told. Was that burner phone yours?" Still no reaction. "It had been used only once, two days ago, to receive a call from an encrypted satellite phone that was used in the Manhattan or Queens area. Did you take that call, Angela? Who was it from?"

Anger swirled in Vasser's eyes, but she said nothing.

Bright leaned forward, resting his elbows and forearms on the table. "Here's the thing. Either you're a patriotic diplomat and you inadvertently got caught up in this mess—which is what I'm inclined to believe—or somewhere along the way you received training in clandestine intelligence from an entity other than the US government. Those paths lead to very different outcomes for you. If I were you, I'd start trying to convince us of your innocence."

Vasser had been watching his face intently as he talked. She looked down at her hands now, which were wrung with silent frustration. She shook her head. "You're missing the bigger picture. Someone is murdering people—Americans. They tried to kill me too."

"That may be true," Bright said, leaning back as if they'd reached a stalemate that Vasser alone could end.

"I won't talk about Kera."

"I'm sure your lawyers have informed you of the plea bargain. Immunity for someone in your situation could be very valuable."

"I don't need immunity. I haven't done anything wrong."

"You had very close associations with two of the deceased. In fact, it was very fortunate for you that you were not on the ambassador's plane that night. Too fortunate, some might say."

"Greg never would have been on that plane either had the CIA not asked him to form ties with Hu Lan," Vasser countered. The chill in her voice was getting to Bright.

"That still doesn't explain why you weren't on the plane."

"I was doing my job."

"Were you? I thought you were spending the night with Conrad Smith, who, it turned out, perished just weeks later. Meanwhile, here you are. Your survival skills, relative to your friends', are remarkable."

"What are you suggesting?"

"I'm suggesting that you start explaining yourself. Specifically, talk to me about your associations with Kera. What is she up to?"

"That won't happen. I don't need your immunity. You know the government's case is weak; their release of my private photos and e-mails and other records suggests that. A judge already released me once." Her stare, those piercing eyes, pinned him against the back of his seat. She kept going. "But I get it: You need scapegoats. If you have villains like me and Kera Mersal, you can still pretend to be the good guys. You don't care about laws or due process, and you certainly don't care about the truth. All you care about is secrecy and covering up your own messes. What you don't seem to understand is that I'm the one who's been wronged here."

Bright shook his head. "What you don't understand is that you're not the one who decides who's been wronged. You've been charged with very serious crimes. I, for one, don't think you wrote those e-mails discussing classified programs with a foreign citizen. But the e-mails exist. Right now, that doesn't look good for you. The benefits of cooperating with us have been explained. It's very clear: take the plea deal and the immunity, prove your patriotism, and avoid a very public trial."

Vasser's eyes burned with a clear conviction that did not allow her to be intimidated by him. "Mr. Bright, this ordeal has indeed made something very clear to me: there is a difference between the courageous people who leak information because it is newsworthy—that is, because it is in the public's interest to know—and the cowards who seek only to tarnish someone by destroying their privacy, in order to cover the asses of people like you, who get to bury their mistakes in secrecy and claims of patriotism. I don't want to avoid a trial. I welcome it. I will talk about Kera Mersal only after everyone involved with accessing, storing, and releasing my private communications has been named publicly in that trial, and every agency involved has admitted to abusing their powers by spying on an American citizen. Then we can talk about the evidence against me and Kera Mersal, if any exists."

Bright had tried to interrupt her but found that he could think of nothing to say. Now suddenly he wanted out of the room. "I didn't come here to be lectured. If you don't want help, I can't make you accept it. Good luck, Ms. Vasser."

Instead of rejoining Director Ellis in the observation room, Bright hurried down the fluorescent-lit hallway toward the nearest exit. He needed air. Outside he wiped sweat from his forehead. He was furious, mostly at himself for taking this case so personally. He'd let Vasser get under his skin. Not just because she was difficult, but because she was right—they were still missing something big.

Henry Liu peeked cautiously through the exit door a minute later.

"Lionel," he said, opening the door and stepping out to join him.

Bright didn't say anything at first. He just stood staring out at a parking lot. And then he spoke.

"We didn't have anything to do with this Vasser privacy leak, did we? This stuff about the photos and medical history?"

"No, sir, not that I'm aware of."

"Find out who did."

# Hong Kong

When Ren Hanchao knocked on Kera's hotel room door the following morning, he was dressed as a hotel manager in a crisp button-down jacket and pressed gray pants. Kera let him in and closed the door.

"Have you had adequate time to consider my offer?" Ren asked.

"I have," Kera said. "And I've decided it's quite unusual. Why are you offering me help? I was under the impression that China is wary of volunteers. The common wisdom among US intelligence analysts is that the MSS is disinclined to accept the risk. If you want to know a secret, we've always kind of admired you for that."

"Your talent for analysis no doubt made you a valuable asset to the CIA, Ms. Mersal. Your information is accurate."

"Then why are you so eager to trust me?"

"Believe me, I am no more eager to trust you than you are to betray your country. But you know many things about your CIA's interest in China. And you need a place to stay. Think of it as a partnership."

"I appreciate your offer of hospitality, and I will accept it"—she saw pleasant surprise flicker in his eyes—"on a few conditions. I will meet with whomever you wish me to meet with, though I cannot promise to give them everything they ask for. I will cooperate with your requests for intelligence—up to a point. I'm not willing to discuss subjects that will harm innocent people. In exchange for my knowledge, I will not be detained and no media outlets will learn that I am here. I don't want to be in Hong Kong; the CIA's presence here is too great. I will stay in and around Beijing on my own recognizance. Maybe I'll go and visit the Great Wall. I've never been. You will pay for a safe place for me to stay and a weekly stipend of twenty thousand yuan. I imagine that you will have to get approval for this from your minister of state security. If he will not grant me this deal, exactly as I've requested, I will disappear. If you try to stop me, you will find that I've changed my mind about sharing intelligence."

Ren smiled. "You must have had a very comfortable night's sleep. You have done some big thinking." The smile faded. "You are asking for a lot."

"I know a lot."

"Very well. I will try to convince my colleagues that we can build trust with you, Ms. Mersal. You understand, they are skeptical."

"I'm sure you and your colleagues have strategies to mitigate those risks. I will oblige them, so long as it doesn't involve prison time or causing harm to innocent people."

Ren nodded. "I will take your proposal to Mr. Feng."

"Thank you. I will wait here for up to three hours. I'm sure you're aware that I've made arrangements to continue on to Malaysia this afternoon should our partnership not work out."

At her mention of traveling out of the country, he gave her a little smile that made her question whether she was overplaying her confidence. They knew as well as she did that she'd involuntarily traded in her passport for round-the-clock surveillance. On the matter of if and when she ever made it out of the country, she could no longer pretend to have much say.

An hour later, one of Ren's bodyguards knocked on Kera's door. She collected her duffel bag and was led down the hall toward the elevator bank.

"Don't take this personally," Kera said, "but I don't ride elevators with people below a certain rank." She opened the stairwell door. "I can meet you downstairs, or you can come with me."

The bodyguard glanced back at the elevator, perhaps considering whether she could possibly know something about the elevator that he didn't and weighing that against the idea of taking thirty-nine flights of stairs. He decided to follow her into the echoing stairwell. They descended quickly, Kera taking two stairs at a time and opening a two-flight gap between herself and the winded bodyguard. As she approached the landing at the lobby, the man called out for her to wait. He caught up to her, sweating from his brow and breathing heavily. Then he continued down another two flights.

She followed him to the first level of the basement parking garage. When they emerged from the stairwell, an SUV with heavily tinted windows was idling by the elevator bank—not a place it would have parked had they planned to crater an elevator car into the bowels of the building. Kera took that as a good sign.

Ren was smiling when the bodyguard opened the door for her.

"Mr. Feng is pleased to honor your requests. Welcome to the People's Republic of China."

# LANGLEY

The MIRAGE team began to hit their stride as they closed in on evidence of how Reese Frampton, the blogger, had obtained Angela Vasser's private photos, medical records, and other documents. The trail led them to a man named Rick Altman, a wealthy defense contractor who worked closely with the NSA. Using Vasser's phone number and e-mail address, a friend of Altman's at the NSA had easily targeted and mined Vasser's private files. Altman himself had filtered through the payload first, selecting files that contained information that had the greatest potential to damage Vasser's reputation. These he handed over to Frampton, who was eager to claim the story as his own.

That was easy enough to determine, but it had done little to reveal the motives behind the smear campaign. So they kept digging, tracing the web of contacts that fanned out from Altman and his NSA insider. This steered them to someone very interesting—Larry Wrightmont, the chairman of the Senate's intelligence committee. Wrightmont was known to have designs on becoming the next head of the NSA, a post that would put him in a position to funnel lucrative contracts back to Altman.

Bright wasn't sure yet what he would do with this knowledge, but there was at least one strategic option. If he played it straight and turned over the findings to Director Ellis at the FBI, so that the Department of Justice could launch a formal investigation, it might isolate the NSA as the primary culprit of Vasser's misery. Then maybe she'd consider talking to Bright or the Feds about Kera Mersal.

Bright and Henry Liu were gaming this out in Bright's office when his assistant knocked on the door. The ops center had just called. They said it was urgent.

"I'll head down there," Bright said. He was almost to the door when Liu caught up to him.

"So you want me to reach out to the attorney general's office?"

"Yes. About all of it except Wrightmont's role. Let's sit on that, see how things play out."

· · · · ·

"What have we got?" Bright said as he entered the LED glow of the ops center.

"It's Vasser's burner phone, sir," one of the analysts said. "The one they found in that refrigerator." He explained that, after a subpoena was issued to the cellular company demanding records associated with the number, the NSA had determined that the sole call Vasser received had originated from a vehicle on the Van Wyck Expressway in Queens.

"Heading to JFK?" Bright asked.

"Yep."

"And?"

"There was no Abigail Dalton on any flights out of the tri-state area, but when we searched facial recogs, we got a partial for the name Sabina Francis. This is her at the JFK security checkpoint."

Bright studied the monitor. He noticed the way the woman avoided putting her face in direct view of the security cameras. In areas where that was impossible—such as the TSA screening zone, where cameras cased the area from every direction—the woman kept her head tilted awkwardly at a fifteen-degree angle, a tactic that usually stumped the software. "That's Kera. Where's she headed?"

"That's where it gets weird. We intercepted this footage from the customs hall at HKG. She landed there yesterday morning, local time. Her itinerary had her booked through to Kuala Lumpur, same day, tight layover. But as you can see, she disappears here with a customs agent and we lose her. Wherever she went, she never got on the flight to Malaysia."

Bright asked the analyst to roll the video again, just the part where Kera approached the customs agent and was then led away. He squinted at the monitor as if that might make it clearer—as if making it clearer would tell him something about what Kera was thinking.

"Lionel?" Henry Liu said. He'd been standing next to Bright the whole time, taking in this new development like everyone else. "Do you think it's time we treat the Mersal case as a defection?"

Bright said nothing. He just squinted at the monitor.

•  •  •  •  •

By that evening Bright had sunk into a foul mood. Kera resurfacing in Hong Kong was big news inside the agency, which had been tracking her in vain since her disappearance. Before Bright could make any determination about how his team should pursue the lead, he was summoned by CIA Director Cal Tennison to the seventh floor. In his corner office, Director Tennison—a tall, graying man with unusually broad shoulders—commended Bright on the fresh lead. But he made it clear that full congratulations were not in order just yet. Bright should be aggressive, Tennison said; he should spare no effort to bring in Kera Mersal. Pressure from the White House was building, and the director was as eager as ever to make an example out of Mersal's treason.

Anxious, Bright left the office early. He considered going somewhere to have a drink, but decided instead to walk two miles on the high school track near his house. It helped a little. Not much.

They were having dinner in Bright's dining room when Karen, sensing a weight on his mind, finally called him out on it, encouraging him to vent. They had been dating now for over a month, and with relative ease, considering the circumstances. He suddenly felt them plunged into new territory: the first headwinds, the first choppy waters. He considered dismissing her outright, but fearing that that tactic was hopeless, he conceded to her that he was having a minor crisis of conscience. He didn't know whom to trust and whom to distrust. He had meant this in the context of work, but as soon as he'd said it, he knew the words hung in the air, equally applicable to their relationship. He didn't correct that notion. Instead, he retreated back into himself, claiming it was something he couldn't talk about.

Bright started at the loud clank of her fork against her plate. At first he mistook himself as the source of her anger.

"They ask too much of us," Karen said. Her voice wasn't loud, but it quavered with emotion.

Bright grew defensive. "It's not as if I'm the only one who doesn't share everything about my life."

"Is that what's eating you? Good. Then you know how I feel."

He parted his lips to speak again, but she stopped him.

"Don't. We can't let this poison what we've managed to create." Her tone was softer now, almost pleading. She exhaled, as if to preface something difficult. "But we can't just ignore it either. Clearly, that isn't working. Look, I know you've checked into my background."

He couldn't suppress an instinct to jump in here and what—deny it? Or defend himself? But he didn't get the chance. She cut him off again.

"I don't have proof. Nothing like that. I can just tell. And honestly, that's fine. I just hope you were able to learn enough to know that I'm not a spy or anything like that."

He had not, in fact, learned enough to make him confident about that. But any suspicion he had about her, he realized, was professional, the sort that had been trained into someone who must live his life trusting no one. He didn't know what to say.

"If you must know, Lionel, I work at DARPA," she said, referring to the Defense Department's secretive scientific research agency. "I'm a scientist. My work needs to be classified for a variety of reasons. And I have the cover identity to protect myself from becoming a target. But what I'm doing is not devious." She made a point of meeting his eye here. "Secrets aren't always evidence of bad deeds."

"I know that," he said. "I'm sorry if I ever implied the opposite."

"Is it too late for us?"

"Is what too late?"

"Sometimes I think I never understood what I was giving up when I was recruited into this career. They don't tell you about this part of it. About how there might never be a way out. Lionel?"

His mind had spun reflexively to all the research tools at his disposal, and whether any might be able to confirm her employment at DARPA. Then, just as quickly, he felt a flush of shame for having a mind that worked like that. "I'm sorry," he said.

She grew quiet and practical then, clearing the table and rinsing the dishes, while he sat thinking in the dining room, marveling actually, at the fact that he'd gotten close enough to a woman that she moved so comfortably in his house. She appeared in the doorway wearing her jacket.

"I'm going to sleep at home tonight."

He didn't try to stop her. But he felt an urgency he'd never experienced when she opened the front door.

"Karen," he said, stopping her in the threshold. "It's not too late."

He thought he saw her head move, the slightest nod, and he decided it was a sign of hope, if not full agreement. She closed the door behind her.

# Beijing

They drove her blindfolded to a safe house somewhere near the airport. The drive had been short, and from inside she could hear the not-too-distant roar of jets departing at regular intervals. First they put her in a windowless room where one of Ren's colleagues asked her a series of benign questions about her background. Then she was escorted to a smaller windowless room where a thin white-haired man sat at a computer. She understood immediately why they'd brought her here: they were going to flutter her.

The old man rose when she entered but didn't greet her. With a stony face, he gestured to his instruments. She slipped cooperatively into the pneumograph vest, which would record her respiratory activity. The old man tightened a blood-pressure cuff around her left bicep, and immediately she could feel her pulse throbbing against its grip. Finally, the tips of her fingers were fixed with electrodes calibrated to detect electrodermal responses.

Everyone else left the room. When the old man finally spoke, his clear English surprised her. The questions he asked fell into three categories. The first were basic questions—"Were you born in El Salvador?" and "Did you go to university at Dartmouth?"—designed to establish a psychophysiological baseline from which to compare her responses to the two other types of questions.

The second category consisted of control questions, such as, "Have you lied to your parents?" and, "Did you ever cheat to get ahead?" Kera knew to goose her body's responses to these by imagining anxiety-inducing thoughts in visceral detail. For example, when asked a control question, she transported her mind to the moment she'd entered the apartment she'd shared with Parker and smelled gun smoke in the air. She relived the awful sinking feeling that came from knowing she was too late. Right on the heels of that, she thought of Rafael Bolívar pushing her naked back against the table of her cabin in the valley. Her heart rate increased, her breath wavered. Not overkill, but just enough.

Control questions, she knew, were designed to tease out the inevitable anxiety one faces when asked to assign truthfulness to past events and behaviors—situations that anyone is likely to reflect on with uncertainty. This way, when she was asked the crucial third type of questions—what polygraph experts call the "relevant" questions, such as, "Are you an intelligence agent of the US government?" and "Did you establish contact with Ren Hanchao under false pretenses?"—her apparent lack of anxiety surrounding these matters would shine in comparison to the control questions, which had caused her to exhibit a physiological spike.

That was how you beat the polygraph. If your physiological responses to the control questions were greater than your responses to the relevant questions, you'd be ruled nondeceptive.

There was no clock in the room, but Kera guessed that the questions had been coming for at least half an hour. She felt sharp and able to focus on each of the old man's syllables as they were delivered, helping her maintain a calm command of the signals her brain sent into her nervous system.

That is until, in the same monotonous drone the old man had used throughout, he said, "Do you know Rafael Bolívar?"

She flinched with surprise—internally if not outwardly. But it must have been enough. She thought she felt a stutter in her chest,

a little spike in her blood pressure. These subtle but revealing signals rippled through her vitals like surface rings caused by a stone
dropped into a still lake. She'd expected questions about her time at
the agency and whether she maintained ties with anyone at Langley.
And she'd been prepared to answer questions about surviving on
the run and, for example, whether Kuala Lumpur had really been
her intended destination. But she had not anticipated Bolívar's name
coming up.

"We've met," she managed to say.

"Yes or no answers, please."

"Yes."

She coached herself to a quick recovery and braced for more
questions about Bolívar. But the old man moved on to other topics,
probing her biography. Then he announced that the polygraph test
had concluded and he disconnected his instruments.

She was invited into a bare conference room. Now that she
was no longer hooked up to a computer, she could let loose on her
internal self-criticism for botching the response to the question
about Bolívar. It was a potentially disastrous mistake. If she gave her
Chinese hosts even the slightest reason to doubt her motives, it could
imperil her chances at gaining more access.

A few minutes later, Ren Hanchao entered and offered her tea.
"Yes, thank you," Kera said, searching his eyes for any change in the
way he regarded her.

"What do you know about Gnos.is?" Ren asked. His voice was
free of tension, full of genuine curiosity.

"The news site? I know that it's a thorn in the side of the US government," Kera said.

"Gnos.is is a nuisance to many governments."

Kera nodded and looked down at her lap. "The classified files
that were published a few months ago, the ones about HAWK and
the CIA. I uploaded them to Gnos.is. It's what forced me to flee the
United States."

"I am aware. How did that process work?"

"Leaving the country?"

"No. The files. How did you hand them over to Gnos.is?"

*Was he kidding?* Kera thought. *He had a fugitive CIA operative sitting in front of him and he wanted technical details about file uploads?*

Kera shrugged. She explained that submitting documents to Gnos.is was simple: anyone could upload files, anonymously, from any device with an Internet connection. If someone happened to live in a country where Gnos.is was blocked by government censors, there was an e-mail address where sources could send files. Either method of exchange, she continued, took place via an "onion router" that shed the source's identity and encrypted the data, which was bounced around to several different servers, each one adding an additional onion layer of encryption. These layers could only be peeled away by Gnos.is's decryption key.

"Did you ever speak to anyone at Gnos.is?" Ren asked.

"No, that wasn't necessary. In fact, my understanding is that Gnos.is prefers to avoid direct contact with sources, to preserve anonymity."

"But you do know Rafael Bolívar, the man who runs Gnos.is?"

"I did, yes. And then he . . . disappeared."

"Yes, I know. Do you know where he is?"

Kera shrugged and shook her head.

"What about your former colleague from HAWK, Mr. Jones?"

"We parted ways. I haven't heard from him since then. You understand, I've been avoiding making contact with anyone."

"Yes, of course." Ren was silent for a few moments, and Kera couldn't tell whether he was weighing her sincerity or simply thinking about what to ask her next. It was apparently the latter. "Does the CIA have an affiliation with Gnos.is?"

Kera nearly laughed. "No. The CIA and NSA have tried for years to understand Gnos.is's operations. But as far as I know, no one knows where Gnos.is's servers are located. Gnos.is had an office in Manhattan. But two days ago . . ."

"Yes, we are aware of the death of Charlie Canyon."

There was a knock at the door, and Ren excused himself and stepped out of the room. He returned a minute later.

"If you'll indulge me, Ms. Mersal, there is someone I would like you to meet."

• • • • •

She was blindfolded again for the first fifteen minutes of the drive, and then Ren told her she could uncover her eyes. Blinking against the afternoon light, she could see that they were in a town car and had moved into the city. The driver was a plainclothes guard she recognized from the safe house. Ren was beside her in the backseat.

Between a gap in buildings, Kera caught a glimpse of Beijing National Stadium, venue of the awe-inspiring and highly nationalistic opening ceremonies of the 2008 Summer Olympics. Nicknamed the Bird's Nest for its thatched-metal exterior, Kera thought the building resembled a giant silver saddle in profile. Using the stadium as a landmark, she pictured a map of the city to get her bearings. They were on the north side of Beijing, just outside the Fourth Ring Road, the outermost of the "ring roads" that, like the DC Beltway, encircled the capital.

The car advanced through traffic in painfully short bursts. Kera sensed Ren was growing impatient. Then, without warning, the car pulled to the side of the road, partially blocking the crowded bike lane that flowed along many of Beijing's streets.

Ren suddenly had an envelope in his hand. He set it on her leg and explained that it contained the address and a key for her new apartment. There was also five thousand yuan inside, "for the cab fare," he said, not actually with a wink but in that way. Ren looked across the car, out Kera's window, and nodded at a modern residence tower across the street.

"The man you will meet with is in apartment number 1501. The penthouse suite," Ren said. "He will give you instructions."

"Instructions?" Kera raised her eyebrows defiantly to remind him that they'd agreed she wasn't to be ordered around.

Ren held up his hand as if to allay her concern. "You understand, there are certain procedures we all must endure, to establish our partnership. To build goodwill. If this goes well, it will make things easier for you in China."

Kera looked out the window, her mind ticking through a checklist of precautions. The building was large enough that there would be fire exits on each side, she guessed. A vehicle ramp descended from the street and disappeared into a subterranean parking garage. On the other side, a narrow alley served as a buffer between the tower and a sprawling construction site. Dozens of men under hard hats swarmed towers of scaffolding, spread concrete, and guided beams lowered from cranes.

"If what goes well?" Kera asked, turning back to him.

"You will see. He will present you with a task, and you will understand its importance," he said with a note of finality. His gaze shifted from the building back to her. Kera could tell there was something else. She waited. "I have another request, which you must not discuss with the man you will meet. You are to please encourage him to confide in you. I don't think it will be very difficult. He studied for a few years in America, and he speaks English very well. But he is not trained like you in human intelligence, and"—Ren paused, trying to find an appropriate phrase—"well, he has not seen an American woman in a very long time."

"What do you want to know about him?"

Ren smiled. "The same thing we want to know about you. We want to know if he's playing both sides."

# Beijing

Kera got out of the car and did not look back. The air was muggy, drawing perspiration to her face and neck almost immediately. As she crossed the street to the building's entrance, she picked out two of Ren's men, one browsing magazines at a sidewalk kiosk, the other loitering near the alley. They were dressed in plain clothes, like Ren's driver, but their positions were deliberate, out of step with the march of other pedestrians.

The building's air-conditioned luxury hit Kera as soon as she stepped through the lobby's revolving glass doors. Two doormen, laughing together by a reception desk, snapped to attention when they saw her. She announced herself as a visitor to number 1501. One of the men gestured toward the elevators after calling up to confirm the resident was at home.

Kera's breath caught as the elevator accelerated skyward, and she had to remind herself that her fear was irrational. Her Chinese hosts wouldn't have wasted their time giving her a polygraph test if they intended to drive her across town and drop her down an elevator shaft. But rational knowledge didn't feel very relevant to her so long as she was trapped in a box hanging by cables from a fifteen-story building. Exhaling as the doors finally parted, she wondered if she'd ever feel safe in elevators again.

Apartment 1501 was easy to find. There were only two units on the fifteenth floor, separated by the length of a short hallway. At either end of the hall was an exit door that led to a stairwell. As she approached 1501, she could hear loud electronic dance music coming from behind the door. She knocked. Then she rapped harder and in counterpoint to the bass thump from inside.

Until she'd heard the loud music, she'd been expecting to meet a middle-aged Chinese man, another of Ren's type. But the person before her when the door opened was a waifish, pasty Caucasian. And he was young, very young. They stared at each other for a long moment.

"Hello," he said, stepping back to let her in. He seemed to realize then that the music was too loud. He rushed over to the kitchen's bar counter and tapped at a tablet screen. The music faded.

From his pocket he removed an object that was about the size of a deck of cards. She recognized it immediately as a radio frequency signal detector. He held it up, seeking permission to sweep her. She held out her arms, crucifixion style, and he approached, nervous, a flare of excitement and terror in his eyes. Without touching her, he waved the scanner through the air around her torso and each limb. Then, satisfied that Ren hadn't bugged her, he stepped back.

They were standing between the dining area and what Kera assumed was meant to be a living room with sweeping views of the city. Instead, every drape had been pulled across the windows to block out the sunlight. The large dining table had been shoved into the middle of the room. On its surface, six computer monitors formed an inward-facing semicircle in front of a swivel desk chair. A closed laptop lay near four empty cans of Red Bull that were lined up on the table's edge, as if for target practice. She drew her gaze around the rest of the room. A commercial-grade server tower sat on the far side, where a bookcase might have been. On a stand in the corner was a sparse bonsai plant in a large ceramic pot. A blanket and pillow were bunched on the couch as if the young man slept there often, though the twitchy glaze in his eyes made her think he didn't sleep much—or at least that he hadn't slept much lately. She noted the duffel bag on the floor by the couch, unzipped, revealing clothes and toiletries within.

The young man scratched at the matted hair on one side of his head. For a moment he saw the apartment through her eyes and appeared to be debating whether it was too late to straighten the place up a bit. Finally, he gestured to one of the tall kitchen barstools.

"You can sit down," he said, dropping into his chair and swiveling his back to the computers so he could face her. He spoke with a Russian accent. For a moment he studied her with wide eyes, as if still in disbelief at what he was seeing. "When they told me they were sending someone who could help me access the CIA's personnel database, I thought they were kidding." Despite his accent, he had a confident ease with English. He wasn't a native speaker in the traditional sense, but English was the predominant language of the Internet, which she guessed was his only real home. Ren, she remembered, had said he'd gone to school in the States.

"That's what they want?" she asked. "Access to Langley?"

"They already know I can access Langley—parts of the network, anyway." He shrugged, not at all rattled by the implications of the request. "What they really want to know is whether you can." He looked up at her. "Whether you will."

Kera understood now. They were testing her, just as Ren said they would. She could guess what they hoped to learn from this test: whether she was actually willing to cooperate with them, and what sort of intelligence she was capable of providing.

"Who are you?" she asked.

"No names." The young man shook his head. "But I am not one of them."

"One of whom?"

"Our crafty Chinese hosts," he said, turning to his keyboard.

His tone was derogatory, which surprised her. "You've clearly earned their trust—and then some," she said, admiring his penthouse full of hacker toys.

"No, not trust. They are too smart for that. But they happen to be in the unenviable position of needing something that I can provide."

She glanced up at the light fixture on the ceiling, which was dark. "You aren't worried that they're watching?"

"No. Though I'm sure they are worried about why they can't see and hear us. Eventually they'll figure out they're not just having technical difficulties. But for now, it's just us." He resumed typing on the keyboard.

She stood and moved closer to him, studying his monitors. Three of them were lit. Two displayed lines of neon text on a black background, evidence that he'd been programming. The other lit screen displayed what looked like the building's closed-circuit surveillance feeds. Black-and-white squares glowed with rotating images of the stairwells, lobby, hallways, elevator banks, and parking garage.

The Russian lit up a fourth monitor and began typing. She was close enough now to see the URL he entered in the address bar of an Internet browser. When the page loaded, Kera felt her chest tighten. She stared at the screen. It was the CIA's secure remote log-in site.

"That URL is classified," she whispered. "How did you get it?"

"Please," he said dismissively. He stood and stepped aside, leaving the chair free for her.

"Do you know who I am?" she asked.

"Of course." His grin exposed crooked teeth; one had gone yellow.

"Then you know I was terminated from the agency. I can't just log in anymore." But she couldn't take her eyes off the screen. It triggered a pang of nostalgia for a time when entering her username and password on this site was part of her daily routine.

Skepticism darkened his eyes. "I think our hosts expected that you might have other, more creative ways of getting in. But if not . . ." He made a move to sit down again.

"Wait," Kera said. She reached out and gripped his thin forearm. They were testing her. If they were looking for a sign that she was willing to meet the challenge, she could give them that. The cursor blinked at her from the username field. Her only hesitation was over the risk that it might not work. What would Ren do with her if he decided she was less valuable than he'd expected? And then: What if it *did* work? That might be the riskiest outcome of all.

Kera sat down in the Russian's chair. Resting her fingers on the keys, she entered "David.Cornwell" into the username field and then paused, probing the ephemeral reaches of her long-term memory in an attempt to retrieve the password. She'd memorized hundreds of PINs and passwords, phone numbers, addresses, and authentication phrases—that had been part of her job. This particular username-password combination had been set up a good three years earlier. "David.Cornwell" was a handle that the agency's Information Operations Center had created to test an experimental counterintelligence tactic—a false backdoor into the network that they could dangle in front of malicious hackers. Kera had participated in simulations for the IOC program, but she'd never actually had the opportunity to use the false backdoor in the field. It was possible—likely, even—that the David Cornwell backdoor had been closed and the username and password scrapped.

She typed in the numbers and letters as she recalled them and hit the "Enter" key. The agency's internal landing page appeared immediately.

The young Russian leaned forward. "Who is David Cornwell?"

Kera could not suppress a smile. "Just an old colleague who was careless with his passwords." Her fingers had started moving again. She navigated into the agency's searchable personnel database, which is what the young Russian had claimed was their target.

But she didn't stop there. She clicked on the search bar and entered Lionel Bright's name.

"What are you doing?" the Russian said, wising to her determined keystrokes.

"I'm spying. Did you have something else in mind?"

He eyed her strangely. "Let me see that," he said, and she got up so he could take over.

# LANGLEY

A ringing woke Bright. He stirred, confused at first about why Karen wasn't beside him in the bed, and then about the source of the disruption. Karen hadn't stayed over, he remembered. He rolled onto his side to reach for his work phone on the nightstand. The clock said it was 3:50 AM.

"What is it?" Bright said.

"Remember David Cornwell?" It was Henry Liu.

Through the fog of half sleep, it took Bright a moment to clarify why that name was familiar. He swung his legs off the mattress and found the floor. "Are you at the office?"

"On my way there now. It might be nothing. Want me to call you back when I have a better idea?"

The still-asleep part of Bright did want that. But he already knew that wasn't possible. The full context of those words—"David Cornwell"—became clearer every second. If this was for real, it needed to be monitored in real time.

"No. I'll meet you there."

· · · · ·

"Let's clear the room, please," Bright said, wide-awake now as he breezed into the ops center. The room was half-full. The overnight shift usually presented the best opportunity for analysts and surveillance techs—who often had lower security clearances—to get routine work done, as opposed to regular business hours when higher-ups came crashing into the room, barking at people to leave every time they got the idea that they needed to watch a live satellite picture of a terrorist. "You, stay." Bright pointed at one of the satellite techs he'd worked with before. "And you too, Hank. Everyone else get up and walk out." When they were gone, he asked Liu to start at the beginning.

"The session was initiated at 1547 hours local time. In Beijing, that is."

Bright's pulse spiked as the tech put up a live satellite image of China's capital. He knew the city well from this perspective.

"Our geolocation sats put the access point at this address," Liu said, nodding at a red circle superimposed over the image. He did not need to explain to Bright that the accuracy of the satellites ran within a few meters. "It's a fifteen-story residential building. Vertical positioning is less accurate, but most likely the user is on an upper floor."

Bright nodded, but he'd turned his attention to the adjacent screen, which displayed a freeze-frame image of the CIA's remote log-in page. "Is this a record of the activity?" he asked.

"Yep. Cued up to the moment the Cornwell session was activated."

Access to large swaths of the CIA's nongapped network—that is, the CIA computers that had not been separated from the Internet—via the David Cornwell username and password had been a highly classified experimental counterintelligence effort, rolled out a few years back by the Information Operations Center. It was designed to look like a backdoor to a mix of classified and unclassified sensitive files that would serve as a honeypot to lure hackers. In fact, the actual cache accessible through the backdoor was a mix of publicly available data and completely fabricated misinformation. Meanwhile, any session initiated through the David Cornwell backdoor triggered an alert in Langley, where analysts could pinpoint the location of the session and view the intruder's activity in real time without them knowing.

The time stamp at the beginning of the playback said 15:47:13. From the digital clocks that were spaced along the upper portion of the walls, Bright noted that local time in Beijing was now 16:14.

"Is the session still active?"

"Yes."

"What are they after?"

"Hard to say, exactly. So far they've run a dozen queries targeting the personnel files of Chinese Americans employed by the agency. They've already downloaded scores of records—all fake, of course. There is no way they can get actual employee records this way. But there was something strange . . ." Liu pointed to the paused screen, indicating to the tech that he could start the playback. "Watch this. This is what happened immediately after the session was initiated."

Bright watched. Within a dozen seconds, his own name was searched for. It returned no results in the spoofed database, and after a few seconds, the intruder moved on to other queries.

"Any idea what that's about?" Liu asked.

"It's her," Bright said softly.

"Sir?"

"It's Kera."

"Kera Mersal knows about David Cornwell?"

Bright nodded. "She helped us test it."

Liu looked up at the screens again. "What is she up to?"

"I don't know. But she's trying to get our attention."

"Sir, the coordinates are holding. The user is in that building," the technician said, looking up at Bright as if anticipating an order for what to do next.

"Keep an eye on her," Bright said quickly. He turned to Liu. "Get me Beijing."

Within three minutes, Bright was on the phone with the station chief, who insisted he hadn't authorized any of his people to engage the David Cornwell backdoor. This only strengthened Bright's conviction that it was Kera.

"Could someone else be acting without the knowledge of the Beijing station chief?" Liu asked, still not buying into Bright's hunch. Liu had been read into the David Cornwell file, but he didn't know its history the way Bright did. When Bright didn't reply, Liu turned to the technician. "Show me who else we have in Beijing." Looking over the man's shoulder, he scanned the short list. "BLACKFISH. He returned from Shanghai a few days ago."

Lionel shook his head. He'd already thought of that. "BLACKFISH doesn't know about Cornwell." And then he had another thought. "But maybe he can help us out. See if we can get him on the phone."

When they had BLACKFISH on the line and determined he was within a short cab ride from the address, Bright gave him the green light to move in on the coordinates for a closer look.

"I'm on my way. What am I looking for?" BLACKFISH asked.

"Someone on a computer," Bright said. He paused. "A woman on a computer."

# BEIJING

Kera was beginning to second-guess her instinct to engage the David Cornwell backdoor. Over the last twenty minutes, she'd watched the Russian download thousands of personnel and other files and save them to a flash drive. She knew they weren't actually classified, but she also knew that they weren't infinite. If the Russian bumped up against the limits of the false cache, he would immediately suspect her of tricking him.

"What's all this?" she asked, trying to distract him and slow him down. She tapped the monitor that was filled with the rotating surveillance feeds.

"That's the building's security network," he said, without looking up.

"Do they know you have access to that?"

He made a *pfft* sound with his lips that left no doubt that he thought her question was ridiculous. And still he kept copying files to the flash drive.

The only time he paused, briefly breaking concentration, was when she moved closer to him so that her arm brushed slowly against his shoulder. He glanced up at her with raised eyebrows, as if to say, "Oh?" And then, with an unappealing little smirk, he returned his eyes to the screen and his fingers resumed their play across the keys.

To keep herself calm, Kera reasoned that if the network's backdoor was still open, someone in Langley must be responsible for monitoring it. But how long would a response take? She kept eyeing the rotating black-and-white squares on the surveillance monitor. The lobby, the elevators, the hallways—she saw no sign of anything unusual; no one moving in on their location.

When she turned back to the Russian's active screen, her anxiety flared again. He'd stolen the entire personnel database and was now browsing through lists of IP addresses. The IP addresses were spoofed, of course, and didn't actually correspond to terminals inside the CIA's Information Operations Center Analysis Group, but she suspected he could discover that quickly. She didn't want to be around when he realized he'd been duped.

"You got your personnel files, OK. Now what are you doing?"

"I'm getting some insurance," he said, not diverting his eyes from his screen. "I'm impressed by your access. I've penetrated isolated areas of unclassified networks at Langley before, but nothing like this."

"Look, I didn't agree to this. It's time to shut it down."

He ignored her. More files streamed into his flash drive.

She weighed the benefits of taking him out. A strike to the throat would disable him before he knew what was happening, allowing her to escape. But where would that leave her? It would spoil whatever trust she'd earned with the Chinese and dash any hope that she could learn who had killed the ambassador and the others.

Instead she said, "You going somewhere?"

"Huh?"

She nodded at the duffel bag by the couch. "You have this spacious luxury condo, and yet you're sleeping next to your computers with a go bag packed and ready. Something have you on edge?"

He grimaced slightly at her remark, but it didn't bait him into a response.

She rested a hand on his shoulder and felt him tense. "You never told me what kind of work you do for our Chinese friends," she said. He didn't reply. It was time to go for broke. "Would you like me to guess? Say I wanted to hack the flight-management system of an airplane. Would you be someone I could hire?"

His fingers froze over the keyboard.

"What about elevator software?"

"It wasn't like that," he said, his voice thin and high with defiance.

"Are you doing it for the money, for this penthouse apartment? Or is it just a fun challenge?"

"I would think someone like you would be a little more sympathetic to my cause."

"Your cause?"

He scratched sheepishly at a red blemish on his cheek. "What I'm doing is no different than what you did with the CIA. You were once complicit in their dirty espionage, but eventually you chose your conscience over your career."

"Bullshit. You don't know a thing about my motivations. Besides, nothing I did got innocent people killed."

"I didn't know who would be on the plane. That wasn't my choice." She saw that his hands had gone to the edge of the table. His knuckles pulsed white. "It was their choice, and I'll make them pay for it."

"Who?" she said, to keep him talking. She'd managed to pull his focus from the computer tasks, but she still had the feeling she was dealing with a short fuse.

"Our hosts. China's MSS—just like the CIA—they think they are better than everyone because they have power and secrets. They censor the Internet or they use it to spy on their citizens. And they support corporations that do the same. Both China and the United States want the same thing: control. They want it too much. They have no right to control the Internet."

Kera felt a chill roll through her, not for the idealistic content of his little speech, but for the starkness with which it revealed his naïveté. He'd fallen into the trap of all hackers who become amateur philosophers. He'd glimpsed his own power, power wielded at his fingertips because he had a skill that few had and that so many depended upon, and that had got him thinking. He thought, inevitably, about right and wrong; he got big ideas about evil governments and corporations. And without realizing it, his own narrow perspective had become his only standard for what was right. And with his computers' ability to spy, to keep him anonymous, and to attack asymmetrically, how could he not be tempted—not just tempted; he felt *justified*—to take hostile action every time the world fell short of his vision of what it could be.

With a clear image in her mind of Ambassador Rodgers and Charlie Canyon and his other victims, she made the decision to grab him by the throat and pry him physically from his weapons. But at that moment one of the surveillance feeds caught her eye.

# BEIJING

Kera squinted at the black-and-white image on the monitor. A man was jogging down the ramp that descended from the street to the building's parking garage. Even on the small surveillance feed, he was hard to miss—Caucasian, tall, and thickly built, with a bald head and a goatee. Within seconds, he disappeared into the garage. *Did he have a car parked down there, or was he avoiding Ren's men posted near the lobby entrance?* She scanned the other feeds, hoping to pick him up.

The Russian was watching both Kera and the surveillance monitor with a mixture of confusion and anticipation.

Before Kera could spot the tall Caucasian on another camera, a second figure appeared on the vehicle ramp in pursuit of the first. She recognized this one—he was one of Ren's men, one of the two she'd made out on the sidewalk. *Shit,* Kera thought. *Here we go.*

"Shut it down. We have to move," she said to the Russian while still watching the monitor. The surveillance feeds rotated, and the Caucasian could be seen sprinting up the stairwell, taking each flight in three bounds. A moment later, Ren's man swung around the railing and into view, looking up as he continued his pursuit. "Come on, let's go."

But the Russian just sat there, either paralyzed or transfixed by the surveillance monitor. He only flinched when the sound of two muffled pops reached them, ringing with a stairwell echo. They both looked instinctively to the door, registering the sounds as gunfire. After a beat, they leapt to action.

The Russian, now appreciating the threat, yanked the flash drive from his computer and nearly tumbled out of the swivel chair as he pushed it back. Kera took a breath and concentrated on the security-camera images one last time, trying to determine which stairwell the men were in. It was impossible to say. Then the feeds rotated again, giving her two new stairwell views. In one, the Chinese agent who'd followed the intruder was slumped motionless against the wall on a landing. On a lower floor, Ren's second man had joined the pursuit, ascending the stairs with his weapon drawn cautiously, as though he'd heard the exchange of fire from above. The Caucasian was out of sight.

When Kera swung around to head for the door, she saw the Russian standing over the bonsai in the corner. He had a laptop under his arm, and he was brushing off a plastic baggie that he'd apparently dug out of the planter's dirt. She saw him slip whatever had been in the plastic bag into his pants pocket.

"Come on," Kera said from the door. This time, the Russian listened. When they were in the hallway, Kera moved toward the nearest stairwell exit. She held a finger over her lips, instructing him not to speak.

She opened the door in a swift, fluid motion and stuck her head in. There was no visible danger. She paused, listening. At first she could only hear her own heartbeat, so strong it seemed to echo off the walls. Then footsteps. The echo made it difficult to gauge the distance, but she guessed the sound was coming from three or four floors below—and closing fast. She guided the door shut softly and pushed the Russian toward the exit sign at the opposite end of the hall.

Once she'd checked for footsteps there, and heard nothing, she told the Russian to run as fast as he could and fell into step on the descent behind him. They were both out of breath when they reached the ground floor.

Kera had intended to descend as far as the parking garage to avoid the lobby doormen, who might have already noticed the carnage under way from the surveillance feeds covering the opposite stairwell. But when she reached ground level, she saw that there was an exterior exit door. She remembered the alleyway that separated the residential tower from the adjacent construction site. This suddenly seemed like a better option than going to the underground parking garage where, if Ren's men had had a chance to call for backup, she and the Russian might be trapped.

"Follow me," Kera said. "Keep moving."

She pushed through the door and sprinted straight across the alley, where she slipped between the exposed wall beams of a half-finished structure. She could hear the noise of hammers and saws a few levels above her, but the ground floor where she entered seemed deserted. When the Russian caught up with her inside, she crossed to a doorless threshold and worked her way down a dim hallway, deeper into the construction site. Only about half of the rooms had walls, but from the load-bearing skeleton she guessed that the structure was on its way to becoming a shopping mall.

Nearing a multistory atrium, the sound of male voices grew louder, even as they were muffled by hissing welders' torches and screeching power saws. Choosing an opening at random, Kera ducked into an unfinished retail space and motioned for the Russian to continue ahead of her through a door that led to an adjacent stockroom. He did so without thinking. As soon as he was through the threshold, she delivered a leg swipe that connected with the outside of his right ankle, which locked behind his planted left foot. His own forward momentum brought him down, hard, sending the computer clattering to the ground a few feet away. In an instant she was on top of him, using one hand and her shin to pin his hands against his tail-bone. Her knee drove into his spine. He hollered in shock and pain and wriggled violently for a few seconds. He was strong for someone who didn't look like he'd spent much time in the gym, but she'd gained the advantage through surprise. When he stopped struggling, realizing for the moment that it was useless, she reached back with her free hand to begin untying his shoelaces.

He kicked her away. "No!" he hissed, part panic and part anger.

She ground her knee into his spine until she forced a mewling sound from him. "Shut up," she said, "or I'll snap it. Don't be an idiot. You'll get us both killed."

She stripped the laces, then suddenly spun atop him and pinned both his arms beneath her knees as she bound his hands behind him with the laces. Without the ability to free an arm for leverage, he could be restrained with just her body weight and a carefully placed knee to his back. He realized this too late, and as she spun back around, he tried again to regain some advantage from her by flailing his shoulders and legs. But once she'd replaced her knee against his spine, he struggled more quietly and without much enthusiasm, as though simply trying to retain a shred of self-respect. Then he fell still but for his heavy breathing.

Kera looked around. A dozen unused cinder blocks were stacked up just inside the door. Two buckets filled with nails and screws sat against the wall. The small room was one of the few spaces fully enclosed by drywall. She was satisfied that for the moment they were hidden in the shadows.

"Who were those guys?" the Russian managed to ask, grimacing.

"Two of them were Ren's. I'm not sure about the other," she lied. If the David Cornwell backdoor had worked the way she understood it would, then the tall Caucasian man had been sent by Lionel. His arrival would have been much more welcome had they not been trapped at the top of a fifteen-story building with MSS agents in pursuit. She eyed the Russian's laptop lying on the ground nearby.

She had to get the David Cornwell session up and running again. It would lock in on their location and give Lionel's man—if he'd made it out of the building—a second chance to get to them.

She leaned away from the Russian and grabbed the laptop, then rode him out for a moment as he thrashed before realizing that it only made the pain at his spine worse. He gave up on the wasted effort and she opened the computer. This deep inside the construction site, it detected only three open Wi-Fi signals. All of them were weak. She picked one and then abandoned it after it was unable to load a web page. The second one she selected got her online.

"What's your name?" she asked the Russian as she typed in the classified URL for the CIA's remote log-in page. Then she entered "David.Cornwell" in the username field, along with the password.

"No names," the Russian said.

"You know my name."

He lay silent beneath her at first, but then reconsidered, perhaps seeing an opportunity to establish enough goodwill to get her off his back.

"I go by Allegro," he said softly.

She rolled her eyes. When she clicked the log-in button to initiate the David.Cornwell session, the screen cleared, as if to load the page, but then it froze on the blank page in a frustrating web limbo. It was difficult to tell whether the operation was laboring under the weak connection or if the Internet link had been dropped altogether.

Leaving that to resolve itself, she slipped a hand into the Russian's pants pockets until she felt what she was looking for. She pulled out two flash drives—the standard-looking black one that he'd used to copy the dummy CIA files, and a sturdy carbonate one that she figured had been the object in the baggie he'd dug out of the bonsai planter.

She flipped the flash drive with the stolen backdoor files to the concrete and reached for one of the loose cinder blocks nearby.

"Wait!" the Russian protested.

But she didn't hesitate. It took only a few seconds to pulverize the plastic storage device to an unrecoverable pile of shards and dust.

"What's on this other one?" she said, examining the flash drive he'd kept hidden in the planter. When he didn't reply, she set it aside to free up a hand. She pressed her palm into his cheekbone and repeated the question.

The Russian tried to shake his head, but that was more painful than holding it still, so he just gritted his teeth defiantly. She could open the drive on the laptop and have a look for herself, but first, while she had him in this position, she wanted some information. She leaned toward his ear and spoke coolly.

"Why did they hire you to bring down Ambassador Rodgers's plane?" On the last word, she increased the pressure on the point where her knee dug into his back between his narrow shoulder blades. His one visible eye popped a little, and he made a futile effort to speak. She let up on the pressure, just enough so that he could talk.

"Get off me. I can't breathe." He wriggled beneath her.

"What about the people in those elevators? You murdered them too, didn't you? Why?" She sent a new surge of pressure through her knee where it ground into his spine.

"OK, stop! Please. I did it," he mumbled. She eased up on his skull. "But it's not like you think. I didn't know that innocent people would die. It wasn't until after the plane and the first two elevators that I figured it out. After that I started working against them."

"Working against whom?"

"Have you heard of Unit 61398?"

"Of course. They're the elite cyberspies of the MSS. They target computer networks, though, not people."

The Russian shook his head. "They follow orders like everyone else. This time their expertise was called upon to take out human targets."

"Orders from the MSS?"

"Yes. All the way at the top."

"Bullshit." Kera shook her head. Even if he was privy to the knowledge he was claiming—which she doubted—what he was saying didn't make sense. Assassinating an American ambassador invited some hefty consequences. There was no way Beijing would take a risk like that. "If you stopped working with them after the first round of attacks, what happened to Conrad Smith? He was killed in an elevator two weeks after the others."

"They were going to kill him anyway. He was on their list. They were planning to shoot him. But by using the elevator, I—"

"Established a trend," Kera whispered, understanding. "It made it obvious that the string of elevators falling out of the sky wasn't a coincidence—or an accident."

"Yes."

"But didn't that anger your MSS handlers?"

"Of course. But I knew they wouldn't do anything to me. Not yet."

"Why?"

"They don't realize just how much I've figured out about their plans. I know, for example, that they need me alive and they need my fingerprints all over these assassinations. That's the real reason they granted me asylum in China. If a lone Russian hacker with anti-American motivations can be blamed for these attacks, then there will be no retaliation from the United States. And China won't be responsible for starting a major conflict between the world's two largest superpowers."

She thought about this for a few moments before she found a hole in his story. "What about Charlie Canyon? He was killed after Conrad Smith. Did you have anything to do with that?"

His voice was softer this time when he replied. "That one I couldn't stop."

She rocked forward, digging the sharpest part of her knee into his back. The Russian moaned.

"Please! I tried, I promise. The MSS are desperate to take out Gnos.is. I didn't want to help them with that, but I had to at least appear to be going along with their attempts. The problem was that Gnos.is couldn't be fully infiltrated remotely. We needed to get someone physically in front of one of their machines to log in and keep a session going long enough to exfil all the files. The MSS has an agent in New York who got a meeting with Canyon by posing as a tech-industry lobbyist. When Canyon visited the cover website we built for the lobbyist, malware was transferred to his computer. This malware sat dormant until Canyon's meeting with the agent. Once the agent was in the room and could prevent Canyon from logging off, I woke up the malware."

"You did that remotely?"

"Yes. From the Unit 61398 facility in Shanghai."

"You've been *inside* Unit 61398?"

"Yes." The Russian's eyes flicked briefly to the flash drive that Kera had set down next to the laptop.

Kera suddenly had a hundred new questions for him. But first she had to know what happened to Canyon. "How did this agent get Canyon to log in? Did he just put the gun to his head?"

"No. We were afraid Canyon wouldn't log in if he felt threatened, or that maybe he could use a decoy account or something. We had to be sure he logged in for real."

"Go on."

"We couldn't get into his computers remotely, but his phone was more vulnerable. I designed a way to ping his phone with a fake cybersecurity alert, which I did once his meeting with the MSS agent had begun. It compelled him to log on."

"Then what happened?"

"The malware started queuing Gnos.is files to send to us—"

"No. I mean, what happened to Canyon?"

"The agent attempted to take control of the computer. It's not totally clear to me what happened next, but apparently Canyon did not surrender the machine to the agent. The outcome was that he got shot, though he must have survived long enough to perform some sort of operation that encrypted everything on the network. Canyon died and the MSS got nothing from Gnos.is. It couldn't have gone worse for anyone."

She looked down at him. She still had his hands pinned behind him with her body weight, but she'd let up on his head and back so he could speak freely. "Why are they so desperate to take out Gnos.is? There are news organizations all over the world. They can't take them all out."

The Russian parted his lips to speak, then decided to remain silent.

Kera rocked forward, reapplying the pressure that had been so persuasive up to this point.

"Ow. OK. But are you sure you want to know more? The people they've killed didn't know half of what I can tell you."

"Tell me."

"It's on the flash drive," he said quickly, to prevent her from administering another pulse of discomfort with her palm or knee.

Kera weighed whether they had time for this. What if he was bluffing, hoping to stall her until Ren's men could find them? On the other hand, he'd admitted his involvement in the death of the ambassador and the others, including the attempt to hack Gnos.is that had resulted in Canyon's murder. He even claimed to have been inside Unit 61398. Was it possible that he had on this flash drive an explanation for why all of these victims had been targeted by the MSS?

Without freeing him, she pulled the laptop closer. Immediately she saw that the David Cornwell session was running. At some point while they'd been talking, the Wi-Fi connection had been strong enough to get through.

# LANGLEY

"Where are you? Do you have eyes on them?" Lionel Bright said into his satellite phone. After waiting out a series of tense moments in which the only signs of BLACKFISH had been the two bodies he'd left in his wake, Bright was relieved to hear the man's voice.

"Negative. I found an apartment full of computers and Red Bull. Someone left in a hurry."

"What was on the computers?" Bright stepped to a corner of the ops center so he could speak freely in private.

"I didn't have time to look around. I'd just shot two MSS guys; I had to get the fuck out," BLACKFISH said. Lionel heard the adrenaline in his voice.

"You're out now?"

"Yeah, I'm out. And not afraid to say I got lucky. The building's hot. They've got an army of plainclothes assholes with firearms searching the site bottom to top. Who's this subject that everyone's so interested in?"

Bright exhaled. "We lifted some footage from the building's security system. Facial recog confirms that a11Egr0, the Russian hacker we like in the ambassador's assassination, lives in a unit on the top floor. And it looks like Kera Mersal paid him a visit today." He paused to let this sink in. "You just missed them. They exited together through the east stairwell door. It leads to an alley. You copy?"

"Yeah, I heard you. But I don't like it. They're together in one spot? And they did something to tip us off to their location? Doesn't that seem a little too good to be true?"

"I don't know what it means, but I think she's trying to send us a message."

"A message? Are you sure it's not a trap?"

Bright grit his teeth. "I'm not sure of anything. For what it's worth, it doesn't feel like a trap to me."

"You're not the one getting fucking shot at," BLACKFISH said, and he had a point.

"I know, I know. Listen, we think they may have slipped into that construction site just east of the building. Can you get in there?"

"I can try. But Lionel, I'm not super psyched about risking my life for this woman. You might have reason to trust her, but from where I sit, she's no great American hero. First she leaked classified files, and now she's cozy with MSS assets."

"Believe me, I understand. But with Kera it's . . . complicated. I know I'm in the minority, but I actually think she went over there looking for some way to redeem herself. Now she seems to be trying to get our attention, and I'm more than a little curious to find out why."

"All right. But if I have to choose between my own life or hers, I'm coming out of there alive."

Bright shut his eyes. "Understood. Proceed with caution."

Five minutes later, Bright was standing nervously in the middle of the ops center, bathed in the glow of live satellite images, when the room's pass code–protected doors parted. Bright turned at the sound to find Director Tennison walking toward him. This was unexpected. Bright's first instinct was to look at the clock. Was it already eight in the morning? He'd never seen the director on campus earlier than that. It was only 5:28.

"What've we got?" the director grumbled.

"Sir?"

"Is it true? We have eyes on Kera Mersal in Beijing?"

The director now stood before Bright, though his gaze was trained beyond him, up at the satellite and video surveillance images on the ops center's main tactical display.

"That's our understanding. We're still trying to confirm the circumstances." Another of Bright's sudden understandings was that someone on his team must have the ear of the director—at least on the issue of Kera Mersal. This was only a minor surprise. The role of CIA director often included making calculations that were political. Ever since Kera's disappearance, Bright had been aware that the director was eager to make an example of her, to bring her very publicly to justice in order to create a precedent that might deter any future would-be intelligence leakers. So it made sense that he'd recruited an informer among Bright's team to keep him intimately apprised of the Kera Mersal case. The surprise was how quickly he'd been rustled from bed and rushed to the ops center.

The director had two men with him, senior ops-center techs Bright recognized vaguely. When the director nodded to them, they went directly to two open terminals.

"What are they doing?" Bright asked.

"They're mobilizing people who are going to get Kera Mersal for us."

"That isn't necessary."

"The hell it isn't." The director's glare, when he swung it in Bright's direction, was part surprise, part anger. "This is the woman who, maybe you remember, dealt herself a royal flush of espionage charges. Leaking those HAWK files made her a pain in our ass. The company she's keeping now makes her an imminent threat to national security."

"I know what this looks like," Bright said, willing himself to deal coolly with his superior and keep the panic from his voice. "But hear me out. I think she's got something there and she's trying to let us know."

"Forget it. We've been waiting for her to make a mistake. Now she has. We're not missing another chance to bring her in."

"We won't miss anything," Bright said. "I've got a man on the ground there who's trying to do just that."

"This isn't an operation for your man, Bright. This has gone way beyond that."

"Sir, please."

"Sit this one out, Lionel," the director snapped. "You're too attached."

"No, sir. It's my duty to give you an honest assessment, even if it's not the one you want to hear. We need to give Kera a chance to come to us. We need to see what she's got."

"You misunderstood me. I'm ordering you out of this facility. We've got a job to do here, and you clearly aren't fit to do it."

"Sir—"

"Out!"

Bright glared at the director, permitting his eyes to express the insubordination that he knew he wouldn't be able to get away with voicing aloud. The worst part was that he knew it was hopeless. The director's mind could not be changed, least of all by him. Bright turned for the door. He was halfway across the room when he heard one of the analysts address the director.

"Sir, they're back up. The signal's spotty, but it's coming from inside that construction site."

That was the last thing Bright heard before the ops center door locked shut behind him.

# Beijing

"It's encrypted," Kera said, staring at the window that had appeared on-screen when she slid the Russian's flash drive into the USB port. She angled the screen so he could see it. "What's the key?"

The Russian attempted to shake his head. "We can't open that here. It isn't secure."

"I don't care." Her knee found his spine again.

"Ah! OK, then let me enter the key."

"You don't understand, do you? You're not in a position to negotiate."

He closed his eyes tight and, out of options, told her the key. It was twelve digits, a mixture of numbers and case-sensitive letters. She pictured the characters in blocks of four to help herself commit them to memory. The flash drive, once she was behind the encrypted security wall, revealed two folders. The first had been named MAYFLOWER, the second BYZANTINE. The latter jumped out at her. The MSS's Unit 61398 was widely referred to as BYZANTINE CANDOR. She steered the cursor toward it.

"No, the other one first," he said.

She flashed him a warning glance—a reminder not to waste time—but then did as he'd suggested. Inside the MAYFLOWER folder she found only one document, an Excel spreadsheet file, also named MAYFLOWER. When she opened it, the screen filled with columns and rows of numbers and dense text entries, all in Mandarin. Kera started to read as fast as her passable grasp of Mandarin would allow. The title at the top of the page translated to "OPERATION MAYFLOWER." She was about to start making sense of the column headers when he stopped her.

"Click the second tab. I'm still in the process of translating it, but you'll get the idea."

The spreadsheet listed over twelve hundred entries, nearly eight hundred of which had been translated into English. Alongside each name were columns of data: home and work addresses, employer names, and the names of relatives with addresses in China. Also recorded were IP addresses, phone numbers, e-mail addresses, and, most telling, a field called "Date of Recruitment." Some of the dates stretched back nearly a decade. Scrolling through the entries, she felt a chill as she read the employers associated with each name: General Electric, Boeing, Lockheed Martin, Apple, Amazon, Google, AT&T, BP, InspiraCom, and so on.

"What is this?" she said.

"The Chinese have been assembling OPERATION MAY-FLOWER for over a decade. This is a list of the people they have in place, working inside American companies."

"These people are spies?" She lightened the pressure on his back. "Twelve hundred of them?"

"Not exactly. Not by choice. Most of them aren't even aware that the Chinese government is using them. They're business executives, engineers, scientists. You can see, they happen to have family who still live in mainland China. Naturally, these people want to help to modernize China and improve life for their loved ones. So the government asks them to do a small favor here and there, like plug a certain thumb drive into their computer at work or copy a few files. Those who hesitate are soon reminded that they're vulnerable. It is not so hard to blackmail people if you have the resources of the MSS. One way or another, they've all been recruited and cultivated."

Kera shook her head as she scrolled through the list. "They've convinced or coerced *twelve hundred* people to participate in a spy network this big?" She kept going back to that number. "How are they keeping it secret?"

"It is not a network. These people are not working together—at least they're not aware that they are. And given the nature of the relatively small favors they're encouraged to do, it never occurs to them that they are acting on behalf of the MSS. Individually, these people don't present a danger; they are not motivated to harm the United States. So it has remained a secret. But—" He paused to gauge whether she understood where this was going. When she didn't react, he continued. "But if Beijing were to coordinate the timing of these coerced 'favors' and leverage them toward one malicious end, the cumulative effect could be devastating to America's infrastructure and economy."

"The thousand grains of sand," Kera whispered.

"Huh?" the Russian asked.

"How did you get this file? Can you be sure it isn't a fake?"

"I'm sure. I stole it—as insurance against what they were doing to me."

"You stole it how?" She wanted to make sure that the Russian hadn't been duped into the MSS's version of the David Cornwell backdoor, which led only to spoofed data.

"Like everyone else, I knew it was more than suspicious when the American ambassador died on a jet owned by Hu Lan. But unlike everyone else, I knew that the Chinese had recently asked me to write a bug for the flight-management system of a specific model of Gulfstream jet—the same model that Hu Lan owned."

"A bug?"

"Yes. A plane like this relies on its computerized flight-management system to fly. And because of that, it has four redundant systems to prevent an in-flight catastrophe. That's standard on modern aircraft, and it ought to be sufficient, at least for combatting the odd unlucky software glitch. If the main system malfunctions, the plane easily switches to one of the three backup systems. It's unlikely that all three backup systems would fail. Unless, of course, you program them to. If you know how the FMS is built, you can design a logic bomb. That is, a—"

"I know what that is." What he meant was that MSS hackers had written a bug that had been inserted into the jet's flight-management system. When the trigger was activated—for example, when the plane reached a predetermined altitude—the bug woke up, crashed all the backup flight-management software, and sent a mishmash of commands through the avionics systems before simply cutting all power. The plane would be transformed into an erratic hunk of metal that the pilots would be unable to control manually. "OK. How did that lead you to these OPERATION MAYFLOWER files?"

"I followed a digital trail. The MSS had provided me with files that contained the code and specs for the Gulfstream's flight-management software. I traced those files back to a man who worked for Gulfstream in the United States. Using a backdoor I'd discovered in the Unit 61398 network, I ran a search for both Hu Lan and the Gulfstream employee. Mr. Hu has a large file with Unit 61398 and the rest of the MSS, but MSS's interest in the Gulfstream employee was much narrower. In fact, they've apparently used him only for that one task. There was just one document in which both men were listed, and you're looking at it." He pointed to the names of the two men on the spreadsheet.

Kera had been listening closely for the Russian to utter a contradiction that would reveal he was making this all up. But she'd only spotted one such flaw in his claims. She shook her head. "Beijing has little to gain by crippling America's economy—and too much to lose."

"They may not want to actually cripple America's economy, but they most definitely want the ability to do it. It's the same reason every nation wants nuclear weapons, even though the consequences of using them would be catastrophic. The MSS simply wants the same thing that's coveted by your CIA and NSA—more power and control."

Kera was about to retort that the CIA wasn't assassinating foreign diplomats and innocent civilians to get it—but she knew better. She'd seen firsthand the lengths the agency went to in order to serve its interests.

"But what threat did the ambassador pose? Or any of the others you've helped them kill?"

"The threat isn't any individual. It's Gnos.is."

"You mean the articles Gnos.is has published about China?"

"No. Not the articles it *has* published. The ones it might publish next."

Kera froze, remembering the TERMITE story, the way Gnos.is had pieced together the existence of the secret TERMITE program using information that was scraped from the Internet. The MSS had caught on to that, and they were anxious that Gnos.is might do the same to expose OPERATION MAYFLOWER.

"But why did they go after the ambassador, Angela Vasser, and Conrad Smith? They have nothing to do with Gnos.is."

"Sure they do. They may not have a direct involvement with Gnos.is or OPERATION MAYFLOWER, but they leak data that makes its way online, just like everyone else. The unlucky problem for them is that, because of their positions, they were the likeliest people to possess key pieces of information—whether they knew it or not—that Gnos.is could analyze and use to potentially discover OPERATION MAYFLOWER. To counter this, the MSS made a cool calculation: if they could remove a few key data points from Gnos.is's intake, it might prevent, or at least delay, the discovery of their plot."

"Data points? We're talking about innocent people," Kera said.

"Innocent people die in war," the Russian said, a little too nonchalantly, as if he knew anything about the real consequences of war.

But that's what this was, wasn't it? A war. A war that had escalated in secret to a point so dangerous that killing an ambassador—an offense that by any other standard might have *started* a conventional war—was viewed by China as a justifiable, if desperate, attempt to prevent an even worse conflict. That told her one impor-tant and horrifying thing: China was as afraid of the consequences of OPERATION MAYFLOWER as the US ought to be.

"What's in the second folder?" she asked him, clicking open the file labeled BYZANTINE. He said nothing, as if he wanted to watch her discover it on her own. The folder contained hundreds of documents. She chose one at random. When the file opened, she found strings of numbers that she immediately recognized as IP addresses. She didn't dare let herself hope it was what it appeared to be. "Are these—?"

"More files I stole."

"These are from Unit 61398's internal network?"

He nodded, unable to disguise his pride for this achievement, even as a woman was pinning him to the pavement.

Kera clicked through a few more documents. In addition to scores of IP addresses, the files contained personal data on Unit 61398 employees, including their e-mail addresses and pass codes. Kera could hardly breathe. At the CIA, she'd worked on a handful of task forces that had tried to breach Unit 61398, known in US intelligence circles as BYZANTINE CANDOR. None of those attempts had succeeded. The US intelligence community was dangerously in the dark when it came to the capabilities of Chinese cyberespionage. What she was looking at on the screen represented a quantum leap in that knowledge.

"How did you get this?"

He made the familiar *pfft* sound. "Unit 61398 is a complicated organization. They are not impenetrable. They have weaknesses, just like airplanes do, and elevators, and even your CIA. After they lied to me and framed me for a crime I never intended to commit, I needed something to level the playing field with them." His mouth was a crooked grin. "So I went after the secrets they thought they'd guarded most carefully."

"Do they know you have this?"

"Not yet. But it's time." He looked up at her with a grin that exposed a discolored row of neglected teeth. "I've been preparing this for a reason. This will be Gnos.is's biggest scoop yet."

She shook her head. "None of this can be made public."

"But it has to. That's why I stole it. You of all people should understand that."

She disconnected the computer from its weak Wi-Fi source, suddenly afraid to have opened these files on a computer that had access to the Internet, potentially within Gnos.is's reach. If there was one thing that could not happen, it was for him to release these files to Gnos.is. Given the precarious state of diplomacy between China and the United States in the wake of the ambassador's death, a news story exposing OPERATION MAYFLOWER would almost surely force China's hand. The United States would retaliate. Within hours, the world's largest superpowers would be crippled by their own vicious cycle of attacks and counterattacks.

She removed the flash drive and tucked it into her pocket. The Russian squirmed beneath her.

"I have backup copies," he protested. "If you take those, I'll just release them myself."

"You're too inexperienced for this work. Get up." She untied his hands and then lifted herself from him, grabbing the computer. He sat up, rubbing his wrists and arching his back. Finally, slowly, he stood.

"Let's go," she said, gesturing for him to walk ahead of her out of the small room, back the way they'd come.

"What are we doing?" He looked down at the shoelaces as if debating whether he needed them.

"I'm going to get us out of here."

He lingered for a moment, his eyes frantic and distrusting. She thought he looked suddenly paler than before.

"Let's go," she repeated.

He took a few steps ahead of her and crossed through the door into the half-finished retail space. He wasn't halfway across the room when he bolted.

She wasn't surprised, exactly, but the suddenness of his move caught her off guard, giving him enough of a gap to escape her grip when she lunged for him. He sprinted toward the wide opening at the store's entrance and cut sharply right, grabbing the wall with his inside hand to swing himself around the corner. Two pops burst from out of sight as soon as he disappeared, followed by a hard thump. Her own momentum carried her through the doorway, and, reeling defensively, she dropped the laptop, which clattered end over end into the corridor. When she came to rest, she was staring at the hot end of a Sig Sauer P229, trained chest high at her from about ten yards away.

The man holding the firearm was without question the same man she'd seen on the building's surveillance feeds. His features were much more visible now. He was sturdy and bald-headed with a ginger goatee, dressed in jeans and a black T-shirt. Definitely American.

Slowly, Kera raised her hands. A surreal silence filled the air in the wake of the gunfire.

"We're on the same team," she said.

"Oh yeah? What team is that?"

"Lionel's team." The American hesitated. She'd gotten his attention.

"Most of Langley thinks you're working with him," he said, nodding down at the ground but keeping both his eyes and the Sig Sauer trained on her. Kera glanced down at the young Russian. He lay facedown and motionless on the concrete between them. Both shots had struck him, rendering two exit wounds—rough edged and ringed with glistening pink, white, and black flesh—one at the back of his head, the other at the base of his neck. She guessed that either would have been fatal on its own. A bright pool of blood expanded slowly from beneath his face.

"I can prove that I'm not," she said.

"I don't care. If it were up to me, I'd just as soon shoot you. You leakers have put a lot of my colleagues in danger."

"I didn't—" Kera started, but then thought better of trying to defend herself here. "Listen. I have a flash drive on me with some sensitive files." She held up her hands higher to stop the thought that she knew had immediately entered his head. "Files that I don't intend to leak. Files that must not be leaked. The files were stolen from a secret cyberespionage division of the MSS known as Unit 61398."

"I know what Unit 61398 is."

She could hear a change in his tone; even if he didn't fully believe her, he seemed to understand the implications if she was telling the truth.

"Good. These files provide, among many other things, an explanation for what happened to Ambassador Rodgers. They are very time sensitive. I need your help to get them to Lionel Bright at Langley."

The American squinted, unconvinced that she wasn't trying to play him.

Kera pressed on. "Here's your dilemma, though. The data is on an encrypted flash drive. It's a long encryption key, one that might take the guys at the NSA weeks to crack." She paused to make sure she still had his attention. "I, however, memorized the key. And I'm not going to give it up until I can personally deliver the files to Lionel Bright. So it's your call. You can shoot me and then explain to Lionel why you weren't able to deliver intel that's going to be pretty valuable in the wake of this clusterfuck. Or, my personal preference, you can give me a lift to the embassy so we can catch a goddam flight out of here."

The American had fallen into a silent deliberation with himself. But like her, he'd been trained to make tough decisions quickly.

"OK," he said. "Let's go. But we can't go to the embassy. The MSS will anticipate that. We'll never make it. Besides, you don't have any friends at the embassy."

# LANGLEY

Bright was in his office, sitting on the back of the couch and watching the dawn light seep into the courtyard outside his windows. It was now past six in the morning and he was still wearing the jeans and untucked collared shirt he'd dressed in hastily when he'd been summoned to the ops center in the middle of the night. After the director kicked him out, he'd retreated to his office, too furious to go home and get some sleep.

Maybe it was the sleeplessness, or the lingering effects of the previous evening's unsatisfying exchange with Karen. Or maybe it was just the sting of being chastised and suspended from his own case—but suddenly he felt the pull of a dark undertow threatening to upend his whole world. He pictured the agency's immense, color-coded parking lots beginning to fill, badge-wearing bureaucrats taking up positions in cubicles and conference rooms. This was how a multibillion-dollar bureaucracy brought itself to life. Every day.

It all felt suddenly so *routine*. Maybe, he thought for the first time with real conviction, maybe it was time for him to get out.

Bright could sit no longer. He looked at his desk phone, willing it to ring with a conciliatory call from the director. But the phone was quiet. He got up, fuming again, to pace his office while he gamed out his options.

Finally a phone rang. He looked hopefully at the secure phone on his desk. But the call wasn't coming from the director or anyone else in the ops center. The ringtone, he realized, was coming from the pocket of his jacket on the couch—his personal satellite phone.

BLACKFISH.

"Did you find her?" Lionel asked immediately. He had to know that first. He shut his eyes, bracing for grave news.

"Yes. I have her here with me."

"She's unharmed?"

"Yes."

"What about the hacker?"

"He didn't make it."

"Where are you?"

"At a safe house."

Bright's mind raced. "Did she come in voluntarily?"

"Sort of." BLACKFISH gave a brief summary of the encounter at the construction site and, particularly, the files Kera claimed to have, which she would only deliver to Bright in person. "She might be bullshitting about the files. But I figured that wasn't my call to make."

A calm clarity possessed Bright's mind. "Does anyone know she's with you?" he asked.

BLACKFISH assured him that he had not yet checked in with the station chief at the embassy; no one was aware that he'd brought in Kera Mersal.

"Good," Bright said. Then he gave BLACKFISH careful instructions.

# Andrews Air
# Force Base

On the plane, Kera had slept in short fits. She awoke picturing life in a cell, where she was visited only by lawyers and let out only to give sealed depositions or to attend secret hearings. Eventually, she might hope for the opportunity to agree to a plea bargain that would give her a life to look forward to. She knew these were not dreams—they weren't even nightmares. They very probably were glimpses of her future after she set foot on American soil.

The American had driven her to the airport in a beat-up Peugeot that was parked in the safe house's driveway. At a gated entrance to a cargo terminal, he produced a magnetic card that got them past the perimeter fence. The car rolled right onto the tarmac and dropped her off almost directly at the base of a stairway that had folded out of a small jet with no tail markings. The American never told Kera his real name. When she asked, he said only that she could call him BLACKFISH, which she assumed was the cryptonym assigned to him by the agency. Then he said good-bye and wished her luck.

. . . . .

The plane touched down at Andrews after dark. A fresh pulse of adrenaline—mustered from where, Kera couldn't imagine—woke her body from the fourteen-hour flight. The stone-faced steward, with whom Kera had exchanged at most a dozen sentences throughout the duration of the flight, opened the cabin door. When the stairway extended to the tarmac, Kera disembarked. A charcoal-suited man waited for her beside an idling black SUV. She noticed the clear, coiled wire running from his ear down into his collar. There was not another human being in sight. By the time he opened the backseat door for her and she climbed in, the plane's stairs had already retracted, the cabin had been sealed, and the aircraft began to taxi away.

The man climbed behind the wheel and steered the SUV in the opposite direction. He left the headlights off. They glided through the dark for only a minute or two before the vehicle turned off the taxiway and onto a wide square of tarmac. Through the blackness, Kera could see a line of UH-1N Huey helicopters. The birds rested quietly in the humid night, with no hint that they were tuned to spring to life at a moment's notice.

The SUV pulled up to a hangar. The driver got out, but only to open her door. "Here you are, ma'am." He pointed to the small human-scale door set within the towering, sectioned hangar wall designed to slide open for aircraft. A dim light illuminated the door, but otherwise the hangar's exterior, like the tarmac, was dark. Kera walked toward the light.

The hanger housed two Hueys, their fuselages partially disassembled for maintenance. The scale of the cavernous room made the helicopters look like miniature toys. Seated at a break table between the two birds was Lionel Bright. Walking toward him, she scanned the office doors along the walls and the overhead catwalks. As far as she could tell, they were alone.

Lionel stood when she approached. "Kera," he said. They'd not seen each other in weeks. With everything that had happened, it felt like years.

"You look good," Kera said.

"Do I? I've been seeing someone. It's kind of an ordeal, but maybe it keeps me young. Welcome home," he said, appraising her cautiously.

"Is that where I am?"

He stepped back and looked at her with sad eyes.

"How's this going to work?" she said. "We talk for a bit and then you give a signal and the building's surrounded?"

"There's no one here but us," Bright said. "I've taken precautions to protect you."

"And to protect yourself, I'm sure. It's OK. You want cover if the files I claim to have aren't legit. Go ahead, say it. You don't trust me. No one does anymore, and you're not willing to be the last one to go down with my ship. That's fine. I've changed my mind about Langley. I don't think I'd go back anyway. Not after what you guys did to Angela Vasser."

"That wasn't us, Kera. Not the pictures and the private files."

"Bullshit. That was never about pictures, not really. Why can't anyone see that? She's innocent, Lionel. She always was. An American diplomat, and she was treated like a traitor." She looked right at him. "I know how that feels."

"Kera—"

She held up a hand to stop him. "Do you have a computer? Let's get this over with." She felt the snap in her voice and regretted it. It was the fatigue, closing in around her.

Bright produced a laptop from a shoulder bag lying on the table. He pushed it toward her, inviting her to sit. She did, after taking the small flash drive from her pocket. She slipped it into the USB port. When prompted for the encryption key, she entered it without hesitation and turned the computer back to Lionel, who started scrutinizing the contents of the files immediately.

Kera sat back. For the first time, she felt real relief—relief for learning the cause of so many deaths, for getting out of China, for recovering the flash drive and delivering it to Lionel. Especially for that. It felt surreal being here with him. The dramatic events of the last few months had taught her that Lionel Bright was not the man she'd believed he was when she'd worked under him at the agency. But didn't that mean she knew him better now, just like she knew herself better too? In a weird way, having cause to question their trust in each other had brought them closer.

She watched Bright for a few minutes as the expression on his face changed from curious to astonished. The files were legit, all right.

"What is Vasser saying?" Kera asked.

"About you?" he said without looking up. He was engrossed in what he was seeing on-screen. "Nothing. She's driving everyone crazy."

Kera smiled. "She did everything right."

Then she fell silent for several minutes and let Bright absorb the details of OPERATION MAYFLOWER and the stolen Unit 61398 files.

"Do you think a war can be avoided?" she asked him. "Or is it already too late?"

"That depends. Does Beijing know these files were stolen?"

"I don't think so."

"Then I like our chances. If we do it right, we might be able to unwind this thing before they even know it's blown. As long as no one panics, we can all wake up tomorrow morning."

"And me?"

He pointed at the computer screen. "Do you realize what you've done here? Not just getting us details of this operation in time for us to diffuse it. But this other stuff on Unit 61398. It's like a decade's worth of work, dropped right in our lap."

"You'll be a character witness at my sentencing hearing, then?" It wasn't a joke exactly, just sarcasm.

His eyes grew serious. "All the things that were done to Vasser after she was falsely accused—they'll be done to you too. And worse, probably. I can't bear to see that."

"It's not up to you, I guess."

"I'm being serious. Do you have somewhere you can go?"

"To go?" she said, finding his eyes. She didn't fully understand what he meant until she saw the steadiness in his gaze. "I . . . I don't know." And then, after a moment of catching up, she said, "Who knows I made it out of Beijing?"

"No one. Just BLACKFISH. I told him that his internal report of the incident in Beijing should suggest that you'd been killed in the gunfight that got a11Egr0. Of course, if you prefer, you can turn yourself in. I'd be honored to be a character witness at your hearing. But I hope I never have to."

Kera stepped back, studying his eyes for a hint that she'd misunderstood him. But he was serious. He was telling her that he'd left her a way out. It felt dangerous to want something as badly as she wanted to believe him. "Remember what you used to tell me?" she said. "'Never forget that there's a difference between your undercover life and your real life. And your real life matters more.'" He nodded. "I don't have a real life anymore."

"Well, now you have a chance. You deserve that much."

She nodded. And suddenly, now that she'd glimpsed the potential for a new life, a life that wouldn't be defined by the four close walls of a prison cell, she couldn't look back. Her mind had already begun to formulate a plan.

Bright held up the flash drive. "I need to get this back to Langley right now. Is there somewhere I can find you, if I need to?"

Kera shook her head. The beginning of a smile formed at the corners of her mouth. "No. You won't be able to find me. But when you want to be in touch, leave a five-star review on Amazon, using your initials, for *The Spy Who Came in from the Cold*. When I see it, I'll find you."

He chuckled. "That was a smart move, getting our attention with the David Cornwell backdoor."

"It only looks smart now because it worked. Thanks for recognizing it for what it was," she said.

"We used to be a good team. I hadn't forgotten that."

"See you around, then?"

He nodded. She gave a little wave, and then she turned and he watched her cross the hangar floor. She never looked back.

# CAPITOL HILL—TWO WEEKS LATER

Before this moment, Angela Vasser had never set foot inside room 219 of the Hart Senate Office Building. She'd been in other Sensitive Compartmented Information Facilities before, of course. The embassy in Beijing had no fewer than three. But no SCIF—outside of the White House's situation room and those at the CIA's headquarters in Langley—had hosted as many discussions about the United States' most closely held intelligence secrets as Hart 219. Upon entering through a vault-like door, she was immediately struck by the simplicity of the room—all beige-paneled walls and utilitarian furniture. The room didn't pretend to be anything other than what it was: a soundproof box full of men and women with very high security clearances.

The twenty-four members of the Senate Select Committee on Intelligence were present, arranged according to seniority in a horseshoe formation on a platform from which they peered down at the speaker. Not one of them made a sound as Vasser took her seat. Whatever else was on their minds, whatever else their busy schedules had in store for them that day—they seemed to forget it when she entered. The tension in the room climaxed as Vasser took a sip of water from the glass on the table before her and then set it down.

"Good morning, Ms. Vasser," said Larry Wrightmont, the intelligence committee's chairman. "Thank you for being here today. I know you have not found many champions on Capitol Hill, but I'd like to be the first here to commend you, in an unqualified, nonpartisan manner, for your continued service to this country. As I'm sure you're about to highlight, our diplomatic relationship with China has never been so delicate. We're relieved to have you back in Beijing."

"Thank you, Chairman," Vasser said, adjusting the microphone in front of her. She felt the room exhale, as if there was universal relief that this exchange would remain civil. The previous weeks had provided good reason to doubt that.

Following the discovery of China's espionage plot, along with evidence that exonerated Vasser from any wrongdoing, the secretary of state had lobbied the president to nominate Vasser to replace the late Ambassador Rodgers. He made a strong case that her presence at the embassy in Beijing was invaluable. But while many of the adults in Congress had voiced support for the Vasser nomination, they were immediately drowned out by waves of vitriol from their political opponents. The past revelations of Vasser's sex life, her associations with Kera Mersal—it was all too much for the politicians to defend to their constituents. Vasser herself had ended the controversy by asking the president to withdraw her from consideration.

"What do you *want* to do?" the president had asked her during a fifteen-minute meeting in the Oval Office after a classified ceremony at which she had been honored by the State Department and the CIA.

"I'd like to go back to China. But I don't want to go through a confirmation hearing, and I don't want a position that's merely ceremonial. The new ambassador, whomever you choose, will need me on the ground there, doing real work to repair this damage. And I'm told the CIA has an interest in having me there too."

With a new ambassador yet to be nominated, Vasser was the only person qualified to brief the Senate's intelligence committee on the diplomatic challenges the United States faced in China. Besides the CIA and FBI, only the men and women gathered in Hart 219 knew the full scope of the tensions with China, including the discovery and careful dismantling of OPERATION MAYFLOWER.

"I understand you've been briefed by the FBI on the foiled Chinese espionage plot," Senator Wrightmont said, tacking straight to business.

"Yes, I just came from there," Vasser said, locking eyes with Wrightmont. "And by foiled you mean foiled except for the assassinations of Ambassador Rodgers, Conrad Smith, Charlie—"

"Yes, of course, Ms. Vasser. No one is forgetting that," Wrightmont said. His voice was clipped, resentful of her approach. "But surely you appreciate the incomprehensible damage that was avoided because our intelligence community discovered OPERATION MAYFLOWER before it could be used against us."

"Let's not sugarcoat the intelligence community's role here, Mr. Chairman. An ex-CIA operative, Kera Mersal—working on her own—led us to that intelligence, and she gave her life in the process." Vasser studied the senators; she didn't owe them anything.

Since her nomination, Vasser had been briefed three times by the FBI and twice by the CIA. Each time, she pleaded to know more about what Kera Mersal had been doing in China and why she hadn't come back. She was told that Kera had been killed during a mission to apprehend her and bring her into US custody for questioning. This was more than what the general public knew, but the information was still vague. When she pressed for details, she was told the case was classified. She had begun to doubt whether anyone actually knew what had happened to Kera after all. Surely it must have been on the minds of the senators before her. If it couldn't be discussed by them in *this* room, it meant the senators had nothing to discuss.

The briefings she received had been much more enlightening about everything else that had happened. The missing link, which neither Vasser nor Kera had been aware of at the time they were on the run together, was OPERATION MAYFLOWER. When a powerful faction of spooks inside the MSS began to sense that their secret operation was slipping from their control just as it was becoming big enough to do real damage, they panicked. In a desperate attempt to keep evidence of the plot from surfacing, they tried to eliminate the potential sources of such evidence. These included people such as Ambassador Rodgers, Conrad Smith, and even Vasser herself, among others, who were unaware of the operation but happened to have close associations with assets involved with OPERATION MAYFLOWER.

The young man who'd been contracted to carry out the assassinations, a Russian hacker called a11Egr0, who ultimately turned against his Chinese handlers, was himself killed on the same day as Kera. Whatever had happened in the final hours of their lives, Kera had somehow stolen classified Chinese intelligence files from the hacker and passed them on to the CIA. Those files led the FBI to systematically question nearly twelve hundred people who lived in the United States and remained in contact with operatives of China's Ministry of State Security. A few dozen of those people had been arrested, and dozens more had been deported, but the vast majority had pleaded complete ignorance of the plot and were happy to cooperate with the FBI. Details they turned over led intelligence officials to identify the network of MSS handlers responsible for orchestrating the plot.

A senator three seats over from Wrightmont jumped in with a question intended to get the conversation back on track. "Are you back in communication with your Chinese counterparts?"

"I am. The willingness of both sides to continue diplomatic relations has, I believe, saved us from entering a much larger conflict."

"What is your interpretation of China's response to all this? What are they admitting to? And how much do they know about the intelligence that we—or, Ms. Mersal was able to recover?"

"There remains plenty of uncertainty about who in the Chinese government knew what—at least with respect to the MSS's lethal attempts to keep OPERATION MAYFLOWER secret. But in just the last few days, the Chinese government has arrested several MSS officials who had been linked to the assassinations or who assisted the Russian hacker. Such a crackdown on spies within their own intelligence service is an unprecedented step for Beijing. I interpret it as a conciliatory and profound gesture of their desire to restore workable levels of trust with the United States."

"Excuse me," one senator said when Vasser finished her statement. "Are you not recommending any sanctions or military action against China?"

"At this time, no."

"Are you not concerned that doing nothing makes the United States look weak?"

"With respect, Senator, we are not doing nothing. We are doing what is in America's best interest. Our strength comes from recognizing that our priority is to work with other world powers to build a healthy global economy and encourage more transparency. How we act now will determine whether the global technology race benefits humanity or precipitates its destruction. We demonstrate that strength by engaging in frank diplomacy with Beijing, not by continuing a tit-for-tat confrontation that, in any event, will not bring back Ambassador Rodgers."

The hearing was adjourned at the conclusion of Vasser's testimony. Several senators approached her to thank her personally for her service and to offer condolences for the loss of Ambassador Rodgers. A few others had remained in the room, huddled in their own private conversations. And a few had left in a hurry to make their next appointments. Once outside the soundproof vault, Vasser waited for her turn to collect her phone from the security guard. When she had that in hand, she pushed through the outer door and into the hallway.

She froze. Standing in the center of the hall with an attentive eye on the door were five men in blue FBI windbreakers. She felt a tightening in her chest, a mix of alarm and anger.

"It's OK, babe," a voice said from her left. It was Ben. He'd planned to meet her and take her to lunch. It was the last meal they'd have together before she left for Beijing. Sensing her distress, he added, "They're here for someone else."

Had she grown so accustomed to being pursued by law enforcement that just the sight of a few Feds made her heart race? Vasser looked back over her shoulder, but the door to Hart 219 had already closed behind her. "Who are they here for?"

Ben didn't know the answer to that. He'd been waiting for her, he said, when the Feds approached one of the security guards. They said they needed to see one of the senators who was inside. They weren't happy to be told to wait, but the guard assured them that they didn't have a security clearance high enough to enter the room while a closed hearing was in progress. If it was any consolation, there was only one way out of the room, and no communication could get in. Their senator wasn't a flight risk.

A few moments later, the question was answered. The outer door opened and Senator Larry Wrightmont emerged, powering up his newly reclaimed phone. He took two steps before he looked up and stopped in his tracks.

"Senator Wrightmont?" the lead agent said, moving with his colleagues toward the senator. "You are under the arrest for abuse of power. Specifically, conspiracy to steal and distribute private, classified information about a private US citizen."

"What is this about?" Senator Wrightmont said, his instinct to fight kicking in. "Hold on. You can't do this. Not here." He brushed away the agent's first attempt to cuff him, but when the four other agents took a step closer, he seemed to concede that he was not going to win a physical altercation. As he was being cuffed, his eyes darted around the hallway. When they found Vasser's, they hesitated. And then they looked quickly back to the agents. "This is a big mistake, gentlemen. I want to speak to my lawyer before you take me anywhere—"

"It was *you*?" Ben said. His voice boomed. "*You* were behind all this?" He took a few steps toward the senator before Vasser could put a hand on his shoulder to stop him. She looked him in the eye.

"It's OK. It's over now," she said. And for the first time since all this had begun, she really believed that it was.

# THE VALLEY

Kera crested the pass and put the rental car in park just in front of the gate. She got out and stood for a minute, looking up at the peaks and down at the lake while a breeze blew hair across her face. After a minute she heard a click, and the gate swung slowly open. She was smiling as she climbed back behind the wheel.

It was Jones who greeted her with a hug when she found him in the driveway outside Bolívar's cabin. His pickup was parked nearby, its engine clicking as it cooled. He must have hauled ass to get here from the mine.

"We thought you'd—" Jones stuttered. "Gnos.is was never able to confirm it, but everyone else was reporting that you'd been killed. In China? We didn't know what to think."

"I know. I'm sorry. I couldn't risk being in touch."

"What happened?"

Kera didn't know how to answer that. She shrugged. "Most of the pieces are all out there in the world now. Don't you have a little toy that can put them all together?"

"Who knows you're alive?"

"Lionel. And one of his guys in Beijing, plus the small flight crew who transported me back. And now you."

"Lionel let you go?"

"It was his idea. I brought him something very valuable." Jones looked at her, wanting more. But she just shook her head. "That part is something Gnos.is is not going to get its hands on."

"I see," he said. And then, after a pause, his tone took on an air of regret. "I'm sorry for dragging you into all this."

"It wasn't your fault. And look, I came out of it OK." She paused. "I'm sorry too. About Charlie."

He nodded. "I keep wondering if we should have seen it coming. If we should have gotten him more protection. We're still not entirely sure what happened. Near as we can tell, his last conscious act was to save Gnos.is from a major security breach." Jones exhaled. "Rafa took that hard. Almost as hard as he took not knowing what had become of you."

Kera nodded. "Is he here?"

"Yes. He must be swimming. He didn't answer his phone." Jones nodded in the direction of the path that led around the cabin and down to the lake. He let Kera go on her own.

Rafael Bolívar was standing on the dock, drying his hair with a towel. He wore khaki shorts and an unbuttoned white shirt that billowed around his torso in the light breeze. He was facing away from the shore, looking out over the water, and so he didn't hear her approach until she stepped on the dock. When he turned and saw her, his arms fell to his sides.

"I was just passing through," she said. "Thought I'd stop by." The last word caught unexpectedly in her throat. She felt her guard crashing down—either because she was too tired to keep it up any longer, or because she didn't care if he saw.

"Come here," he said, walking toward her.

She gripped his back tightly when he hugged her, at first clenching her jaw tight against a surge of emotion.

"You're all right?" he asked.

She nodded into his shoulder. She was afraid to speak, afraid that if she tried, she'd lose her composure.

"What happened?" he asked, pulling back to look at her. "After they got Canyon, you were angry. I understand that. We thought you were with Angela Vasser. But then they found her and there was no sign of you. Until . . . they said you were killed."

"I was in China. They got that part right. But I found a way out." She leaned into him and closed her eyes. One side of her face was against his, the other felt the warmth of the sun. "I wanted to see you."

After a moment she heard him ask, "Are you really just passing through?"

She shrugged without opening her eyes. In her mind, the reason she'd come to the valley was to let them know she was all right. She'd intended to go after that. But standing there on the dock with him, she felt something new. There was no urgency; there was nothing in the world she had to do. She had nowhere to go, and there was nowhere she had to be.

"Stay awhile," she heard him say.

She opened her eyes.

"Yeah," she said. "OK."

# ACKNOWLEDGMENTS

If the goal here is to assign credit where it is due, this page seems woefully insufficient. Merely acknowledging the people named below is actually the least I can do. Let it be known: I don't take any of these smart and talented people for granted. Readers shouldn't either.

Chris consistently goes above and beyond the call of duty in tolerating the bizarre and relentless daily routine of someone who is writing a novel. And he's always smiling. His patience, love, and support are essential to my sanity and productivity. And my parents, Pattie and Dick Quinn, have always been and continue to be proud supporters of this venture. I love you all.

The first line of defense against humiliating errors, vagary, and fatal plot holes are my early readers. Not only did these people save me from myself, but they challenged me to make every page better. They are: Chris Fajardo, Kelly Quinn, Gretchen Newell, Jon Bergman, Phil Buiser, Marc Valera, and Zac Hug.

After that layer of editorial brush was cleared, my editor David Downing stepped in and did his thing. "His thing" is the real deal. I've had the pleasure to work with David on three novels. Each time, he has added real value, line by line, and I am forever grateful for his wisdom, humor, and talent.

Throughout this process, I've benefited immeasurably from the hard work of the outstanding people at Thomas & Mercer. They are doing big things. The following people deserve special recognition for their efforts in making this book possible: Gracie Doyle, Alan Turkus, Jacque Ben-Zekry, Kjersti Egerdahl, Alison Dasho, Timoney Korbar, Tiffany Pokorny, and Sarah Shaw. And a special shout-out to Lindsey Alexander, the superb copyeditor who handled the final manuscript with great care and a sharp eye.

# Sources

*If I was able to create any illusion that I know what I'm talking about when it comes to cutting-edge cybertechnologies, it is mostly due to the following books and articles.*

Bamford, James. *The Shadow Factory: The Ultra-Secret NSA from 9/11 to the Eavesdropping on America.* New York: Doubleday, 2008.

Bowden, Mark. *Worm: The First Digital World War.* New York: Atlantic Monthly Press, 2011.

Clarke, Richard A., and Robert Knake. *Cyber War: The Next Threat to National Security and What to Do About It.* New York: Ecco, 2010.

Greenberg, Andy. "How the NSA Could Bug Your Powered-Off iPhone, and How to Stop Them." *Wired*, June 3, 2014. Online version, accessed September 2014: www.wired.com/2014/06/nsa-bug-iphone/.

Greenberg, Andy. *This Machine Kills Secrets: How WikiLeakers, Cypherpunks, and Hacktivists Aim to Free the World's Information.* New York: Dutton, 2012.

Greenwald, Glenn. *No Place to Hide: Edward Snowden, the NSA, and the U.S. Surveillance State.* New York: Metropolitan Books, 2014.

Huslin, Anita. "If These Walls Could Talk..." *Washington Post*, May 28, 2006. Online version, accessed July 2014: www.washingtonpost .com/wp-dyn/content/article/2006/05/27/AR2006052701153 .html.

Matthews, Jason. *Red Sparrow*. New York: Scribner, 2013.

Mayer-Schönberger, Viktor, and Kenneth Cukier. *Big Data: A Revolution That Will Transform How We Live, Work, and Think.* Boston: Houghton Mifflin Harcourt, 2013.

Wise, David. *Tiger Trap: America's Secret Spy War with China.* Boston: Houghton Mifflin Harcourt, 2011.

# ABOUT THE AUTHOR

*Photo © 2015 Sean Marier*

A native of Alaska, Ryan Quinn was an NCAA champion and an all-American skier while at the University of Utah. He worked for five years in New York's book-publishing industry before moving to Los Angeles, where he writes and trains for marathons. Quinn is also the author of the bestseller *End of Secrets*, as well as *The Fall*, a finalist in the 2013 International Book Awards. For more, please visit ryanquinnbooks.com.